The Various Flavors of Coffee

Also by Anthony Capella

The Food of Love

The Wedding Officer

The Various Flavors

BANTAM BOOKS

OF COFFEE

Anthony Capella

THE VARIOUS FLAVORS OF COFFEE
A Bantam Book / September 2008

Published by Bantam Dell
A Division of Random House, Inc.
New York, New York

This is a work of fiction. Names, characters, places, and incidents either are the product of the author's imagination or are used fictitiously. Any resemblance to actual persons, living or dead, events, or locales is entirely coincidental.

Title page art by Stephen Youll

Book design by Helene Berinsky

Library of Congress Cataloging-in-Publication Data

Capella, Anthony.
The various flavors of coffee / Anthony Capella.
p. cm.
ISBN 978-0-553-80732-5 (hardcover)
1. Coffee industry—Fiction. 2. Coffee—Sensory evaluation–Fiction. 3. Senses and sensation—Fiction. 4. London (England)—Fiction. 5. Africa, North—Fiction. I. Title.
PS3603.A64V37 2009
813'.6—dc22
2008025625

Printed in the United States of America

www.bantamdell.com

BVG 10 9 8 7 6 5 4 3 2 1

Yesterday
a drop of semen,
tomorrow
a handful of spice
or ashes

—MARCUS AURELIUS, Meditations

The Various Flavors of Coffee

PART I

Much about coffee's flavor still remains a mystery.

—TED LINGLE, *The Coffee Cupper's Handbook*

[ONE]

WHO IS HE, THIS YOUNG MAN WHO STROLLS TOWARD US down Regent Street, a carnation in his collar and a cane in his hand? We may deduce that he is well off, since he is dressed in the most fashionable clothes—but we would be wrong; we may deduce that he likes fine things, since he stops to look in the window of Liberty, the new department store devoted to the latest styles—or is that simply his own reflection he is admiring, the curling locks that brush his shoulders, quite unlike the other passersby? We may deduce that he is hungry, since his footsteps speed up noticeably as they take him toward the Café Royal, that labyrinth of gossip and dining rooms off Piccadilly; and that he is a regular here, from the way he greets the waiter by name, and takes a *Pall Mall Gazette* from the rack as he moves toward a table. Perhaps we may even conclude that he is a writer, from the way he pauses to jot something down in that calfskin-leather pocket-book he carries.

Come along; I am going to introduce you. Yes, I admit it—I know this ludicrous young man, and soon you will know him, too. Perhaps after an hour or two in his company you will consider you know him a little too well. I doubt that you will like him very much: that is of no consequence, I do not like him very much myself. He is—well, you will see what he is. But perhaps you may be able to see past that, and imagine what he will become. Just as coffee does not reveal its true flavor until it has been picked, husked, roasted and brewed, so this particular specimen has one or two virtues to go along with his vices, although you may have to look a little harder to spot them. . . . Despite his faults, you see, I retain a sort of exasperated affection for the fellow.

The year is 1896. His name is Robert Wallis. He is twenty-two years old. He is me, my younger self, many years ago.

[TWO]

IN 1895 I HAD BEEN SENT DOWN FROM OXFORD, HAVING FAILED my Preliminary Examinations. My expulsion surprised no one but myself: I had done little work, and had chosen as my associates young men notable for their idleness and dissolution. I learned very little—or perhaps it is fairer to say that I learned too much; those were the days, you will recall, when undergraduates chanted Swinburne as they rioted down the High—*Could you hurt me, sweet lips, though I hurt you? / Men touch them, and change in a trice / The lilies and languors of virtue / For the raptures and roses of vice*—and the college servants still talked in shocked tones of Pater and Wilde. Among the monkish cloisters a mood of languid romanticism prevailed, which prized beauty, youth and indolence above all things, and the young Robert Wallis imbibed this dangerous doctrine along with all the other heady aromas of the place. I spent my afternoons writing poetry, and my father's allowance on silk waistcoats, fine wines, brilliant peacock feathers, slim volumes of verse bound in yellow vellum, and other *objets* essential to the artistic life, all of which were available on ready credit from the tradesmen of the Turl. Since my talent for poetry, like my allowance, was actually rather more meager than I cared to acknowledge, it was inevitable that this state of affairs would eventually come to a sorry end. By the time I was sent down I had exhausted both my funds and my father's patience, and I was soon faced with the necessity of finding a source of income—a necessity which, I am ashamed to say, I intended to ignore for as long as possible.

London at that time was a great, seething cesspit of humanity; yet, even in that dung-heap, lilies grew—indeed, they flourished. Out of nowhere, it seemed, there had come upon the capital a sudden outpouring of frivolity. The Queen, in mourning, had retired from public life. Released from her attention, the Prince began to enjoy himself, and where he led, the rest of us followed. Courtiers mingled with courtesans, dandies moved among the *demi-monde,* aristocrats dined with aesthetes, and rough trade mixed with royalty. Our house magazine was the *Yellow Book;* our emblem was the green carnation; our style was what came to be known as *nouveau,* and our mode of speech was the epigram—the more paradoxical the better, preferably tossed into the conversation with a certain practiced, weary melancholy. We celebrated the artificial above the natural, the artistic above the practical, and, Oscar Wilde notwithstanding, laid claim to extravagant vices which few of us had any intention of actually indulging. It was a glorious time to be young and in London, and I was to miss most of it—curse it!—all because of a chance remark I happened to make in the hearing of a man named Pinker.

[THREE]

The primary factor affecting the taste is the selection of the beans.

—LINGLE, The Coffee Cupper's Handbook

I WAS HAVING BREAKFAST IN THE CAFÉ ROYAL—A PLATE OF OYSters and a dish of thickly sliced ham with green sauce—when the waiter brought my coffee. Without looking up from my newspaper I drank some, frowned, and said, "Damn it, Marsden, this coffee tastes rusty."

"It's ver same as all ver other customers is drinking," the waiter said haughtily. "None of vem, as I'm aware, have seen the necessity for complaint."

"Are you saying I'm pernickety, Marsden?"

"Will there be anyfink else, sir?"

"As a waiter, Marsden, you have mastered every skill except waiting. As a wit, you have mastered every requirement except humor."

"Fank you, sir."

"And yes, I am pernickety. For a well-made cup of coffee is the proper beginning to an idle day. Its aroma is beguiling, its taste is sweet; yet it leaves behind only bitterness and regret. In that it resembles, surely, the pleasures of love." Rather pleased with this *aperçu,* I again sipped the coffee that Marsden had brought. "Although in this case," I added, "it seems to taste of nothing much except mud. With, perhaps, a faint aftertaste of rotten apricots."

"My pleasure, sir."

"I don't doubt it." I turned my attention back to the *Gazette.*

The waiter lingered a moment. "Will ver young gentleman be paying for his breakfast this morning?" he inquired, with just a trace of fashionably weary melancholy.

"On my tab, please, Marsden. There's a good fellow."

AFTER A WHILE I became aware that someone had joined me at my table. Glancing over my newspaper, I saw that my companion was a small gnome-like gentleman, whose sturdy frock coat marked him out from the usual swells and dandies who frequented that place. I was myself expecting to be joined at any moment by my friends Morgan and Hunt, but since the hour was early and the room mostly unoccupied, it would be no great inconvenience to move to another table when they arrived. I was, however, somewhat curious, since the same surfeit of tables made it all the more surprising that the stranger should sit at mine uninvited.

"Samuel Pinker, sir, at your service," the gnome-like gentleman said, with a slight inclination of his head.

"Robert Wallis."

"I could not help overhearing your remark to that waiter. May I?" And without further ado he reached for my cup, raised it to his nostrils, and sniffed it as delicately as I had that morning sniffed the flower I had chosen for my buttonhole.

I watched him, unsure whether to be wary or amused. Many eccentric characters frequented the Café Royal, to be sure, but their eccentricity was generally of a more affected kind, such as carrying a posy of violets, wearing velvet knickerbockers or twirling a diamond-topped cane. Smelling another customer's coffee was, so far as I knew, unheard of.

Samuel Pinker seemed unperturbed. His eyes half closed, he inhaled the aroma of the coffee twice more, very deliberately. He put it to his lips and sipped it. Then he made a curious sucking sound, together with a tiny snake-like flicker of his tongue, as if he were swilling the liquid around his mouth.

"Neilgherry," he said regretfully. "Over-brewed, not to mention over-roasted. You are quite right, though. Part of the batch was spoiled. The taste of rotting fruit is faint, but quite pronounced. May I ask whether you are in the trade?"

"Which trade?"

"Why, the coffee trade."

I think I laughed out loud. "Good heavens, no."

"Then may I ask, sir," he persisted, "what trade you *are* in?"

"I am in no trade at all."

"Forgive me—I should have said, what is your profession?"

"I do not profess anything very much. I am neither a doctor, nor a lawyer, nor anything useful."

"What do you *do,* sir?" he said impatiently. "How do you support yourself?"

The truth was that I did not support myself just then, my father having recently advanced me a further small sum against literary greatness, with strict injunctions that there would be no more. However, it seemed absurd to quibble over definitions. "I am a poet," I confessed, with a certain weary melancholy.

"A famous one? A great one?" Pinker asked eagerly.

"Alas, no. Fame has not yet clasped me to her fickle breast."

"Good," he muttered, surprisingly. Then: "But you can write? You can use words well enough?"

"As a writer I consider myself the master of everything except language—"

"Confound these epigrams!" Pinker cried. "I mean—can you describe? Well, of course you can. You described this coffee."

"Did I?"

"You called it 'rusty.' Yes—and 'rusty' it is. I should never have thought of it—the word would not have come to me—but 'rusty' is the, the . . ."

"The *mot juste*?"

"Exactly." Pinker gave me a look that reminded me of my Oxford tutor—a look which combined doubt with a certain steely determination. "Enough talk. I am going to give you my card."

"I shall certainly accept it," I said, mystified, "although I believe I am unlikely to have need of your services."

He was scribbling something briskly on the back of his business card. It was, I could not help noticing, a rather fine card, made of thick ivory paper. "You misunderstand me, sir. It is *I* who have need of *you*."

"You mean, as some kind of secretary? I'm afraid I—"

Pinker shook his head. "No, no. I have three secretaries already, all extremely proficient in their duties. You, if I may say so, would make a very poor addition to their number."

"What, then?" I asked, somewhat piqued. I had absolutely no desire to become a secretary, but I had always liked to believe that I was capable of it should the occasion arise.

"My need," Pinker said, looking me in the eye, "is for an aesthete—a writer. When I have found this gifted individual, he will join me in an enterprise which will make fantastically wealthy men of us both." He handed me the card. "Call on me at this address tomorrow afternoon."

IT WAS MY FRIEND George Hunt's opinion that the mysterious Mr. Pinker intended to start a literary magazine. As it had long been an ambition of Hunt's to do exactly that—principally because no existing literary magazine in London had yet seen fit to accept his verses—he believed I should take up the coffee merchant's offer and call.

"He hardly seemed a literary type." I turned the card over. On the back was written in pencil, *Admit to my office, please. S.P.*

"Look around you," Hunt said, waving a hand at our surroundings. "This place is full of those who clutch at the petticoats of the Muse." It was true that there were often as many hangers-on in the Café Royal as there were writers or artists.

"But he particularly liked it that I called the coffee 'rusty.' "

The third member of our group—the artist Percival Morgan, who had so far taken no part in the speculation—suddenly laughed. "I know what your Mr. Pinker wants."

"What, then?"

He tapped the back page of the *Gazette.* " 'Branah's patented invigorating powders,' " he read aloud. " 'Guaranteed to restore rosy health to the convalescent. Enjoy the effervescent vigor of the alpine rest cure in a single efficacious spoonful.' It's obvious, isn't it—the man wants you to write his advertising."

I had to admit that this sounded much more likely than a magazine. Pinker had specifically asked if I was good at describing—an odd sort of question for a magazine proprietor, but one that made perfect sense for someone who wanted advertisements composed. Doubtless he simply had a new coffee he wished to push. *Pinker's pick-me-up breakfast blend. Richly roasted for a healthy complexion,* or some such nonsense. I felt an obscure sense of disappointment. For a moment I had hoped—well, that it might be something more exciting.

"Advertising," Hunt said thoughtfully, "is the unspeakable expression of an unspeakable age."

"On the contrary," Morgan said, "I adore advertising. It is the only form of modern art to concern itself, however remotely, with the truth."

They looked at me expectantly. But for some reason I was no longer in the mood for epigrams.

THE FOLLOWING AFTERNOON saw me sitting at my desk, working on a translation of a poem by Baudelaire. At my side, a goblet of pale Venetian glass was filled with golden Rhenish wine; I was writing with a silver pencil on mauve paper infused with oil of bergamot, and I was smoking innumerable cigarettes of Turkish tobacco, all in the approved manner. Even so, it was utterly tedious work. Baudelaire, of course, is a great poet, and thrillingly perverse, but he also tends to be somewhat vague, which makes the translator's job a slow one, and were it not for the three pounds a publisher had promised me for the work, I would have jacked it in several hours ago. My rooms were in St. John's Wood, close to the Regent's Park, and on a sunny spring day such as this I could hear the distant cries of the ice-cream sellers as they paced back and forth by the gates. It made staying inside rather difficult. And for some reason, the only word I could think of that rhymed with "vice" was "strawberry ice."

"Hang it," I said aloud, putting down my pencil.

Pinker's card lay on one side of the desk. I picked it up and looked at it again. *Samuel* PINKER, *coffee importer and distributor.* An address in Narrow Street, Limehouse. The thought of getting out of my rooms, if only for an hour or two, tugged at me like a dog pulling at its master's leash.

On the other side of the desk was a pile of bills. Of course, it was inevitable that a poet should have debts. In fact you could scarcely call yourself an artist if you did not. But just for a moment, I grew dispirited at the thought of eventually having to find the means to pay them off. I fingered the top one, a chit from my wine merchant. The Rhenish wine was not only golden in color: it had cost damn nearly as much as gold as well. Whereas if I agreed to do

Mr. Pinker's advertisements . . . I had no idea what a person charged to write those bits of nonsense. But then, I reasoned, the fact that Pinker had resorted to hanging around the Café Royal in search of a writer suggested that he was as much a novice at this as I was. Supposing he could be prevailed upon to give me, not just a lump sum, but a retainer? Say that it was—I reached for a reasonable sum and then, finding it not enough, quadrupled it—forty pounds a year? And if the coffee merchant had other friends, business acquaintances, who wanted the same sort of service—why, it wouldn't be long before a man had an income of four hundred pounds a year, and all from writing lines like "Enjoy the effervescent vigor of the alpine rest-cure in a single efficacious spoonful." There would still be plenty of time left over for Baudelaire. True, the Muse might feel somewhat slighted that one was prostituting one's talents in this way, but since one would have to keep the whole business secret from one's literary acquaintances in any case, perhaps the Muse might not find out either.

I made a decision. Pausing only to pick up Pinker's card, and to pull on a paisley-pattern coat I had bought at Liberty the week before, I hastened to the door.

LET US TRAVEL now across London, from St. John's Wood to Limehouse. Put like that, it does not sound so very exciting, does it? Allow me, then, to rephrase my invitation. Let us cross the greatest, most populous city in the world, at the very moment when it is at its peak—a journey on which, if you are to accompany me, you will have to employ every one of your senses. Up here by Primrose Hill the air—smell it!—is relatively fresh, with only the faintest sulphuric tinge from the coal fires and kitchen ranges which, even at this time of year, burn in every house. It is once we get past Marylebone that the real fun begins. The hansom cabs and coaches exude a rich smell of leather and sweating horse;

their wheels clatter on the stones; gutters are thick with their soft, moist dung. Everywhere streets are brought to a halt by the press of traffic: carts, coaches, carriages, broughams, cabriolets, gigs, coupes, landaus, clarences, barouches, all struggling in different directions. Some are even constructed in the shape of colossal top hats, with the hat makers' names emblazoned in gold letters. The omnibus drivers are the worst offenders, veering from one side to the other, drawing up next to pedestrians, trying to tempt them inside for thruppence or, for a penny less, up onto the roof. Then there are the velocipedes and bicycles, the flocks of geese being driven to the markets, the peripatetic placard-men pushing through the crowds with their boards advertising umbrellas and other sundries, and the milkmaids who simply wander the streets with a bucket and a cow, waiting to be stopped for milk. Hawkers parade trays of pies and pastries; flower sellers thrust lupines and marigolds into your hands; pipes and cigars add their pungent perfume to the mix. A man cooking Yarmouth bloaters at a brazier waves one, speared on a fork, under your nose. *"Prime toasters,"* he cries hoarsely, *"tuppence for a toaster."* Immediately, as if in response, a chorus of other shouts rises all around. *"Chestnuts, 'ot, 'ot, a penny a score . . . Blacking, an 'aypenny a skin . . . Fine walnuts sixteen a penny . . ."* yell the costermongers' boys. *"Here's your turnips,"* roars back a farmer on a donkey cart. Knife-grinders' wheels shriek and sparkle as they meet the blades. Cadgers offer penny boxes of lucifers, their hands mutely outstretched. And on the outskirts of the crowd—always, always—shuffle the spectral figures of the destitute: the shoeless, breadless, homeless, penniless, waiting to take whatever chances might come their way.

If we ride the underground railway from Baker Street to Waterloo, we will be sharing the narrow platforms with the hot, wet, sooty steam from the locomotives; if we walk down the grand new thoroughfares such as Northumberland Avenue, built to cut through the slums of central London, we will find ourselves amongst a crush of unwashed humanity—since each fine avenue is still surrounded by tenements, and each tenement is a rookery containing up to a hundred families, all living cheek-by-jowl in a fetid stew of sweat, gin, breath and skin. But the day is fine: we shall walk. Though many eye us as we hurry through the back streets of Covent Garden, searching for an exposed handkerchief or a pair of gloves to relieve us of, only the teenage whores in their cheap, gaudy finery speak as we pass, murmuring their lascivious salutations in the hope of fanning a momentary spark of lust. But there is no time for that—no time for anything; we are already horribly late. Perhaps after all we will take a cab; look, there is one now.

As we clatter down Drury Lane we become aware of a faint odor, hardly pleasant, which creeps up these side streets like a poisonous fog. It is the smell of the river. True, thanks to Bazalgette's sewers the Thames is no longer responsible for a stink of rotting waste so foul that Members of Parliament were once forced to souse their curtains with sulphate of lime; but sewers are only effective for those whose modern lavatories are connected to them, and in the tenements great putrid cesspits are still the norm, leaking their malodorous ooze into London's underground streams. Then there are all the other smells from the industries clustered, for reasons of access, along the waterfront. Roasting hops from the breweries—that's pleasant enough, as is the scent of exotic botanicals from the gin distilleries; but then comes a reek of boiling horse bones from the glue factories, of boiling fat from the soap makers, of fish guts from Billingsgate, of rotting dog-dung from the tanneries. Small wonder that those with sensitive constitutions wear nosegays, or keep brooches filled with eucalyptus salts fixed to their lapels.

As we approach the Port of London, we pass beneath great towering warehouses, high and dark as cliffs. From this one comes the rich, heavy smell of tobacco leaves, from the next a sugary waft of molasses, from another the sickly vapors of opium. Here the going is sticky from a burst hogshead of rum; here the way is blocked by a passing phalanx of red-coated soldiers. All around is the chattering of a dozen different languages—flaxen-haired Germans, Chinamen with their black hair in pigtails, Negroes with bright handkerchiefs knotted round their heads. A blue-smocked butcher shoulders a tray of meat; after him comes a straw-hatted bos'n, carrying a green parakeet in a cage of bamboo. Yankees sing boisterous sail-making songs; coopers roll barrels along the cobbles with a deafening drum-like cacophony; goats bleat from their cages on their way to the ships. And the river—the river is full of vessels. Their masts and smokestacks stretch as far as the eye can see: sloops and schooners and bilanders, bafflers full of beer barrels and colliers laden with coal; hoys and eel boats, tea clippers and pleasure cruisers, gleaming mahogany-decked steamers and grimy working barges, all nosing higgledy-piggledy through the chaos, which echoes with the piercing shrieks of the steam whistles, the coalwhippers' shouts, the klaxons of the pilot boats and the endlessly ringing bells of the barges.

The mind would be moribund indeed that did not feel a stirring of excitement at the boundless, busy energy of it all; at the industry and endeavor which pours out all over the globe from this great city, like bees hurrying to and from the laden, dripping honeycomb at the center of their hive. I saw no moral force in it, though—it was exciting, but it was thoughtless, and I watched it go by as a man might cheer a circus parade. It took a man like Pinker to see more to it than that—to see that Civilization, and Commerce, and Christianity, were ultimately one and the same, and to grasp that mere trade, unfettered by government, could be the instrument that would bring a great light to the last remaining dark parts of the world.

[FOUR]

"Cedar"—this lovely, fresh, countrified aroma is that of untreated wood, and is almost identical to that of pencil shavings. It is typified by the natural essential oil of the Atlas cedar. It is more pronounced in mature harvests.

—JEAN LENOIR, Le Nez du Café

THE YOUNG MAN ABOUT MY OWN AGE WHO OPENED THE DOOR to the house in Narrow Street was clearly one of the proficient secretaries Pinker had spoken of. He was impeccably dressed; his white collar was neatly starched, and his hair, which gleamed with Macassar oil, was short—much shorter than my own. "Can I help you?" he said, giving me a cool glance.

I handed him Pinker's card. "Would you tell your employer that Robert Wallis, the poet, is here?"

The young man examined the card. "You're to be admitted. Follow me."

I followed him into the building, which was, I now saw, a kind of warehouse. Bargemen were unloading burlap sacks from a jetty, and a long chain of storemen were hurrying to various parts of the store, a sack on each shoulder. The smell of roasting coffee hit me like a waft of spice. Oh, that smell . . . The building held over a thousand sacks of coffee, and Pinker kept his big drum roasters going day and night. It was a smell halfway between mouth-watering and eye-watering, a smell as dark as burning pitch; a bitter, black, beguiling perfume that caught at the back of the throat, filling the nostrils and the brain. A man could become addicted to that smell, as quick as any opium.

I only got the briefest glimpse of all that as the secretary led me up some stairs and showed me into an office. One window looked onto the street, but there was another, much larger, which gave onto the warehouse. It was at this window that Samuel Pinker was standing, watching the bustle below. Next to him, under a glass bell jar, a small brass instrument clattered quietly, unreeling a spool of thin white paper printed with symbols. The tangled loops, falling like a complicated fleur-de-lys onto the polished floorboards, were the only untidy thing in the room. Another secretary, dressed very like the first, was sitting at a desk, writing with a steel safety pen.

Pinker turned and saw me. "I will take four tons of the Brazilian and one of the Ceylon," he said sternly.

"I beg your pardon?" I said, nonplussed.

"Payment will be freight on board, with the proviso that none spoils during the voyage."

I realized he was dictating. "Oh, of course. Do carry on."

He frowned at my impertinence. "Ten percent will be held back against future samples. I remain, et cetera, et cetera. Take a seat." This last comment clearly being addressed to me, I sat. "Coffee, Jenks, if you please," he told the secretary. "The four and the nine, with the eighteen to follow. I'll sign those while you're gone." He turned his gaze back to me. "You told me you were a writer, Mr. Wallis," he said sourly.

"Indeed."

"Yet my secretaries have been unable to find a single work by you in any Charing Cross bookshop. Mr. W. H. Smith's subscription library has never heard of you. Even the literary editor of *Blackwood's Magazine* is strangely unfamiliar with your work."

"I am a poet," I said, somewhat taken aback by the diligence of Pinker's researches. "But not a published one. I thought I had made that clear."

"You said you were not yet famous. Now I discover you are not yet even heard of. It is hard to see how you could be the one without being the other, is it not?" He sat down heavily on the other side of the table.

"I apologize if I gave the wrong impression. But—"

"Hang the impression. *Precision,* Mr. Wallis. All I ask from you—from anyone—is precision."

In the Café Royal, Pinker had seemed diffident, even unsure of himself. Here in his own offices, his manner was more authoritative. He took out a pen, uncapped it and reached for the pile of letters, signing each one with a rapid flourish as he spoke. "Take me, for example. Would I still be a merchant if I had never sold a single sack of coffee?"

"It's an interesting question—"

"It is not. A merchant is someone who trades. Ergo, if I do not trade, I am not a merchant."

"But a writer, by the same token, must therefore be someone who *writes,*" I pointed out. "It is not strictly necessary to be read as well. Only desirable."

"Hmm." Pinker seemed to weigh this. "Very well." I had the feeling I had passed some kind of test.

The secretary returned with a tray on which were four thimble-sized cups and two steaming jugs, which he placed in front of us. "So," his employer said, gesturing to me. "Tell me what you make of these."

The coffee was evidently freshly brewed—the smell was deep and pleasant. I tried some, while Pinker watched expectantly.

"Well?" he demanded.

"It's excellent."

He snorted. "And? You are a writer, are you not? Words are your stock-in-trade?"

"Ah." I realized now what he wanted. I took a deep breath. "It is completely . . . invigorating. Like an Alpine sanatorium—no—like a seaside rest cure. I can think of no better, balmier, more bracing pick-me-up than Pinker's breakfast blend. It will aid the digestion, restore the concentration and elevate the constitution, all at once."

"What?" The merchant was staring at me.

"Of course, it needs a little work," I said modestly. "But I think the general direction is—"

"Try the other one," he said impatiently.

I started to pour from the second jug. "Not in the same cup!" he hissed.

"Sorry." I filled a second thimble-sized cup and sipped from it. "It's different," I said, surprised.

"Yes, of course," Pinker said. "And?"

It had not really occurred to me before then that there was coffee and *coffee.* Of course, coffee might be watery, or stale, or overbrewed—in fact, it was often all those things—but here were two coffees, both palpably excellent, whose excellence varied from each other as chalk from cheese.

"How might one deal with such a difference in words?" he said, and although his expression had not changed I had a sense that this was the nub of our conversation.

"This one," I said slowly, gesturing at the second cup, "has an almost . . . smoky flavor."

Pinker nodded. "It does indeed."

"Whereas this one," I pointed at the first, "is more . . . flowery."

"Flowery!" Pinker was still staring at me. "Flowery!" But he seemed interested—even, I thought, impressed. "Here—let me make a—" He pulled the secretary's pad toward him and jotted down the word *flowery.* "Go on."

"This second cup has—a sort of tang."

"What sort of tang?"

"More like pencil shavings."

"Pencil shavings." Pinker wrote this down, too. "Exactly."

It was like a parlor game, enjoyable but pointless. "While the other—chestnuts, perhaps?" I said.

"Perhaps," Pinker said, making a note. "What else?"

"This one," I indicated the second cup, "tastes of spice."

"Which spice?"

"I'm not sure," I confessed.

"Never mind," Pinker said, crossing out *spice.* "Ah, there you are. Capital. Pour it, will you?"

I turned. A young woman had entered with another jug of coffee. She was, I noted automatically—in those days I considered myself something of a connoisseur on this particular subject—rather attractive. She wore the Rational style of dress that many professional women were adopting just then. A tailored jacket, buttoned high up to the neck, worn above a long skirt without a bustle, revealed little of the slight figure underneath. Her features, though, were alert and lively, and her hair, although carefully pinned, was elegant and golden.

She filled one of the cups and handed it carefully to me. "My thanks," I said, catching her eye with a frank smile as I took it. If she noticed my interest she did not reveal it; her face was a mask of professional detachment.

"Perhaps you would take notes, Emily," Pinker said, pushing his pad toward her. "Mr. Wallis was just trying to decide which spice our finest Brazilian reminded him of, but inspiration has temporarily deserted him."

The secretary seated herself at the table and raised her pen. For a moment, as she waited for me to resume, I could have sworn I discerned a hint of amusement—of mischievousness, even—deep in her gray eyes. But it was hard to be sure.

I drank some of the new coffee, but to begin with I could taste nothing at all. "I'm sorry," I said, shaking my head.

"Blow on it," Pinker suggested.

I blew, and drank some more. It was, I realized, very ordinary compared to the other two. "This is what they serve at the Café Royal!"

"Very like it, yes." Pinker was smiling. "Is it—ha!—is it rusty?"

"A little." I tried some more. "And dull. Very dull. With a faint aftertaste of—wet towels." I glanced at the stenographer. She was busy writing it all down—or rather, I now saw, making a series of curious, almost Arabian squiggles on her pad. This must be the Pitman's Phonographic Method I had read of.

"Wet towels," Pinker repeated with a chuckle. "Very good, though I'm afraid I have never actually tasted a towel, wet or dry."

The secretary's pen stopped, waiting. "And it smells like—old carpet," I said. Immediately, my words were translated into more dashes and strokes.

"Carpet!" Pinker nodded. "Anything else?"

"A whiff of burnt toast." More squiggles.

"Burnt toast. Well. That will do, I think, for the moment."

The girl's notations did not even occupy a full page of her notebook. I felt a foolish desire to impress her. "So which one of these is yours?" I asked the merchant, gesturing at the jugs.

"What?" Once again Pinker seemed surprised by the question. "Oh, all of them."

"And which do you want to advertise?"

"Advertise?"

"Of this one," I said, pointing to the first jug, "you might say . . ." I raised the cup. *"A choice concoction, the cream of the colonies, with an ambrosial chestnut taste."* Was it my imagination, or did the secretary give a faint snort of laughter, instantly suppressed? "Though I've noticed most advertisements do tend to stress the health side of things. Perhaps: *It's the choice chestnut taste that cheers the constitution."*

"My dear Wallis," Pinker said, "you would make a truly terrible advertising man."

"I don't believe I would."

"People want their coffee to taste of coffee, not chestnuts."

"We could tell them how good the chestnut part of it is."

"The essence of advertising, of course," he said thoughtfully, "is to conceal the truth, by revealing only those parts which coincide with what the public wants to hear. The essence of a code, on the other hand, is to fix the truth precisely for the benefit of the few."

"That's very good." I was impressed. "That's almost an epigram. Er . . . what's this about a code?"

"Young man," Pinker said, looking at me intently, "listen carefully to what I am about to say. I am going to make you a very important proposal."

[FIVE]

"We live, Mr. Wallis, in an Age of Improvement." Pinker sighed and pulled a watch from his fob pocket. "Take this timepiece," he said, holding it up by its chain. "It is both more accurate than any watch produced in previous decades, and less costly. Next year, it will be cheaper and more accurate still. Do you know how much the latest Ingersoll sells for?"

I confessed myself ignorant on this score.

"A single dollar." Pinker nodded. "And then consider the benefits. Consistency—the first requirement of trade. You doubt it? More accurate timepieces mean more accurate railways. More accurate railways mean more trade. More trade means cheaper, more accurate timepieces." He picked up a pen from the table. "Or take this safety pen. It has its own inkwell, ingeniously contained within the barrel—do you see? Which means my secretaries can write more speedily, so we can do more business, et cetera, et cetera. Or—" He reached into his fob pocket again and dug something out with his thumb and forefinger. "Look at this." He was staring intently at a tiny nut-and-bolt. "What a remarkable thing this is, Wallis. The bolt was made in—oh, Belfast, shall we say. The nut, perhaps, was made in Liverpool. Yet they fit together exactly. The threads, you see, have been *standardized.*" The stenographer's pen was flying across her pad by now—she must have been under instruction to record all these extempore speeches of her employer's, or perhaps she was doing it for her own education. "A few years ago every workshop and machine room in the country produced their own design of thread. It was chaos. It was impractical. Now, thanks to the impetus of Improvement, there is only one. Are you a believer in the theories of Mr. Darwin?"

Taken aback by the abrupt change of topic, and cautious of giving offense—Darwin was a topic on which my Oxford tutors had tended to become heated—I said that, on balance, I probably was.

Pinker nodded approvingly. "What Darwin shows us is that Improvement is inevitable. For species, of course, but also for countries, for races, for individuals, even for nuts and bolts. Now. Let us consider how Mr. Darwin's ideas may benefit the coffee trade."

I tried to look as if I might conceivably have some useful suggestions to contribute to this subject, and had only chosen not to voice them out of deference to the greater wisdom of my companion. It was a look I had often been required to employ in my tutors' rooms at Oxford. However, it was not needed now: Pinker was in full flow.

"First, the brewing. How may this process be Improved? I will tell you, Mr. Wallis. By steam."

"Steam? You mean—a mill?"

"In a manner of speaking. Imagine if every café and hotel had its own steam engine for making coffee. Just as in the manufacture of cotton or corn, we would see consistency. Consistency!"

"Wouldn't it make the cafés rather—well, rather hot?"

"The engine I am describing is a miniature one. Jenks, Foster," he called, "bring in the apparatus, will you?"

After a brief pause, and a certain amount of banging, the two male secretaries wheeled in a trolley on which sat a curious mechanism. It seemed to consist of a copper boiler, together with a quantity of brass pipes, levers, dials and tubing.

"Signor Toselli's steam-powered coffee-machine," Pinker said proudly. "As demonstrated at the Paris Exhibition. The steam is forced through the grounds one cup at a time, giving a much superior taste."

"How is it heated?"

"By gas, although we anticipate an electric model eventually." He paused. "I've ordered eighty."

"Eighty! Where will they all go?"

"To Pinker's Temperance Taverns." Pinker jumped to his feet and started pacing. Behind him, Jenks was lighting the boiler: the apparatus hissed and whistled softly as its owner spoke. "Oh, I anticipate what you are about to say. You wish to point out that there exists, at this time, not a single Pinker's Temperance Tavern in the land. But they will come, Wallis; they will come. I intend to apply the principles of the safety pen and the Ingersoll timepiece. Look at London. A pub on every corner! Gin palaces, most of 'em, where the working man is fleeced of his hard-earned wages. What does his intoxication benefit him? It makes him a drudge, a wife beater. It makes him so incapable that he is often unable even to stagger home, and must spend the night in the gutter, ruining him for employment the following day. Yet coffee—coffee!—offers no such drawbacks. It does not incapacitate: rather, it invigorates. It does not dull the senses, but sharpens them. Why should we not have a coffee-house on every street instead? It would be an Improvement, would it not? Yes? Then, if it is an Improvement, it must happen—it *will* happen. Darwin says so! And I will be the one to *make* it happen." He sat down, dabbing at his forehead with his sleeve.

"You mentioned a code," I said. "I still don't quite see—"

"Yes. Demand and supply, Mr. Wallis. Demand and supply."

He paused, and I waited, and the secretary's dainty hand paused on her pad. She had exceptionally long, elegant fingers. One could imagine them playing a violin or pressing on the keyboard of a piano. One could imagine them, in fact, doing all sorts of things, some of them deliciously improper . . .

"The difficulty with my plans," Pinker explained, "is cost. Coffee is expensive stuff—much more costly than beer or gin. Well, it comes from further away, of course. You order it through an agent, who in turn gets it from another agent—it's a wonder it reaches us at all." He looked at me. "And so we ask ourselves—what?"

"We ask ourselves," I suggested, dragging my attention back to him, "how the supply could be Improved?"

Pinker snapped his fingers. "Exactly! We've made a start with this Exchange. You've heard of the Exchange, I take it?"

I had not.

He placed his hand on the bell jar in which the printing machine still clicked and clattered quietly to itself, spooling its line of symbols endlessly onto the floor. "The London Coffee Exchange will revolutionize the way we do business. It's linked by submarine cable to New York and Amsterdam. Prices will standardize—all across the world. The price will fall—it's bound to." He shot me a crafty look. "Can you spot the difficulty, Mr. Wallis?"

I thought. "You don't actually know what you're getting. You're buying by numbers—on cost alone. You want to find the good stuff—for your taverns—and pass on the rest. That way, you get the benefit of the lower prices, and other people get the dross."

Pinker sat back and regarded me with a smile. "You've got it, sir. You've got it."

The apparatus suddenly emitted a wheezing, bubbling screech. Jenks pulled some levers, and an unpleasant gargling sound issued from its several throats as liquid and steam together hissed into a miniature cup.

I said, "If you have a code—no, *code*'s not quite the word—if you have a trading *vocabulary,* a way of describing the coffee you and your agents have fixed in advance, then even though you're in different countries—"

"Exactly!" Pinker picked up the bolt, took the nut in his other hand, and placed them together. "We have our bolt and we have our nut. The two will fit together."

Jenks placed two tiny cups in front of Pinker and me. I picked mine up. It contained no more than an egg-cup's worth of thick black liquid, on which floated a honeycomb of hazelnut-brown froth. I rotated the cup: the contents were dense and sluggish, like oil. I raised it to my lips—

It was as if the very essence of coffee had been concentrated into that tiny morsel of liquid. Burnt embers, woodsmoke and charred fires danced across my tongue, caught at the back of my throat, and from there seemed to rush up directly to my brain . . . and yet it was not acrid. The texture was like honey or molasses, and there was a faint, biscuity sweetness that lingered, like the darkest chocolate, like tobacco. I finished the tiny cup in two gulps, but the taste seemed to grow and deepen in my mouth for long moments afterwards.

Pinker, watching me, nodded. "You have a palate, Mr. Wallis. It is rough and somewhat untutored, but you can apply yourself in that sphere. And—more importantly—you have the gift of using words. Find me the words that can capture—can *standardize*—the elusive taste of coffee, so that two people in different parts of the world can telegraph a description to each other, and each know exactly what is meant by it. Make it authoritative, evocative, but above all *precise.* That is your task. We shall call it . . ." He paused. "We shall call it The Pinker-Wallis Method Concerning the Clarification and Classification of the Various Flavors of Coffee. What do you say?"

He was looking at me expectantly.

"It sounds fascinating," I said politely. "But I could not possibly do what you suggest. I am a writer—an artist—not some manufacturer of phrases." My God, the coffee from that machine was strong: I could feel my heart racing from its effects.

"Ah. Emily anticipated that this might be your response." Pinker nodded toward the secretary, whose head was still lowered demurely over her notebook. "At her suggestion, I took the liberty of establishing your father's address and sending him a telegram about this offer of employment. You may be interested to see the Reverend Wallis's reply." Pinker pushed a telegram slip across the table. I picked it up: it started with the word *Hallelujah!* "He seems quite keen to be relieved of the burden of supporting you," he said drily.

"I see."

" 'Tell him allowance terminated stop. Grateful opportunity stop. God bless you sir stop.' "

"Ah."

"And in the light of your being sent down—your father mentions it in passing—taking orders or indeed schoolmastering are avenues now probably closed to you."

"Yes," I said. My throat seemed to have gone dry. Jenks placed another tiny cup of coffee in front of me. I threw it down my throat. Fragrant charcoal and dark chocolate flooded my brain. "You mentioned fantastic wealth."

"Did I?"

"Yesterday, at the Café Royal. You said that if I entered into your . . . scheme, we would both become fantastically wealthy men."

"Ah, yes." Pinker considered. "That was a figure of speech. I was employing . . ." He glanced at the secretary. "What was I employing?"

"Hyperbole," she said. It was the first time she had spoken. Her voice was low, but again I thought I discerned a faint note of amusement. I glanced at her, but her head was still bent over the notepad, recording every word with those damn squiggles.

"Exactly. I was employing hyperbole. As a literary person, I'm sure you appreciate that." Pinker's eyes glinted. "Of course, at the time I was not fully apprised of your own somewhat straitened circumstances."

"What remuneration—exactly—are you suggesting?"

"Emily here informs me that Mrs. Humphrey Ward was paid ten thousand pounds for her last novel. Despite the fact that she is the most popular writer in the country and you are completely unknown, I propose to pay you at the same rate."

"Ten thousand pounds?" I repeated, amazed.

"I said the same *rate,* sir, not the same *amount*—once again I have to warn you of the dangers of imprecision." Pinker smiled—the brute was enjoying this. "Mrs. Ward's opus is approximately two hundred thousand words long—or six shillings and thruppence a word. I will pay you six and thruppence for every descriptor adopted for our code. And a bonus of twenty pounds when it is complete. That is fair, is it not?"

I passed my hand across my face. My head was spinning. I had drunk far too much of that damn coffee. "The Wallis-Pinker Method."

"I'm sorry?"

"It must be called the Wallis-Pinker Method. Not the other way round."

Pinker frowned. "If a Pinker is the originator, surely Pinker must have the greater share of the credit."

"As the writer, the bulk of the work will fall to me."

"If I may say so, Wallis, you have not yet fully grasped the principles by which business is conducted. If I want to find a more amenable employee, I can simply go down to the Café Royal and get myself one. I found you within five minutes, after all. Whereas if you want to find yourself another employer, you will be hard pushed to do so."

"Possibly," I said. "But no two writers are exactly the same. How can you be sure that the next man will do as good a job?"

"Hmm." Pinker considered. "Very well," he conceded abruptly. "The Wallis-Pinker method."

"And, as this is a literary work, I will need an advance. Thirty pounds."

"That is a very considerable amount."

"It is customary," I insisted.

To my surprise, Pinker shrugged. "Thirty pounds it is, then. Do we have an agreement?"

I hesitated. I had been going to say that I would have to think about it, that I must take advice. I could already imagine the sneers of my friends Hunt and Morgan if I ever told them of this commission. But—I could not help it—I glanced at the girl. Her eyes were shining, and she gave me . . . not a smile exactly, but a kind of tiny signal, the eyes widening with the briefest nod of encouragement. In that moment I was lost.

"Yes," I said.

"Good," the merchant said, standing up and offering me his hand. "We start in this office tomorrow morning, sir, sharp at ten o'clock. Emily, will you be so good as to show Mr. Wallis out?"

[SIX]

"Acerbic"—an acrid and sour sensation on the tongue.

—LINGLE, The Coffee Cupper's Handbook

AS WE REACHED THE BOTTOM OF THE STAIRS I STOPPED HER. "Would it be possible to look round the warehouse? I am curious to know more about the business to which Mr. Pinker has decided I am to be apprenticed."

If she understood that I was inviting her to make fun of her employer, she did not show it. "Of course," she said simply, and led me into the vast storeroom I had glimpsed earlier.

It was a curious place—devilish hot, from the line of roasting drums that stood to one side, the flames of their burners bright in the gloom. The boat had been unloaded now, and the big doors onto the jetty were closed, with only one fat blade of sunlight pushing through the crooked gap between them. There were windows, high above, but they admitted little illumination. Rather, the air was full of a peculiar mistiness; caused, I now saw, by a thick dust of cotton-like fibers which floated all around us. I reached into it; the air eddied around my hand.

"Coffee parchment," she explained. "Some of the beans we receive have not yet been milled."

Her words meant nothing to me, but I nodded. "And all this coffee belongs to Pinker?"

"Mister Pinker," she said, with a little emphasis on the title, "owns four warehouses, of which the two largest are in bond. This is merely the clearing house." She pointed. "The coffee comes in along the river, by boat. Then it is sampled, weighed, milled, roasted and placed in its proper location, according to its country of origin. In this store we have, as it were, the whole world. Over there is Brazil; over here is Ceylon. Indonesia is behind us—there is not so much of that: the Dutch take most of the crop. The pure arabicas we keep over here, for safety."

"Why must pure arabicas be kept safer than the rest?"

"Because they are the most valuable." She took a step toward a stack of plump jute sacks. One was already open. "Look," she said. Her voice seemed to thrill with excitement.

I looked. The sack was filled with beans—iron colored, gleaming, as if each one had been individually oiled and polished. She scooped up a handful to show me. They were small, each one notched like a peanut, and as they fell back through her fingers they hissed like rain.

"Mocca," she said reverently. "Every one a jewel." She pushed her arm in up to the elbow, swirling it around with a soft, hypnotic gesture that was almost a caress, releasing a great waft of that dark, charred aroma. "A whole sack like this is like a sack full of treasure."

"May I?" I slid my arm in beside hers. It was a curious sensation: I saw the beans closing around my wrist, as liquid might, but they were dry and light, as insubstantial as chaff. The rich, bitter smell filled my nostrils. I pushed deeper. Amongst the slippery, oiled smoothness of the beans, I thought I felt, for an instant, something else—the soft dry touch of her fingers.

"Your Mr. Pinker is quite a character," I said.

"He is a genius," she said calmly.

"An impresario of coffee?" As if by accident, I slid my thumb gently over her wrist. She stiffened and withdrew her arm, but otherwise she did not react. I had been right: there was a curious kind of mischief here, or perhaps, it would be truer to say, a kind of confidence: this was a woman who did not simper and shriek for the sake of it.

"A genius," she repeated. "He means to change the world."

"With his Temperance Taverns?"

I must have sounded amused, because she said abruptly, "That is part of it, yes." As if drawn back by some sensual force, she dipped her hand into the sack again, watching the beans drip between her fingers, dark as beads of ebony or jet.

"And the rest?" I prompted.

She looked at me coolly. "You think him ridiculous."

I shook my head. "I think him misguided. The working man is never going to prefer arabicas to gin."

She gave a dismissive shrug. "Perhaps."

"You disagree?"

Instead of answering she scooped another handful of beans, letting them spill slowly from her palm as she tilted it from side to side. I suddenly realized what that dim, sepulchral warehouse reminded me of. The overpowering smell of coffee was like the smell of incense, and the dim, dust-filled light was like the gloom of some great cathedral.

"These are not just beans, Mr. Wallis," she said, her eyes fixed on the tumbling black drops. "They are seeds. The seeds of a new civilization."

She glanced up. I followed her gaze, toward the window that

looked down from Pinker's office. The coffee merchant was standing at the glass, watching us.

"He is a great man," she said simply. "He is also my father."

SHE WITHDREW HER HAND from the sack, wiping it daintily on a handkerchief as she stepped toward the burners. "Miss Pinker," I said, catching her up. "You must allow me to apologize—I had no inkling—if I have offended—"

"If you should apologize to anyone, it is to him."

"Your father, though, is not aware of my remarks."

"Well, I shall not tell him if you do not."

"And I must apologize for . . ." I hesitated. "For my behavior toward yourself. It was hardly appropriate to someone in your position."

"What behavior was that?" she asked innocently. Overcome with confusion, I did not reply.

"I hope, Mr. Wallis," she said, "you will treat me no differently from any of my father's other employees."

A rebuke—or an invitation? If so, it was a heavily coded one. She held my gaze for a moment. "We are both here to work, are we not? Any personal feelings must be put on one side. 'In the morning sow thy seed, and in the evening withhold not thy hand.' Ecclesiastes."

I inclined my head. "Indeed. Then I shall look forward to the evening, Miss Pinker."

"And I to the morning, Mr. Wallis."

I LEFT THE WAREHOUSE exhilarated and confused in equal measure. On the one hand, I seemed to have blundered into gainful employment. On the other, there was a nascent cockstand rolling around in my trousers as the result of my flirtation with the lovely

Emily Pinker. Well, that was easily taken care of. I took a boat to the Embankment, then crossed the Strand to Wellington Street. Here there were several cheap and cheerful establishments I had frequented before, all of a reliably high standard. Tonight, however, was a night for celebration: I had the promise of my thirty pounds advance.

Pausing only to eat a meat pudding at the Savoy Tavern window, I entered the grandest of the bagnios at Number 18. On the second floor, behind heavy curtains, was a receiving room lined with red damask where half a dozen of the prettiest girls in London reclined in their négligés on upholstered divans. But which to choose? There was a girl with glorious red ringlets; another whose powdered face was like the face of a marionette. There was a strapping six-foot German beauty, a dark-skinned French coquette, and more besides.

I chose the one whose long, elegant fingers reminded me of Miss Emily Pinker.

[SEVEN]

Pinker looks up as his daughter comes into his office to clear the cups and jugs that litter the desk.

"Well?" he says mildly. "What do you think of our aesthete, Emily?"

She takes a cloth and wipes some spilled grounds from the polished mahogany before she replies. "He is certainly not quite what I expected."

"In what way?"

"Younger, for one thing. And somewhat full of himself."

"Yes," Pinker agrees. "But after giving the matter some thought, I decided that may not be a bad thing. An older man might be more fixed in his opinions. This one, I hope, will be less inclined to run away with your idea."

"It is hardly my idea," she murmurs.

"Do not be too modest, Emily. If you are to work with Mr. Wallis, I suspect that modesty will be a luxury you cannot afford. Of course it is your idea, and must remain so." He twirls his safety pen between his fingers. "I wonder that he did not consider that—

did you notice, when I talked about a Pinker being the originator, he assumed that it was me?"

"A reasonable assumption, surely? Particularly as he had not realized at the time I was your daughter."

"Perhaps." Pinker watches her as she places crockery on the tray. "Will you tell him? That the Guide originated with you, I mean?"

She stacks up the cups. "No," she says after a moment.

"Why not?"

"I think at this stage the less Mr. Wallis knows of our plans, the better. If I tell him, he may want to know more about the purposes for which the Guide was conceived. And anything we say might somehow get back to our competitors—even, perhaps, to Howell."

"As ever, you are very wise, Emily." Her father turns his head, watching the stock ticker as it stutters and pecks at its endless flow of tape. "Let us hope, then, that young Mr. Wallis is up to the job."

[EIGHT]

Keep the cupping room free from outside interferences, especially sights, sounds, and smells. In addition, completely concentrate on the task at hand.

—LINGLE, The Coffee Cupper's Handbook

THE NEXT MORNING IT WAS THE TURN OF JENKS, THE SENIOR secretary, to show me around. If the warehouse had seemed on the previous evening like a cathedral or a church, in the company of Jenks it soon became clear that it was actually a machine—a vast but very simple mechanism for the accumulation of profits. "The material," as he called the coffee, came in on the high tide; was swept from point to point around the great box of the warehouse; was hulled, milled, roasted and in some cases ground, before being swept out again on another tide, its worth quadrupled. Jenks showed me the books, all kept in his own hand; vast ledgers that recorded the movement of every bag, every bean, as they made their inexorable progress from one column to another.

Most of the coffees that came to this store were destined for one of just four blends: Pinker's Mocca Mix, Pinker's Old Government Java, Pinker's Ceylon, and Pinker's Fancy. These blends were not quite what they seemed. Old Government Java, for example, was so called because the Dutch government aged their coffees before releasing them, creating a mellow taste popular on the continent. However, because of the duties on Dutch coffee, the actual proportion of Java in Pinker's blend might be as low as one-third, with the rest coming from estates in India and Brazil. Similarly, Jenks explained, the Ceylon blend had originally been sourced from Pinker's own plantations in that country; now, blight having all but wiped out the crop, the name was more of a descriptor of the style than an indicator of origin, with cheaper Brazilian coffee making up more than eighty percent of the mix.

I must have looked surprised, because he said sternly, "It is a standard business practice—there is nothing unscrupulous about it."

"Of course."

"Other merchants commonly adulterate their blends with foreign substances. Chicory, oats, roast maize, even sorghum, flavored with wood ash and molasses. Pinker's never does that."

"Even though it is, as you said, a standard business practice?" I said innocently.

He glared at me. "I said it was common. Amongst the lower sort of merchant, I meant. Such as Seymour, or Lambert's. Even Howell's, for all that they carry the Royal Warrant." He spoke the names, particularly the last one, with a kind of angry sneer.

"I see." To change the subject—I had ribbed him enough—I said, "The failure of your estates in Ceylon must have been a blow."

"Not really. The land was cheap, and the labor was easily redirected to other crops such as tea. There was a small book loss, which we have written off against our assets."

These were terms, of course—*book loss, assets, written off*—that meant nothing to me then. I nodded, and we moved on.

In the office, Jenks showed me how a merchant samples, or

"cups," as he called it. An exact amount of ground beans was placed directly in a standard-sized cup. After water was added, one waited precisely two minutes before pushing the grounds to the bottom with a spoon and tasting the result.

"Like this," Jenks said. He dipped his spoon into the cup with a practiced, dainty flick, then raised it to his mouth and slurped it noisily. It seemed a coarse sound for such a man to make, until I realized that he was deliberately sucking in air with the liquid—much as Pinker had done at the Café Royal.

"How does it taste?" I asked.

He shrugged. "I don't know. I have little palate." Again, there was a note of disdain in his voice, as if to say that the actual taste of the stuff was best left to people like myself.

"That must be a disadvantage, for someone in your position."

"My concern is with the business side of things."

"But a poor business it would be, if the coffee did not taste of anything."

"Then it is fortunate for us all that you're here," he said with a sniff. I looked at him, surprised by his tone: it had not occurred to me before that Pinker's existing employees might have had their noses put out of joint by my appointment.

At that moment the merchant himself joined us. "Ah! I see our new pupil is hard at work," he commented. "I am delighted to find you so industrious, Mr. Wallis. I confess I had a moment of anxiety last night. From here, after all, one cannot be 'sent down.' " He picked up the cup the secretary had just tasted, pushing his nose into it and sniffing deeply. "You will observe," he said thoughtfully, "that the smell differs here in the cup and"—he moved his nose a little further away—"from a distance of a few inches. Moreover, tilting the nose to one side—*thus*—appears to intensify the aromas. While rotating the liquid with a gentle motion"—he swirled the cup—"release a different set of volatiles. These will all be matters for us to consider in due course."

"Mr. Wallis was just expressing his reservations in the matter of blending," Jenks piped up caustically.

Pinker looked at me with a frown. "Is that so?"

"I was just observing," I said mildly—damn that sneak Jenks!—"what a trouble it must be, to buy coffee in so many varieties, yet to sell so few."

"True, true. The aficionado will find something to admire about the coffee from any estate, just as a lover of wine will delight in comparing the clarets of Bordeaux with the Riojas of Spain and so on. But we must make a profit, and unlike wines, coffee once roasted does not improve with age."

He went to the window that overlooked his warehouse, and for a moment he looked down at that great space, brooding. "Think of them as an army," he said, almost to himself—I was compelled to stand at his shoulder to hear him. "Each regiment has its place of origin, its character, yet each regiment is composed of individuals—fighting men who have given up their own identity to the whole. Out there I have my Highlanders, my Irish Irregulars, my Gurkhas. And just as an army deploys its cavalry or its engineers, depending on the task, so the blender might balance a dull Brazilian with a small amount of Sumatra, or mask the deficiencies of one lot with the best attributes of another."

"Then, if they are an army, you must be their general, ready to send them into war," I said. I was joking, but Pinker's expression as he glanced at me then betrayed not a whit of humor: rather, his eyes were fierce with the thought of what his battalions might achieve.

"Exactly so," he said softly. "Exactly so."

WE BEGAN work immediately. A burner was brought in and connected to the gas. We were supplied with a copious quantity of cups and kettles of water, as well as a rough fellow called South whose job was to fetch samples of coffee as we required them. There were also two steel buckets, the purpose of which I was initially unclear about.

"For the coffee," Pinker explained. "If you actually drink it all, you'll jump out of your skin."

We were also supplied with Emily, who took up her position at the side of the table with her notepad. I smiled at her, but although she nodded back it was a professional greeting, nothing more. Of course she was not to know that the previous evening we had copulated at some length on a velvet-covered divan at Number 18 Wellington Street. (The girl I had chosen was pretty enough, but lethargic, her natural lubriciousness clearly augmented by a generous dollop of Clayton's Grease. Much later, after I had returned to my own rooms, I found my detumescent member to be thickly coated with the stuff. It is a curious thing with whores that one pays a premium for inexperience and lack of ability—surely the only profession in which this is the case. But I digress.)

"I suggest we take as our starting point the remarks Linnaeus makes on the various categories of odor," Pinker said. He consulted a pocket-book. "Here we are. Linnaeus groups scents into seven classes, depending on their hedonic, that is to say pleasant, properties. Thus we have *Fragrantes,* the fragrant smells, such as saffron or wild lime; *Aramaticos,* aromatics, such as citron, anise, cinnamon and clove; *Ambrosiacos,* ambrosial or musky smells; *Alliaceous,* the smells of garlic or onion bulbs; *Hircinos,* goatish smells, such as cheese, meat or urine; *Tetros,* foul smells, such as dung or walnuts; and *Nauseosos,* nauseating smells, such as the gum of the asafoetida plant. Are you in agreement?"

I gave it a moment's thought. "No."

Pinker frowned.

"Linnaeus's system may have suited his own purposes," I said airily, "but aesthetic principles dictate a different approach. We must deal first with sight—with color and appearance—and only then proceed to smell, taste, aftertaste and so on."

Pinker considered. "Very well."

Having thus established that we were doing this my way, I sent South off to get a handful of coffee from every sack in the warehouse. Eventually the beans were arranged in little heaps on the table before me.

"So," I said, more confidently than I felt, "these ones over here are as black as despair, whereas these are as golden as virtue—"

"No, no, no," Pinker interjected. "This is far too poetical. One man's despair is another man's gloom, and who is to say whether gloom and despair are the same color?"

I saw his point. "Then we will have to decide on words for several different shades of black."

"Exactly, sir—that is my purpose entirely."

"Hmm." I considered. It was, when one thought about it, a rather vexing issue. "We shall begin," I declared, "by fixing the very blackest form of black there is."

"Very well."

A silence fell upon us. It was, in fact, quite hard to think of a word to describe the pure blackness of the darkest beans. "The pure black of a cow's nose," I said at last. Pinker made a face. "Or the glistening black of a slug at dawn—"

"Too fanciful. And, if I may say so, hardly appetizing."

"The black of a Bible."

"Too objectionable."

"The black of a moonless night."

Pinker tutted.

"Too poetic for you? What about charcoal, then?"

"But charcoal is not quite black. It is a kind of gray, somewhere between the gray of Cornish slate and the gray of a mouse's fur." This was from Emily. I glanced at her. "My apologies," she added.

"You probably don't require another person's opinion, when your own is already so pronounced."

"No—you make a good objection," I said. "And besides, the more . . . collaborative we are, the better our chances of eventual success." Inwardly, of course, I was deeply regretting not having stipulated that this Guide should be something I produce entirely on my own. We had been debating the color black for ten minutes, and I had not even made back the ten shillings I had spent so energetically the night before.

"Sable?" I suggested.

"Crow," Pinker countered.

"Anthracite."

"Tar."

"Jet," I said.

Pinker nodded reluctantly. No one could argue that jet was indeed very black.

"We have our first word," Emily said, writing it down. "But you should perhaps bear in mind that these beans are only black because we have roasted them to be that way. In their natural state they are actually light brown."

"Yes, of course," I said. "I was aware of that." And, needless to say, I had forgotten. "The roast is, naturally, something else we must consider. In the meantime we ask ourselves—if those are jet, then what are these?" With my finger I pushed at some more beans.

"Those are . . . iron," Emily said.

"Indeed," I agreed. "Iron they certainly are."

"This is getting easier," she commented as she wrote it down.

"And these?" Pinker said, pointing at a third pile.

"Those are pearl."

"Pearls are white. Any fool knows that."

I picked up one of the beans and scrutinized it closely. It had a sort of opalescent sheen, like a polished coin. "Pewter, then."

"I agree," Emily said, writing it down.

"And so we come to brown."

"But there are many different shades of brown, and all of them are simply called brown," Pinker objected. "There are no words to distinguish between them."

"Not so. Consider, for example, the brown of different kinds of wood." I glanced at the beans. "Some of these might be called mahogany, some ash, some oak."

Abruptly, Pinker stood. "I have other affairs to attend to. You two carry on." I was to discover that this was typical of him—he was unable to persevere at any task for more than an hour or so; the consequence, in part, of having so many calls upon his time, but also because he was predisposed to the excitement of novelty. Now he strode to the door and pulled it open. "Jenks?" he called. "Jenks, where are you?"

Then he was gone.

I looked at Emily. She kept her gaze on her pad. "I have been trying," I said softly, "to fix in my mind a word which would describe the precise color of your eyes."

She stiffened, and I saw a little color rise in her cheeks as she bent over her notebook.

"They too are a kind of gray," I suggested. "But brighter, I think, than charcoal or Cornish slate."

There was a moment's silence. Then she said, "We should continue, Mr. Wallis. We have much to do."

"Of course. In any case, it is not a question that should be hurried. I shall need to give the matter much further thought."

"Please, do not do so on my account." There was a hint of ice in her voice. "There is no need to put yourself to the trouble."

"No, it will be a pleasure."

"But perhaps in the meantime, we might return our thoughts to the color of these beans."

"You are a hard taskmaster, Miss Pinker."

"I am merely aware that the task before us is a considerable one."

"Considerable, perhaps, but not irksome," I said gallantly. "No labor could be tedious in such company."

"But I fear I am becoming a distraction to you." The hint of ice had become positively arctic. "Perhaps I should see if Mr. Jenks or Mr. Simmons is free to take my place—"

"No need," I said hastily. "I will attend to my duties all the more conscientiously because you have commanded it."

We stared at the heaps of gray-green raw beans. Neither of us, I am sure, was thinking about coffee. I stole another glance at her.

"Whereas the color of your cheeks," I said, "puts me in mind of the ripening of an apple—"

"Mr. Wallis." She slammed her pad forcefully on the table. "If my cheeks have color in them, it is because I am angry at you for continuing to tease me like this."

"Then I apologize. I meant no harm. Quite the reverse, in fact."

"But you must see," she said in a low, urgent voice, "that you are putting me in an impossible position. If I leave the room, my father will want to know why, and then he will dismiss you, and the Guide will not get written, and that is a responsibility I do not want. Yet if I stay, I am effectively at your mercy, and from your conduct so far this morning I cannot help but suspect you will take advantage of that to tease me even more."

"I swear on my honor that I shall do no such thing."

"You must promise to disregard my sex entirely."

"I had thought you too modern to shrink like a violet from a perfectly natural attraction on my part. However, if you prefer it I shall in future try to think of you as if you were a boy."

She gave me a suspicious look, but lifted her pencil over her pad.

"These beans . . ." I picked up a handful and closed my fist around them, shaking them. "We might compare their color to leaves."

"In what way?"

"New leaf is pale green. Summer leaf, of course, is darker. Autumn leaf is more like the paler, more yellow beans."

"Very well." She wrote it down.

"And so we come to aroma. For that, I think, we must prepare some samples."

"I will light the burner."

She busied herself boiling water, and I watched her. I had been wrong when I considered that those Rational garments of hers did not flatter her. Rather, the absence of a corset, whilst it might deprive her of the voluptuous silhouette which until recently had been the fashion, allowed one to appreciate what her natural shape would be—in other words, her naked figure. She was slender: bony, some might say. Even her haunches, as she leaned over the table, were so insubstantial that the comparison with a boy was quite apt. Half closing my eyes, I mentally compared her with various whores I had been with, and was thus able to create a sort of composite image of her unclothed body, a pleasant reverie which Emily might well have taken for studious concentration.

Just then Pinker came back into the room and found me looking at his daughter. He must have been able to guess what was going through my mind.

"Does the work progress?" he said sharply. "Is Mr. Wallis proving industrious, Emily?"

Now, of course, was the time when the least hint from her would have had me thrown out. Inwardly I cursed my recklessness. I needed that advance, particularly after the inroads I had made into it the previous night.

She gazed at me coolly. "Mr. Wallis is progressing quite well, Father. Though not as rapidly, I believe, as he would like. I fear my girlish chatter has been a distraction."

"On the contrary, Miss Pinker has been an inspiration," I said smoothly. "As Beatrice was to Dante, or Maud to Tennyson, so is Emily Pinker to the Wallis-Pinker Guide."

Pinker's eyes narrowed. "Very well. Perhaps, Wallis, I might help you cup your first sample."

"There is no need," I said airily. "Jenks has already explained the principles."

"I shall observe, then."

He took up a position next to the door, arms folded, and watched me as I measured the beans, ground them in a handmill, and added the hot water. I waited exactly two minutes by my watch, then pushed the thick, foaming crust of grounds to the bottom with the spoon. I was not as practiced as the secretary had been, however, and when I lifted the spoon, the liquid was still thick with tiny grains of coffee. I put it to my lips anyway and tried to slurp it in the same manner that Pinker and Jenks had done, pulling in a quantity of air along with the hot liquid. The inevitable and immediate result was that I choked, spluttering coffee all over the table.

Pinker roared. "My dear Wallis," he cried, "you were meant to taste it, not to spray it like a surfacing whale!"

"A catch in the throat," I said, or rather croaked, when speech was possible. "My apologies. I will try again." I was very embarrassed. Again I tried to slurp the coffee as I had seen others do, but it was harder than it looked: this time I managed to keep the liquid in my mouth as I coughed and choked, but it was a close thing.

"Emily, my dear, I fear your new colleague will be unable to speak for the rest of the morning," Pinker chortled.

"That will be no great hardship," Emily said. Her lips twitched. "At least, for everyone but Mr. Wallis."

"Perhaps . . . Perhaps . . ." Pinker wiped his eyes with his finger. "Perhaps his waistcoat will speak for him!"

Now it was the turn of Emily Pinker to splutter. I looked at the two of them in astonishment. I understood that in some way I had caused them this amusement, but I could not for the life of me understand how. It was true that my waistcoat that day was, like my shoes, a vivid hue of yellow, but even a Limehouse coffee merchant could surely see that it was *à la mode.*

Pinker wiped his eyes. "Forgive us, my dear Wallis. We mean no harm. Here, let me show you. There is a knack, which those of us who are accustomed to the thing take for granted. Observe." He spooned a little coffee into his mouth, slurped it noisily with a kind of gargling motion. "The trick is to aspirate the liquid with the lips and tongue. Aspirate, aerate, and ultimately expectorate."

I followed his lead, and this time I managed to control the liquid a little more—at least, the reaction of my audience was a little more restrained. Their hilarity returned, however, when I was called upon to master the art of spitting the tasted coffee into the bucket. Pinker demonstrated, efficiently ejecting a thin stream with a pinging sound as it hit the metal, but even before he turned to me I knew that this was going to prove difficult.

"Imagine that you are whistling," he explained. "And whatever you do, be decisive."

I glanced at Emily. Her face bore an expression of studied disinterest. "Perhaps your daughter would prefer . . ." I suggested.

"Prefer what?"

"Not to be present at what might, I fear, prove a somewhat indelicate display."

Pinker turned to his daughter, who responded, "Oh, come, Mr. Wallis. Let us be thoroughly modern, and not shrink like violets from what is only natural."

"Yes," I said. "Of course." I turned reluctantly back to the table.

"Together?" Pinker said. He spooned some coffee into his mouth. I followed suit. We aspirated and aerated, and then he pinged a thin stream of brown liquid with deadly accuracy into the bucket.

I leaned toward the bowl, paused to collect my thoughts, and expectorated as delicately as I could. Unfortunately, my delicacy was counterproductive: it simply meant that I squirted coffee randomly in the general area of the receptacle. Most missed the target altogether.

"I do apologize," I said, my face as red as beetroot. Neither Pinker heard me. The father's shoulders were shaking. His eyes were closed, and from underneath the lashes tears squeezed. Emily had jammed her hands under her armpits, and was rocking herself backwards and forwards on her chair, while her bowed head nodded vigorously with the effort of containing her laughter.

"I see this is amusing for you," I said stiffly.

Pinker put a hand on my shoulder. "If you ever fail as a poet, Wallis," he gasped, "you have a certain future in the music halls. It is the preparatory pose, sir—the pose is wonderful. As if you were about to declaim, rather than dribble."

"I don't believe I dribbled."

"And the facial expression!" he continued rapturously. "The solemnity! The look of comic surprise you contrive!"

"I'm not sure I know to what you are referring." I was still rather red in the face.

"My dear young fellow," he said, suddenly serious, "we have baited you enough. Forgive us. I will let you resume your duties."

He went to the door. When he had gone there was a silence. I said bitterly, "I suppose you think me ridiculous."

Emily said quietly, "No, Robert. But perhaps you now think yourself ridiculous, and that, I think, is what my father intended."

"I see."

"If we are to work together we must be comfortable with one another. And we cannot do that if either of us is attempting to get the upper hand."

"Yes. I understand."

"I will promise not to laugh at you, if you will promise not to flirt with me."

"Very well. You have my word." I sat down heavily.

"Believe me," she added, her mouth twitching, "it is I who lose most by the deal."

[NINE]

The basic difficulty in coffee flavour terminology is inherent in our language. Although many words describe the sensations of sight, sound and touch, few words describe the sensations of smell and taste.

—LINGLE, The Coffee Cupper's Handbook

PERHAPS PINKER REMAINED SUSPICIOUS OF MY INTENTIONS. AT any rate, we were soon joined by a dark-haired young woman, a couple of years younger than Emily. She placed a large pile of books on the table with a thump.

"My sister, Ada," Emily explained. "Ada, this is Robert Wallis."

Ada's terse "Pleased to meet you" suggested that she probably wasn't. I picked up one of the books and glanced at the spine. *"Water Analysis for Sanitary Purposes.* Good heavens."

She removed the book from my hand. "Professor Frankland's work is the standard text on the valency of compounds."

"Ada hopes to go up to Oxford," Emily said. "That's where you were, Robert, wasn't it?"

That got Ada's attention. "Oh? Which college?"

"Christ Church."

"Are the laboratories any good?"

"I have absolutely no idea."

"What about the Clarendon? Is that an asset?"

For ten minutes she cross-questioned me about the new science rooms, the women's colleges, the Examination Halls and so on. I was a disappointment to her. I could describe walking across the college deer park at dawn, arm in arm with a couple of drunken fellows, or punting to Wytham for a lunch of grilled trout, but of the lecture halls and academics she named I knew almost nothing.

However, it was useful to have a third person in the room. The object of our glossary was, after all, to communicate, and we were able to test our progress on Ada. She proved useful in a more practical way, too, when it came to the creation of the sample case—but I am getting ahead of myself.

AT AROUND TWELVE O'CLOCK, Emily stretched. "Perhaps it is a consequence of this unaccustomed scrutiny I am giving to my own perceptions," she said, "but I find I am actually quite ravenous."

"That is to be expected," I said. "Just as music must be studied and practiced before one can sit down and sight-read, so one must diligently practice all the scales and arpeggios of pleasure before we may claim to be proficient."

She rolled her eyes. "Is that a rather long-winded way of saying you too are hungry?"

"Exactly. Where is good round here?"

"There's a place in Narrow Street that does excellent eel pies. In fact, I have been thinking of little else these last twenty minutes. They serve them with mashed potatoes, and a little of the eel liquor as a sauce—"

"I have to go to Hoxton, to buy some chemicals," Ada interjected.

"Then it looks as if it will just be you and I," I said to Emily.

"Emily, may I have a word?" Ada said quickly.

The two sisters conferred on the landing in low voices. Of course, I went to the door to listen.

"—promised Father nothing objectionable would take place."

"Don't be such a nincompoop, Ada. There is about as much chance of me succumbing to Mr. Wallis's purple compliments over a harmless lunch as there is of that river freezing over. But if you're really so concerned, come with us."

"You know I can't. You'll have to take the Frog."

I heard Emily sigh. "I'd rather not."

"Why not?"

"We can't possibly talk with the Frog there."

"Wallis does nothing *but* talk, as far as I can see. But very well—if you can really bear to go with him, then go."

AS WE WALKED along Narrow Street a silence fell upon us. To tell the truth, I was still smarting from Ada's remark that I did nothing but talk.

"How long have you been working for your father?" I said at last.

"Almost three years now."

"Three years!" I shook my head. "It is a longer sentence than poor Oscar got at his trial!"

"You don't understand. For me to be able to work is a luxury." She gave me a sideways look. "Whereas for you, I suppose, it is a novelty."

"Certainly. To paraphrase that great writer, the only work worth pursuing is a work of art."

"Hmm. You have clearly lit your torch at that man's flame, like so many of our artists at present."

"Oscar Wilde is a genius—the greatest man of the age, whatever anyone says."

"Well, I hope you have not been too much influenced by him."

"Whatever do you mean?"

"Only that it would be a shame if you were to copy him in . . . certain respects."

I stopped. "Are you flirting with me, Miss Pinker?"

"Certainly not," she said, blushing.

"Because if you are, I shall have to complain to your father. Or possibly to Ada, who is even more terrifying."

I WOULD NEVER have believed such a delicate creature could put away so much food. I watched open-mouthed as she finished off an eel pie with liquor and mash, a dozen oysters, a slice of trout pie, and a plate of whelks with parsley butter, all washed down with half a pint of hock-and-seltzer.

"I told you I had an appetite," she said, wiping parsley butter off her lips with a napkin.

"I am most impressed."

"Are you going to finish those oysters? Or shall we order some more?"

"I had not realized," I said as she reached for my plate, "that lunch with you was going to turn into a competition."

OVER THE COURSE of that meal I learned rather more about her family. The girls' mother having died many years before, Pinker was left with a prosperous business that he inherited from his father-in-law, and three daughters, of whom Emily was the eldest.

These girls he resolved to bring up in the most advanced way possible. The governesses and tutors all came from the various societies—the Society for the Advancement of Knowledge, the Royal Scientific Societies, and so on. The children had been encouraged to read books and attend public lectures. At the same time their father was busy stripping their home of its old-fashioned furnishings, installing electric lights, bathrooms and a telephone, replacing the furniture with the latest styles, and generally embracing all things modern.

"That is why he is amenable to the idea of us working," she explained. "Having invested so much in our education, he wants to see us give something back."

"That seems a somewhat . . . prosaic attitude to take to his own flesh and blood."

"Oh, no—quite the opposite. Father believes in business—believes in its principles, I mean, its power to do good."

"And you? Is that how you see it?"

She nodded. "As I said, working is a luxury for me, but it is also the expression of my moral beliefs. It is only by showing that women can be worth as much as men in the workplace that we will prove we are worthy of the same political and legal rights."

"Good Lord." Suddenly, working to pay off my wine merchant seemed rather ignoble.

TOWARD THE END of the meal I pulled out my cigarette case. "Mind if I smoke?" I said automatically.

"I do, rather," Emily replied.

"Oh?" I said, surprised.

"We will not be able to taste my father's coffees accurately after breathing a fug of tobacco," she explained.

"These make no fug." I was a little offended. My cigarettes were from Benson's in Old Bond Street; slim ovals of fine Turkish tobacco that filled a room with a drowsy, perfumed mist. "Besides, smoking is one of the very few things I am good at."

She sighed. "Very well, then. Let us have one each before we go back."

"Excellent," I said, although this was even more surprising—for a well-brought-up woman to smoke in front of a man was considered quite a racy thing in those days. I offered her the case, and struck a lucifer.

It is a sensual pleasure to light a woman's cigarette: her eyes are on the kiss of flame against the tip, which means that yours are on the downward sweep of her lashes and the delicate shape of her upper lip, pursed around the paper tube. "Thank you," she said, blowing a little trumpet of smoke from the side of her mouth. I nodded, and lit my own.

She took another drag, and looked thoughtfully at the cigarette in her hand. "If my father notices the smell on us," she said suddenly, "you must say that it was only you, not me, who was smoking."

"He doesn't approve?"

Her eyes held mine as she took another pull. "He doesn't know." Small barks and puffs of smoke eddied around each word.

"A woman is entitled to her secrets."

"I've always hated that expression—it makes it sound as if we're entitled to nothing else. You'll be saying we're the weaker sex next."

"You don't think so?"

"Oh, Robert. You really are quite hopelessly old-fashioned, aren't you?"

"On the contrary. I am every inch *à la mode.*"

"One can be fashionable and still be old-fashioned—underneath your fine clothes. I'm sorry, am I making you blush?"

I said quietly, "I didn't think you cared for what is under my clothes."

She gazed at me for a moment. It is a phenomenon I have noticed on many occasions, that smoking makes a woman bolder in her manner, almost as if one freedom begets another. "I was referring to your thoughts."

"Oh, I try not to have any of those. I find they get in the way of my fine feelings."

"What does that *mean,* exactly?" she asked with a frown.

"I have absolutely no idea. It is much too clever for me. I find that at least three-quarters of what I say goes completely over my own head."

"Then you must be too clever by three-quarters."

"Do you know, if I had said that it would have been quite amusing."

"But a woman, of course, cannot be witty."

"Not when she is as beautiful as you are."

She breathed smoke into the air. "You are flirting with me again, Robert."

"No, I am flattering you, which is not the same thing at all. Women are an ornamental gender. It is the secret of their success."

She sighed. "I doubt if I will ever be as ornamental as you. And unlike an ornament, I do not intend to sit on a mantelpiece gathering dust. Now, shall we put these out and get back to work? Our palates will be no good to us, but perhaps we could make some notes."

It was a great shame, I reflected, that Emily Pinker was a respectable middle-class bourgeois and not a bohemian or a whore. There was something combative, even challenging, about her manner which I was finding quite irresistible.

WHAT I LEARNED, in those first weeks at Pinker's offices, was something that is quite obvious to me now: the absolute treachery of words. Take a word like *medicinal.* To one person, it might mean the sharp tang of iodine; to another, the sickly-sweet smell of chloroform; to a third, the rich, spicy warmth of a balsam or cough mixture. Or *buttery.* Is that a positive attribute, or a negative? To which my answer is: when it describes the moist feel that freshly ground coffee beans should have between the fingers—like crumbled cake—it is a positive; when it describes the feel of a brewed coffee in the mouth—viscous, thick, the opposite of *watery*—it is also good; but when it describes a taste, as when a coffee is over-rich in oils, verging on *rancid,* it becomes undesirable. Our job was thus to define not only the tastes of our coffees, but also the words and phrases we used to describe them.

Or take these words: *scent, fragrance, bouquet, aroma, odor, nose.* Do they mean the same thing? If so, why? Lacking the words that described different kinds of smell—the smell of the beans, the aroma of the grind, the bouquet of the coffee in the cup—we apportioned existing words according to our needs. In this way we soon left ordinary language behind, and began to speak in a private dialect of our own.

I learned something else, too: that our perceptions become more substantial when we start to examine them. Pinker had spoken of my palate becoming trained, an obvious enough expression, except that I had at the time no inkling of what it really meant. Day by day I became more confident in my judgments, more precise in my terms. I seemed to enter a state of synaesthesia, that condition in which all the senses become interlinked, so that scents become colors, tastes become pictures, and all the stimuli of the physical world are felt as strongly as emotions.

Does that sound fanciful? Consider these tastes. *Smoke* is a fire crackling in a pile of dead leaves in autumn; a chill in the air, a crispness in the nostrils. *Vanilla* is warm and sensual, a spice island warmed by a tropical sun. *Resinous* has the thick pungency of pine cones or turpentine. All coffees, when considered carefully, have a faint smell of *roast onions:* some, without a shadow of a doubt, also have *soot, fresh linen,* or *mown grass.* Some will yield the fruity, yeasty smell of freshly peeled *apples,* while others have the starchy, acidic taste of *raw potato.* Some will remind you of more than one flavor: we found one coffee that combined *celery* and *blackberries,* another that married *jasmine* and *gingerbread,* a third that matched *chocolate* with the elusive fragrance of fresh, crunchy *cucumbers.* . . . And all the time Pinker was rushing in and out, checking on our progress, crying, "What have you found?" and "Shall we fix its Soul? Roses, is it? Let us Improve—what kind of roses?"

It became a kind of obsession. I was walking along the Strand one evening when I heard a shout: "Get them roasted!" and smelled the odor of hot nuts, their shells scorched by burning coals. I turned: an urchin was standing by a brazier, shoveling walnuts into a paper cone. It was exactly the aroma of a Java as the water first hits the beans. On another occasion I was in a bookshop in Cecil Court, examining a volume of verse, when I realized that the smell of beeswax on well-preserved leather bindings is almost identical to the aftertaste of a Yemen mocca. Or the simple smell of buttered dark-brown toast would prompt a memory of an Indian Mysore, and then nothing would satisfy me but a cup of the same brew—I had taken samples back to my rooms by now, so that I could indulge my addiction the moment I woke up, and clear my head as well.

For my head, most mornings, was generally very thick. I spent my days with Emily and Ada; I spent my evenings, and my advance, with the girls of Wellington Street and Mayfair. There was one memorable occasion when a dollymop at Mrs. Cowper's, in Albemarle Street, asked me what I did, and when I explained that I was engaged in the organoleptic analysis of tastes and aromas, nothing would do but that I smell her cunny and tell her what I discerned there (for the record: musk, peaches, Pears' soap, crayfish); when she proudly told the other girls, they all demanded I do the same for them, too. I explained the principles of side-by-side tasting, and got four or five of them onto a bed together. It was an interesting experience, not least because they were all subtly different—the base note, as it were, of musk, present to a greater or lesser degree in all, was accompanied by a range of individual scents, from lime to vanilla. One girl had an elusive fragrance I could not identify, although I knew that I knew it; like a forgotten name, it nagged at me all evening. It was only the next day that it finally came to me: it was the aroma of blackthorn blossom, that fragrant, honeyed scent of country lanes in springtime.

That evening had two important consequences. First, I realized that just as the human body has some of the same aromas as coffee, so some coffees have a musky, feral odor that is almost erotic—certain African coffees, in particular, have something about them that is dark, earthy, even clay-like, evoking the stamp of naked feet on sun-baked ground. I did not mention this to Emily or Ada, of course, but in my own mind I used Linnaeus's term to describe it: *hircinos,* goatishness. Second, I realized that if we were to make the Guide truly practical as a way of spanning distances, we would have to have a box of samples.

The issue was a simple one: the code only worked if two people meant exactly the same taste or smell when they used a certain word. For some tastes this was not a difficulty: tar, for example, or cloves. But blackthorn blossom, vanilla, even walnuts—these were smells which it was easy to summon up in the calm of Pinker's offices; but we could assume that in the future at least one of the parties to each communication would be in the field, in Africa or Ceylon or Brazil, where blackthorn blossom might well be in short supply. The answer was to create a small, stout traveling box containing a dozen or so of the key scents, to which the taster could refer.

It was Ada who grasped the practical aspects of this. As a scientist, she understood the techniques by which an aroma could be distilled, and I think she was pleased to have found a role for herself. Just as a painter's palette does not need to have every color on it, since the various shades may be mixed from combinations of primaries, she worked out that our sample box did not have to contain every scent: an essence of oranges, for example, was enough to remind one of the general qualities of all citrus fruit, and so on. A perfumer, Mr. Clee, was found and briefed. From then on Ada dealt with the technical issues of fixing scents in a way which would withstand the heat of the tropics.

ONE AFTERNOON I was striding up and down the office, talking volubly—I was, I think, attempting to elucidate the qualities of a particularly astringent Brazilian; despite the presence of the bucket, I still tended to ingest more coffee than I should, and consequently became quite excitable; in addition, I had just that morning purchased a splendid ivory-topped cane, and a splendid new cane is no use for twirling unless you are in motion—when I glanced down and saw a leg under the table.

I looked up. Emily was sitting at one end, taking notes; Ada was at the other, deep in a science book. I glanced down again. The leg must have realized that it was visible: it shifted surreptitiously, like a snail pulling in its horn.

"I smell . . ." I sniffed the air ostentatiously. "I smell an *intruder.*"

Emily looked at me curiously.

"There is a whiff," I explained, "of . . . of . . ." I sniffed again. "Of disobedient puppy dogs and wickedness. *Fe fi fo fum.*"

Emily clearly thought I had taken leave of my senses.

"It is the smell," I announced, "of little children who are hiding where they should not." With my cane I solemnly rapped the top of the table. "Who's there?"

A small, frightened voice issued from beneath the wood. "Me."

"It's only the Frog," Emily said.

"Go away," Ada said without looking up from her book. "Begone, troublesome amphibian."

A small child hopped out from under the table. She squatted on the floor like a frog and croaked.

"Why aren't you in the schoolroom, Frog?" Ada said sternly.

"Mrs. Walsh is ill."

"Mrs. Walsh is only ill because you make her so," Emily scolded. "The governess," she explained to me. "She suffers from neuralgia."

"Anyway, I'd much rather be in here with all of you," the child announced, springing up. She was about eleven years of age: her legs seemed much too long for her body, and her eyes had a slightly pouched quality that did indeed make her look very like a frog. "Can't I stay? I shan't be trouble, and I can help guard Emily from Robert's poetic licenses as well as anyone."

"He's Mr. Wallis to you," Ada said. She looked a little embarrassed. "And there is no question of guarding Emily from anything."

The girl frowned. "But why must I always be left out? I'll be good."

"You'll have to ask Father."

"Then I can stay," the girl said triumphantly. "Because Father said I could stay if I asked you."

". . . on condition you don't say a word," Emily added sternly.

The girl squatted down and croaked.

"Or make that ridiculous croaking sound."

"I'm a frog."

"In France," I said mildly, "frogs are boiled and eaten with green sauce."

She turned her big eyes on me. "I'm not really a frog," she said excitedly. "I'm Philomena. When she was little Ada couldn't say Philomena, so she called me Frog instead. But actually I quite like being a frog." She hopped up onto a chair. "Don't mind me. You had just got to where you were saying it was like lemons."

Thereafter, there was often quite a crowd in our little cupping room. Ada ignored me whenever possible, but the porter, South, and the child, Frog, both stared at me open-mouthed while I tasted, as if I were a creature from some exotic country—a gallery, I'm ashamed to say, to which I occasionally played, coming up with fanciful descriptions and wordplay that elicited from the Frog gasps of admiration, and from Emily the faintest of sighs.

"DO YOU MEAN to ravish Emily?" the Frog demanded. Emily and I had just returned from one of our lunches; Emily had gone to hang up her coat, so I was alone with the child.

"I'm not sure that's altogether a polite question."

"Ada thinks you do. I heard her ask Emily if she'd been ravished by Lord Byron yet. That's what Ada calls you, you know." She was silent a moment. "If you do ravish Emily, you'll have to marry her. That's the rule. Then I can be a bridesmaid."

"I think your father might have an opinion on that subject."

"Shall I ask *him* if I can be a bridesmaid?" Frog said hopefully.

"I meant, an opinion on whom Emily marries. It's rather up to him, you see."

"Oh, he's very keen to marry her off," she assured me. "I'm sure you'll do. Are you rich?"

"Not in the least."

"You *look* rich."

"That's because I'm a spendthrift."

"What's a spendthrift?"

"Someone who doesn't earn as much as they ought to. And who keeps buying nice things even when they oughtn't."

"Like wedding rings?"

I laughed. "Not wedding rings. Wedding rings aren't nice things."

[TEN]

I HAVE SOMETHING TO SHOW YOU," PINKER ANNOUNCED ONE day, bounding into the office where Emily and I were working. "Put on your coats—it cannot wait."

Outside, his carriage was waiting, and we set off at a smart trot through the crowded streets. I was sitting next to Emily, facing backwards. The carriage was a narrow one, and I could feel the warmth of her thigh where it lay against mine. As we went round corners we were gently swung together: she shifted to avoid being thrown into my arms, but there was little either of us could do.

"Have you heard about the latest autokinetics, Robert?" Pinker said. He gazed out of the window at a snarl of traffic. "I've ordered one from France. Four wheels, a small combustion engine, and as fast as a mail cart at a gallop. There will be none of these ridiculous hold-ups once they become the norm."

"I will miss the horses, if that is so," Emily said. "Where will they all go?"

"I am sure horses will always be in demand on farms," her father said. "Ah! Here we are."

We drew up not far from Tower Bridge, in Castle Street. On the corner was a public house—or rather, what had once been a pub. Workmen were putting the finishing touches to a smart new door; there were clear windows where once there would have been frosted glass, and above it all was a black-and-gold sign proclaiming that this was a Pinker's Temperance Tavern.

We dismounted and inspected the property. Pinker senior was bursting with pride, and took us on a tour at breakneck speed. Inside, everything was painted black and gold. "It is not so much a color scheme, you see, as a livery. The colors will be replicated in every establishment, as they open."

"Why, Father?"

"So that they all look the same, of course. And the staff—the waiters—will all have black uniforms, with a gold motif. And white aprons, as they wear in France. I took that idea from the Café Royal." He nodded at me. "The tables—here is one—are topped in marble. Like Florian's in Venice, I believe."

I looked around me. The place was extraordinary; smart enough, in its way, but strange. Every inch of wood was painted black, and the only other color was the gold. It was more like the inside of a hearse-carriage than a tavern. At the rear, behind what had once been the bar, was the contraption Pinker had demonstrated at our first meeting in his office, chugging quietly to itself. Next to it Jenks, kneeling, was making some adjustments to the dials.

"Are we operational?" Pinker called.

"Almost, sir." As Jenks spoke a gust of steam hissed out of a valve, making Emily jump.

"Well?" Pinker turned to us, rubbing his hands with excitement. "What do you think?"

"It's wonderful, Father."

"Robert?"

"Remarkable," I agreed. "Most impressive. There is just one thing . . ."

"Yes?"

"The name."

"What of it?"

"Do you think people—ordinary people—will want to go and drink coffee somewhere that is actually called a Temperance Tavern? One might as well advertise a foodless restaurant or a grape-free wine."

Pinker frowned. "Then what would you call it?"

"Well, anything. You could call it . . ." I looked around. My eye fell on the sign that said "Castle Street," and I recalled his predilection for military analogies. "You could call it Castle Coffee."

"Castle." Pinker considered. "Hmm. Castle. Castle Coffees. Yes—it has a ring. It sounds dependable. Emily? What do you say?"

"I think Robert has a point when he says that Temperance may be off-putting to some customers," she answered carefully. "So Castle would, perhaps, be better."

Pinker nodded. "Castle it is, then. Thank you, Robert, your contribution has been most valuable. I'll have the workmen change the sign immediately."

So was born one of the most famous trademarks in the history of coffee—a name as well known in its time as Lion, Ariosa or Maxwell House. But something else was conceived that day as well, amid that bustle of industry; the workmen, the marble table-tops, the smell of new paint mingling with the rich coffee-scented steam that issued from the twin nozzles of Signor Toselli's apparatus like smoke from a dragon's nostrils. . . . As Pinker stalked outside to find the foreman, his daughter turned to me. "Yes, thank you, Robert. That was tactfully done. And Castle is undoubtedly the better name."

I shrugged. "It's hardly a big matter."

She smiled at me—a smile that lingered a fraction longer than it might have done. Then, suddenly bashful, she dropped her gaze.

"Come along!" Pinker urged from outside.

In the carriage, as we returned to Limehouse, it seemed to me that the pressure of her thigh against mine was withdrawn just a little less than it had been before.

[ELEVEN]

"Earthy"—this is the characteristic of freshly dug earth, of the soil after storms, and is not unlike that of beetroot.

—LENOIR, Le Nez du Café

THAT EVENING, AS I WALKED DOWN PICCADILLY, I PASSED A carriage horse trying to copulate with a mare. Most carriage animals were geldings, of course, but this was obviously some rich person's mount, docile enough in the ordinary way to be shackled to a brougham. The mare had been tied up outside Simpson's department store, and the driver of the carriage was nowhere to be seen.

It made a strange sight: the stallion, still harnessed to the shafts of the carriage, was attempting to clamber on to the mare's back, prodding his great pizzle into her hindquarters. Each time he slipped off, pulled backwards by the unwieldy weight of the brougham; yet, nothing daunted, he immediately returned for another attempt, pulling himself clumsily up again with his front hoofs, like a Chinaman trying to clasp a piece of meat with chopsticks. The mare, for her part, stood for it patiently, barely moving even when the stallion took the skin of her neck between his teeth. The back end of the carriage had tipped up, and was being crashed around on the road with every staggering thrust of the stallion's rear legs.

A small crowd had gathered. The more respectable ladies hurried on by, but amongst the onlookers were several young women who were rather more daring, and I alternated between watching the congress of the beasts and the wide-eyed, giggling fascination of the girls.

Eventually the driver of the brougham returned and began shouting at his beast, trying to force it off. Of course the stallion had no intention at all of stopping, even when its master began laying into it with a whip—at considerable risk to himself, I might add: the stallion's front hoofs were flailing wildly as he struggled for purchase on the mare's back, and his hind legs were doing a kind of dance as he tried to kick free from the crinoline of the carriage. It almost looked as if the man were whipping the animal on. Eventually the stallion was done, and slid off the mare of his own volition, the battered brougham returning to the level with a crash. The horse's pizzle was still dripping onto the cobbles when the owner finally succeeded in trotting him away, to an ironic cheer from the watchers.

A couple of doxies, meanwhile, had hit on the idea of going round the crowd touting for business. One brushed by me, with a muttered "Are we feeling gay, sir?"—"gay" being London slang in those days for a prostitute. She glanced back at me: a pretty enough girl, more common than I usually liked, no more than sixteen or so. I shook my head. She said, "My sister's here." I must have looked interested then, because she beckoned to another girl to join her. Sure enough, they did resemble each other, brown-eyed and brown-haired, both with cheeky round faces. It was a novelty; I had never had sisters before, and my blood was up from watching the stallion. "Quick," she said, sensing she'd made a sale. "In here."

There was a note in the tobacconist's window behind us, *Rooms for rent.* I followed them into the shop and up some stairs: when I had given them half a crown each and another for the shopkeeper, I unbuttoned and had them both, one after the other in quick succession, without even pausing to take my trousers off.

> *Ah, that's the thrill!*
> *First drink the stars, then grunt amid the mire,*
> as Richard Le Gallienne puts it.

I SUPPOSE I should explain something about myself here. I have not, in this account, made any attempt to paint myself in an attractive light—rather the opposite. When I think back to what an affected, vainglorious young *poseur* I must have been in those days, I am quite astounded that any girl could have fallen in love with me: if I make myself sound ludicrous, it is because I think I probably was. On that, I am happy to be judged. But I am aware that you will be judging me now on a quite different account, for my morals.

I would only remind you that things were different then. Yes, I went with prostitutes—good ones, when I could afford it: ugly ones when I could not. I was a healthy young man, and what was the alternative? Abstinence was believed to be injurious to the health, while self-abuse was thought even more dangerous, causing weakness, lassitude and foul temper. Prostitution was not illegal, although the Contagious Diseases Acts, which allowed the police to apprehend any woman and have her examined for signs of venereal disease, had caused a great outcry amongst respectable ladies, who felt slighted by association. Nor was sleeping with a prostitute grounds for divorce (although a woman's adultery, conversely, would be grounds for the husband to instantly divorce *her*).

Whoring was not something one discussed in polite society—but there were many things that were not discussed, or at least not until the ladies had risen from the table. Then, amongst one's own, it might be murmured: one did not necessarily have need of such creatures oneself, but it was scarcely startling that there were those who did. It was one of the great benefits of living in a society in which the poor were so very poor: servants, workers and women were all cheap and plentiful—a circumstance which made most men instinctively resistant to social reform, just as most women were instinctively supportive of it.

MANY OF MY lunchtime conversations with Emily were about this very subject—reform, that is: for her, modernity was synonymous with a social conscience, and she took it for granted that, as a poet, I was as keen to change the world as she. Was it not Shelley who had said that poets were the unacknowledged legislators of the world? Had not Byron taken on the armies of the Turk?

I dared not tell her that, whilst I might admire Byron's haircut and Shelley's flowing shirts, their political consciences were something alien to me. Mine was a generation of frippery and baubles: we sought only for "experiences"; our one aim was to "pass swiftly from point to point, and be present always at the focus where the greatest number of vital forces unite." But I was happy to make it seem to Emily as if I was more of a radical than I really was. What can I say? I wanted her good opinion, and I thought that if I revealed myself to be uninterested in such matters, she would think me superficial and shallow—which, of course, I was, although the same superficiality which had seemed so gloriously decadent at Oxford was now starting to feel a little *jejeune.*

I did try to tell her. When she first raised the matter of Social Evil, I replied that I had no interest in politics, adding: "In this, surely, I am like most politicians."

She did not respond, although her face bore a pained expression.

I said airily, "Wealth, of course, would be quite wasted on the poor. One only has to look at the ghastly things the lower classes spend their money on to be thankful that no one has given them any more of it."

She sighed deeply.

"And I cannot think why any woman would want the Vote, when one sees what ghastly people already have it. One would approve so much more of democracy were it not so frightfully common."

"Robert," she said, "do you ever speak seriously?"

"Only when I care absolutely nothing for the subject under discussion."

"I don't believe you do so even then," she muttered.

"I shall take that as a compliment, dear Emily. How I should hate to get an undeserved reputation for sincerity."

"Robert, shut *up.*"

I fell silent.

"These epigrams. Not only are they deeply unoriginal, they are barely even amusing. I cannot help feeling that they are nothing but a verbal tic or habit—a way of showing off, with no more sense to them than that awful croaking noise the Frog has learned to make."

I opened my mouth. "Wait," she said, holding up her hand. "You are about to say that sense is greatly overrated: what is needed in the world is more nonsense; or that all epigrams are meaningless: that is why they are so profound; or that showing off is the basis of all art: in that lies its genius; or—or—some other silly construction that sounds impressive but actually has no more wit or sense to it than a fart."

I stared at her. "Did you just say—?"

" 'Fart.' Yes. Did you really imagine that a modern girl wouldn't know such a word?" She pushed her chin defiantly in the air. "Well, I shall fart at you every time you make an epigram."

"You will not!"

"I will. You think I don't know how to fart, perhaps? Believe me, my sisters and I are quite expert at it."

"What an extraordinary girl you are."

"If it will cure you of epigrams I would do much worse."

"You would risk being accused of immodesty?"

"Not something that you have ever been accused of, I am sure."

"True," I said thoughtfully. "Yet in a woman immodesty has nothing to do with boastfulness, only with indelicacy."

There was a sound like a wet raspberry from Miss Pinker's direction. I stared at her. "Did you just—?"

"I caught a distinct whiff of epigram."

"My epigrams, I think you'll find, smell of violets and roses, whereas—" There was another eruption. "Good God!"

"I mean it, Robert. Every time you pontificate, I shall flatulate."

"Do you know, that's rather—"

"And now you had better open a window," she interrupted, "or my father will wonder why his finest Java smells like a privy."

AND SO I learned not to epigrammatize, and to speak seriously on serious matters. But of course, it was the speaking seriously that was the pose; the epigrams, for all their shallowness, were much closer to my real nature. Still, who would not want to wax lyrical about Reform, when those sparkling gray eyes were drinking in your every word? Who would not pretend to care about the Poor, when your reward was such a smile? And who would not agree that something must be done about Fallen Women, when the woman who was talking with such passion on the subject was causing you to become so very aroused with every soft syllable that shaped her pretty lips?

Does it seem strange to you that I could pass so easily from flirtation with Emily Pinker in Limehouse in the afternoon, to fornication in the evening with a Covent Garden whore? But the two were as different as breakfast and dinner, east and west. The fornication meant far less than the flirtation, but at the same time it was far more necessary—oh, I can't explain this: all I know is that, were it not for the prostitutes, I would surely have embarrassed myself even more than I did during the flirting afternoons.

In any case, there was less time for flirting now: Miss Pinker had me attending Meetings. Oh, how she loved a Meeting! There were Meetings of the Society for the Promotion of International Civilization, Meetings of the Fabians, Meetings of the Society for the Dissolution of the Contagious Diseases Act . . . I began to suspect, in fact, that I was being Improved. There were Midnight Meetings at which we dispensed sweet tea to prostitutes—I found a rather wonderful fuck that way, as it happens, a young moll with the sweetest smile: I quietly followed her onto the street, and we had a quick ten-shilling stand-up in an alleyway before I strolled back to rejoin my fair companions. There were luncheon Meetings of the Theosophists. There were Temperance dinners, at which we discussed the need to raise the tax on gin while cradling glasses of fine claret. There was even a deeply uncomfortable meeting at the Fellowship of the New Life, where a strange creature with a high, fluting voice talked incessantly about the Transitional Sex, the future of Homogenic Love, and other forms of Inversion. I was puce with embarrassment the entire two hours, but to my amazement Emily and the other ladies seemed hardly more perturbed than if he—she? it?—had been discussing a trip to the seaside.

AT SOME OF these meetings there was much earnest discussion about what a Rational Marriage might look like. People often quoted with approval those lines of Shelley's in the *Epipsychidion:*

I never was attached to that great sect
Whose doctrine is, that each one should select
Out of the crowd a mistress or a friend,
And all the rest, though fair and wise, commend
To cold oblivion. . . .

I noticed, however, that the men and women tended to take it different ways—the women wanted equality and independence, by which they meant equal status with their husbands, while the men wanted equality and independence, by which they meant something less like a marriage and more like the freedom of being a bachelor. For my part, I offered no opinions. If pressed, one could always quote Shelley.

EMILY'S OWN views on marriage were rather more complicated. I remember an argument we had as we were walking back to the office after one of these meetings. I cannot now recall what started it—I suppose I had made a flippant remark about the speaker. She turned to me and said crossly, "Do you actually believe that, Robert, or is it just another pose?"

"It is one of my most strongly held opinions, and I shall certainly have discarded it by teatime."

"The question," she said, ignoring me, "is whether men and women should have the same political rights."

I recalled now that we were talking about that old chestnut, votes for women, and with a sigh I prepared to be serious. "But men and women have separate spheres—"

"Oh, yes," she interrupted. "The woman has the drawing room, and the man has politics and business and the whole of the rest of the world. That isn't equality—it's like saying the prisoner has the freedom of her cell."

"But any woman has to accept the authority of her husband—"

"Why?"

I must have looked confused, because she added, "Oh, it's never talked about, of course. We're supposed to say suffrage can't possibly undermine a man's right to be master of his own home. It's just that no one can give me a good reason why men have to be masters in the first place."

"But look at men's achievements—"

"That's a circular argument. Men have had the opportunities."

"But your argument is circular too, my dear Emily. You're saying that women would have achieved more if they had been given the opportunity, yes?" She nodded. "So why did men have the opportunities in the first place? Because they took them, that's why."

For some reason this incensed her even further. "So it all boils down to brute force and rape?"

"Rape? Where does rape come into it?"

"Because by *your* definition, marriage and rape are one and the same. Whereas *I* happen to believe that men and women can love each other fully only when they are equals."

"But men and women are different," I pointed out. "The fact that we're having this extraordinary argument proves it."

She stopped and stamped her foot on the pavement. "And if we were married, you would be able to tell me that as my husband you were right, and that would be an end of it?"

"I can tell you I'm right now. I don't see you agreeing."

"Because you haven't proved your point." She was flushed and angry. "And I suppose you think I shouldn't have a job?"

"Emily—how did we get onto jobs? I thought we were talking about votes. And then somehow we got onto marriage—"

"Don't you see—it's all the same?" And then she would not talk to me, and walked on in a furious silence.

I lit a cigarette and caught up with her. "I'd offer you one," I said, "but . . ."

". . . But a woman shouldn't smoke in the street?"

"I was going to say, but you're already fuming."

LATER, when she had calmed down, I said to her, "I'm sorry we quarreled."

"We didn't quarrel, Robert. We argued."

"Is there a difference?"

"As my father would say, a distinction. Arguing is a pleasure and quarreling isn't." She sighed. "The limitations of a woman's rights in marriage is a subject on which I tend to become heated. It is a long-standing disagreement I am having with my father. He is completely modern in every way but that. I think it may have something to do with not having a wife—he feels that choosing, or at least approving, our husbands is his last responsibility toward us."

"What sort of husband does he intend for you?"

"That's the problem. In his head he wants someone modern—someone like himself, a man of industry. But in his heart he wants someone with connections and social standing."

"It's a rare combination. And you? What sort of man will capture your heart?"

She rolled her eyes. "Robert!"

"What?"

" 'Capture your heart'—you sound like something from a novel. No one's going to capture any bit of me, thank you very much. My hand, and my affection, will be bestowed on someone . . ." She thought for a moment. "Someone whom I can admire. Someone who has already achieved something in the world, and intends to go on achieving things—*great* things. Someone who can see what's wrong, but who also knows how to put it right; someone with so much passion he can make other people see things his way simply by speaking—I always imagine him with an Irish accent, actually, but that may just be because I know he will have very determined views on Home Rule. He's probably the sort of person who doesn't have much time for women, but that doesn't matter, because I'm not going to sit around being decorative in any case. I intend to be his helpmeet, you see, and although no one else will ever know it, privately he will always acknowledge that he couldn't have done any of it without me."

"Ah," I said. It is always disconcerting to realize that someone else finds admirable exactly the sort of person one would least like to be. "And what if you can't find that man?"

"Then I shall just have to settle for someone who captures my heart," she answered, linking her arm in mine.

"Sure, and dat's a very foine way of tinking."

"Why are you speaking in that ridiculous Irish accent, Robert?"

"Air, no reason."

[TWELVE]

Understanding coffee's flavour is further complicated by the intricate method by which the human palate responds to multiple sensations.

—LINGLE, The Coffee Cupper's Handbook

EMILY STANDS IN HER FATHER'S OFFICE, LOOKING DOWN ON Robert as he leaves Pinker's for the evening. She continues to watch until he is out of sight, leaning progressively closer to the window so that she can follow him down Narrow Street. When he has gone she finds that her breath has left a coffee-scented blossom on the glass.

It is just one of many things she would not have noticed a few weeks ago.

Without thinking she touches the tip of her tongue to the cool, hard glass. The blossom acquires a tongue-tip-shaped pistil in its center. With the end of her finger she traces four petals, then a stalk. When she rubs it out, the side of her hand squeaks on the windowpane.

Something is happening to her. She is not sure whether to be intrigued or alarmed, whether to approve or disapprove of these changes, this physical awakening that is slowly taking hold of her, warming her like an apricot in a glasshouse.

She turns back to the desk, picking up her most recent notes. Apricot—that is one of the flavors they have discovered today, in some of the moccas and the better South Americans; the concentrated golden aroma of an apricot preserve. It will take its place on the chart of flavors, in between blackberries and apples. And then, this afternoon, the Colombian Excelsos yielded a truly remarkable discovery: the precise smell of fresh peas, just as they are snapped out of their crisp, juicy pods. . . .

Straw. The aroma of barley stalks just before harvest, rustling softly in sun-baked fields. Licorice, dark and soft and sweet. Leather, rich and old and polished, like her father's favorite armchair. Lemon, so astringent it puckers the lips . . . As her eyes travel down her notes she finds she can recall each one of them, the tastes bursting across her palate like exotic flowers, each one more powerfully real than the last.

Each one coaxing open the hard, closed bud of her senses a little more.

When she first had the idea for the Guide, many weeks ago, what interested her most was the potential for *systemizing:* for taking the chaotic, ever-shifting world of human perceptions and bringing to it order and the calm discipline of rational investigation. She had never imagined that it might work the other way round as well: that she would find her own inner calm—her systematic, practical nature—shifting and stretching like some unruly, enchanted plant.

She has not told anyone what working on the Guide is doing to her—not her sisters, and certainly not her father. He has already had cause once or twice to suspect his oldest daughter of dangerous passions: he must suspect nothing now. Besides, he has his own reasons for commissioning this work; not just the obvious ones he has mentioned to Robert, but certain other plans—commercial schemes—in which it might play a part; it would alarm him to think that its accuracy could be compromised by wayward, schoolgirl emotions.

Schoolgirl—that is exactly it, that is the whole problem. It is because she is a female that she feels this ridiculous sensuality, this weakness for physical gratification. And that is precisely why she must fight it, or—since she has already tried to fight it, and has already found, paradoxically, just how powerful, how strong, this female weakness is—she must disregard it.

She has discovered that she is not altogether a Rational person, yet she intends to go on behaving as if she were.

No man, she is sure, will ever allow women to work alongside him—to vote alongside him—to shape the future with him—if he believes them to be as foolish as she has realized that she is.

Of course, there are women who delight in being foolish. They are the sort of women of whom Emily disapproves. Indeed, Robert Wallis is the sort of young man of whom she disapproves. The realization that her heart—not to mention various other, more secretive organs—seems to be incapable of seconding the judgments made by her head is deeply irritating to her.

She picks up one of the tiny cups in which they have been cupping today's samples. It contains, still, a tiny morsel of Excelsos, long since cold. But more than that: as she sniffs it she fancies that she can just discern, caught in the cup, the soft aroma of Robert's breath.

She inhales it, allowing her eyes to close, allowing the brief delicious fantasies to flit through her mind. *His breath and mine, mingling together, like a kiss . . .*

She turns back to the window and breathes it back onto the glass, over her rubbed-out flower.

Like something written in invisible ink, the flower slowly reappears, just for a moment, before fading once again from view.

[THIRTEEN]

"Green"—a sourish flavour imparted by green beans, immature.

—MICHAEL SIVETZ, Coffee Technology

EMILY AND I DID NOT ONLY TASTE HER FATHER'S COFFEES; AT Pinker's insistence, we also ranked them. Initially I had been reluctant to do this, pointing out to my employer that good and bad are moral judgments, and as such have no place in Art.

He sighed. "But in Commerce, Robert, one makes such decisions every day. Of course one cannot directly compare a heavy, resinous Java with a delicate Jamaican. But it is the same coin that pays for them, and so one must ask oneself where that coin is best spent."

It was true that some coffees seemed to be consistently of higher quality than others. We noticed that when we particularly liked a coffee, it was often labeled "mocca"—and yet that word seemed to cover a multitude of styles; some heavy, some light, some with an intriguing floral aroma.

One day I found myself alone in the office, tasting a small lot.

There was no label on the sack, although there was a mark in what I took to be Arabic, a mark I had seen on many of the bags we shipped from that region:

ي

I knew as soon as I opened it that this was something special. The dry scent was honeyed, almost fruit-like: when I took the beans up to the office and waited for the water to boil, my wait was accompanied by a delicate perfume of woodsmoke and citrus. I ground the beans in a little hand-grinder: the smell intensified, adding a deep, *basso profundo* note of licorice and clove. Then, carefully, I poured on water.

Suddenly, so thick and full I could almost see it, the bouquet took life. It was like a genie escaping from its lamp, or a gush of steam snorting from an engine, or a fanfare of trumpets, majestic yet piercingly simple. The aroma of exotic flowers filled the room—and not just flowers: there was lime, tobacco, even mown grass. I know this must seem fanciful—to find so many disparate elements in one smell—but my palate was by now attuned to the task, and these were no will-o'-the-wisps: they were precise and distinctive, as real in that room as the walls and windows.

The steeping time was done. I pressed the grounds down with a spoon and lifted the cup to my mouth. For once I did not aspirate: there was no need. The taste was exactly as the smell had promised—the mouthfeel was solid and substantial, with the barest hint of brightness, and the floral flavors filled my head like heavenly choirs. I swallowed. There came a delicious sensation of natural sweetness and a long, mellow aftertaste of green tea and leather. It was as near to perfection as any coffee I had come across.

• • •

"THE COFFEES of mocca," Pinker said when I asked him about it, "are not as other coffees. Have you found it on a map?"

I shook my head. He went to the shelf and pulled out a great atlas, its pages big as circus bills.

"Now then." He flipped impatiently through that vast tome until he had found the page he wanted. "Yes. *There.* What do you see?"

I looked at where his finger was pointing. Where Persia and Africa met, separated by an arse-crack of water, there was a fly-spot. I looked harder. The fly-spot was labeled "Al-Makka."

"Mocca," he said. "Or as the Arabs call it, Makka. Source of the greatest coffees in the world." He tapped it. "This is where it was born. This is the cradle. Not just of coffee—of everything. Mathematics. Philosophy. Storytelling. Architecture. When Europe was lost to civilization, it was the Ottoman Empire which kept Christian learning alive. And yet, today, it is as if they are living through their own dark ages, waiting for history to come and set them free."

"Why are their coffees so particularly fine?"

"It's a very good question, Robert. Damned if I know the answer." He was silent a moment. "Some merchants swear that moccas have a faint chocolate taste. Some even adulterate other beans with cocoa powder to replicate it. What do you think?"

I searched my memory. "Some have a note of chocolate, certainly. But not the very finest—those seem to me to have an extraordinary fragrant quality, more in the range of honeysuckle or vanilla."

"My feelings exactly. Which would tell us what?"

"That mocca is not one coffee but several?"

"Precisely." His finger made a circle around the Red Sea. "The Arabs, of course, used to have a monopoly on growing coffee. Then the Dutch stole some seedlings and took it to Indonesia, and the French stole from them and took it to the Caribbean, and the

Portuguese stole from *them* and took it to Brazil. So. Let us be logical for a moment, and assume the Arabs stole it, too. Where might they have stolen it from?"

"Can we ever know?"

"Perhaps not. Did you ever meet Richard Burton?"

I was accustomed by now to the abrupt turns which a conversation with Pinker took—his mind was always racing ahead, seeing where he wanted to take you and then leading you there by easy steps. I shook my head.

"I was introduced to him at a reception," Pinker said. "There were above five hundred of us there, and he was a great man—fêted, at the time, for his explorations of the Islamic world. He's less favored now, of course. There were rumors about his private life . . . well, never mind. When he heard I was in coffee, he made a point of talking to me. Held me spellbound, as it happens, as well as the small crowd who soon gathered around us to listen.

"Burton had not long returned from one of his Arabian jaunts—he had darkened his skin with walnut juice, taken Arab dress, and passed himself off as an Islamic holy man. His Arabic was almost perfect, of course, and his scholarship of their texts considerable. He told me of a magnificent walled city he had found, in a part of East Africa that was lush and temperate—a coffee-growing region. In fact, he claimed the coffee there was so plentiful it had never actually been cultivated—the bushes grew wild, propagating themselves wherever the surplus fruits fell to the ground. Coffee traders were considered so important to the economy they were forbidden to leave the city on pain of death. It was a place of great wealth, apparently; Burton talked of ivory, precious stones, gold . . . and what he called some darker transactions. Slavery, one presumes.

"So closed is that city the traders even developed their own language, quite separate from that of the surrounding countryside. But the coffee, Burton said, was the best he had tasted in all his years of wandering. And—this is what sticks in my mind—he said it smelled fragrant, like honeysuckle blossom."

"Like that mocca?"

"Exactly. And something else that interested me—the town is called Harar, but the name of that region in the local tongue is *Kaffa.*"

"As in 'coffee'?"

"Burton was convinced the words must surely share a root."

"So the coffee beans that grow wild in Kaffa—"

"—are sold, perhaps, by the merchants of Harar to traders, who bring them, eventually, to Al-Makka. From where they are shipped to the rest of the world. If you were a trader in, say, Venice or Constantinople, you might well label the coffees you purchased by their port of origin, not the place they were grown in. Given the Arab mania for secrecy, you might not even be told which country a particular lot had come from. So you would call everything that passed through Al-Makka 'mocca,' just as today, some people refer to all South Americans as 'Santos.' "

"Intriguing. And where did Burton say this Harar was?"

Pinker ran his fingers over the map. In those days atlases were updated and reissued every year or so, the new countries tinted with the colors of the empires that had claimed them. Most of the world, of course, was red—British red—with a certain amount of blue, purple, yellow and so on. When I was a child, Africa was almost blank. As travelers returned with news of territories explored, named, and added to the tally, so the white had shrunk and the red expanded, nudging inward from the edges of that great continent toward the center. Not all was red, by any means: the French and the Dutch were not going to let us have everything our own way, and the boundaries between the different colors had often been drawn in blood.

Pinker had the very latest atlas—of course. Yet there was still a small part of Africa that, although it was no longer completely blank, had not been colored, a space the size of a man's hand in the mid-part of the continent.

He tapped it pensively. "Here," he said. "Burton places it here."

We both stared at the map.

"What an extraordinary thing coffee is, Robert," he said at last. "To be able to do good at both ends—temperance in England, and civilization elsewhere."

"Remarkable," I agreed. "And even more so when one considers the profit generated in the middle."

"Exactly. Remember Darwin: it is the profit which makes all else possible. It is not charity that will change the world, but commerce."

I DID NOT think any more of that conversation at the time: we were all talking of Africa in those days. Yet Pinker was someone who did not waste his assets. Every shilling must be put to use, and when the Guide was finished, I would be a coin no longer in hock.

THE MONEY was flowing through my own hands like water by now. Wellington Street was not all divans and chignons: any girl would do pretty much anything for an extra sovereign or two, and if your palate was becoming jaded with the possibilities and permutations of *that,* all sorts of other treats were available nearby. Just as London had a flower market and a fish market, a street of silversmiths and a street of booksellers, so establishments in different areas specialized in the different arts of love. In this quarter one might find Houses of Sappho; over here, Houses of Youth. I feasted on these pleasures as one might feast on the dishes of the Orient: not because I preferred them to my native fare, but because they were previously unfamiliar to me.

And sometimes I found myself being drawn to more dangerous pastimes. I was passing along a quiet quayside one afternoon when I discerned a faint, spicy waft of poppy smoke. It was the work of a moment to identify where the smell was coming from. I slipped down an alleyway in that direction and found myself on a deserted wharf. The aroma led me, as if along a well-marked trail, to a nondescript doorway. From the shuttered windows of the warehouse there came no sound, but when I knocked, the door swung open a crack. A wizened Chinese face looked out. I showed some coins. The door was opened wordlessly and I was allowed inside. On numerous berths and bunks that lined the inside of that storeroom like giant pigeonholes, reaching up into the gloom as high as the eye could make out, men lay wrapped in their coats like Egyptian mummies, or sat propped up on one arm, puffing at the curved clay pipes with unseeing eyes.

In the center of the room, laid out on a trestle, were the instruments of the trade, watched over by an old Chinaman: more pipes, some as long as walking sticks, a small brazier of glowing coals, a set of scales. I paid my shilling, and a pipe was plugged with resin, then plunged into the fire to be lit; when it was going, I clambered into the berth that was indicated to me and surrendered to the opium's effects. After a few puffs I felt a great weariness come over me, and my body relaxed so fully I could barely hold the pipe. Colors seemed to become more colorful, sounds more precise; that silent, dingy warehouse suddenly seemed like the most luxurious palace, full of shimmering, subtle sounds and gorgeous half-heard melodies. Intrigues and ideas flittered around me. I caught exhilarating snatches of conversation. I felt inspired. Brilliant rhymes began to spin through my head, rhymes that were all tangled up with algebra. I remember realizing that mathematics and poetry were one and the same, and both were astounding. Then for some reason I imagined a sea voyage. I could taste quite clearly the salt on my lips, and the fresh turtle I had eaten for lunch, washed down with a tot of rum. I could even smell a faint waft of spice in the warm African wind on my face. Then I fell into a deep sleep.

I woke up with the old Chinaman roughly shaking me, demanding more money: when I staggered to my feet I discovered that eight hours had passed. Needless to say, I could not remember a single one of those brilliant phantasmagorical rhymes. I stumbled outside and found a cab to take me home. Next day I was still so lethargic and nauseous that Emily grew exasperated and sent me away. I vowed never to repeat the experience, but even so I found myself yearning for those shimmering, inspired visions; like Caliban, having woken, I cried to dream again.

AND THEN my advance was gone. I had somehow got through thirty pounds in about the same number of days.

The pawnshop on Edgware Road was a foul place. Ike, the old Russian who ran it, would take anything from jewelry to rag-and-bone. As you walked in, you were hit by a sour, fungal smell that dealers call "mother," an odor not unlike wet, rotting fur.

Behind the counter Ike rubbed his hands. "Good morning, young man," he said with a quick smile. "What have yer got?"

I showed him—a vellum-bound edition of Coventry Patmore, three silk waistcoats I no longer wore, two beaver-skin top hats, a cane carved out of ivory.

"These are fine," he said, running his hands lasciviously over the goods. "Very fine."

"How much?"

He produced a stub of pencil and scratched his head with it, all the while regarding me craftily. I knew his game: the sum he named would depend not so much on the value of what I was selling as on how desperate he considered me. I did my best to look unconcerned.

"Three guineas," he said at last, writing it down on a filthy scrap of paper, as if that somehow made it more immutable.

"I was hoping for six."

He smiled and shrugged. "I'll have to sell them on."

"Perhaps this is the wrong place. I can easily take them up to the West End."

"They're specialist, sir. You won't find a better price." He brightened. "Of course, if you was wanting more cash, I could always advance you a sum."

"I didn't know you offered such a . . . service."

"Not in the usual way, sir, oh no. But for someone like yourself, someone with prospects . . . My fees are quite reasonable."

"You'd charge interest?"

Another shrug. "A small percentage, payable weekly."

"How much could I borrow?"

His smile broadened. "Step into my office, and we can look through some paperwork."

[FOURTEEN]

"Toasted almonds"—this superb aroma is reminiscent of candy made from sugared almonds, or chocolate-covered almonds called pralines.

—LENOIR, Le Nez du Café

EMILY HAD DECIDED SHE WANTED TO BE TAKEN OUT FOR DINner. There was a masked ball at Covent Garden, and she was greatly desirous of seeing, as she put it, my former bohemian haunts, not to mention some of the beautiful actresses of whom she had read in the newspapers. I could not decide where to take her: the private rooms at the Savoy were too large for a *tête-à-tête,* the private rooms at Romano's, with their Japanese print wallpapers, were very fine and intimate, but the Trocadero had those lovely corner rooms overlooking Shaftesbury Avenue . . .

"You seem remarkably familiar with the private salons of these establishments," she commented. "I suppose you use them for your assignations."

"Oh, one just gets to know about them," I said vaguely. "I have an invalid aunt who prefers to dine *à deux.*"

"Well, I *don't* want to dine in private. I want actresses."

"Your father would never forgive me if I took you somewhere unsuitable."

"I think I can stand an actress or two, Robert. Unless the urge to go on the stage has somehow become contagious, I shall be quite safe."

She was in a lighter mood with me these days—we were becoming easy with each other, although she still pretended to scold.

"Very well," I said. "If it is actresses you want, then it is to Kettner's we must go. It will be handy for the ball, too."

The following day I went to arrange the *menu* with Henri, the dapper Frenchman who, as *maître d'hôtel,* administered the warren of dining rooms off Church Street. Together we pondered the options. *Hors d'oeuvres,* of course, amongst them oysters and a dish of caviar, and then for the soup a silky *velouté* of artichokes. We deliberated whether sole or trout was better suited to the delicate appetite of a lady: the trout being, I was assured, particularly fine just then, trout won the day. *Côtelettes de mouton Sefton* was Henri's next suggestion, to which I immediately acquiesced, but I rejected his roast pheasant, which sounded greedy for two people, in favor of *perdreau en casserole. Épinards pommes Anna, haricots verts à l'Anglaise* and a *dauphinoise* to accompany. Then salad, of course. Asparagus with a *sauce mousseline.* A board of cheeses, vanilla ice *en corbeille,* and *petits fours* wound up our bill of fare. As for the wines, we settled on an Amontillado, the '82 Liebfraumilch, a pint of iced Deutz and Gelderman champagne, claret, and curaçao to close. I selected the table—positioned in a curtained alcove, it gave the option of privacy should the necessity arise, but had a view along the largest of the upstairs dining rooms when the curtains were open. Then, our preliminaries concluded, I bade farewell to the *maître d'* until the following day.

That still left the question of what to wear. Evening dress was an option—a dull one. We had opted to take our domino to the restaurant and change for the ball after the meal, but even so evening dress would look as if one were hardly making an effort.

Barely had I left Kettner's when my eye fell on a window in Great Marlborough Street. In it was displayed a fine jacket of dark blue otterskin. It was a magnificent thing—and it would look more magnificent still when paired with a cravat of French lace, such as the one I had spied a few days before in Jermyn Street. The exchange with Henri had left me feeling munificent, and I walked into the shop and inquired the jacket's price. Three guineas—a considerable sum, but as the tailor pointed out, reasonable for so unique a garment, when one could pay almost as much for a coat indistinguishable from that worn by every dullard in the room.

"Ah, Master Wallis," Ike greeted me. "And only a day late, too."

"Late?"

"With your interest. Two pounds, although next time there will have to be a small additional charge to cover the delay." He shrugged. "You are a man of business yourself now. You know how it is."

"A man of business? In what way?"

"You have become, like me, a trader, I hear. In the world of coffee?"

"Oh—yes. Yes, I suppose I have."

"But I am sure your enterprise fares rather better than my own little operation."

"It does fare tolerably well—but I have need of a little more cash."

"More?" Ike raised his eyebrows.

"Shall we say—another fifteen pounds?" I prompted.

"Certainly. Although," he said thoughtfully, "if it were twenty, the rate of interest would be rather less. A discount for the larger sum, you see."

"Oh. Very generous. Twenty it is then."

We concluded the paperwork, and I handed him two pounds back. "Your interest."

He bowed. "A pleasure doing business with you, Mr. Wallis."

I ARRIVED at Kettner's early, and chose Emily's buttonhole from the flower stall at the door. I had promised actresses, and the clientele did not disappoint; there were more pretty thespians on hand than in the green-room of many a Drury Lane theater. I spotted the pert lead of the latest brilliant comedy, dining in a booth with a member of the House of Lords. A notable agent was giving supper to a theatrical journalist; a colonel was entertaining his catamite, or possibly his subaltern; and a dainty young actress called Florence Farr was pretending not to recognize me as she smiled dutifully at her beau for the evening—who would, I knew, be paying five pounds for the privilege of being seen out with her: the tumble later would be thrown in for free.

Then Emily arrived, and my heart stood still. I had never before seen her out of her office clothes—her Rational garments. Tonight she was wearing a dress of black velvet embroidered with tiny steel sequins, cut low about the bust, and a cloak of red cloth trimmed with gray fur. As she greeted me she shyly allowed the cloak to slip off her shoulders, which were bare: as I took it I caught a tantalizing whiff of Guerlain's Jicky, and inhaled the perfect mixture of warm fragrance and warm female skin.

A woman's dress is a struggle between modesty and majesty: by the treasures it reveals it must hint at the pleasures it conceals. On this occasion the dressmaker had persuaded her client into a garment that was sensual, succulent, opulent; but which by those very qualities only emphasized the wearer's girlish innocence.

"You may say something, Robert," she said with a hint of—

entirely fetching—awkwardness as she sat down in the chair the waiter was holding for her.

I recovered myself. "You look absolutely beautiful."

"Though as usual I feel woefully underdressed beside you," she commented, taking up her napkin. "Thank goodness. Now, where are my actresses?"

I pointed out the various sights and personalities of the scene. Emily exclaimed over every morsel of gossip. "You should do tours," she said when I had finished. "But tell me, Robert, is this place not rather tame compared to the Café Royal?"

"Oh! No one goes to the Café Royal anymore," I assured her. "It is far too crowded."

"Ah. I suppose I must expect epigrams tonight. Since we have come, as it were, to their spiritual home."

"I shall certainly be talking a great deal of nonsense. It is the only subject on which I can converse with authority."

She looked around the room and frowned. "Can you smell something?"

I sniffed. "I don't think so. What sort—" Then I realized she was pulling my leg.

"Dear Robert," she said fondly. "Who would ever have thought, six weeks ago, that you and I would be sitting here like this?"

Our *hors d'oeuvres* arrived, and I enjoyed watching the gusto with which she tipped the oyster shells up to her mouth: the tightening of her neck, and the delicate convulsions of her throat as she swallowed. One day, I thought automatically, you shall have something in that pretty mouth even saltier than oysters . . . and then I thought, But would she? How does one go about explaining such a lewd act to an innocent young woman? Or would lust itself act as a teacher, prompting her to initiate those explorations for herself? I had a brief but almost ridiculously vivid fantasy of the two of us on a bed together, the black velvet dress thrown to the floor, and she my willing pupil . . .

"Robert?" Emily was looking at me with concern. "Are you all right?"

"Oh." I pushed the thought away. "Absolutely."

"You seem unusually quiet."

"I was struck dumb by how beautiful you look."

"Now you're just being silly. I don't believe you have ever been struck dumb in your life."

Our soup was excellent, our fish magnificent. Trying to maintain my position as a man of critical tastes, I said I thought the partridge a little dry, but my companion pointed out that I was a pampered sybarite, and we agreed to find it pretty much perfect. Henri came by, like a general marshaling his troops at the midpoint of the engagement, and Emily told him that she had decided to become an actress immediately, if this was how they got treated. "Oh!" that stalwart replied, "but you are far lovelier than any of the actresses here tonight." He glanced at me, and I thought I detected the merest quiver of his left eyelid—a quiver which might in another man have been taken for a wink.

The conversation flowed this way and that. I can barely remember what we spoke about; I was concentrating on being amusing, but I had learned that the way to amuse Emily Pinker best was to be serious occasionally, so I expect we talked a little of important things as well. Eventually our meal staggered to a close. I signed the bill—five pounds four shillings and sixpence—while Emily went to change into her costume. From the activity around the dining room, it was clear that many of the other patrons were also going on to the ball.

Emily returned in the domino of a harlequin, with a Pierrot cap and a half-mask of white silk. For my part, I had a simple eye-mask of black feathers that went rather well with my new jacket.

As we left the restaurant she stumbled and grabbed my arm. "I am a little tipsy," she murmured in my ear. "You shall have to promise not to take advantage."

"We should arrange a time and place to meet. That way, if we are separated, we can find each other again."

"Good! Where shall it be?"

"Shall we say, under the opera clock, at two?"

For reply she squeezed my arm, which she kept hold of as we headed to the street. Shaftesbury Avenue was bustling with carriages heading to the ball, and groups of people in carnival thronged the pavements. Suddenly I heard a shout. "Wallis! Wallis! Wait up!" I turned. A Pantaloon and a Punchinello, their faces made up with copious amounts of greasepaint, were hailing me as they descended from a cab, accompanied by two female marionettes. Despite the make-up, I recognized Hunt and Morgan.

"Where have you been?" Punchinello cried.

"In Kettner's."

"No—where have you *been*? Hunt is published at last—a villanelle in the *Yellow Book*! And you nowhere to be found for weeks!"

"I have been busy—"

Pantaloon snapped his fingers. "We knew inspiration must have struck."

"Not with poetry. I have had employment."

"Employment?" Punch shrank in mock horror. "The last time we saw you, you had been asked by that funny little gnome—what was his name—"

"May I introduce my companion for the evening, Miss Emily Pinker?" I said hastily.

Morgan made an exaggerated "Ah!" with his rouged lips. "Charmed. And this is . . . This is . . . um, Miss Daisy. And Miss Deborah."

The marionettes giggled as I took their hands. They were, I realized with a sinking heart, almost certainly *demi-mondaines.* And I was utterly responsible for Emily's welfare that night. If there was any suggestion of impropriety, it would be me Pinker would blame.

"I've met you before," Daisy said to me under her breath. "Don't you remember me?"

I stiffened. "I'm afraid I don't."

"I didn't look like this, sir, that's for sure." Her friend shrieked with laughter.

"You're an actress?" I suggested desperately.

"You could call it that," Daisy said. "A performer, anyway." Deborah shrieked again.

By now we were all surging into the Opera colonnade, and it was possible to contrive to be separated from our companions. Inwardly I cursed Hunt and Morgan for imbeciles. What had they been thinking of, bringing such women here? Fortunately, Emily seemed not to have noticed anything amiss.

"Isn't this wonderful?" she said, gazing at the crowd.

There must have been over a thousand people present, all disguised. Even the foyer, bars and rehearsal rooms were decked out in carnival-themed sets. A full orchestra was tuning up in the pit, though it was much too crowded to dance, and almost too noisy to hear. Waiters in elaborate costumes pushed through the crowd with trays of wine; acrobats on stilts performed wherever they could find a space; jugglers and dancers jostled us as we moved through the throng. I lost sight of Emily for a second on the stairs, then found her again, and I guided her to a quiet corner on the balcony where we could watch the antics below.

"This would have been unthinkable even a few years ago," I said.

By way of reply she reached for my hand. Then, to my astonishment, she put my fingers to her mouth, biting them hard with sharp little teeth.

"You are very jolly this evening," I said, surprised.

Her hands reached around my head as she brought our lips together. Our masks collided. Laughing eyes looked into my own—laughing eyes that were dark, not gray, and I stiffened as I realized that it was not Emily Pinker in my arms but someone else entirely. With a gasp of laughter she spun away from me: the hair under the Pierrot cap was dark, not fair. It must have happened when we were separated on the stairs.

I hurried back—but everywhere I looked there were harlequins. I grabbed one by the shoulder and said desperately, "Are you Emily?" She cackled. "If you like, m'sieur."

I glimpsed Hunt in the ballroom and struggled across to him. "Have you seen Emily?" I shouted over the din. "I've lost her."

"How perfect," he murmured vaguely. "By the way, how's the writing going?"

I shrugged.

"Lane says he will take a short story next quarter. But I was talking to Max—do you know Max?—and he thinks a sonnet sequence is the way to go. To make a name for myself, I mean."

"Max? You mean—Max Beerbohm?"

He nodded. "Ernest Dowson introduced us. You must know Ernest."

"Only by reputation," I said enviously.

"Yes, we're a jolly lot at the Café Royal these days." He peered around at the crowd with studied insouciance, pulling out a cigarette holder. "I really should find Bosie. I promised him I would look out for him. He does so hate a crowd."

"Bosie!" I exclaimed. "Not—Lord Alfred Douglas?"

He nodded. "Oscar has written him a love letter from prison, had you heard? He is still completely infatuated."

Bosie! Now I was feeling sick. Oscar Wilde's lover—the original wonderful boy—the sonneteer—and Hunt had been socializing with him! Had promised to look out for him! "Will you introduce me?" I said eagerly.

His glance seemed to imply that, as Bosie's great friend, one's first duty was to keep the encroaching hordes of would-be poets away, if necessary by beating them off with a stick.

"Hunt—please," I begged.

"Oh, very well. If I'm not mistaken, that's him over there."

I followed the direction of his gaze—and immediately glimpsed Emily, or what might be Emily, stepping through the crowd. "Blast!" I said.

"What is it?"

"I'll be right back."

I followed the elusive figure into the area behind the stage, a warren of small rooms decorated for the occasion with painted drapes. Here the atmosphere was even less restrained. Men and women were openly embracing—masked women were being passed from mouth to mouth, shrieking; I saw exposed breasts, arms slipping between thighs, a gloved hand fingering a bared nipple. More than one dressing room door was locked, and in some cases couples were queuing for the use of them, barely able to contain their impatience as they kissed and fondled. I felt even more sick: if Emily had come here, there was no telling what she might have seen.

I pushed my way back to the ballroom. Hunt had disappeared, nor could I see anyone who looked like an innocent young woman searching frantically for her lost partner. I thought: if I cannot find her, perhaps she will be able to find me, at least. I walked desperately through the crowd, back and forth, trying to make myself visible. After a few minutes I glanced up at the balcony. A harlequin with a Pierrot cap was being passionately embraced by a masked male figure in an otterskin jacket. Then more figures came between us; when I looked again, they were gone.

• • •

AT A QUARTER to two, ill with anxiety, I went outside. She was under the clock, waiting. I hurried forward. "Are you all right?"

"Of course." She sounded surprised. "Were you worried?"

"A little."

She slipped her arm through mine. "Did you think I had taken offense?"

"At what?"

She leaned in close. "I know quite well it was you, so don't pretend it wasn't."

"I don't know what you're referring to."

Her only answer was a laugh. A remarkably filthy laugh, as it happens.

"WHERE ARE WE going now?" she asked as we walked down Drury Lane.

"I'd rather thought of putting you in a cab."

"I want to go to the Cave of Heavenly Harmony," she announced.

"Oh, Lord—however do you know about that place?"

"I read about it in the *Gazette*. It's quite near here, isn't it?"

"Just around the corner. But it really isn't suitable—"

"If I hear one more time what isn't suitable for me, I shall run away," she said. "Really, Robert, for a poet you take a remarkably conventional view of womanhood. We aren't all quite as delicate as you seem to imagine."

"Very well," I said with a sigh. "The Cave of Heavenly Harmony it is."

The Cave was a dingy cellar bar which, having realized it was a place not worth visiting for any other reason, had installed a piano player and a stage. The idea was that you told the pianist what you would perform, and he would accompany you while you sang for whoever happened to be there. It was a favorite of young aristocrats, who loved to go and roar out the verses of bawdy music hall ditties. Sure enough, there was a group of swells there when we arrived. One of them was singing, with help from his friends on the refrain:

A pretty little novice in her convent woke at dawn, dawn, dawn,
And looking from her lattice she spied upon the lawn, lawn, lawn,
A handsome shepherd, quite intent
On playing with his instrument,
His instrument so long, long, long!

I glanced at Emily. She seemed oblivious to the innuendo of the lyrics.

"I'm going to put my name down," she said. "Whom do we speak to?"

"The waiter, I suppose." I beckoned to the man, who presented us with a list of songs. The swells finished their final chorus, to cheers and applause. A portly Italian man got up and sang a mournful lament in his native language, one hand clasped to his heart throughout. Then Emily's name was announced—I should have reminded her to give a false one. She stood by the piano, looking suddenly rather nervous. The audience whooped. She swallowed. There was a brief, agonizing silence. Then the piano player launched into his music, and she into the song.

It was a piercingly beautiful ballad—sentimental perhaps, but in her mouth the romantic clichés became sweet and genuine:

It is not wealth and state that smooth the way,
Nor bid the desert bloom;
The ploughman at his furrow can be gay,
The weaver at his loom. . . .

It was very lovely. However, it was not an ideal choice as far as the Cave's regular patrons were concerned. They had come here for coarse choruses and carousing, not sentimental ballads. Soon they were catcalling, whistling, and generally making a nuisance of themselves, and it was all poor Emily could do to finish. The moment she had done so, a blade jumped up on stage and launched into a music hall number, to roars of appreciation.

"Oh," said Emily, returning to the table somewhat crestfallen. "Perhaps this place is a little low after all."

"I thought you were wonderful," I said, patting her shoulder.

"Anyway, it is probably time to go now."

"Capital. I'll pay the bill."

As WE LEFT the Cave, I spied a cab coming round the corner, and whistled to it. "Limehouse," I told the cabman, handing Emily up.

"Good-night, Robert," she said, smiling at me. "I've had the most wonderful time."

"And I too."

She leaned down and kissed me quickly on the cheek, and then the cabman flicked his whip. I breathed a sigh of relief. The night had passed off without any major disasters, thank God.

I retraced my steps through the crowds to Wellington Street. I had never seen Covent Garden like this. It was as if a kind of madness had taken hold. The streets were thronged with drunken people in costumes and masks, chasing each other through the colonnade. Couples were openly embracing. I entered the relative calm of the brothel at Number 18 with a sigh, as another person might sigh with relief on reaching their club. But even here, it seemed, all was chaos. In the waiting room I found half a dozen girls naked except for blindfolds, playing a kind of blindman's buff: they were wandering around with outstretched arms trying to catch the men, the idea being that whoever they caught would have to go with them. Of course, being blindfolded they were mostly blundering into each other, and groping with their hands to ascertain each other's sex, much to the amusement of their watching quarry. I sat a little while, watching and drinking a glass of absinthe, but I wasn't in the right frame of mind for these frolics. It was a relief when I was finally able to take one of the girls upstairs, conclude my dealings with her rapidly, and return by cab to St. John's Wood.

[FIFTEEN]

Mouthfeel: firmness, softness, juiciness, or oiliness are measured in the mouth much as they would be measured by the finger.

—LINGLE, The Coffee Cupper's Handbook

❧

I WAS IN NO BETTER A MOOD WHEN I AWOKE THE NEXT MORNING. The cause of my bad temper was not hard to pinpoint. So Hunt was published. I should have been pleased for him, but actually all I could feel was a dull throb of envy. Beerbohm—Dowson—Lane—even Bosie! While I had been flirting and drinking coffee, my friend had been getting on with the serious business of forging a reputation.

Ignoring my thick head, I pulled a stack of mauve paper toward me. Damn it, I would write a villanelle myself, just as a warm-up.

Half an hour later I had six lines composed. But it is one of the features of villanelles that they become harder, not easier, as you go on. And I had to be at Pinker's.

I glanced at the clock. Perhaps my employer would excuse me a morning's work, given that I had taken his daughter to a ball the night before. I decided to continue for another hour.

At the end of that time I had crossed out three of my six lines. And now I was ridiculously, hopelessly late. I put the poem to one side, intending to pick it up when I returned.

Needless to say, when I came back that evening I looked at what I had written and immediately saw that it was worthless. I tore it up and told myself I had had a lucky escape—were it not for the necessity of going out, I might have wasted the whole day trying to make something of it.

Or, alternatively, a small voice in my head reminded me, I might have succeeded.

OVER THE DAYS that followed I made a concerted effort to do some writing. My feelings for Emily, apparently just the kind of thing in which poets had found inspiration for centuries, provoked only some flat, insipid sonnets which I burned at once. My real poem to her was the Guide. I am certain that it became subtly altered as a result of our growing affection; my passion scenting its prose, as a cask of wine is said to take on the flavors of the air in which it is stored.

Pinker, however, was always on hand to sniff out any taint of the fanciful or ornate. When I wrote that a Mysore had "the scent of curries, a whiff of arid Indian streets, elephant dung topped by a Maharaja's cigar," he packed me off to the zoo, pointing out that I had never smelled an arid Indian street, never eaten curry, and was no doubt unfamiliar with elephant dung as well. He was right, of course, although I kept the reference to cigars. He was equally indignant when I tried to compare the floral bouquet of a Yemeni mocca with "the rose-petal vapors of a maiden's breath." "There is no such aroma, Robert. You only wish it to be so," he cried, exasperated. But I noticed that he did not call Emily over to prove it. The same thought had obviously occurred to her: when her father had left us, her cheeks were quite pink.

"WHAT ARE YOU doing, Robert?" the Frog demanded one lunchtime.

"I am writing poetry," I said with a sigh, knowing that any such thing was now going to be impossible.

"I like poems. Do you know *Alice in Wonderland*?"

"Know it? I used to live in the wretched place." This reference to my alma mater went over her head, but it did not stop her pestering.

"Robert, please will you write me a poem about a crocodile?"

"Oh, very well. If you absolutely promise to go away afterwards."

Within two minutes I had dashed something off, and read aloud:

"The hunger of the crocodile
Is awesome to behold:
For breakfast he eats fifty eggs,
Scrambled, then served cold.

He follows that with toast and jam,
And oysters, tea and juice,
And when he has no more of those,
He likes a roasted goose.

And then he has a plate of ham,
Served with English mustard,
A dozen kippers, smoked of course,
On which he pours hot custard.

But what he likes to eat the most
Is quite another question:
His favorite dish is little girls,
Which gives him indigestion."

She stared at me, open-mouthed. "But that's brilliant! You really are a poet!"

I sighed. "If only real poetry were that easy."

"Now can I have one about a caterpillar?" she said hopefully.

"I thought you had promised to go away."

"I promise to go away for three times as long if you write me one more poem. That's a very advantageous proposition, you know—three aways for two poems."

"Ah, the famous Pinker gift for negotiation. Let's see, then . . .

" 'This is a curious business,'
The missionary said,
'I seem to have a caterpillar
Living in my head.

'He must have been inside those pears
The cook served up for tea,
And since I ate his old abode
His new address is me.

'I hear him singing in my ear;
My mouth is his front door;
And when he has too much to drink
I hear the beggar snore.' "

The Frog clapped. Emily, who had come into the room as I was extemporizing this nonsense, said, "That is really very sweet, Robert. You should send it to a children's publisher."

"I am a poet," I said tersely. "Heir to a glorious tradition of rebels and decadents. Not a composer of nursery rhymes and doggerel."

DETERMINED TO find the time to write, I tried doing without sleep, keeping myself up with the help of vast quantities of Pinker's product. The first time I did this, I was elated to find that I had completed twenty lines of lyric ode. The next night, though, caffeine and fatigue battled each other to a stalemate, producing only a dull headache and some even duller couplets. Moreover, I was too exhausted the next day to do my job properly. I was so fatigued, in fact, that I was somewhat short with Emily. We had a silly argument over the wording of a paragraph, and she promptly burst into tears.

I was astonished. She had never given any sign of being the sort of girl who cried at small provocations—quite the reverse, in fact.

"I'm sorry," she said, drying her eyes on a handkerchief. "I'm just a little tired."

"So am I," I said with feeling.

"Why is that, Robert?" she asked, and it seemed to me that she looked at me a little oddly.

"I have been trying to work."

"We both have."

"I mean my *real* work. Writing."

"I see—and that is the only reason you have been so," she hesitated, "so off recently?"

"I suppose it must be."

"I thought perhaps that you were tired of *me*."

"What on earth do you mean?"

"At the ball—Robert, when you kissed me—I thought perhaps . . . but of course, you are a bohemian, a kiss means rather less to you—"

"Emily," I said, exasperated. "I did not—" I stopped. I had been about to say, "I did not kiss you." But something made me pause.

I thought: I *would* have kissed her, if I could. If I had known she would not have rejected my advances, or gone running to her father. And now, it seemed, because of some ridiculous mix-up she had been kissed by a stranger she had believed was me.

And had not minded. Had apparently rather liked it, in fact.

I had a choice.

I could tell her the truth, which would both heartily embarrass her and give her the impression that I did not want to kiss her; or I could accept the greater truth of what had happened that evening.

I said slowly, "If I have been short with you, darling Emily, it is because I could not be sure whether I had overstepped the mark."

"Did I give that impression—in any way?" she said quietly.

I had absolutely no idea. "You did not," I said. I took a step toward her. I hoped to God my stand-in had been a good kisser. Though not, of course, so good that I could not live up to his example. "But we had both of us had much to drink that night. I was not certain . . ."

"If you overstep," she said, "I will be sure to tell you."

She tasted of cream, of meringues and vanilla and milky coffee, with a faint far-off tang of cigarettes.

I paused. "Have I overstepped yet?"

"Robert," she cried, "can you never be serious?"

I kissed her again. This time I pressed my hand into the small of her back, gently drawing her in to me. It seemed to me that, even in the midst of that wonderful kiss, she gasped with pleasure. I slipped my tongue between her lips, and after a moment's resistance, felt them parting, inviting me deeper. . . . Good heavens, I thought, astonished: she is more passionate than I had ever imagined.

Footsteps! We drew apart just as the door opened. It was Jenks.

We both took a step back—Emily turning away in confusion, her color high. The secretary threw us a suspicious glance.

"I am getting honeysuckle, floral aromas, very bright and smooth," I said quickly. "Perhaps a little citrus. But the mouthfeel is excellent."

Jenks's eyes raked the room. He saw, I am sure, that there was no coffee on the table, but he said nothing.

"Emily?" I said.

"Yes?" She turned back toward me.

"What did you think?"

"It was—it was quite pleasant, Robert. Though perhaps a trifle strong. Excuse me—I have left something—something downstairs."

IT WAS MUCH LATER when she returned carrying a thick folder of papers, which she placed in front of her at the table and ostentatiously began to review.

"Every minute you were not with me was an age," I began.

"Not now," she interrupted. "We have work to do."

I was baffled. "I thought—before—you seemed to prefer my attentions to work."

There was a brief silence. "That was before Jenks surprised us. It has brought me to my senses."

"Jenks? What does Jenks matter? What does anyone matter?"

"We are both my father's employees. We should not—we must not—do anything unprofessional. We cannot betray his trust."

"Now you're being inconsistent."

"There must be no more kissing." She said it firmly. "Promise me that, at least."

"Very well. I will try not to think of kissing you more than—what? Once every—six or seven seconds?"

Silence.

"That's twice already—three times, now."

"Robert!"

"I cannot help the way I feel, Emily. And no more, I think, can you. But if you wish it, I will refrain from kissing you again."

WE KISSED beside the river, we kissed behind her sisters' backs, we kissed with the *crema* of a freshly made coffee still mustachioing our lips. Sometimes she would murmur, "Robert—we mustn't," but she kissed me anyway.

Once she said, "I wish I did not like it so much, and then I might find it easier to stop."

"But why should we stop?"

"Because it is wrong."

"But how can it be wrong? Art shows us, surely, that life should be a succession of exquisite sensations. Of course you must kiss me."

"I am not quite sure if you are flattering me now, or yourself," she muttered. "You are a good kisser, but 'exquisite sensations' may be pushing it a bit."

"We must seize the moment, for joy is fleeting, and besides, I think I hear Ada clumping up the stairs."

[SIXTEEN]

"WHERE SHALL WE EAT TODAY?"

"Unfortunately, I shall not be able to have lunch with you today, Robert."

"Is it something I said?"

"No, something I have said. A promise to the Suffrage Society. I am to go out selling their leaflets."

"You mean, in public?"

"Yes. Don't look so surprised. Someone has to do it."

It would have been easy enough to have a disagreement about that particular statement, I reflected. But I saw the look on Emily's face and kept my own counsel. "Then I will come with you. We can have lunch afterwards."

She frowned. "I suppose you could stand next to me and look helpful. But you will have to promise not to pass any of your flippant remarks."

WE TOOK UP position next to the entrance to the Underground station on King William Street in the City. Emily held up one of her leaflets, and in a querulous small voice called: "Votes for women! The truth for a penny!"

A couple of people glanced at us curiously, but no one stopped. "Oh dear," she said anxiously. "They don't seem terribly keen. Votes for women!"

An elderly gentleman with muttonchop whiskers paused. "What have we here?" he said in a kindly voice, taking the pamphlet from her and examining it.

"The truth for a penny," she said promptly. "The case for woman suffrage."

"And how much for a fuck?" he said in the same kindly tone.

For a moment neither of us reacted. Then Emily gasped, and I said furiously, "How dare you?"

"Are you with this creature?" he said to me.

"I am with this woman. And you have insulted her."

"She is standing in the street peddling her wares, is she not? In my experience only one sort of woman does that." He walked away, not bothering to return the pamphlet.

"I'll kill him," I said hotly, starting after him.

"Robert, don't." Emily caught at my arm. "We are under instruction not to make trouble."

"So you may be, but I won't stand by—"

"Please, Robert. In any case, I've heard worse language used by my father's porters." She raised her arm, and her voice, simultaneously. "Votes for women! The truth for a penny!"

An urchin ran up to her and shouted, "I'd vote for yer, love!" He accompanied his comment with an unambiguous gesture of the hips, dodging my foot as I lashed out at his scrawny buttocks.

"Remind me," I said grimly, "why we are doing this."

"Because men and women need to have the same rights before they can truly communicate with each other as equals."

"Oh yes, of course. And how long do we have to do it for?"

"Until the leaflets are gone," she said firmly.

I held out my hand. "You had better give me half."

"Are you sure?"

"If it means I get some lunch, most certainly. In any case, you are doing it all wrong. There is an art to selling things."

"I am doing it exactly as the Society instructed."

"Then we shall see who is more successful." I crossed over the road. There was an elderly lady coming along the pavement. I stopped her. "Excuse me, madam—may I sell you this pamphlet? It contains everything you need to know about the suffrage movement."

"Oh." She smiled without examining the leaflet. "How much is it?"

"One penny, though you can give more if you like."

"Here's a sixpence—I shan't want change," she said, giving me a coin.

"Thank you," I said, pocketing the money. "Have a pleasant day."

"Votes for women," Emily called on the other side of the road, waving her pamphlet aloft. There was a frown on her face. I laughed: I knew that frown; she was irritated that I had been proved right.

Two young women with their hands pushed deep into fur stoles walked past me. "Excuse me," I said, catching them up. "You look as if you ought to read about votes for women." I pushed two pamphlets into their hands. "That'll be tuppence, please."

Smiling back at me, the younger one found me the money. "What is it all—" she began, but once I had the coins I didn't have time to chat. Turning to a young office clerk, I said, "Chum—want to find out what women *really* think? It's all in here." Within moments I had my next sale.

I glanced across the street. Emily had realized that my method of directly accosting people worked better than her shouting, and was now following suit. I saw her make a sale to two elderly ladies, and another to a woman out shopping with her daughter.

A middle-aged man was heading toward me. "This leaflet," I said, walking alongside him and showing him the cover, "contains all the filthy arguments of the suffragists. Sexual equality, free love—it's all in there."

"I'll take two," he said, eyeing the leaflet anxiously.

"Good man. That'll be a shilling." As he walked away I could see Emily giving me a furious look—I had sold almost half my leaflets, and she only one or two. "The one who sells least buys lunch!" I called. She scowled, but I noticed that she redoubled her efforts.

"Good afternoon, ladies," I said to a group of shopgirls. "Sensational stuff, this—everyone's reading it." I quickly made four sales, and turned my attention to a matron who was struggling with her shopping. "No more burst paper bags when women have the vote! It's all in here, and I'll even carry your potatoes to the pavement."

When I had finished picking up potatoes I strolled across the road. "All gone," I reported smugly.

"People are only buying them from you because you're a man," Emily said crossly. "It's the same old problem all over again."

"Well, whatever the reason, I seem to have made a nice profit. And now I shan't even have the expense of lunch, since you're paying."

"Robert, will you tell me a poem?" the Frog asked hopefully.

I was still in an indulgent mood after lunch. "Very well. What sort of poem?"

"The same one you told me last time, the one about the caterpillar."

"You can't have that one. As an artist, I must be original."

"But you didn't finish it. You left the man with a caterpillar inside him, and I have hardly been able to concentrate on arithmetic ever since."

"You see, Robert," Emily murmured behind me. "The artist does have some responsibilities after all. Though since the Frog never concentrates on her arithmetic anyway, you must not feel too guilty."

"I should not want to be liable for poor sums," I assured the Frog. "Let me see . . ."

A moment's thought, a little jotting on a scrap of paper, and it was coming—

"I am timing you, Robert," Emily said. "You have to do it in less than a minute."

"That is hardly fair."

"Was it fair that you sold more leaflets than me because you are a man? Forty seconds left."

"I need a little longer—"

"I should stop protesting, if I were you, and concentrate on writing."

"Oh, very well—"

"Too late—"

"I have it!" I jumped up.

"'This really is most vexing,'
The missionary said,
'That dratted caterpillar is
Still living in my head.'

'I did not offer him free board,
Or ask him here to stay,
But now he is so comfortable,
He will not go away.'

—so said this mournful cleric;
He gave a heavy sigh;
And as he did so, from his mouth
There flew a butterfly."

It was nonsense, of course; but it rhymed, after a fashion, and scanned—almost. The Frog applauded, and Emily smiled fondly, and just for a moment I felt a sense of triumph greater than the publication of any sonnet in the *Yellow Book* could have given me.

[SEVENTEEN]

HER HEART IS SINGING. HER HEAD IS TROUBLED.

Not by the small white lie she has told Robert—Emily knows perfectly well that it was not him who tried to kiss her at the ball, but he was taking his duties as a chaperon so seriously that evening that it had amused her, initially, to tease him a little; and then, when she saw how envious it made him, she had allowed his misunderstanding to develop, and ultimately become something much more—no; what is perplexing her is that this relationship, according to the codes of the time, does not exist.

Those who court might fall in love; those who fall in love might marry. There is no room in the rituals of her class for those who do not officially court, who are thrown together by fate, or—even worse—by work.

She doubts her father will let her marry him; she is not even sure, yet, if that is what she wants herself.

So she does what she can; gently singing his praises, but not so much that her father could suspect her of losing her head.

She tells him that Robert—"although a silly young man, and still quite the most annoying aesthete"—is working not only hard but well; that he would be an asset to the company, when he has only grown up a little. She points out that, as an artist, he has a kind of expertise which none of their other employees has; that he sees things in a way that might be extremely useful to them.

Her father listens, and nods, and does not suspect.

ONE PERSON who does suspect, though, is Jenks. And this presents its own problems, because for some time now she has been aware that her father's senior secretary harbors a certain fondness for her—a fondness bound up, she is fairly sure, with a sincere regard for her professionalism, and her reticence, and the careful way she comports herself in the office; all the things, in fact, which have allowed his affection to remain implicit, and therefore manageable, and which she has now kicked over in the madness of her affair with Robert.

So she feels both a little guilty and a little foolish. But since the nature of her relationship with Jenks is unspoken, she does not think he will embarrass himself by saying anything.

She has not reckoned, however, with the force of his antipathy for Robert. One afternoon, as she is transcribing her shorthand notes, the secretary enters the room and carefully shuts the door behind him. "Miss Pinker," he begins. "I must speak with you."

She knows immediately what he is going to say. She wishes she could somehow just skip to the end of the scene, with him closing the door behind him, without them both having to go through the awkward bit in the middle.

He surprises her.

"I would never dream of telling you what you should or should not do." He speaks fiercely, avoiding her eyes. "And I would never criticize a fellow employee, let alone one who has been fortunate enough to acquire your good opinion. But I have to tell you that on at least two occasions, Wallis has been seen frequenting a certain street in central London, the nature of which leads me to . . . to question his character."

"I see," she says calmly. "And which street is this?"

"A part of Covent Garden well known for its . . . associations."

"And you were there? You saw him?"

"Yes. I have a friend who is performing at the Lyceum. I have been to see the show three times—it is a great success."

"Well, there you are," she says, relieved. "You were there quite innocently, and doubtless Robert was, too."

"I'm afraid not. I was waiting at the stage door—it backs on to the side of the street I am referring to. Wallis was . . . Wallis was not waiting for anything. He was entering one of the buildings. It is a place quite notorious for what goes on there."

"Are you quite sure of this?"

He nods.

"To blacken someone's name without absolute evidence—"

"I would have said nothing!" he cries. "If I had not been sure—if it had been anyone else—but how could I stay silent, knowing what I know? If something had happened—if there had been some," he swallows, "some beastliness on his part toward you. Imagine if that had happened, and I had done nothing."

"Yes," she says. "Yes, I do see that. I must thank you for speaking out."

"I will talk to your father, and have him dismissed."

"No," she hears herself saying, "I will mention this to my father myself, when the moment is right."

"Surely it would be better coming from a man—"

"It is a delicate matter. It should be handled delicately. I will choose the most appropriate time."

He frowns.

"I do not want my father to feel pressurized into acting precipitately. The Guide is very important to Pinker's—essential, even, if we are to steal a march on Howell's. Robert should finish it before any discussion is had."

"So you are going to say nothing?"

"You have spoken to me. That must have been difficult, and I appreciate it, but now it is done, you have discharged your responsibilities. It is I, after all, not my father, who would be at risk—"

"If you will not speak to him, I must."

"Please, Simon," she says. "Let us leave it. Please? For my sake."

He is hurt, she can tell—not because she has rejected his advice, but because he is suddenly seeing her in a different light.

"Well, I have said my piece," he says abruptly, turning to the door.

As he goes she says, "When was this? That you last saw him, I mean."

"The last time was on Friday evening."

She thinks: *Earlier that afternoon, we had kissed.*

A MIXTURE of emotions kick their way across her heart. Anger and disgust, principally. But then—she is a modern woman—she tries to think rationally.

Perhaps it is partly her own fault. Perhaps she is somehow inflaming his passions with her kisses, and he must find release in— She cannot bear to think about what he finds release in.

For a week she cannot bring herself to touch him. And then they discover that muscat grapes and coriander seeds share some of the same floral characteristics: that hazelnuts and freshly churned butter have a similar milky, creamy fragrance. As they join the various parts of the Guide together, so they find the hidden connections between different tastes and aromas—a spectrum ranging from sweet to sour, from flowery to spicy, a palette of the senses. And somehow when Robert takes her in his arms, everything that happens in that other world, that dark mirror-land where men keep their secret desires, seems not to matter, to have no bearing on the guilty pleasure she feels.

And—another emotion she had not expected to feel. When she does think about those other women, the faceless, nameless women who lie with him in the mirror-land, she is surprised to discover that what she feels for them is not pity or even disgust. What she feels is a sudden, disturbing, jolt of envy.

[EIGHTEEN]

AT LAST THE GUIDE REALLY WAS COMPLETE. THE PERFUMER had made up a dozen stout mahogany boxes, which opened at the side to reveal an ingenious series of shelves holding thirty-six glass-stoppered bottles of aroma. Meanwhile, a printer was running off the pamphlet which explained how the scents should be used. I must confess to a touch of vanity here: I insisted the pamphlet be bound in calfskin vellum, ostensibly so that it would withstand the rigors of the field, but actually because this was my first printed work and I wanted it to look as much as possible like a volume of verse.

The conclusion of the Guide left me in something of a quandary. Since I was being paid by the word, there was now no obvious reason for me to remain at Pinker's. But equally, no one could claim that by remaining I was wasting their money. To Emily I muttered something about wanting to refine my phrasing when the first reports came in from Pinker's agents, but we both knew that my motives were quite different.

Pinker never commented on my presence. Occasionally, though, he found me small tasks to keep me busy. This happened so frequently, in fact, that I even began to wonder if it was deliberate.

ONE DAY he placed before Emily and me half a dozen squat tins with roughly printed labels. One bore an elaborate picture of an angel, another a picture of a lion. "What are these?" Emily asked, clearly as unfamiliar with them as I was.

Her father's eyes twinkled. "Shall we taste them, and find out?"

We had boiling water brought up, and cupped the first tin's contents. It was coffee, but of a poor quality.

"Well?" Pinker demanded.

"Very ordinary."

"And the next?"

I proceeded to the second tin. "If I am not mistaken, this has been glazed with sugar water to lend an artificial sweetness."

It was the same with the others: they were either bland, tainted, or flavored with additions.

"Can you tell us where these excrescences came from?" I asked.

"Certainly." Pinker tapped one of the tins. "This is Arbuckle's. I had it sent over by boat. It has a quarter of the entire American market—over a million pounds by weight in a year. When you ask for coffee anywhere from New York to Kansas City, this is what you get."

He pointed to the second tin. "This is Chase and Sanborn's. They have from Boston to Montreal. In that territory, hardly a cup is sold that is not produced by them.

"This is Lion coffee. . . . This is Seal. . . . This is Folgers, of San Francisco and the gold rush lands. And this is Maxwell House, which hails from Nashville and the South.

"In all, just six makes—brands, as they call them over there—share out the coffee consumption of the most vigorous nation on earth. Six! Inevitably, their proprietors wield colossal power. You have heard me talk of the Exchange, I think, Robert?" I nodded. "The Exchange is a remarkable place. But it is also the scene of a great, ongoing conflict—a conflict between those who wish our industry to be free, and those who seek to control it for their own ends."

"How can anyone control an entire industry?"

He went to stand by the ticker machine, still endlessly tossing its chains of white tape onto the floorboards, and gazed at the symbols as he spoke. "These six have made a private arrangement with the Brazilian government. They have effectively bypassed the Exchange; as they say over there, they have cornered the market. If the price is too low, they buy up stocks to create a shortage, and release them only when prices are better. Or if the price is high they simply refuse to sell, and sit back and wait for it to fall to a level that suits them. And all because the public have learned to trust their name."

"It is the standardization of which you spoke, the first time you interviewed me."

"Yes." Pinker pursed his lips. I think he was judging how much to tell me of his plans. "It is the future," he said at last. "And we must beat it, or be left behind. Remember Darwin."

"But they are in America. England is something else entirely."

Pinker shook his head. "We are all one market now, Robert. Just as there is one price for the raw product, so there will eventually be one price for the finished article. And what persuades a housewife in Sacramento or Washington to part with her money will also work in Birmingham or Bristol."

"You don't intend to sell a coffee as poor as these, though, surely?"

Again Pinker hesitated. "I am going to reduce the number of my blends to two," he said. "Both will trade under the brand name 'Castle.' Castle Premium will be supplied to the Temperance Taverns, Castle Superior to the shops. Thus the customer will have the reassurance of knowing they are buying the same trusted name for home use that they enjoy when they go out." The phrases tripped off his tongue, polished and slippery.

"The same name, yes, but not actually the same coffee," I pointed out.

"I suspect that is a distinction that will pass most people by. It is for the greater good, Robert—our success will mean the success of the Taverns, and the success of coffee, and thus of temperance: we will create a sober, more efficient economy that will be of benefit to the whole nation, and to the nations which supply us, but no one will help us do it. We must play the game in order to win it. And so we must look to America, and the new methods."

"But you do not control the market, as the Americans do."

"No."

"Then that is, surely, a flaw in your plan."

"Let us just say it is something which must be factored in."

"In what way?"

"All in good time, Robert. All in good time. In the meantime, will you give some thought to how my blends might be constructed?"

IT WAS A curious conversation, and one which I took up again with Emily when we were alone.

"Your father seems very keen on these blends of his," I commented.

"It is nothing new." She picked up some of the beans we were examining. "This Java, for example, has an excellent body but is a little bland in taste. Mocca is more likely to be the opposite—full of flavor but thin in the mouth. Combining them makes for a coffee that is easy to enjoy."

I glanced at her. "It is a kind of marriage of flavors."

"It is," she agreed. "But . . ."

"What is it?"

She sighed. "I think it is like mixing colors on a palette. It is easy to produce brown by combining the other colors together, but just because it is easy does not mean you should."

"Quite. The colors are much better appreciated on their own."

She was silent for a moment. It was not often that she criticized her father. "Of course, he has commercial considerations to think of."

"He is clearly very good at making money."

"He has plans—such great plans. If you only knew the half of them."

"I should like to."

Another sigh. "He has to be careful whom he tells, and when."

"Of course. And you are family, and I am not. Although I hope that one day I may be considered more close than I am."

At that, she blushed.

"And now," I said, "let us perform a marriage of our own." I held out my hand to her.

"What *do* you mean?"

"I mean, between these two coffees," I said, pointing to the mocca and the Java on the table in front of us. "Their flavors have been flirting for such a long time now, ever since they were introduced at a dance. Let us bless their union, and assist them in consummating it."

"Robert!"

I raised my eyebrows innocently. "I am speaking metaphorically, of course." I put the beans together into the grinder and worked it vigorously. "It will be interesting, as you say, to see how the two bodies combine—"

"Robert! Stop it."

"Very well."

I spooned the grounds into the cups and added the water. The mix, in fact, was not bad. "A happy union after all," I said, but she was trying to ignore me. I smiled at her, until eventually she grew pert and pretended to hit me.

And so, through flirtations and false constructions, we danced our way in mutual ignorance toward the greatest misunderstanding of all.

[NINETEEN]

"How do we do?" Pinker demanded for the twentieth time, stepping into the room. "Are my blends concluded?"

"Very nearly," I admitted. I was alone there except for the Frog, Emily having taken the afternoon off to go shopping.

Pinker stopped dead. "What on earth are you wearing, Robert?"

"It is a jacket made in the Indian style."

"And in Indian colors, too, I see. Though perhaps it would seem less . . . brilliant under the glare of an Oriental sun."

"Perhaps," I said airily.

"It cost eight pounds," the Frog said eagerly from the floor, where she was squatting in her usual posture. "It's the only one of its kind in all London."

"I am not surprised." Pinker looked at me and sighed. "Leave us, would you, dear Philomena? Mr. Wallis and I have some matters to discuss."

Obligingly the Frog hopped away, croaking.

"I have no idea why she insists on making that extraordinary noise," Pinker muttered. "I suppose she'll grow out of it." He glanced at me. "My daughters—my daughters are each in their own way unconventional, Robert."

"They are a great credit to you," I said politely.

"They are a great worry. Doubtless all parents fret about their children. But when there is only one parent the sum of worry must be doubled, rather than divided."

"I can imagine."

"Can you?" He glanced at me again. "You must think it strange I employ them in the business."

"I had not considered it," I said carefully.

"Emily needs to be occupied. She gets that from me, of course. But even more than I, she needs a sense of purpose—to know that what she is about is creating some good in the world. She would never be happy, for example, running some minor aristocrat's household. Supervising servants and dances and dinner menus and so on."

I thought I began to see where this might be going, now. "Of course," I agreed. "She is a modern woman. She must not on any account be thrown back into the past."

"Exactly!" Pinker gripped my arm. "Thrown back into the past—that is exactly what she fears. You put it well—you have the gift of words."

"I do my best," I said modestly. "But if I am able to express the sentiment, it is because I feel it myself—I too wish to look forward."

"Yes." He released my arm. "You must come to dinner, Robert. We have much to talk about."

"I would like that very much."

"Good. Saturday at six. Jenks will give you the address."

HE WAS THINKING that I might marry his daughter.

I could scarcely believe my luck. He was a wealthy man, and

clearly he was rapidly becoming even wealthier. With a fortune such as his, he could have bought his daughter into the upper classes, or cemented an alliance with another wealthy tradesman. I was an artist, and I was penniless. True, I was educated, and—I liked to think—not without talent or charm, but in the normal way of things it was unlikely a man like that would have considered me a suitable match. To have won him over was a great coup.

I would never have to take employment again. I could travel: I had always wanted to do the Grand Tour, like so many poets and artists before me. I could afford a place in town, and somewhere quiet in the country. I would be able to write, freed from domestic worries.

That evening I celebrated this fortuitous turn of events by purchasing a syringe and a cocaine solution and taking them along to Wellington Street. It was not a great success. While the drug made me eager, it seemed to have an anaesthetic effect on my performance, slowing me down to the point where I eventually just longed to get the whole thing over with. However, on this occasion the girl did not mind, as she took for herself what I did not use. Apparently it is rapidly becoming the stimulant of choice among the better sort of whore: it does not put the customers off, as the smell of gin does, and makes the girl appear more enthusiastic, unlike morphine, which makes them drowsy. One can now get cocaine in lozenge form from any Covent Garden chemist. As Pinker would say: *And so we Improve.*

[TWENTY]

"Pungent"—a prickling, stinging or piercing sensation, not necessarily unpleasant, e.g. pepper or snuff.

—SIVETZ, Coffee Technology

❧

I CONSIDERED CAREFULLY WHAT TO WEAR FOR DINNER AT Pinker's. On the one hand it was almost one's duty, as an aesthete, to make a striking show at table. On the other, I wanted Pinker to think of me as a possible future son-in-law. I should wear something impressive, I decided: something that declared that I was, if not quite his equal, then somebody of distinction within my own sphere. After some consideration I found the very thing: an ornate jacket of green Jacquard silk, inlaid with gems, which seemed to shimmer with the opulent iridescence of a mallard's neck. It was on display in Liberty, along with a magnificent turban in blue, at the fastening of which was a sumptuous brooch of red garnet. The only problem was that the ensemble cost six pounds, a sum I could no longer afford.

I went to Ike and explained that I was in need of a little more cash.

Ike raised an eyebrow. "More? But if you do not mind me pointing it out, Mr. Wallis, you are a little behind with the loans you already have."

"This is for an—investment."

"Ah?"

Ike seemed to be waiting for more information.

"I am hoping to make a proposal of marriage," I explained.

"*Ahh.* And is this a union which we might expect to have good prospects—financially, that is?"

I was tempted to tell him that it was none of his business; but of course, it was his business now. "Indeed. The lady in question—her father—has funds. Ample funds. But in the meantime, I shall inevitably have some further expenses."

He nodded thoughtfully.

"Shall we say—another forty pounds?" I suggested.

Once again I signed some papers, and once again, when he handed me the money, I handed him two pounds back. "Your interest."

He bowed. "And may I be the first to wish you, and your enterprise, every success. Though I should perhaps point out that the loan will be repayable in either case." He laughed. "Not that I am suggesting you will be unsuccessful in your suit, Mr. Wallis. I am sure you and the lady will be very happy."

PINKER LIVED a short distance from his warehouse, in a fine square of black-stoned Georgian houses. The door was opened by a liveried footman, with a maid standing at his side to take my coat and cane. I was impressed. If this was how Pinker lived, then this was how his son-in-law could expect to live, too. To have a footman as well as a maid would be most satisfactory. And the maid, I noticed, was quite pretty.

"They are in the drawing room, sir," the footman murmured, handing me a glass of Madeira.

I stepped through the door he indicated. The drawing room was lit by electric lamps, casting a flattering glow across the faces of the three Pinker daughters, who were all dressed up for the occasion. Even Ada did not look quite so plain as usual, while the Frog—uncomfortable in a schoolgirl's frock—was scowling, but at least looked for once like a girl. Pinker, seated in a high-backed chair, was talking to a thickset man in a sober black coat. Emily, next to them, looked ravishing in a gown of green velvet.

"Ah," Pinker said. "Robert, there you are. May I introduce Hector Crannach?"

"Wheel," the thickset man said in a heavy Scottish accent, looking me up and down as he crushed my hand, "they'd warned me that ye were a pote, Wallish, but they'd no' warned me that ye might forget your clothes."

"I beg your pardon?" I said, frowning.

"Ye've turned up to dinner in your dreshing gown, man."

Pinker chuckled. "Hector, you must curb your famous plain-speaking tonight. And Robert, you will have to forgive Crannach if he is not quite *au fait* with the latest Regent Street fashions. He has just recently returned from Brazil."

"Hector is father's general manager," Emily added, offering me her hand. "Hello, Robert. Are you in fact a Mughal or a Mikado tonight?"

"Tonight," I said, kissing her fingers, "I am a triumph of style over style. Although if you are referring to my jacket, I think you will find the design is Persian."

"Ay've traveled extensively in Pusha," Crannach announced. "And ay've never sheen a jacket lake *tha'*."

I was by now forming a strong dislike for this Scot.

"Though I did once shee a carrrpet quite like it, in Morocca," he added, turning to Ada and Frog. I laughed politely along with them.

"Father has been explaining your Guide, Robert," Emily interjected quickly. I saw now that one of the mahogany sample boxes had been placed upon the table. The sides were open, revealing the tiers of bottles. "Hector's most impressed."

"Oh, aye," Hector said dismissively. "I dinnae deny—"

I snorted.

He stopped. "Shorry?"

"Nothing."

"I dinnae deny—"

I caught Emily's eye and tittered. She pulled a furious face at me, but I could tell that she was trying hard not to laugh as well.

"Wha'?" Hector snapped, looking from one to the other of us.

"Nothing," I repeated, although in fact the wonderful clash of mangled vowels as Crannach managed to make the words "do not" and "deny" sound almost identical had been deeply amusing. "Please continue. What do you not deny?"

"Tha' such a shkeem may be of shome yuice," he mumbled furiously.

"But?" That was Pinker. "You have a reservation, Hector?"

"Out there in the feelt," Hector said portentously, "and in particular the truppics, I fear yon guide'll nae last six month."

"And why not?" I asked.

"Terramites," he said brusquely. "Truppical terramites as big as ma fist. They'll do fae the box. And the heat, man—the terrabull heat—that'll boil those fine pearfumes of yoursh away to nothin'."

"Well," I said, "I am not as intimate as you evidently are with termites. But the principles should remain sound whatever the conditions. And the written word—the pamphlet—should be able to withstand even the terra-bull heet o' the truppics, I imagine."

I felt a sharp pain in my ankle. I looked down. Emily's sharp-pointed shoe was just withdrawing back under her gown.

"In any case," I continued smoothly, "you are wrong to call it my Guide. It is as much the work of the elder Miss Pinker, who has been my willing assistant and indefatigable secretary these past few weeks." I took her hand and kissed it again. Hector glowered. It occurred to me that he was not terribly pleased to return from Brazil and find me nestled firmly in the bosom, as it were, of the Pinker daughters.

"Ha' ye ever been tae the truppics, Robber'?" he asked sourly.

It was then that I made the first of many mistakes that evening.

"Not yet. I fully intend to, though, to get some writing done," I replied casually. "It seems to be the last place where one can avoid being bothered by one's friends."

So I was, you see, undone by an epigram. Oh, the irony.

THE EVENING proceeded well enough. Hector bored us all with an account of his travels around Malaya, Ceylon and the Caribbean; or, as he put it, "M'lair, Shillon and the Carrybeena." I really cannot be bothered to record his conversation phonetically from now on: you will just have to use your imagination.

You will have to use your imagination, too, to picture Emily's succulent beauty at the dinner table that night. In the soft glow cast by Pinker's electric lights, the globes of her milky bosom, accentuated by the cut of her gown, were quite mesmerizing. I noticed Hector glancing surreptitiously at them as he spooned soup into his mouth: I was immediately determined not to do anything so vulgar.

It transpired that Hector's job was to go from one equatorial country to another, starting up plantations for Pinker and checking on his existing ones, making sure that each was run along exactly the same lines whether it was situated in Bangalore or

Buenos Aires. At one point the sour Scot launched into a long explanation of the difficulties of growing coffee in the mountains of Jamaica.

"Come now," I muttered. "It can hardly be that challenging."

He glared at me. "Wha'?"

"Listening to your account," I said, "I am struck by an obvious inconsistency. On the one hand you tell us that coffee is now the most cultivated crop in the world—more plentiful even than cotton or rubber. On the other, you wish us to believe that it is fiendishly difficult to grow. Surely it cannot be both."

"Robert," Emily murmured reprovingly.

"No, he makes a good point," Hector said equably. "But I'm afraid, Robert, you reveal your ignorance—your ignorance of conditions in the field. Aye, coffee's easy enough to grow. But that disnae mean it's easy to make a profit. It's four years from clearing the forest to picking your first crop—four years of planting, weeding, tending, irrigating, before you see so much as a penny. Four years in which ye have to pay your workers, unless of course you're—" He stopped.

"Unless what?" I asked.

"I will not have slavery, or anything approaching it, on a Pinker's plantation," Pinker said firmly. "That is never negotiable."

"Aye, of course," Crannach said, recovering himself. "Quite right, too. As I was saying, you have obligations for years before you take a crop. And by its very nature coffee is grown in mountainous regions. It has to be dried, transported—that's the biggest cost of all: not so much the last two thousand miles by sea, but the hundred miles getting it to the sea in the first place."

"Which is why, increasingly, we are establishing plantations in areas that already have good trading routes," Pinker added.

"And why we must ensure that—" Hector began, but Pinker interrupted him.

"Hector, we have talked business long enough. My daughters are getting bored."

"I'm not bored," the Frog said. "I like hearing about all the different countries. But I should most like to know if you met any cannibals."

Hector, it seemed, had not only met cannibals, but had been received into the very highest echelons of cannibal society. After ten minutes I stifled a yawn. "What adventures you have had, my dear Crannach. And you relate them so thrillingly. You shot them all, you say? How I do envy you. I myself have never shot anything more exciting than my cuffs."

The Frog giggled. Hector glared. Emily merely sighed.

THE FOOD was excellent. Pinker had served us a proper meal—none of these *à la Russe* sideboards for him: there were enough forks, knives, silverware and so on to supply a whole team of surgeons. By each plate there stood a handwritten menu. If I remember rightly, the bill of fare was as follows:

Huîtres natives
Petite bouchée norvégienne
Tortue claire
Crème Dubary
Homard sauté à la Julien
Aiguillete de sole. Sauce Germanique
Zéphir de poussin à la Brillat-Savarin
Selle d'agneau à la Grand-Veneur
Petits pois primeur à la Française
Pomme nouvelle persillade
Spongada à la Palermitaine
Jambon d'York braisé au champagne

Caille à la Crapaudine
Salade de saison
Asperges vertes en branche. Sauce mousseuse
Timbale Marie-Louise
Soufflé glacé Pompadour
Petits fours assortis

What with one thing and another, it was several hours before the ladies excused themselves. The footman placed a box of cigars on the table and withdrew. Crannach took his leave. I think he had probably had rather too much to drink; if so it was fortuitous, as I needed to speak to Pinker man to man.

My employer poured himself a tumbler of port. "Tell me, Robert," he said thoughtfully, "where do you see yourself, say, five years from now?"

I took a deep breath. "Well—married, I suppose."

"Married?" Pinker nodded. "That's good. Marriage is a wonderful thing. It makes a man more settled—gives him purpose."

"I'm glad you approve."

"Of course, a man with the expense of a household needs money."

"He certainly does," I agreed, pouring myself some more port.

"And tell me something else," he said humorously, clipping the end off a cigar. "I have noticed that, while the specific task for which I engaged your services is now essentially completed, you are still coming to my office almost every day."

"I cannot deny it," I answered with a faint smile.

"And there is, perhaps, a reason for this—a particular reason?"

"There is," I agreed.

"I thought as much." He puffed at a candle to get his cigar going, then chuckled. "I was the same at your age."

"Really?"

"Yes. I was—oh—burning with ambition. I had met Susannah—the girls' mother—and I only had one thought in my head."

This was an unexpected stroke of luck. If Pinker had once been in the shoes of an impoverished suitor himself, my job would be that much easier.

"So." He puffed contentedly. "Pinker's is, as you'll have observed, a family business. More than that: our business *is* our family."

"Of course."

"It's something we pride ourselves on. And you"—he pointed with the cigar—"fit into that family very well."

"Thank you," I said. This was going far better than I could have hoped.

"You are a little—well, shall we say when I first met you I had my doubts. I wondered . . . to be frank, I wondered if you were quite man enough for the job. But you are an amusing young fellow, Robert, and I have become increasingly fond of you."

I nodded modestly.

"Let me get to the point. I want you to become a permanent part of the Pinker family."

I could hardly believe what I was hearing. Far from me having to convince Pinker of my suitability as a husband, it almost seemed that he was trying to convince me of it!

He puffed on his cigar. "Perhaps you are wondering if you are up to it."

"No, I am confident—"

He chuckled. "Of course you are. And why not? You have the energy of youth." He leaned forward, underlining his words with the glowing tip of his cigar. "*Energy.* It's the critical ingredient. Never forget it."

"I won't."

"Every morning you have to wake up and say to yourself: I

am ready. I am equal to this challenge. I am man enough. Every morning!"

"Quite," I said, slightly taken aback by Pinker's unexpectedly physical attitude to matrimony.

"What you are considering is an adventure—a great challenge. There will be times when it is difficult."

I nodded.

"You will think, why am I here? Why am I doing this?"

I laughed along with him.

"My advice," he said, suddenly serious again, "is not to ask too much of yourself, Robert. No one expects you to be a saint, eh? Not in those conditions. Give yourself a few days' holiday every once in a while. Then come back to the task with your vigor renewed. You understand what I'm saying?"

"I think so," I said cautiously. This was certainly rather more man-to-man than I had been expecting. But Pinker might simply think that encouraging his son-in-law to visit prostitutes occasionally was the Rational, modern thing to do.

"Of course, your lack of experience will make it harder. You have none whatsoever, I suppose?"

"Well, I've, er, actually there has been the odd occasion—"

"Believe me, it will still be a shock. Oh yes—I've been there, and it's a shock. But we were all inexperienced once—and what I wouldn't give to be in your shoes, a young man again, setting out on this great journey! Now then. Let's talk money."

"Very well." I took a deep breath. This was the point at which it could all become unstuck. "I really don't have very much."

To my surprise, Pinker grinned. "I thought as much."

"You did?"

"Everything I've paid you so far has been spent, hasn't it?"

"I'm afraid it has, yes."

"Do you have debts?"

"A few."

Emboldened by his unexpectedly indulgent smile, I explained about Ike and his loans.

"So you've been borrowing more principal to pay the interest?" Pinker winced. "Oh, that's bad. That's very bad." He glanced at me shrewdly. For a moment I was struck by how much his own expression resembled the moneylender's. "But it's a detail, it can be taken care of when you have an income. Shall we say—three hundred a year? With another three hundred for your expenses? And a year's money in advance?"

It was not quite as much as I had hoped, but it seemed ignoble to haggle. "Very well."

"There'll be a bonus after four years if the enterprise is as fruitful as we both expect."

I stared at him. The coffee merchant was actually proposing to give me a bonus for getting Emily pregnant! Just for a moment I reflected what a shame it was that I was forced to marry into such a family. Then I remembered the three hundred a year, with three hundred expenses. And all for doing nothing more onerous than fornicating with his beautiful daughter on a regular basis. "I accept with pleasure."

"Excellent."

"I just hope Emily does," I joked.

Pinker frowned. "Emily?"

"I'd better go and ask her, hadn't I?"

"Ask her what?"

"If she'll marry me."

The frown deepened. "You will do no such thing."

"But—now you and I have agreed these terms—what is left to delay us?"

"Oh, my God." Pinker passed his hand over his brow. "You prize fool—you surely didn't imagine—what do you think I am offering you?"

"Well—your daughter's, er, hand—"

"I was offering you a career," he snapped. "You said you wanted to go abroad—said you were ambitious—that you needed employment in order to become marriageable."

"I was rather hoping that marriage would mean the end of needing to be employed," I said nervously.

"Of course you can't marry Emily. It's unthinkable." He stared at me, aghast. "What does *she* know of this?"

"Um . . ."

"If you have so much as touched her," he hissed, "I'll have you whipped from here to Threadneedle Street." He put his hand to his forehead. "Your debts—oh Lord—that bastard moneylender must be hoping—we must avoid another scandal." He picked up the tumbler of port, looked at it, then put it down on the table again. "I need to speak to Emily. I will see you in my office, sir, at nine tomorrow morning. Good-night."

Misunderstandings, cross-purposes, mixed messages. Yes, yes, I know—how droll that the first consequence of producing the Guide should be muddle on such an epic scale.

[TWENTY-ONE]

I WALKED AS FAR AS THE CITY. IT WAS RAINING: THE JACQUARD jacket and turban were soon drenched, the cloth heavy as a doublet and barely more waterproof. Eventually I found a cab that would take me as far as Marylebone. I trudged back to my rooms through the drizzle, wondering how the evening could have gone so disastrously wrong.

There was a public bar on the corner. From the outside it was all warm lights, gleaming brass, and glowing windows etched with the names of the brewer's products. I could not face the silence of my rooms. I stepped inside.

It was almost empty. I ordered brandy and sat down. There were a few girls in there, sheltering from the rain: one of them caught my eye and smiled. I suppose I must have smiled back, because she picked up her glass, said something to her companions, and came over.

"Do you tell fortunes?" she asked.

"No," I said brusquely.

"Are you a Hindoo, then?"

"No, I'm as English as you are."

"Oh. Why are you—?" She indicated my clothes.

"I went to a dinner." I pulled off my sodden turban and gulped the brandy.

"Would you like me to sit with you?"

I glanced at her. She was pleasant enough, but I did not find her remotely attractive. "Not for business, I'm afraid. Sorry. Not in the mood."

She shrugged. "For company, then?"

"How much do you charge for company?"

She sat down and pushed her glass across the table. "If you fill that up, you can watch me drink it for free. On a night like this, I'd rather be in here with a beer than out there looking for trade."

I waved to the barmaid and pointed at both our glasses. "What's your name?" I asked my companion.

"Mary. What's yours?"

She had a directness I rather liked. "Robert."

"Why're you here, Robert?"

"What do you mean?"

"No one wanders around on a night like this without a reason."

"Ah." I finished my first brandy and started on the second. "Tonight I asked the father of the girl I love for his permission to marry her."

"It didn't go well, then?"

She was no fool, this Mary.

"About as badly as it could have gone," I said sourly.

Mary placed a hand on my arm. "Buy us both another drink," she suggested, "and you can tell me all about it."

Needless to say, a little more than half an hour later I had her in a room upstairs, up against a washstand, my hands clasped around her solid, rippling thighs, while for her part she panted and gasped into the basin, and I watched my own reflection in the mirror.

• • •

As I NEARED my rooms I noticed two men lurking in a doorway. I ignored them, but as I pushed the key into the lock I heard footsteps. Something small, hard and very heavy, like a billiard ball in a sock, smashed against my neck. As I spun round I was felled by another colossal crack across the side of my head. My first thought, as I hit the ground, was that Pinker had sent thugs to warn me off, but even in my semi-concussed state I knew that was unlikely.

One of the men bent over me. In his hand was a blackjack.

"Don't even *fink* of leaving the country without payin' your debts," he hissed.

A big house like Pinker's, of course, was no more private than Trafalgar Square. Anyone could bribe a servant to send word when something important occurred. News of my falling-out with Pinker had probably spread by now to every interested party in London.

"Are you from Ike? Tell him I'll pay—" Abruptly, I realized I could not pay. "I'll borrow some more from him tomorrow."

"Don't be *fick,*" the ruffian spat. "Why would Ike want ter lend you any more?"

"So that I can pay his interest."

"I don't fuckin' *fink* so." He raised the blackjack. It was no longer than a pair of gloves, and he glanced over me casually, selecting where to use it. He tapped my stomach, and I was seized by an excruciating pain.

"Ike's calling in the debt," he said. "All of it. Yer've got a week ter pay."

THE FOLLOWING morning I had an equally painful interview with Pinker. No cudgels were involved, but only because there was no need for them.

To my surprise, when I was shown into his office Emily was there, too. She was standing in front of the desk at which her father was sitting, so after a moment's hesitation I went to stand beside her. She said nothing, although her eyes widened when she saw the bruise on my forehead.

"Emily and I have spent much of the night talking," Pinker said. He watched me with hooded eyes. "There are certain things I think you need to be made aware of." He addressed his daughter. "Emily, are you in love with Mr. Wallis?"

"No, Father."

The words were like a hammer, smashing all my hopes like glass beads.

"Have you ever suggested to him that you might be in love with him?"

"No, Father."

"Do you wish to be married to Mr. Wallis?"

"Perhaps, Father."

I looked at her, bewildered. This was making no sense.

"Explain, if you will, the circumstances in which you would consent to take him as your husband."

She hesitated. "I am not in love with Robert, but we are friends—good friends. I believe he has the makings of a kind, able man. I believe that he wants to do good in the world. I should like to be able to help him."

There was more—much more, all perfectly phrased: it came out of her beautiful lips like a speech. She had not found anyone else in her life to love and be loved by; she must marry someone: the question was, therefore, what marriage would most advance those causes and interests which were dearest to her heart, as well as to her father's? She and I liked each other; we were both believers in the Rational Marriage, we were concerned with the greatness of Humanity; we were not looking to retreat from the world into some lover's bower, "and all the rest, though fair and wise, commend to cold oblivion"; more than this, she knew that the thought of our eventual union would sustain me and lift me through the long, difficult years ahead, and thus she felt it was her duty to make this contribution to the cause of Civilization—a small contribution, to be sure, but all she had to give.

I listened, stunned, to all this noble nonsense. She appeared to be saying that she wanted to sacrifice her virginity on the altar of my Improvement, as if goodness and virtue were some sexually transmitted bacterium, like syphilis.

"Very well," Pinker said. "Emily, please leave Robert and me alone now. And if I may say so, your words do you, and this family, great credit." He pulled a handkerchief from his sleeve as she left and blew his nose.

"You have heard Emily," he said when he could speak again. "I am sure that if you loved her before, you love her even more now that you fully understand the fineness of her feelings. You are a very lucky young man." He paused. "I am prepared to give my permission for the two of you to be married after all."

"Thank you," I said, astonished.

"But first, you will have to be in a position to settle a thousand pounds on her."

It was like some fairy-tale riddle. "But—how can I possibly do that? I have no money whatsoever."

"Africa, of course. You must go and make your fortune."

He laid it all before me, like a general briefing a subaltern whom he is sending on a mission of certain peril. The plan had clearly been formulating in his mind for some time; my wanting to marry his daughter was simply an obstacle which had now been turned to advantage.

His plantations in Ceylon had failed, and would shortly have to be replanted with tea. His plantations in India were becoming too expensive—the sepoys had turned rebellious; there was even talk of independence. No, Africa was the coming place. In the

Protectorate, in Uganda, in countries as yet unnamed, men of vision and energy were establishing vast coffee gardens which one day would rival those of Sumatra and Brazil. It was a rush, of course, to get the best places—part of the Great Scramble, as the newspapers were calling it. But he, Pinker, had stolen a march. Thanks to our Guide, and Burton's inside knowledge, he had been able to establish that the very best coffee-growing conditions were in that part of Abyssinia known as Kaffa, southwest of Harar. It was land that no one else wanted—for the moment. It was not even owned by anyone: the Italians had failed to hold on to it. So Pinker had bought it from them.

"Bought it? How much?"

"Fifty thousand acres."

I stared at him. I could not conceive of an area of land so vast.

He waved his hand airily. "Of course, you don't have to plant it all. I am simply protecting us from competition in the future."

"It is the size of London," I said.

"Exactly." He jumped up, rubbing his hands. "And you are its ruler—its regent, I should say. You will go down in history, Robert: you will be the man who brought civilization to Kaffa."

For there was more, of course. With Pinker there was always more. I was not being sent to Africa merely to grow coffee beans. I was on a mission: "A Trade Mission, if you like; but the most precious seeds you plant will be those which are invisible. When the natives see what you achieve with your modern methods of cultivation—when they see how you behave; how you govern them properly, as you govern yourself, through the principles of free trade and fair dealing; when they see the wonders which prosperity can bestow—then, Robert, it is my belief that they will turn to God, as surely as a growing plant turns to face the sun. There are those who say that we must change the savage mind before we can change his beliefs. I say there is a step that must come before both, which is to change the pitiful circumstances in which he finds himself. Give a heathen charity and he remains a heathen, and the charity is soon gone; but only give him a contract of employment and you have pointed him on the road toward eternal life—"

"How do I get there?" I asked, my mind now on roads.

"By camel, I believe. There is a trade route from the coast."

"And what shall I do while I am waiting for the coffee to grow? It takes four or five years to get a crop, I understand." *Four years,* I thought as I said it. *My God—I am being sent away for four years.*

"You will trade as well, as Pinker's buying agent in that part of Africa. After all, no one knows the Guide better than you. I am arranging for you to operate under the auspices of a local merchant—you may have seen his mark on some of our moccas." Pinker pulled a piece of paper from the shelves behind him and laid it on the table. At the top was the same Arabic sign I had seen on the sacks of Harar coffee:

ي

"His name is Ibrahim Bey," Pinker continued. "A great man—his family have been merchants for generations. And Hector will accompany you as far as your destination, to assist you in picking out the right spot for the farm, employing a headman and so on, before he goes on to India. If you are a success, as I am sure you will be, then on your return you will have both my daughter's hand and my blessing." He frowned. "Needless to say, until that time, nothing is official. It is a private understanding between us—a probation, as it were; a chance to show what you are made of." Then his mood abruptly lightened again. "All this expertise at your disposal, Robert. And a fortune to be made, a fair lady to be won, history to be written. How I envy you."

Part II
The Road of Skulls

The character of the nose depends primarily on the degree of roast given the green beans.

—LINGLE, The Coffee Cupper's Handbook

[TWENTY-TWO]

SS Battula
8th June 1897

My darling Emily,

I write this to you from the good ship Battula, *presently making steady progress along the northern shore of Egypt. Five days ago we put in to Genoa to take on stores—our stay was only a brief one, but what a pleasure it was to see Italy at last, and to stand on dry land after so long at sea! My plan to go overland, see the Venice of which Ruskin has written so beautifully, and then rejoin Hector at Suez has, as you predicted, proved impossible—it seems we are in a race against the coming of the rainy season, and Hector is impatient to get the plantation up and running this year rather than next. (My observation that I have packed my umbrella, and so shouldn't be bothered by a bit of rain, prompted another of those heavy sighs of his. Apparently I have a lot to learn, or even to* larrun*—his accent, I am sorry to report, becomes no more comprehensible on close acquaintance.)*

We dine each night at the Captain's table, where we are sixteen, including the Captain and First Officer. Hector is very thick with the nautical fraternity, and spends many hours discussing nor'westers, spinnakers, bilges and other manly concerns with the gravest of faces. Then we have a brace of missionaries, destined for the Sudan; four fellows who are going out to set up an ivory-collecting concern in Mombasa; and no less than six ladies who are off to India, visiting relatives.

As the only one amongst us with any experience of the regions for which we are destined, Hector is in great demand as an authority, and settles many an argument with a brief but definitive utterance on subjects as diverse as the correct headgear for a visit to a mosque, or whether the white man need carry a pistol in the jungle. Dearest Emily, I have not forgotten the promise you extracted from me before I left, but sometimes one is sorely tempted to mock him just a little. I think you would like the missionaries, though—they are completely in agreement with your father's idea that we must, as it were, convert the savages to Commerce and Christianity at one and the same time. One of them asked me if I intended to build a church on my plantation! I must admit, it was not a question that had occurred to me before, but I suppose I probably shall, in good time. And perhaps a theater, too, for culture.

In good time . . . as I write those words I realize how very long I shall be away. Being apart from you for almost five years is going to be so very hard. Of course, I do not complain—you are completely right that it is our duty to remain cheerful—and it will all be worth it to marry you at the end. It is wonderful to be able to think of you as my partner in this great project of saving Africa, and as you say, being physically together in the same place is not as important in the long term as this togetherness of mind and purpose.

Anyway, I had better go now as it is time to dress for dinner. I have not had much occasion to wear my alpaca suit—we are not really in the tropics yet, although the days are quite warm—and the Captain is a bit of a stickler for protocol. I came down on the first evening in my green waistcoat and was taken aside for a "word of advice" about "the need to keep up appearances in foreign climates." I tried to explain that a white-

tie dinner suit is considered a little old-fashioned now in polite circles, but no dice.

With much love from your future husband,

Robert

SS Battula

The North Pole

12th June 1897

Dear Frog,

Well, here I am at the North Pole. Admittedly, it is a funny sort of Pole, being surrounded by warm blue sea on three sides, with the coast of Egypt just visible to the south, and the occasional palm tree poking up on the skyline, but Hector has got me practicing with my sextant and theodolite, learning how to plot our position; and since the North Pole is where the sextant informs me we are, at the North Pole we must be. I have surprised my travel companions by attempting to converse with them in Polish—Northern Polish, that is—so far without much success.

Why, you may ask, is it necessary to know precisely where one is? A good question, you perspicacious Frog, and one which I put to Hector myself. It seems that we are soon going to be living in the Bush, and that this Bush, moreover, is not a nice English laburnum, or a well-pruned magnolia, or even a prickly bramble, but an altogether larger and more fearsome species of Bush, in which it is possible to get oneself quite lost. And when we come to plant our Coffee, Hector informs me, it is extremely important to plant it in absolutely straight Lines, so that everyone can see how neat and well-regulated a White Man's Plantation is, and for this too we will need to know how to Survey. I had thought myself quite able to Survey already—I am surveying a large whisky-and-soda at this very moment—but apparently I am a Flippant Egypt, or possibly a Flipping Eejit, I forget which.

Dearest Frog, will you do a favor for me? Look up "Hectoring" in your dictionary, and tell your sister what it says. Don't tell her I put you up to it, though.

Regards,

Robert

Hotel Pension Collos
Alexandria
20th June 1897

My dear Hunt,

Landed at last! The voyage was tedious beyond belief, made worse of course by the fact that it was entirely without female company—or rather, without female company of the necessary kind, for there was in fact a large consignment of twittering women on board, who were clearly being sent to India for the sole purpose of finding a husband. One of them even tried to flirt with Hector, which shows you how desperate she must have been. He told me brusquely later that he'd once considered marriage, but had decided it was "incompatible with a life of adventure and travel." I forbore from pointing out that if it wasn't for marriage, I would be tucked up in the Café Royal as we speak.

Mindful that my prospects in that line may soon be somewhat limited, once we were ashore I gave Hector the slip and made for the city's cat-houses. It was an interesting experience—the thing here is dancing: the prettiest girl in the place comes and performs in front of you while you sit back and smoke a narghile, *which is a pipe of tobacco filtered through a kind of bubbling apple-scented liquid. The girl who danced for me was wearing a snood of gold piastres—a helmet made of metal discs fastened together with chain, which glittered and clinked as she writhed. She was clothed when she started, but soon rolled her girdle down to her hips, where she knotted it very low. The "dance" simply consisted of raising the edge of each hand alternately to her forehead, while the pelvis quivered and shook in imitation of the sexual act. It was strangely effective, and by the time she was done I had a cockstand like an iron bar. A choice of women then paraded before me in a line. They were mostly on the plump side—apparently the dancing girl is chosen for her looks and dancing abilities, while the* poules de luxe *are chosen for their superior abilities in the bedroom. I insisted on having the dancer, which caused much merriment—I was, I suppose, behaving in their eyes like a typical greenhorn. And so we went upstairs, to a room draped with woven silks, with a window open to the night breeze and the shouts of the people in the street just below us. She had to shoo a litter of kittens off the bed before we got down to it, then she crouched over a silver basin to wash. My first dark-skinned girl. Completely shaven, incidentally. She was pleasantly flexible, I thought, in comparison to London girls, though a little dry.*

If you want to write to me, the best place is via Aden. I'll be there in a fortnight—we have to wait here for a Suez boat, a delay which is bothering my traveling companion greatly, and me somewhat less so.

Best,
Wallis

✱

Hotel Pension Collos
Alexandria
27th June 1897

Dear Frog,

Greetings—I write to you these quickly scribbled lines
Composed in what are sometimes called "Alexandrines."

Actually I don't do anything of the sort—an Alexandrine is much too difficult and tedious for a letter. And I don't have the energy to think of rhymes today: it is far too hot.

There was an old man of Peru
Whose poems all stopped at line two.

Instead, I shall tell you about Alexandria. We landed here very early on Friday morning, just as the muezzin were calling the faithful to prayer. All the passengers were up at first light to see the city. First the inky blue-black of the sea, with just a few twinkling lights on the horizon. The sky lightening . . . the salmon-colored mist of an African dawn . . . an impression of towers and minarets; palaces with onion-shaped windows . . . and then, instantly, the sky brilliantly and fierily alight as the sun hoisted itself like a huge sail over our heads, while before us the great white city of the East slipped serenely past our bow. As we edged into harbor a host of tiny black children dived for the sixpences we tossed into the water. The gangplank was quickly surrounded by dozens of rubbery-lipped camels, gargling and spitting and being beaten about the head by yelling Arab gentlemen in long white shirts. Most of the women go about veiled, but that is as far as their modesty extends: it is considered no more shocking here to show your breasts than it would be for us to go bare-headed.

Today I saw a man who had stuck iron spikes through his chest; on the end of each spike he had placed an orange, though whether this was to prevent anyone else from accidentally piercing themselves, or because it was a convenient place to keep his lunch, I could not say.

With best regards,
Your future brother-in-law,
Robert

❧

Hotel Pension Collos
Alexandria
28th June 1897

Dear Mr. Pinker,

I am writing this preliminary report from Alexandria, where we are awaiting the next stage of our transport. I have busied myself cupping various coffees, and also testing the efficacy of the Guide. The local beans are predominantly arabica, with a small amount of African longberry available in the better markets. I bought all I could find of the latter, as its quality is very fine. Most of the coffee for sale here is good, although every merchant seems to keep back a quantity of inferior stuff for the sole purpose of fleecing European visitors—an inquiry for the "finest lot you have" will instigate a lengthy pantomime, in which the shop or stall is closed up with many looks to left and right, as if fearful that a competitor will spot what is going on; then a storeroom is unlocked, a sack is dragged out from the back and opened with great ceremony. A handful of beans is placed on a silver dish and passed to you for your approval—but not before the merchant has smelled them himself, his eyes closed in ecstasy, informing you in bad French that this particular lot is more precious to him than his own children. He then offers you the chance to taste them, and a brew is prepared, usually by an assistant. No instructions are given, but the factotum knows exactly what to do: the beans in front of you may resemble a handful of rancid rat's droppings—and smell as if they had lately been swept off the merchant's floor—but the sample cup that is presented a few minutes later will taste as if it contains the very finest coffee that Yemen can supply, as indeed it probably does. All the while the merchant will be making conversation, inquiring after your journey, your family, where you have embarked from and so on, and generally treating you like a long-lost friend. When confronted with the accusation that beans and brew are entirely dissimilar, he will appear mightily offended, and claim that you have insulted him. One merchant even went so far as to "discover" that his assistant had been swapping the sacks around, whereupon he cudgeled him soundly about the head! Quite why they persist in this performance is a mystery, since they have a perfectly good supply of high-quality moccas available. It is almost as if attempting to short-change the White Man has become a ritual.

The Guide has already proved itself useful. One is overwhelmed with such a plethora of unfamiliar scents, tastes and other sensations here that it is quite easy to forget what, say, a simple slice of fresh apple tastes like. Yesterday I found in the market a grand lot of mocca, which I cupped in my hotel. Scents of blueberry, cedar, and peat smoke—I ordered three hundredweight. I have also been on the lookout for some of that remarkable coffee you and I tasted back in Limehouse, though as yet my nose has not led me to any.

With best wishes,
Your future son-in-law,
Robert Wallis

❧

SS Rutalin
30th June 1897

My dearest, dearest Emily,

Your letter reached me just before we left Alexandria. Your exhortations are unnecessary, I assure you: I am being perfectly charming to Hector. Only last night at dinner I amused him by reciting nursery rhymes in a Scottish accent. And the day before we left Alexandria, I accompanied him on a shooting expedition into the desert—we shot cormorants and water-magpies, and lunched on dates we bought from a Bedouin. As we set off again on our camels an Arab trotted past us on a donkey, his feet nearly brushing the ground, calling out a greeting in his own language. Hector, I am sorry to say, was so affronted at being overtaken that he tried to make his camel go faster, fell off, and had to be hoisted back up by our porters. But just to show you how good I am being—I did not laugh once, even though the people at our table in the hotel thought it must have been very amusing when I described it to them, later.

And yes, I am sorry about that letter to the Frog. I promise not to mention ladies' bare chests to her again. I suppose it was a bit indelicate, but really, if you see the lack of concern with which people display themselves here, you would understand why I did not think anything of it at the time.

Anyhow, we are now back on board ship, passing through Suez. One of our new fellow passengers is a journalist called Kingston, who has written a fine piece describing us as "the lantern bearers of civilization, bringing their precious candles of light into the great darkness of Africa." As he puts it, "some of the lights may flicker, and some will go out; but others will catch and become great beacons, lightening the darkness which currently envelops whole populations of savages." I believe he has sent it to the Telegraph.

Talking of darkness, I have been watching some splendid dawns. Every morning the sky is streaked with the colors of an English hedgerow—primrose pink and daffodil yellow: with the first glimpse of the sun all color is instantly burnt out; everything turns white, and soon the only colors to be seen are the dazzling green of the water and the dazzling silver-blue of the sky. The glare is so bright that one's eyes hurt. Hector has taken to wearing an eyeshade, which makes him look a bit like a sickly parrot.

I only wish that you were here, but the thought of you is more than enough. My love for you will sustain me during the long years ahead.

Your ever-loving,

Robert

❧

Grand Hôtel de l'Univers
Prince of Wales Drive
Aden
2nd July 1897

Dear Mr. Pinker,

I have made contact with the coffee wholesalers here in Aden, as you suggested. The Bienenfeld brothers had some extremely good lots: the one that impressed most I rated fr-1 bou-4 no-4: *a light mocca, small-beaned, mahogany brown after roasting, with notes of blueberry and lime and a very low acidity. Overall, I gave it a five. I purchased all they had, and ordered it shipped as soon as possible.*

I am very keen to meet Ibrahim Bey: he has a reputation amongst the merchants here as being quite a character, although there are also rumors that his business is in some unspecified trouble. At present he is on a trading trip in the Interior: we may catch up with him when we cross to Zeilah, on the African side.

With best wishes,

Robert Wallis

Grand Hôtel de l'Univers
Prince of Wales Drive
Aden
2nd July 1897

Dear Hunt,

You will see from this notepaper that I have arrived at the Grand Hôtel de l'Univers, which probably conjures up a vision of a pleasant palace set amidst rolling lawns. In which case, get out your atlas. Aden is that small pimple on the right buttock of Arabia, and the Grand Hôtel is nothing but a cockroach-infested shack. Honestly, this place is hell—an exposed expanse of volcanic rock, lying at sea level, sheltered from every breeze but utterly exposed to the pitiless glare of the sun. This is not even the hottest part of the year, and the mercury still reaches 130 degrees every day. There isn't a blade of grass, or even a palm tree, in the whole damned place.

The truth is that the British are only here because it's the mid-point between Africa, India, Australia and home—a sort of military-cum-mercantile staging camp for British Empire Incorporated. No one actually lives here, though some people will tell you they have been "stationed" here for a few years. Most are passing through—and yours truly is no exception. The quicker I can get out of this oven, the happier I'll be. Even the locals call the straits here "Bab al Mandeb"—the Gate of Tears.

The fact is, my friend, I am at a bit of a low ebb. On the one hand, I suppose all this travel & experience will somehow be useful for my writing one day. On the other hand, I still cannot quite believe that I have blundered into the kind of bourgeois existence that I always absolutely swore I would avoid at all costs. I now seem to have all the responsibilities and disadvantages of marriage and employment, without even benefiting from the domestic comforts and financial rewards which should accompany them! How I am ever to become an artist while stuck in a fetid, stinking jungle I have no idea. It is enough to make one want to weep. If there were only somewhere to run away to, I think I should probably give it all up. But as my future father-in-law (a.k.a the jailer-in-chief) would probably say, from this predicament one cannot be "sent down." . . .

Yours in adversity,
Robert

SS Carlotta
Zeilah Creek
Africa!
7th July 1897

Dear Morgan,

Thank you for your letter, which reached me in Aden. We have now left that hell-hole, thank God, in a tiny steamer barely bigger than a biscuit tin. It was quite a squeeze to get our luggage on board—we have accumulated enough for over thirty porters, including:

- *fishhooks, beads, snuff, for dish-dash*
- *nails, for building me a bungalow*
- *a Remington rifle, for shooting me my lunch*
- *six bottles of beer, for washing said lunch down with—which by my reckoning works out at one-and-a-quarter bottles per year*

- *a bottle of Baillie Scotch Whisky, for emergencies*
- *a Gasogene Rechargeable Sodawater Maker, ditto*
- *a wooden lavatory seat*
- *white tie and tails, for entertaining foreign dignitaries*
- *Kuma, our cook. Kuma is a fine fellow, and comes with a letter of recommendation from one Captain Thompson of Bengal, who says, "Kuma is not the bravest of boys, and cannot be relied upon to hold your second gun should the animal you are engaged in stalking be simultaneously engaged in charging you, but he cannot be faulted in his ability to get hot food ready after a day's march. Occasionally I believed him to be stealing from me, which he always denied. Twenty-five strokes from an ox-whip seemed to solve the problem. Please do not pay him more than one dollar a month, and leave him in Aden when you have finished with him, as I hope to return for another safari in a year or so's time." This "boy," incidentally, is around forty years old. Kuma is remarkably unenthusiastic about returning to the Interior, which is, he says gloomily, "full of savages, sah."*
- *my library. This consists of Pater's* Renaissance; *a volume entitled* Coffee: Its Cultivation and Profit, *which Hector assures me contains everything there is to know about that fine crop; an actor's stage script of* The Importance of Being Earnest; *six blank pocket-books; the* Yellow Book *for April 1897, and Francis Galton's* Hints to Travelers. *From the last I learn that "a young man of good constitution, who is bound on an enterprise sanctioned by experienced travelers, does not run very great risks. Savages rarely murder new-comers; they fear their guns, and have a superstitious awe of the white man's power: they require time to discover that he is not very different to themselves, and easily to be made away with." What a good thing it is that I am only to be here five years. I also have a book, issued by the Society for the Propagation of the Christian Gospel, entitled* Phrases in

Common Use in East Africa: *these include "Six drunken Europeans have killed the cook," "You have no more brains than a goat," and "Why has this body still not been buried?"*

- *a crate containing hoes, spades, axes, measuring lines, and other mysterious farming tools.*
- *a sturdy cash chest, with padlock, containing eight hundred silver dollars. These are Austro-Hungarian dollars bearing an image of the late Queen Marie-Thérèse, which for some unknown reason have become the universal currency hereabouts, possibly because each one is about the size of a small dinner plate. Amongst the British, rupees are also in use, although the natives sometimes grumble about taking them, since they have no intrinsic value anywhere except India.*
- *two alpaca bush-suits from Simpson's, and a great quantity of trousers, both long and short, made out of flannel, which is considered to be the most hygienic material for hot climates. And my red velvet smoking jacket, of course.*
- *a medicine chest. This has been stocked as per Galton's instructions, and contains many items which are mysterious to me, viz: (1) emetic, for poison, (2) Warburg drops, for fever, (3) Dover's Sudorific Powder, for infections, (4) Chlorodyne, for wounds, (5) "one large roll of diachylon"—I have absolutely no idea what this is for, and Galton does not elucidate, (6) lunar-caustic, in a holder, "to touch old sores with, and for snake-bites," (7) needles, to sew up gashes, (8) waxed thread, ditto, (9) Moxon's mild effervescing aperient, and (10) a large bottle of Caldwell's Preparation of Laudanum (full strength), for when other remedies (and flannel trousers) prove ineffective.*
- *Twelve very fine small Wedgwood coffee cups, white, of lustrous bone china, a present—surely ironic?—from my future father-in-law.*
- *Hector—who, it has to be said, becomes visibly more cheerful the*

> *nearer he gets to the Equator. He has been striding about manfully organizing everything, shouting at the natives and making lists. It makes me tired just to look at him.*

What on earth am I doing here? *Whatever happened to beauty, and truth, and the contemplation of wonderful things? Sometimes I think I am going to wake up and find it was all some terrible dream.*

The only consolation are the sunsets, the most glorious I have ever seen. The moon rises first, through a bank of mist that covers the mangroves like a layer of tracing paper: a blood-orange orb that seems to change shape as it rises, elongating as it separates from its reflection in the oil-black river. On the other side, the sun sinks down into the mist, touches the water and bursts. Flushes of gold, amethyst, carmine and violet color the sky, and then those, too, fade into the darkness, leaving only the dazzling frost of the moonlight and the utter blackness of the swamp . . . Oh, and a million small flying creatures that instantly come and bite your skin with all the ferocity of piranhas.

Regards,
Robert

✻

?
??
???
????

Dear Frog,

You will notice this letter bears no return address: that is because we are now Nowhere. Nowhere is a topsy-turvy sort of place: trees grow in the water, as casually as if they were on dry land: the fish, meanwhile, have forgotten that they are meant to be sub-aquatic, and skip about on top of the mudflats, possibly to escape the crocodiles, who spend more time in the water than the fish do.

Our little boat measures no more than twenty feet from brass bow to mahogany stern. We eat outside, under a kind of awning, with the Captain and his Mate, a Russian. Progress is slow: we are chugging against the current, a wide, mocca-brown, silt-filled creek that appears not to move at all but which occasionally shoots a sunken log past us at great speed toward the sea. Occasionally we pass a village, and then the natives come out onto the bank and stare. You can tell Ada that she is not doing at all the right thing pinning her hair back, if she wants to make herself marriageable. Here the accepted way to do it is to knock a couple of your front teeth out, smear your scalp with ochre paint, and carve a pattern of zigzags into your forehead with a hot knife. Then you're considered quite a beauty, and asked out to all the dances. These take place most evenings, to the accompaniment of a jolly rump-a-tump tune not a million miles from Wagner. The children all have big tummies, as if they had been blown up with a pump.

As for me, I am looking quite the Arab these days—before leaving Aden I had my hair cut by a local barber. Now I am completely shorn except for a single lock at the occiput, by which Mohammed lifts you up on Judgment Day. Hector sighs when he looks at me and calls me a "fullish pup." Which, no doubt, I am.

Yours fullishly,

Abu Wally (as Kuma calls me! It is Arab, I think, for "Master Wallis")

Zeilah

July

Dearest Emily,

I cannot tell you how much I am missing you. Five years is such a very long time—when I think back to the brief period we spent together, those innocent days cupping coffees in your father's office, they already feel like another lifetime. Will you still remember me in half a decade? Will we still be able to laugh with each other? I am sorry to sound despondent—it is just that being out here, everything back in London feels like a dream; a very dim, distant dream. Sometimes I even wonder if I am going to come back at all. . . . I know you told me to think optimistically, but really it is almost impossible not to wallow sometimes.

These gloomy thoughts were, I suppose, partly prompted by an accident that occurred when we landed here. There is only one jetty in the harbor, a very rickety one at that, and as we unloaded our luggage one of the crates somehow got dropped into the water. It was the one containing my books, my best clothes, and the Wedgwood cups your father gave me. The books have dried, although some of the pages have stuck together. The clothes, though, are somewhat the worse for their experience: anything made of velvet now exudes a distinct smell of mold. Remarkably, only six of the cups were broken—I am trying to think of that as a good sign.

Today I opened the sample bottles in the Guide and smelled some of the scents that most remind me of home—apples, and gingerbread, and tea roses, and hazelnuts . . . And then I tried to mix up a scent that reminded me of you—that "Jicky" you sometimes wore: a mixture of lavender, rosemary and bergamot. It made me feel—well, quite emotional, I suppose. I cried like a child for a few minutes.

Dearest Emily, please don't mind me missing you. I will buck up tomorrow, I expect.

Your loving,

Robert

[TWENTY-THREE]

"Soft"—affecting the senses in a gentle and pleasant way.

—ROSE PANGBORN, Principles of Sensory Evaluation of Food

EMILY SITS AT THE OFFICE TABLE, COPYING FIGURES FROM A great pile of receipts into a ledger. She can see, from the evidence in front of her, that the Guide has already proved its worth. Pinker's is buying more high-quality coffees than ever before—principally Maracaibos and moccas. Many coffees from regions previously thought to be the finest have turned out to have quite low scores: Jamaican Blue Mountain is actually thin and watery, whilst the Monsooned Malabar so prized by many connoisseurs is surprisingly rank. But other regions have thrown up some gems: notably Antigua and Guatemala, with notes of smoke, spice, flowers and chocolate, and a lively brightness on the tongue. . . .

She frowns. Along with the fine coffees that Pinker's has been buying in such quantity, there also seems to be a large amount of inferior stuff, particularly the very cheapest coffee of all—African Liberica, dense, thick and flavorless, with a tarry mouthfeel and no acidity to speak of. It can be picked up for almost nothing: indeed, there is a glut of it on the market at the moment: no reputable merchant would be stockpiling it, unless—

Her father is showing a visitor round the warehouse, a well-dressed man with quick eyes and a lively smile.

"Ah, Emily, there you are. Brewer, may I introduce my daughter?"

The man steps forward and shakes her hand. "I am very pleased to make your acquaintance, Miss Pinker. I believe we have a friend in common—Millicent Fawcett?"

Emily is surprised, even impressed. "I do not know Mrs. Fawcett very well. But I am a member of her Society, and a great admirer of hers."

"Mr. Brewer is the Member of Parliament for Ealing," Pinker explains. "He has a particular interest, as I do, in Free Trade."

She looks at the visitor with even greater interest. "You're a Liberal?"

"Indeed. And although we currently find ourselves out of government, I have no doubt that with the aid of forward-thinking men like your father"—Pinker inclines his head, acknowledging the younger man's words—"we will soon command a popular mandate again. Our watchword will be Freedom—freedom of thought, freedom to spend your wages as you wish, freedom to do business without government interference."

"Change and Improvement," Pinker agrees. "It is the only way."

"And is your party also in favor of freedom for women?" Emily asks.

Brewer nods. "As you know, there has been a suffrage bill every year for the past five years, and every year it has been talked out by the Tories. That is the kind of abuse of procedure we are determined to stamp out."

"But first things first, eh, Arthur?" Pinker says. "Free Trade, then social issues."

Brewer turns his kindly eyes to Emily. For a moment a gentle glint of amusement seems to pass between them—an acknowledgment, perhaps, that this is the way of the world; that ideals must be achieved step by careful step. "First we need to be in government," he agrees, but he is speaking more to her now than her father. "And for that we need the support of Business. So yes, Free Trade first. It is the nature of the disenfranchised that they cannot help us win the power which we will exercise on their behalf."

They have stopped by the door to the street. Brewer's tour is clearly at an end, and her father impatient to get on, but both she and the MP are lingering.

"Perhaps we might discuss this again," he says.

"I should like that," she agrees. "Very much." She looks at her father.

"What? Oh, yes—you must come to dinner, Arthur. In any case, we have a great deal to talk about."

"SO YOU ARE going to support the Liberals financially?" she asks her father, when the MP has left.

"I am. It seems to be the only way to get any influence. And they need funds, if they are to oust the Tories." He shoots her a glance. "Do you approve?"

"I think it's an excellent idea. But why do we need influence?"

He makes a sour face. "It is as we suspected—Howell has joined his plantations to the syndicate. They control the major part of the world's coffee, now. Even with the Guide, it makes it impossible to compete."

"And your Mr. Brewer can help?"

"A Liberal government will no more want the market run by a few rich men and foreign governments than we do."

"How will they stop it?"

"By regulation, if necessary. But in the short term . . ." He looks at his daughter intently, aware that she will understand the importance of what he is about to say. "Mr. Brewer believes they can help us to smash the cartels."

"Really?"

"It is just the Free Trade cause they have been looking for. They are already working their way onto the key committees, establishing diplomatic ties with Brazil's neighbors."

She sighs. "It seems a very long way from making a good cup of coffee."

"Yes. But it is the way of all business, I suspect, to move from small issues to larger ones."

She remembers now what she came to ask him. "Does this have anything to do with the cheap Liberica we have been purchasing?"

"Ah." He nods. "In a manner of speaking, yes. You'd better come into the office."

HALF AN HOUR later they are still sitting at the big table where she used to work with Robert. The Guide is open on the table, and in front of them half a dozen used cups show where they have been tasting various samples.

"So you see," Pinker is saying, "the Guide has turned out to have a double function. It is the work Robert did for me on blending, in those last weeks." He glances at his daughter: Robert is still a subject on which she is reticent. He points to a cup. "Take a cheap, coarse coffee like this; categorize its deficits, then add just enough of those coffees which you see, from the Guide, will compensate for them." He gestures to three or four other cups. "And then you have a coffee which has no discernible faults."

"But a coffee which also has no particular virtues, surely," she points out.

"Yes—but that can itself be a virtue. You know, Emily, people don't always agree on what flavors they actually like in a coffee. To you and I, perhaps, it will be an African, rich and bright. But to others, the stronger, thicker taste of a South American will be preferable. Robert, I know, likes the fine moccas and Yemenis, but many find those floral attributes too scented for their tastes. By blending a coffee according to the principles of the Guide, we can eradicate all those attributes which might otherwise stop people from buying Castle. We end up with a coffee which no one dislikes. A coffee whose taste is consistent, irrespective of what coffees go into it. And all for a fraction of the cost."

"Robert would be somewhat unhappy to hear you say that, I imagine."

"Robert is not a businessman." He looks at her carefully. "There was a reason why I sent him away, you know, and it was not only to do with money."

"Yes," she says. "I know."

She does not meet her father's eye. Two spots of pink appear in her cheeks.

He says quietly, "Perhaps, once distance has cooled your affection, you will decide that he is not the man for you after all. If that happens . . . You have no obligation to him."

"I would not go back on our understanding, Father."

"In matters of the heart, as in business, we must do what is best. Not necessarily what we had planned. An understanding is simply that: one person's perception of the truth."

She does not reply. Instead she reaches for the Guide, her finger moving along the corked tops of the phials, choosing one. She takes it out, opens it, lets the fragrance fill her nostrils.

"Of course," she says. "You are quite right, Father, to counsel me to be cautious. And I promise I will make no hasty decision."

[TWENTY-FOUR]

Zeilah
31st July

Dear Hunt,

We have been waiting in this godforsaken shit-hole for three weeks now. Only now do I realize what a haven Aden was—it might have been a dump, but it was an orderly, well-stocked, well-run sort of dump, with proper buildings and regular gaps between them that could almost be described as streets. Here there are just huts, mud, and choking swirls of dry red dust. This dust—peppery, pungent, leathery, slightly rancid—is the smell of Africa, it seems: I cannot get it out of my nostrils.

The people here are Somalis, but they are governed by another tribe called Danakils, who control the trade routes. Danakils carry spears or swords and wear necklaces of strange, shrunken, globular things that look like dried dates but are actually their enemies' testicles. Yes, that's correct: the penalty for any minor infringement here—say, failure to pay a bill on time—is to have your bollocks lopped off with a sword. Adulterers get off lightly by comparison, being simply stoned to death. The whole place is under the aegis of a savage called Abou Bekr and his eleven sons. I do not use the word "savage" here in its ethnic sense: the man has personally disemboweled over a hundred people. His cruelty is legendary. Needless to say, we are not going anywhere until we have his permission.

Every few days we are shown into his courtyard—sic: a patch of red earth, surrounded by palisades, which combines the functions of a royal court and a farmyard. An elderly man with a wispy beard, he reclines under an awning on a couch of animal skins. Even from a distance, they smell of goat. He wears a filthy white robe and an enormous onion-shaped turban. Behind him stand a Somali or two, in slightly cleaner robes, who whisk flies away from his head with an implement not unlike something you might use at home to sweep out the fire. In his left hand is a necklace of prayer beads, which constantly click under his fingers: with his right he works away at a toothpick. His eyes are dead and weary, the eyes of a tyrant. Periodically during your conversation he will spit, silently and without warning, without much bothering where he is aiming. If you are currently in favor, coffee is brought—excellent coffee, in tiny cups, poured by a kavedjabouchi *who stands ready at all times, a flagon with a tiny spout nestled under his arm. To any question concerning the caravan, Abou Bekr answers* "Insh' Allah"*—if it please God. What he actually means, of course, is "If it please me." And what will please him? We do not know. We are waiting for something—some sign, some request. When we ask Abou Bekr what it will take to allow us to travel, he frowns: when we ask his courtiers, they shrug and repeat the same formula, "Soon,* inshallah, *very soon."*

Sometimes, when we are not in favor or when Abou Bekr wishes to play with us, we are not even granted the honor of being spat at, but are made to stand and watch the business of the court until he decides to send us away again. We are told that he is well disposed toward us, that this interminable wait is simply a formality, like the queue in a post office. There will also have to be a harour, *or assembly of elders, which will debate our application, and sometimes Abou Bekr uses the difficulty of convening this as a reason why nothing is happening. It is a fiction: everyone knows that he alone makes the decision.*

In the meantime, we busy ourselves assembling our caravan. We have enlisted the help of one Desmond Hammond, a former military man who is now making his fortune trading ivory and other goods. He and his partner, a Boer called Tatts, vanish for a week at a time, laden down with Remingtons, Martini-Henrys and ammunition: when they return their camels are festooned with huge tusks, like some strange hybrid mastodon unknown to Darwin.

Another curiosity of this place: you cannot buy the sexual services of a woman. This is not because they have any scruples, rather the reverse—any woman of a nubile age is already purchased. Since there is no limit to the number of wives a man can have, a rich man continues adding them as the fancy takes him. Hammond tells me that before the women here reach puberty they are circumcised, a concept I found quite hard to grasp at first and which still revolts me as I write this. It is different in the Interior, where we are headed. Among the Galla, a woman may take a lover even when married: if a man's spear is left outside her hut, no other man can enter, not even her husband. I cannot help reflecting that this arrangement is preferable to the brutal pseudo-civilization of the coast, and for that matter compares quite favorably to the way we do things back home.

Curious, isn't it, how one can come all this way, see so many things, and yet find oneself reflecting not on what is strange and new, but on what one left behind—the strange and old, as it were. What was that line of Horace that was drummed into us at school? Coelum non animum mutant qui trans mare currunt—*"Those who chase across the sea change their skies but not their souls." I wonder whether it is altogether true.*

Regards,

Wallis

❧

Zeilah
2nd August

My dearest Emily,

We hope to be leaving here soon. Ibrahim Bey, the coffee merchant, is coming to Zeilah, and according to the latest reports will be here in a few days. We are optimistic that with Bey's help the administrative difficulty which has pinned us here will somehow be resolved. Certainly Abou Bekr's courtiers seem to be full of happiness for us: they mention Bey's name and smile.

Poor Hector—he has been fretting about the rains. At one point he was thinking of leaving me here, making his way back to Aden and on to Ceylon before the bad weather comes, but apparently your father's instructions were that he must see me established at all costs. I do not find his company any easier, but I am grateful for it. To be here on one's own would be very harsh.

I have just been watching two cormorants engaged in a courtship dance: it was a hilarious sight. The male is the more brightly—

[TWENTY-FIVE]

AND THAT'S WHEN I SEE HER.

I'm sitting on the deck of our boat, writing a letter, when another boat comes round the bend in the river. A dhow, under human power—four pairs of black oars rising and falling rhythmically, as one. And, on the deck, a tableau:

A man in Arab dress—a white robe—enormously large, is seated on a folding throne-like stool, one hand resting on his knee: putting his weight on it, as if he might be about to spring to his feet. The posture speaks of alertness, eagerness. The sensual, heavy face is that of a potentate, but the eyes—those hooded eyes—miss nothing as they scan the jetty. Big, fleshy lips, an Arab's curving nose. Behind him, standing, is a Negro: a tall man—or rather, a tall boy, for despite his height there is something youthful in the black face. He stands like a sentry, waiting for a command, his hands folded loosely over the pommel of a huge weapon, a kind of sword, the point sticking in the wooden deck, just as in London a man might rest both hands on his walking stick.

And behind *him,* at the Arab's other shoulder, stands a girl.

A saffron-yellow robe envelops her, from her ankles to her hair. The face below the headscarf is delicate, fine-boned, almost Indian, but the body . . . as a momentary breeze along the river ruffles the gown, I see that she is strong and supple, her posture as upright as an athlete's. She is, I realize with a start, quite breathtakingly beautiful, her skin so black that like a piece of split coal it seems almost silver where it catches the light.

A whistle blows. The dhow raises its oars, as smartly as a coxed four on the Thames at Eton, and drifts in toward the jetty. People run to and fro with ropes. From nowhere a crowd appears and surges excitedly toward the boat; the inevitable passionate hubbub begins. The dhow's trajectory takes it near to where our own craft is moored. The two men continue staring ahead, but as the dhow passes, the girl turns her gaze a little and looks directly at me. The effect of making contact with her eyes is extraordinary—it is all I can do not to recoil, to hold her gaze without flinching from that remarkable beauty.

The moment the boat docks the Arab is on his feet. He is a heavy man, but nimble; he needs none of the offered hands to help him onto dry land. The Negro follows, also disdaining help, holding his sword in front of him as a priest might hold a cross. Then the girl comes ashore—a swift, confident stride: a hint of the figure inside the robes pressing against the cotton as she steps up onto the gunwales, balances there for a moment on her bare feet, and then jumps—or rather, steps: there is no discernible effort—onto the jetty, balanced as a cat.

After that comes the usual chaos—porters and the unloading of cargo. I continue to watch her, mesmerized. Her feet are black—so black they are almost gray: but when she stepped from the boat there was a flash of pink at her soles. Beneath the loose-fitting headscarf the hair, one can now see, is long and wiry. Tendrils and dark zigzags escape. The yellow robe—*sari,* one might almost say—blows against her, outlining first one part of her body, fleetingly, then another . . . she puts a hand to her head, adjusting it, and I see that the palm of her hand is pinkish gray as well.

The luggage is not unloaded yet, but the Arab gives an order or two, his voice booming; then the three of them walk up toward the village, still in the same formation, toward the royal compound. I watch the saffron-yellow robe amongst the press of black heads—the way she moves, so unlike them: strong and light and easy, her shoulders pulled back like a runner. Something clicks in my brain, a key turning in a lock I had not even known was there. The sensation is quite acute: there is no mistaking it, although whether it is locking or unlocking I cannot say. I find I have been holding my breath: when I release it, the sound that comes from me is like a gasp. I look down. In my hand is the letter to Emily, half finished. I crumple it in my fist and throw it into the water, where it circles twice before drifting, slowly at first and then with gathering speed, down that black, silent current toward the sea.

[TWENTY-SIX]

"Piquant"—agreeably stimulating to the palate. Pleasant; tart; sharp or biting; pungent.

—PANGBORN, Principles of Sensory Evaluation of Food

I AM STILL SITTING THERE HALF AN HOUR LATER WHEN HECTOR hurries back. "We're summoned," he says shortly. "Ibrahim Bey has arrived. Now it seems the damned nigger king will talk to us after all."

"Well, it's good something's happening. At last."

"It's damned impudence, if you ask me."

I get up from my camp-chair and make to go ashore, but he stops me. "I think we should make a show of this, Robert. We're not just here as individuals, like that thieving scoundrel Hammond. We're here as representatives of British Industry. Even if he won't respect the man, he might respect *that*."

And so it is that we walk into the court of Abou Bekr—the tin-pot tyrant of a godforsaken dung-heap in a tiny fly-ridden corner of savagedom—wearing as much regalia as we can muster: white tie, tails, cummerbunds, and in Hector's case, a rather splendid white hat surmounted with red cockatoo feathers. The Africans look at us incuriously. I suspect that to them, it simply looks as if we have at last started dressing appropriately, as the tribes of the Interior do.

Abou Bekr is lounging on his couch, eating dates. Ibrahim Bey stands in front of him. A silver tray has been placed at the tyrant's feet. On it are a pile of leaves—some kind of spice, perhaps, or drug, a gift from merchant to king. The Negro is at his master's shoulder. I look for the girl but she is nowhere to be seen.

We are spotted and waved forward. Abou Bekr performs the introductions in a language none of us understands, though his gestures are clear enough. Bey, Hector and I all shake hands. The king speaks again; a document is brought; he dunks the royal seal in ink and presses it to the paper, splashing some ink on his white robe as he does so. Then, without a hint of a smile, he holds out his hand to me. I take it: it is leathery and rough, like the paw of a leper, but I shake it all the same. He stares fiercely. We are dismissed.

"Have you been here long?" Bey inquires solicitiously when we are outside. He might be meeting us off a slightly delayed express train.

"Nearly a month," Hector growls furiously.

"Oh. Not so bad then." Bey smiles. "It's good to meet you both. You, I think, must be Crannach. And you," he turns to me, "must be Robert Wallis."

"How did you know that?"

"My good friend Samuel Pinker wrote to tell me you were coming to Africa. He has asked me to help you in any way I can." He bows his head. "I shall be honored to do so."

"What caused the delay?" Hector asks brusquely.

"What delay?"

"Why did his royal lowness need to keep us waiting so long, exactly?"

Ibrahim Bey's big face assumes an expression of bafflement. "I have no idea. But in the meantime, there is still the council of elders to square. Will you make them a gift? I have taken care of Abou Bekr."

"A gift?" Hector's face is sour.

"A couple of goats should do it."

"We don't have any goats," I point out.

"And if we did," Hector says ponderously, "we wouldnae exchange them for travel permits in a country where we are already entitled to pass freely, as subjects of Her Britannic Majesty."

"Of course," Ibrahim Bey says thoughtfully. "There is absolutely no obligation to give anything at all." He catches my eye and winks. "But you may find yourself stuck here for a very long time if you do not."

"I also happen to be of the opinion," Hector says, "that whenever a white man resorts to bribery, he makes things worse for every other white man who follows."

"Then I am fortunate not to be a white man—or at least, not quite," Bey replies. He has, I realize, enormous charm: another man might have taken offense at Hector's tone, let alone his words, but Ibrahim Bey acts as if it were all a great joke. "But assuming that the *harour* give their permission, will you agree to share the costs of a caravan with me? I too need to get to Harar, and the larger the group, the smaller the risk."

"Why? Is it dangerous?" I ask.

"That journey is always dangerous, my friend. Once we are beyond the protection of Abou Bekr"—here Hector snorts contemptuously—"everyone is fighting everyone else. Menelik, the Abyssinian Emperor, is fighting the Italians and subjugating the Galla. The Galla are fighting all the other tribes. The Egyptians are stirring up trouble wherever they can, in the hope that somebody will ask them to invade. But we have guns, and a piece of paper signed by Abou Bekr, and the protection of our passports. We would be unlucky to be killed."

It's a strange thing, but after Bey has made this speech, explaining just how dangerous the expedition is, I feel greatly reassured. That is the charisma of the man, I suppose—I realize with a jolt of surprise that he reminds me, a little, of Samuel Pinker.

"But we'll nae bribe anyone," Hector repeats doggedly.

"You would tip a porter or a waiter," Bey suggests mildly. "Why not a king or a headman?"

"A tip comes after." Hector says it firmly. "A bribe is before."

"Then that's settled. A gift of two goats, to be given *after* the meeting. I'm sure they will accept your word that two goats is what they'll get: an Englishman's promise is notoriously reliable." Bey claps his hands. "And now, may I offer you coffee? I have made camp on the hill—it is a little cooler up there."

Hector says disgustedly, "I have some preparations to attend to."

Bey looks at me. "Thank you," I say. "I'd be honored."

"Typical Arab," Hector mutters as Bey strolls up the hill. "He only wants to travel with us because he knows they won't dare attack a British caravan. I wouldn't mind betting that he paid Abou Bekr to make us wait."

PORTERS ARE ferrying water and a goat is being skinned as I make my way through Bey's encampment. At the center one tent is larger than the rest. The Negro youth is standing outside it, supervising a group of women cooking over a fire. When he sees me he silently lifts the flap and motions for me to go inside.

The interior has been hung with patterned silks, and overlapping carpets cover the floor. There is a pungent, spicy scent, some kind of incense; later, I come to know it as myrrh. In the middle of the space, either side of a low table, are two throne-shaped stools.

"Robert—welcome."

Bey emerges from another chamber. He has changed his clothes; now he wears a flowing pair of cotton trousers, with a shirt of the same material and a waistcoat of patterned silk. He does not move like a heavy man as he steps quickly toward me and clasps both my shoulders in greeting.

"You are very welcome," he repeats. "Samuel has written to me of your venture—your *ad*venture, I should say. And of the Guide, too—I am looking forward to making the acquaintance of that remarkable system. But first—always first!—some coffee. Have you experienced the Abyssinian way of serving it yet?"

"I don't believe so."

He smiles. "Mulu! Fikre!"

The Negro comes into the tent and they exchange a few words in Arabic. Bey points to a stool. "Please, sit," he says to me.

He sits on the other stool, watching me. After a moment the girl comes in. For a moment I actually feel dizzy, such is her effect on me. The cotton robe she is wearing now is darker, almost brown, and it ends at her hips. Underneath she is wearing trousers of pale silk, embroidered with pearls; a long coiled bracelet of copper winds itself about her arm like a snake. Before now, I had not seen her eyes properly. They are extraordinarily light, the only thing in that delicate iron-colored face that is: perhaps she has the blood of some European sailor in her ancestry. Pale, almost gray eyes, that meet mine for a moment—an endless moment, their expression inscrutable—then drop, as she kneels and lights incense in a brazier. Tendrils of perfumed smoke fill the tent. Her lips are dark purple, almost black; the color of pomegranates.

"The coffee ceremony," Bey's voice says, "consists of three cups, *abol, tona* and *baraka,* taken one after the other. The first is for pleasure, the second provokes contemplation, and the third bestows a blessing. Between them, the Abyssinians believe, they effect a kind of transformation of the spirit."

The Negro returns with a copper tray. On it are various implements: cups, a black clay pot, a drawstring bag, a napkin and a dish of pink-colored liquid. The girl dips the napkin in the dish and comes to kneel before me. Just looking at her face makes me want to sigh with pleasure.

Then, surprisingly, she reaches forward and wipes the damp, scented napkin over my own face. It touches my forehead, my closed eyelids, smoothes my cheeks. The aroma of rosewater fills my nostrils, sweet and sharp. I feel her fingers on the other side of the cloth. Her touch is sensual, light, but oddly impersonal. Her perfect face is very close, and then she has moved away again. She pulls at the strings fastening the bag and holds it up to me in both hands.

"Now you must smell the beans, Robert," Bey's voice says.

I take the bag from her and raise it to my nose. Instantly I know I have come across these beans already, in London—or a lot very like it. Honeysuckle . . . licorice . . . woodsmoke . . . apple.

"I've had this coffee before," I say. "You sold some to Pinker."

Bey smiles. "He has trained you well. This is the coffee of the land beyond Harar—the land where you are to make your plantation."

"Does it have a name?"

"Many names or none, depending on where you are. The world calls it *mocca,* though as you have noticed it is quite different from the moccas of my country. It comes down from Harar by the same ancient slave route we will be following." I look at him, surprised. "You didn't know? Yes, the trail we will be following across the desert is one that has been used by slavers for centuries. That, not merely coffee, is the source of Harar's wealth, and the reason why they have not always invited the attentions of outsiders. But the two trades—coffee and slavery—are connected in other ways as well."

He is silent a moment. The beans hiss in their pot as they roast. The girl stirs them with a wooden spoon; a rhythmic, ritualized motion. Her fingers are slender, long; the backs are a deep, even black, while the palms and fingertips are almost as light as a European's.

"How so?" I ask Bey.

"To keep awake as they traveled at night the slavers ate the beans of the *kaffa* bush, mixed with a little butter. In more temperate regions the beans were sometimes discarded—thrown by the wayside whenever the slavers stopped. Where they took root, new areas of coffee production started."

"Then it was fortunate the traders stopped."

"Not for their captives. It was at these halts that the boy slaves would be castrated. Then they were buried up to their waists in the hot sand to cauterize the wound. For an unfortunate few, the wounds became infected, and they were left there in the desert to die a painful death."

Despite the heat, I shiver. "But that's all in the past now."

He does not reply. The beans have reached the point which roasters call "first crack," popping and rattling in their clay pot. The girl tips them onto a plate. The smell intensifies. Scorched tar, ash, peat smoke—but over all of those, a triumphant blaze of that sweet, honeyed, floral aroma. She hands me the plate and I inhale the deep, pan-scorched smell. "These are good," I say to her politely. Her beautiful fine-boned face is as expressionless as a mask.

"I see she doesn't understand," I say as I pass the plate on to Bey.

"There you are wrong, Robert. Fikre knows seven languages, including French, English, Amharic and Arabic. But without my permission she will not speak a word in any of them." He lifts the plate to his own face and inhales deeply. "Ah!"

I look into the girl's eyes. Just for a moment there is something in them—a nod, and something more: a kind of despair; an appeal, a silent plea of desperate intensity.

I frown a little, as if to say, *I don't understand.*

For a moment she seems to hesitate. Then she gives the minutest of shrugs. *I cannot tell you.*

I slide my eyes toward Bey. *Why? Because of him?*

Another tiny, almost imperceptible nod. *Yes.*

She busies herself getting cups, holding them upside down over the smoking myrrh, turning them this way and that to perfume them. Then she pounds the beans in a mortar—quickly, fluidly. Tipping them into a silver coffee-pot, she pours on the boiling water. A gust of steam. The smell is like a fanfare: ecstatic, exultant, a mixture of honeysuckle and spices, lilies and lime.

The pot has a long curved spout like a hummingbird's beak. She pours coffee in a thin, continuous stream into two cups. As she hands one to me she leans forward, deliberately masking our hands from Bey. I feel something being pushed into my hand, surreptitiously—something small and hard. Casually, as I lift my coffee to my mouth, I glance down.

In my palm is a single coffee bean.

What does it mean? I try to catch her eye but she is still avoiding my gaze. I drink the coffee. Yes, it is as good as the last time, when I had it in Limehouse—perhaps even better: this time my nostrils are full of myrrh and rosewater, my senses tingling with the heat and the incense and the presence of the girl.

The second cup is subtly different—the coffee has been left to steep a little: the flavors are deeper, the mouthfeel thicker. I watch her move; the way the flowing cotton shifts around her as she crouches. She is thin-hipped as a cheetah, and her movements have something of the same fluid, rolling gait. She has evidently decided that she is risking too much: she avoids my eyes even when she must dip the napkin in the rosewater and wash my face in preparation for the next cup. But I discern something in her gesture—her hand lingers, minutely, as she smoothes the damp cloth across my face.

She drops the napkin. We both reach for it at once. Our fingers touch. Her eyes widen, startled.

Please. Be careful.

I squeeze her hand once, reassuring her. *Don't be frightened. Trust me. Wait.*

• • •

Bey, meanwhile, talks of coffee. We discuss the different kinds of curing process, wet and dry—"As soon as you can, Robert, move to the wet process: the lots are more consistent, and less of the crop is spoiled." He talks of Harar—"Getting the coffee out is hard, but it will become easier. Menelik is talking of building a railway from the coast to Dire Dawa. You have arrived at the right time: fortunes will be made here soon."

The third cup—*baraka*. Now the coffee is a little salty: evaporation has thickened it. She refreshes it with a sprig of herb that tastes like ginger.

"Do you know what this is, Robert?" Bey asks, taking the sprig and sniffing it.

I shake my head.

"*Tena adam*. The Abyssinians believe it to be an aphrodisiac. The coffee ceremony, you see, has many meanings. Between friends, it is a gesture of friendship; between merchants such as ourselves, a symbol of trust. But between lovers it is a ritual of a different kind. When a woman gives a man coffee, it is a way of showing her desire."

In my left hand, my fingers rotate the bean, small and hard and round. Is this what it means?

"And that is the coffee ceremony. Now I know you will never cheat me. Ha!" His booming laughter fills the tent.

Fikre takes the empty cups and places them carefully on the tray. At the flap of the tent, just beyond his sight, she glances back at me. A flash of white teeth, lips the color of pomegranates, black skin. Then she is gone.

"How long has Fikre been in your service?" I ask, as casually as I can.

Bey looks at me thoughtfully. "She's very lovely, isn't she?"

I shrug. "Yes, she is, rather."

He is silent for a moment. Then he says abruptly, "She isn't in my service, Robert. I own her. She's a slave."

I HAD half-suspected it. But it is still a shock—an outrage.

"I am telling you this," Bey fixes me with a fierce look, "because you would have found out anyway, and because I will not lie to you. But I promise you that it is not what it seems. Someday I will tell you how I came to buy her. But not today."

"What about Mulu?"

He nods. "Him too. Mulu is her *lala*—her maid, protector, servant."

"So he is a—?"

"A eunuch, yes. He was taken from his tribe as a child and castrated on the journey, just as I described."

I shudder. It explains something that had been puzzling me about the way Mulu looks: the height of a man, the hairless face of a boy . . .

Bey says gently, "For you British, slavery is the great evil. But things are different here. It is not a question of simply saying to someone, 'Now you are released, go home.' Where could they go? Even if they knew who their own people were, they would not be accepted—they have no status. I give them a better life than they could otherwise hope for."

I nod. A part of me is appalled at what he is saying. But another part of me is horribly, furiously envious.

[TWENTY-SEVEN]

"Really," Ada says crossly. "I know he is your fiancé, Emily, but I do wish Robert would not write quite such condescending things about me."

Emily sighs. "Is that the one he wrote to the Frog about the villagers and Wagner?"

"It is. I have a good mind to write back."

"He will be in Abyssinia by now. I am not sure when letters will reach him—he does not seem to reply to any of mine. Besides, Ada, I suspect Robert was merely trying to be amusing. It is his way of keeping his spirits up."

"Robert has far too much spirit already, if you ask me."

"All the same, it cannot be easy for him. It is the least we can do to be a little understanding."

"That is all very well for you to say—to you he is writing sweet nothings and billets-doux."

"Actually," Emily says with a wry smile, "Robert is not very good at billets-doux. I think he considers them a corruption of his art."

Ada snorts.

"You really don't like him very much, do you?" Emily says quietly.

"I just can't quite see the point of him. And . . ." She hesitates, for there is a limit to her sisterly disloyalty. "I suppose I'm surprised you like him quite as much as you do."

"I think it is because he makes me laugh."

"Speaking for myself," Ada says primly, "I should not like my husband to be a constant source of hilarity."

Just then their father bursts into the room. He is holding a two-foot-long thread of white paper from the tickertape machine in his office. "My dears!" he cries. "Would you like to see something marvelous?"

"What is it, Father?"

"Get your coats—we are going to the Exchange. Lyle's are trying to break the sugar corner!"

"But how does that affect us?" Ada said, frowning.

"Directly, not at all. But if they can do it for sugar, we can do it for coffee. Whatever happens, it will be a sight!"

Neither of the girls is quite as excited as he is, but they allow themselves to be hurried into their coats and hats. Their father, meanwhile, is hailing a cab, and they set off through the streets toward the City.

"For many years Lyle's have faced a situation similar to us," Pinker explains. "As we are to Howell's, so they are to Tate's. But they refuse to be beaten! By marketing their sugar as a syrup, they have begun to establish a name. Now Lyle's have started to use sugar from their own beet fields in East Anglia: they hope to use it to destroy the corner."

"I still do not see how that will work," Ada says with a frown.

"Lyle's will release a huge amount of sugar onto the market all at once," Emily explains. "Tate's syndicate will have to buy it, if they are to keep the price at its artificial level. Then it just becomes a matter of whose nerve holds longest—if Lyle has to stop selling, they will have lost, and the price will stay high; if Tate has to stop buying, they will lose, and the price will tumble."

"Exactly." Her father favors her with a smile. "Tate is already under pressure because of the harvest. And Lyle has good reserves. . . . It will be a fascinating contest."

At the Exchange they are shown up to the public gallery. It is a bit like a theater, Emily thinks, looking down at the scene below her. She sees a large, echoing hall, around which are scattered half a dozen octagonal raised platforms made of mahogany and brass.

"Those are the pits," her father explains. "The Norfolk pit is this one, just below us." There are dozens of men milling around the pit he indicates, their attention focused on a blackboard. Emily is reminded of children, waiting in front of a Punch-and-Judy for the puppets to appear. The only activity comes from a man in a bright red bowler hat, writing figures on the board; when he reaches the bottom, he rubs it all out with a wave of a duster and starts again.

"Ah! There is Neate," her father exclaims. "And Brewer, too." Emily looks up: the Member of Parliament she met previously with her father is heading their way, along with a young man in a business suit. Arthur Brewer acknowledges her with a smile and a nod before taking a seat. Pinker, meanwhile, is talking urgently into Neate's ear, clapping him on the shoulder as the young man turns away.

"Our broker," he explains as he sits down again. "I have put a small amount on Lyle."

"A wager?" Emily asks.

"In effect. I have placed a sell order. If the price falls, as I hope, I will pocket the difference."

She nods, but she does not really understand this market the way her father obviously does. This is a new side of him, a side she has not seen before: in the past, when he has spoken of his coffee sacks as soldiers and cavalry, it was a different kind of battle she imagined.

On the floor, a bell rings. Immediately a low hubbub starts up around the pit. Men are waving their hands in some kind of sign language; others are writing dockets, passing them back and forth over the counter. Despite not knowing exactly how it works, she is aware of some great drama being played out. It seems to center around two men standing on opposite sides of the octagon.

"Lyle's broker. And Tate's, over there," her father says. "Ah! Here, if I am not mistaken, are their principals, come to watch."

Two separate groups are coming into the public gallery. Each consists of about half a dozen men: they pointedly ignore each other, walking to the rail and focusing all their attention on the activity below.

"The Lyle brothers. And that, I believe, is Joseph Tate, Sir Henry's son." Pinker turns back to the floor, straining to watch the changing figures on the blackboard. "From what I can see, Lyle's are still buying. They must be building up their stocks."

"Even though they hope the price will fall?"

"It is a gesture. They want the Exchange to see how much they are committing."

For twenty minutes or so nothing much happens. Ada catches Emily's eye and grimaces. But Emily, far from being bored, is fascinated. She does not like it, exactly—in fact, she finds it slightly repulsive, the way everything Pinker's does can be reduced to this, to pieces of paper pushed back and forth across a mahogany counter. There is something pack-like about the men around the pit she finds disturbing: she can imagine them turning on one of the two dealers at any minute, like animals, savaging him. . . .

"Remarkable," Pinker murmurs.

He is looking at the side of the public gallery, where a very elderly gentleman is making his way toward Tate's group with the aid of a stick. A younger man stands at his shoulder, ready to assist him should he need it.

"Sir Henry Tate himself," Pinker says in a low voice. "He must be over seventy by now."

As if the appearance of the old man were a signal, the noise on the floor alters. People are shouting at Lyle's broker, waving their hands in front of his face in that strange sign language, pushing what look like scraps of paper into his hands. Imperturbably, he collects them, tapping people on the chest to show that he has taken their contracts, all the while nodding at others, signing the chits and handing them on.

"Lyle's are selling," her father says. "This is it!"

For five minutes the frenzy continues. Pinker glances over at where Sir Henry sits next to his son Joseph, his hands folded on the handle of his cane. The two of them are watching the activity below in silence, their faces impassive. "They must break soon," Pinker mutters. "They have spent a small fortune already."

The noise suddenly seems to falter. Down on the floor, there is a long moment of expectant silence. Then Lyle's broker shakes his head.

As one the men on the floor turn away from him toward Tate's broker.

Her father sighs. "It's over. Tate has won."

"Why, Father?"

"Who knows?" he says brusquely. "Perhaps Lyle's misjudged their moment. Perhaps they had fewer reserves than they were letting on. Perhaps the old man just held his nerve better." He gets to his feet. "Let us go home."

The gallery is already emptying. Lyle's group is the first to leave: amongst Tate's lot a few quiet handshakes are being exchanged. It is hard to believe that a fortune has just been gambled and lost.

"They will not win next time," her father says, looking down at the floor. "Not in the long run. The market wants to be free, and no man is more powerful than the market." He turns to Arthur Brewer. "Don't forget that dinner, Brewer. We must learn the lessons of today, if we are not to suffer the same fate."

[TWENTY-EIGHT]

"Smoke"—the very symbol of volatility, this is the smell given off by certain types of wood and resins as they burn.

—LENOIR, Le Nez du Café

WE LEAVE ZEILAH FOUR DAYS LATER—A CARAVAN OF THIRTY camels, consisting not only of ourselves and Ibrahim Bey but Hammond and Tatts, eager to ride as far as possible in the safety of our party. Fikre and Mulu walk behind us with the other servants. Sometimes, when we are nearing the end of a march, I notice her stagger against the eunuch for support. He puts an arm around her tenderly, holding her upright.

At Tococha we stop for water. We fill the *gherbes,* barrels made of goatskin which are tied to each camel like giant footballs, two to each beast. The water has a rancid, animal taste—*hircinos*—that worsens dramatically after a day in the sun. At Warumbot, ten miles on, we turn inland. This is the very rim of the desert: the village seems to perch on the edge of the hot sands like a small harbor on the edge of a great sea. In the moonlight—we travel from late afternoon to dawn—it is the color of salt, bright, brilliant and glistening, like a vast plain of quartz. If you lick your lips they are coated with salt dust. Black faces sparkle with crystalline specks. According to Hammond we are now actually lower than the ocean. Sometimes there are steam vents, fumaroles, in the featureless, rocky scrub; sometimes just the endless petrified waves of sand. We see only one living thing all night, a thorn tree that could have been dead for all the leaf it showed.

I find myself daydreaming about Emily, replaying scenes from our courtship—the way she stamped her foot when we had an argument in the street; lunch at the pub in Narrow Street . . . But then I catch a glimpse of Fikre, the moonlight catching on her slate-gray skin, and I am instantly, vertiginously aroused. The rhythm of the camel, once you get used to it, is hypnotic, almost sensual, a constant nudging, rocking motion that does nothing to dispel the fantasies flitting through my head.

When the sun rises, soaring like a Montpellier balloon over the sands, we are still in the same featureless desert. I sense alarm among the drivers. To stay out here in the heat of the day means death. The *gherbes* are almost empty, and no one seems to know exactly where we should be. After some debate we keep going as we are. Eventually another tiny village comes into view. The shapeless houses are almost invisible against the shapeless rocks scattered across the desert, which a trick of perspective can make bigger than a ship or smaller than a speck of dust. This is Ensa, our destination for the day. Everyone is relieved. There are a dozen ramshackle huts, a few goats looking for grass among the stones, a Negress feeding a baby from a flat gray tit that is already as empty as a squeezed orange. Big-shouldered vultures stamp around the huts, or pull at the stinking remains of a camel's straw, but there is a well to refill our canteens. We have traveled forty miles.

• • •

THE FOLLOWING NIGHT I ride, a little shamefully—it does not seem right to be sitting on top of a camel when a woman is walking. But there is clearly an etiquette here: I can no more offer my camel to Bey's slave than I could offer a seat on an omnibus to a servant.

Ibrahim Bey sees me glancing at her and steers his camel alongside mine. "I said I would tell you how I found her."

"Yes?"

"Would you like to hear now?"

I think: I am riding a camel through the desert. The moon is very big above me—so big and clear I can almost reach up and touch its mottled surface. I have barely slept in days. I am going to a place where there is absolutely no civilization. These camels stink. An Arab trader is going to tell me about his slave. Surely this is all a terrible dream.

"Please," I say.

{TWENTY-NINE}

FOR NEARLY AN HOUR BEY TALKS, HIS VOICE A LOW MONOTONE. It was an accident, it seems—a slave sale in Constantinople; a curious friend who insisted on attending; Bey dragged along against his better judgment to watch.

"Please understand, Robert: this was not some squalid, dusty bazaar, where plantation laborers are bought and sold by the gross. This was a sale of the most valuable specimens—girls who had been selected in infancy for their beauty, and nurtured in the harem of a prestigious dealer; who had been taught mathematics, music, languages and chess. Some were from the lands to the east—Georgia, Circassia and Hungary—prized for their fair coloring, while others were from the dealer's own family."

Such girls, he explains, might not even be bought by their eventual owner: rather, they would be sold from agent to agent, the very finest ones being passed up the chain toward the Imperial Harem itself. Each agent would add a mark-up: the price of a girl sold into the Sultan's service was astronomical, more than Bey would earn in a lifetime. But these were very few; a girl would be exceptional indeed who reached such heights.

He stares into the darkness. "We were greeted by the trader, who offered us refreshments—sherbets, coffee, pastries and so on—before showing us to our seats, which had been allocated according to the status of the guests. There were only about twenty of us, but it was clear that some were preparing to spend small fortunes that afternoon.

"One end of the room had been screened off, and from behind the screen one caught the flutter of excited faces, peering eyes, a giggle of girlish excitement . . . that was where the goods were waiting. A scribe sat at a table, preparing pens and ledgers to record the payments. The trader's mother, the *hanim,* dressed in her richest clothes, was flitting around making last-minute adjustments. The trader made a short speech of welcome. Then he introduced the first girl, describing her in glowing terms. That was all very well, but we wanted to see her. Eventually she came out, bashful in front of so many men but also rather pleased with herself—it was an honor to be chosen to open the proceedings. She was a Russian by birth, a nice enough thing, barely more than a child. She was wearing a *gomlek,* a coat of glittering, jewel-encrusted silk, left open at the throat; silk trousers, soft bootlets. We looked, and we were impressed. No one touched her, of course—there was a certificate of virginity from a midwife, to reassure anyone who was anxious, but the whole setup was designed to emphasize that these were harem girls, not prostitutes."

I open my mouth to ask a question. I close it again, not wanting to interrupt, but Bey has noticed. "The harem, Robert—perhaps you are imagining some kind of brothel. But a seraglio is nothing like a cat-house. No one would take a girl if she had been pawed by other buyers; sullied, as it were. It is like when you buy a book—you appreciate fine books, I think?"

I nod, though I cannot recall ever having had a conversation with him to this effect.

"When you buy a first edition, you have to cut the pages. Why?

It is a service the bookseller, or the printer, could easily perform for you. But the truth is that we all like to have absolute proof that we are the first to read those words. As with books, so with women."

We have come to a patch of rocky scree. The caravan slows, each animal taking it in turns to negotiate the boulders that lie strewn across our path. I glance back. Mulu is helping Fikre across the rocks, lifting her from stone to stone. Her skin glows like a silver coin, brilliant moonlight on absolute black.

"The bidding started," Bey says softly. "Almost immediately some kind of record was broken—I can't remember the details. I can't remember anything much. Of course, I took no pleasure from seeing human beings go under the auctioneer's hammer. Yet most of the girls seemed childishly happy. Clearly they had never been dressed in such finery before: each girl walked proudly from behind that screen with a kind of dazed delight, almost skipping in her soft silk boots as she made her way to the chair in the middle of the room. No, what was making my blood race was something else. I am a merchant, you must remember; commerce is in my blood. I had been to many sales, but never one like this. The auctioneer was skillful—he did not raise his voice above a murmur, but his eyes were everywhere, nodding as he acknowledged the signal of a raised hand, or with a slight smile invited an underbidder to return once more to the fray. The excitement in that room was exceptional. Girls like this came onto the market only rarely, and for these men, all their wealth was nothing compared to the thrill of being able to buy one . . . and, I suppose, the thrill of beating the other bidders, too. Of course I could not have joined in, even if I had wanted to. The sums being thrown around were far beyond my means. I was a mere coffee trader, an observer. By rights I should not even have been present to watch these wealthy men at play.

"After perhaps half a dozen had been sold, a temporary halt was called to the proceedings; ostensibly for refreshments but actually to increase the tension to fever pitch. And—a clever trick of the *hanim* and her son—while we were taking coffee, they had arranged an entertainment. Nothing vulgar: all that happened was that the girls came out from behind the screen, some to play instruments, some to play each other at chess.

"The men got up and strolled around, apparently to talk to one another or admire the ornate tilework on the pillars, but actually to get a better look at the girls who had not yet been sold. That was when I became aware of a whisper that was being passed around. There was a young man there whose clothes proclaimed him to be a wealthy member of the court. It was being murmured that he was intent on buying the very best girl to present to the Sultan, in the hope of being given a post which was in the Sultan's gift, the governorship of some province or other. The other buyers were speculating which girl it would be.

"I looked around the room, seeing the goods through his eyes. Fair-skinned girls, as I said, were particularly sought after. Perhaps he would favor the Hungarian girl with the long fair hair? The trader's mother evidently thought so: the *hanim* was fussing over the girl, twitching at her clothes, as if she were a bride about to go to the altar.

"And then I noticed another girl, very dark, very beautiful, sitting at one of the chess tables. She was an African—by birth; she had clearly been in the harem some years. She was dressed in a jacket of fine, shimmering red silk, and her expression as she moved the chesspieces across the board was somber. That intrigued me: she was not using the game as an excuse, as the other girls were, darting swift glances at the men: she was concentrating, with fierce determination, on her game. It mattered to her, I could see, whether she won.

"That was her response to the sale, the buyers, the whole undignified circus: she simply blotted them out, focusing instead on the one engagement where she might actually be able to triumph. I admired that in her.

"I paused as I passed by her table. Her opponent was a very poor player, and in any case was barely thinking about the pieces—she was more interested in what was going on elsewhere in the room. When she had been beaten, in no more than half a dozen moves, I stepped forward.

" 'I would be very honored,' I said, 'if I could join you in a game.'

"The African shrugged and reset the pieces. I made a couple of easy opening moves. I wanted to see how she played. The etiquette of the harem demanded that she lose to me, to flatter my ego. For a couple of turns, I thought she might. But then—suddenly—a spark of dogged determination came into her eye, and she began trying to beat me.

"As we played I studied her face. She did not meet my gaze—that would have been an astonishing impudence, at least in that setting. But I could not fail to appreciate her beauty. Well, you have seen her: I do not have to describe what she looks like. Perhaps, though, I do have to describe her spirit. This was a girl who absolutely *refused* to be owned—to be beaten. It was obvious from every muscle in her body that she was seething with anger at what was happening, at the way she was being disposed of. Beating me was her only possible revenge; a tiny revenge, perhaps, but a statement of her defiance nevertheless.

"Then I became aware that someone else had come to stand by the table at which we were playing. It was the young courtier. He watched us, and something about his stillness made me think that he too had seen something in this African girl—something extraordinary. I looked up, hoping to scare him off with a scowl, but he had already walked away.

"After we had returned to our seats, the trader announced the next lots. The fairest-skinned girl would be auctioned last, the climax of the show. First it was the turn of the African. The trader ran through a list of her accomplishments: languages, music, archery, running. It was clear that they were suggesting her as an exotic, a kind of novelty—an educated ape. Two men bid against each other in a desultory way, running the price up to what was in all probability a fairly generous figure. The contest had stalled when suddenly, with a bored wave of his hand, the rich young courtier entered the sale.

"I could see his game immediately—he wanted to suggest that this was an afterthought, that he had decided to make more than one purchase today, and that whilst his real interest lay elsewhere, he would not be averse to taking Fikre away with him as well. His demeanor may have fooled some of the people in that room. It did not fool me. I might not have known much about slaves, but I knew all about auctions. And there was another reason why I understood the young man's motives so well: I shared them.

"In that brief time, over the chess table, I had fallen . . . I will not say in love with her, but perhaps, under her spell. It was remarkable—a visceral, physical, all-consuming thing: I simply *knew* that I could not let that man, or any man for that matter, take her from me and break her spirit.

"There was a brief flurry of bidding. The young courtier shrugged—named a vast price. The other bidders bowed and withdrew. The hammer fell once. And then—a murmur of excitement; or rather, of puzzlement. Another buyer had entered the auction. Someone had had the temerity to try to snatch this unusual purchase from under the courtier's nose. With a start of surprise I realized that it was me. My hand was in the air. The courtier raised his eyebrows, and lifted his hand again to signal that battle was joined. I snapped my fingers—a gesture which smacked of rudeness, but I was past caring. The onlookers sat up. The courtier frowned and doubled his bid. There was no pretense now that this was just some casual afterthought on his part. He wanted her. So did I—but the price was already more than my income for the entire year. Again I raised my hand. Again the other man doubled the price. I knew that if I were successful now I would have to mortgage everything I owned—even her. It did not stop me. I raised my finger, pointed it at the auctioneer, and called out a figure so unimaginably large it meant almost nothing. He accepted my bid with a nod, and turned to the other man for a response. Again, the price doubled. Again, the bidding was against me—until, without a moment's thought, I doubled again.

"Suddenly, the courtier blinked, shrugged, shook his head. It was over. There was a brief smattering of applause—which quickly died when those present recalled that it was hardly politic to clap the success of a poor merchant against a powerful member of the court. The auction moved on.

"Fikre, seated in the middle of the room, had been staring fixedly at the floor during all this. Now she raised her head and glanced at me. I will never forget that look. It was a look of utter contempt.

"I had risked everything to become her owner—the man who would have the power of life and death over her—and she displayed no more fear or interest in the matter than if I had been a foolish young suitor calling compliments after her in the street."

Somewhere behind us in the silvery darkness a camel gargles tremulously, smacking its lips together with a kind of clapping sound. Its owner speaks to it, a low murmur of Bedouin.

"Yes, I was her owner," Bey mutters, almost to himself. "Think, if you can, what that meant. The responsibility—the decisions I had to make. Think what a dilemma I now faced."

"Why?" I ask.

Bey starts. "Why what?"

"Why was it such a dilemma?"

I get the impression he has been talking as much for his own benefit as mine. He certainly seems quite surprised to find me questioning him about it. "That, my friend, will have to be a story for another occasion," he says curtly, kicking his camel forward to the front of the column.

[THIRTY]

ANOTHER STOP, ANOTHER DAY OF ATTEMPTING TO SLEEP through the heat. When the sun finally begins to ripen like a fruit to a deeper red, we load up the camels. The sand underneath us is no longer quartz-colored but black as tiny beads of jet; we are in volcanic country now, the *samadou*.

Desmond Hammond rides alongside me. He has wrapped a Bedouin shawl around his neck, against the drifting sand: with his leathery, sun-lined face, he has something of the air of an African himself. For a long time he says nothing, then, "Forgive me, Wallis, but you don't seem much like a planter."

"Two months ago I would have taken that as the highest praise."

He grunts. "Come out for your own reasons, have you?"

"Pretty much."

"There won't be many Europeans where you're going. Let alone many Englishmen. If you have problems . . . You could try getting a message to us via the Bedouin. They're surprisingly reliable, if a little slow."

"Thank you," I say, with genuine gratitude.

"We could do some trading, if you want. I hear there's ebony, gold, diamonds, up there. Anything you need in the way of trade goods, just send me word."

"I suppose Bey will be my nearest neighbor. In Harar."

"Bey . . ." Hammond almost says something, then appears to change his mind. He nods at where Fikre walks by Bey's camel, one hand resting on his stirrup. "Do you know the story about that woman of his?"

"Yes. He told me last night, in fact. How he bought her in a sale."

Hammond grunts again. "So he says."

"You don't believe him?"

"I don't believe it's the whole story. There's no one slipperier than an Arab, and an Arab merchant's the slipperiest of all."

"My employer's firm has dealt with him for years. I myself have tasted his coffees. His goods are always of an unusually high quality." As I say it, I realize that this may be the real truth about Fikre and the slave auction—Ibrahim Bey simply cannot resist buying the best, whether it's coffee or a slave.

"Do you know what the Bedouin say about Bey?"

I shake my head.

"They say he's a sentimentalist. They believe he bought the girl for the worst reasons—because he fell in love."

"Is that so terrible?"

"It's mixing business and pleasure. Think about it. So he buys her. What then?"

I have already imagined in vivid detail the grunting, ecstatic defloration that would follow such a purchase. Hammond continues, "It's not like buying a whore. Such a girl, in their culture, is very different from a whore, and a great deal more expensive. But her price depends on two things. One is her virginity—and don't forget, he paid a small fortune for her. The moment he has her, she loses her value. That's the way that particular market operates. She's only worth what he paid as long as she remains untouched, by him or any other man."

"What's the other thing?"

"Her youth," Hammond says bluntly. "Rich Arabs buy their wives at puberty, or not much older. By the time a woman's eighteen, she's lost most of her value. By the time she's twenty-five, she's worth nothing—she'll certainly never be taken into a great harem.

"So now think what it must be like to be Ibrahim Bey. You've paid a fortune for this girl—all your wealth is invested in her. You're her owner: you can do with her whatever you like. And you do dream of those things, of course you do. Just look at her—any man would. But you also know, as a merchant, that the moment you do, she's worthless. Your money, your investment, will have vanished as surely as water poured into the sand.

"Sell her, or fuck her? It's an irrevocable decision. So you wait, paralyzed, trying to decide. But—the terrible irony—even as you wait, she's losing her value, day by day.

"Still you can't decide. A year passes. By now everyone knows about your predicament. You've become a laughingstock—and for a merchant, that's a terrible thing. People won't deal with you; or if they do, they try to cheat you. You can't get credit—how could you, when everyone knows you can't bring yourself to sell your only asset? Your rivals joke behind your back. Meanwhile, the girl herself grows ever more spoiled and unruly. You know that the only way out is to grasp the nettle and sell her. But still something stops you . . . sentiment."

"He mentioned his dilemma," I say. "That must be what he meant."

Hammond nods. "I've been knocking around East Africa for quite a while now. You see quite a bit of the different races: Arab, African, European. The Europeans—we decide what we're going to do, and then we get it done. That's our strength. The Africans have a different mentality—they wait and see what happens: they believe life is outside their control. That's their strength, too, in a way—their resilience. But the Arabs—they're the fascinating ones: you never know where you are with them. Their judgment is always being clouded by something: religion, or vanity, or pride." He pauses. "I suppose what I'm saying is, keep Bey at arm's length, Wallis. When all's said and done, he isn't one of them and he isn't one of us."

WE TRUDGE through the shifting black scree all night. Occasionally a wind gets up, warm and dry. It makes the blackness whisper and lift around the walkers' ankles. Sometimes I could imagine that we are trudging through an endless desert of roasted coffee beans.

The water runs low. The camel drivers are rationed: two mouthfuls each. No one dares to suggest that the white men should be rationed, too, but I try to stick to their allowance.

When it is Mulu's turn to drink he only moistens his lips, then passes his cup to Fikre.

THERE IS NO moon tonight; it is necessary to go slowly. Gradually we become aware of a ripple in the air: a vibration, which eventually resolves itself as a sound, like distant thunder. But it is not thunder. It is drums.

In the absolute darkness it is impossible to be sure where it is coming from. Then, with a shock, I realize it is all around us—in front and to either side, the darkness is speaking to itself, the sound echoing across the empty desert much as thunder rolls around the sky.

We fall silent. No one knows what it means.

"It must be a Galla raiding party," Hammond says at last.

We keep going, but cautiously. Then, out of the darkness, comes the sound of chanting. It is very close, but we can see no one. We draw together and travel four abreast, the camels on the outside. The Bedouin loosen their daggers anxiously. Hammond checks his rifle.

"What are they singing?" I ask.

Hammond shrugs. "It's in Galla."

Fikre says suddenly: "It is a war song. They are singing 'Love without kisses is not love. A spear without blood is not a spear.' "

It is the first time I have heard her speak English. Her speech is heavily accented—like the English a Frenchman would speak—but her grammar is oddly correct. Her voice is low: she has a slightly sibilant pronunciation, as if her tongue were catching on her teeth.

"I'll spook them." Hammond raises his rifle and fires four shots into the air. The camels, alarmed, break into a trot, then slow.

The chanting stops abruptly. Now there is only the squeaking, sighing rustle of the black sand underfoot.

AT DAWN we stumble upon a group of bones. First we see the vultures, circling lazily over something ahead of us on the sand. Then we see the humped silhouette of a camel. A bird is sitting on its back, tearing at it methodically with its beak.

As we get nearer we see another camel, then a third. We are almost on them before we see anything else. The vultures hop a few yards away, waiting for us to leave them to their meal.

Between the camels are the remains of four people. The bodies are decomposed—black flesh, through which white bones jut, picked clean by birds. Other bones lie to one side, their ends smashed, as if they have been pulled away and fought over.

"Hyenas," Hammond says abruptly. "But it wasn't hyenas that killed them."

I force myself to look. It is the eyes, face and stomach the scavengers go for first—the soft tissue. One of the mangled faces, I think, is that of a woman. Everything has been eaten away from her jaw but her teeth.

"Bedouin, presumably," Hector says. "Poor brutes."

"They might just as easily have been Europeans," Hammond says curtly. "All flesh is black when it rots."

"We should keep going," Bey says. "Biokobobo is still an hour away."

We move on. Nobody suggests burying the corpses. The sun is already high in the sky. The eyeless faces of the camels, slumped on the sand, watch us leave.

[THIRTY-ONE]

"Spicy"—this aroma is typical of the odour of sweet spices such as cloves, cinnamon and allspice. Tasters are cautioned not to use this term to describe the aroma of savoury spices such as pepper, oregano, and Indian spices.

—INTERNATIONAL COFFEE ORGANISATION,
The Sensory Evaluation of Coffee

BIOKOBOBO IS THE RESTING PLACE—AN OASIS IN EVERY SENSE: a small town of sand-colored houses nestled amongst palm trees. To one side of the village lie three small lakes of sparkling cobalt blue. On one side, we look down on the desert; the other way lies uphill toward the mountains.

We are to stay here several days, to recuperate and to let the Galla war party move on. There is a small market; we eat dates, nuts, coconuts, flat breads, cheese made from camel milk. Hector and I swim in one of the wadis and unpack a few essentials from the luggage. It is extraordinary how, after days with no comforts at all, a pond of sparkling water and a place to put up a camp-bed have become treasured luxuries.

I try to write. *Dear Emily, I am writing this in the heart of a desert. Our supper is cooking on a spit over a fire—another goat: I am becoming quite a connoisseur of goats. . . .* But I cannot finish, and not because of the heat. I cannot remember her properly. I get the Guide out from the luggage and carefully, in the shade of one of the houses, unstop a fragrance or two. They seem insipid, insubstantial. Or perhaps I have no palate—I have had the rank odor of unwashed camel in my nostrils too long.

We eat the roasted goat sprinkled with *berberi,* a powder made of chili: once you get a taste it becomes quite an addiction. Fikre and Mulu do not eat with us, but sit slightly apart. Sometimes he combs her hair for her with a steel comb, and at these times they chatter, quietly but animatedly, in some language I do not recognize. I see her laugh—a quick, easy laugh; when she does so she deliberately bumps his shoulder with hers, like two schoolgirls. He only smiles shyly.

Once or twice I see her glance in my direction, but her eyes are expressionless: there is no sign, now, of that intensity, that silent despair, I sensed back in Bey's tent. I find myself wondering if I could have misread it. . . . But there was that bean, pushed into my hand.

ON THE SECOND morning in Biokobobo, I find myself awake early. With a sigh I get up, stretch, go outside.

In the half-light I see a slim figure hurrying toward the wadi, wrapped in a blue shawl.

Fikre.

She goes between the palm trees and is lost to sight. Of course: she was unable to bathe yesterday, when the men were in the pool, so she has come now, for privacy. Without hesitation I skirt round to the other side of the wadi, just in time to see her unwinding the shawl.

In the light the iron-colored skin seems polished and glowing. I catch a glimpse of the hair between her legs, like dark cloves, as she steps into the water: the nipples too are almost black on the small, muscular breasts. I gulp down the sight of her greedily, thirstily, as if I am taking draught after draught of coffee. Then she turns away from me. Her back is compact, narrow, as flexible as a snake's as she scoops up water to wash her face. Water droplets, in the early sunshine, retract and glitter like showers of diamonds. She dips under the water; resurfaces, spluttering, and swims directly toward where I am.

I pull back before I am seen. Then something makes me change my mind. I step forward, deliberately, so that she can see me watching her.

Just as deliberately, she too stands up. The pool is waist deep. The water streams off her, polishing the black skin. The jewels drip from her breasts.

I can feel the thudding of my heartbeat in my neck.

For a long moment we look at each other. Then, on the morning air, there is the sound of goat bells.

She turns and wades back to where she has left her robe, her legs moving slowly in the crystal water.

Love without kisses is not love:
A spear without blood is not a spear.

They are still the only words in English I have heard her speak. I hear them again—that strange, French inflection she gives the words—and I know that I am hopelessly obsessed.

[THIRTY-TWO]

I AM DESPERATE TO TALK TO HER ALONE, BUT IN THIS I AM HINdered by Hector, who wants to use our rest stop to go through *Coffee: Its Cultivation and Profit* page by page, and Ibrahim, who wants to discuss poetry.

"Your future father-in-law tells me that you are a writer, Robert. Are you familiar with the works of Hafiz?"

"I'm afraid not."

"Perhaps, though, you have come across the verses of Said Aql?"

"Not to my knowledge."

"The sonnets of Shakespeare?"

"Well, yes, of course." I am slightly irked by the implication that just because I have not read some Arab I am a complete philistine.

"Sometime I will recite to you the verses of Hafiz of Shiraz. He was a Persian, but his thoughts are most profound. *'I have estimated the influence of reason upon love, and found that it is that of a raindrop upon the ocean, which makes a single mark upon the water and disappears. . . .'* "

"That would be very interesting."

"Robber'?" another voice rumbles nearby. "Listen to this. *'The writer has planted coffee on Mount Kilimanjaro, and from six months' experience finds the young plants thrive wonderfully.'* "

"That's very reassuring, Hector."

" *'Like Hafiz, drink wine to the sound of harps, for the heart itself is strung with strands of silk.'* How I envy you your vocation, Robert. To be a poet is truly to be a prince among men."

"Indeed, Ibrahim."

" *'Occasionally, when pressed for time, we have known the soil in areas to be planted just levered up and loosened by crowbars, but this is a slovenly and unsuccessful arrangement. Make your planting pits as large as your money and your patience will allow.'* "

"Thank you, Hector. I will certainly bear it in mind."

It is quite impossible. Between Bey's talk of love and Hector's talk of peggings, planting pits, nursery shade and mulch, I can do nothing except wait for the caravan to move on.

I hoard the image of a graceful black body stepping naked into a desert pool. I haven't had a woman for weeks.

"WOULD YOU LIKE some coffee, Robert?"

I look up. It is Bey, coming to sit near me. I am trying to read a short story in the *Yellow Book*—some drawing-room comedy by Meredith. But in truth I have been unable to concentrate, even before this interruption. "You have some here?"

"Of course. I never travel without a sack of beans." He claps his hands. "Fikre—Mulu. Coffee, if you please."

They come hurrying. In no time they have constructed a fire, unloaded the coffee, found the clay pot and the cups, ground the beans. The fire is lit and coaxed to the right temperature. From somewhere a tiny dish of rosewater is produced.

All this, I think, so that we might have coffee.

"Hector?" Bey calls.

"Aye, if you're making some I'll join ye."

Fikre is sweating by the time she comes to wash our faces with the rosewater—tiny, silvery beads on her black skin. I stare into her eyes. But they are blank, unreadable.

Then I feel it: a coffee bean, slipped into my hand.

I reach down and touch the only part of her which is out of sight of Bey and Hector, sliding my hand around her ankle, squeezing for a moment.

There is still absolutely nothing in her eyes. Nothing at all. But suddenly I notice that she is trembling, as if maintaining this composure is costing a terrible effort.

FROM BIOKOBOBO we cross the flat basin of Dahelimale and begin to climb toward the mountains. Sometimes we pass land under cultivation—long, thin strips, scattered apparently at random in the scrub. Tall Negroes stroll across the landscape, always in the same posture: a walking stick sideways across their shoulders, both arms crooked over it, hands flapping. The women wrap themselves in gauzy robes of scarlet, turquoise or green. Their foreheads are adorned with piastres. The children are naked. Their huts are humps of skins and rugs. You get the sense that nothing is permanent here.

The endless traveling is becoming tedious now. There is no longer the feeling of danger that crossing the desert induced, and the mountains seem as far away at the end of each night's march as at the beginning.

DEAR EMILY.

I stare at the blank page. It is like a salt desert—a brilliant white glare from which the sun bounces, dazzling me. Words seem to have deserted me, along with everything else.

I close my eyes. Her face floats in front of me. She is frowning. "Robert, pay attention," she says. I smile, open my eyes. But there is the page still, blank and unyielding.

Bey calls, "Coffee."

As the smell of roasting beans wafts through the camp, I fold the paper and slip it into an inside pocket.

"Coming."

Is it my imagination, or is Bey watching Fikre and me with more than usual concentration today as she prepares the coffee? The hooded eyes are solemn, unreadable. Fikre washes our faces, then hands us the cups. There is no chance to pass anything.

But in the bottom of the cup, as I finish, I find it. A single bean, nestling amongst the grounds.

I SPEND many hours trying to puzzle out what these gifts mean. Is there some clue in the variety of the bean, perhaps? But when I examine them they are simply Harar mocca, the same beans from which all the coffee is brewed.

Then it strikes me. The beans are not the message: it is the passing of them secretly that is. She is telling me that she is giving me her trust—the only thing she possesses in the world, the only thing she has to give.

FINALLY, on the second night after Biokobobo, Bey's attention is distracted by an interminable discussion with Hector about the pros and cons of indenture. I drop back, gradually working my way to the rear of the caravan to where Fikre is walking. She glances around; then she too falls back. As if by coincidence, we are now amongst the Bedouin, their camels hiding us from the others.

There is always the possibility that we will be overheard. We speak in code, or rather in trivialities and nonsense.

"Your English is very good," I murmur.

"My French is better."

"Je suis Robert. Robert Wallis."

"Oui. Je sais. Je m'appelle Fikre. In Abyssinian my name means 'love.' "

"My name, I'm afraid, doesn't mean anything at all."

"But at least it's your real name," she says with a twisted, angry smile.

"Oh. So Fikre . . ."

". . . was what my master decided I should be called. Like a dog I own nothing, not even my name."

For the first time I feel the force of that—what did Bey call it? Defiance? A better word might be "passion." This tiny girl is like a fierce coil of compressed resentment and fight.

Suddenly she darts forward. Bey is looking back along the caravan with a frown. Within moments there is thirty feet between us.

I see now what the other message contained in those beans was. I had misjudged her trembling, that intensity, as fear. But the dominant emotion in this girl's life is not terror. It is a deep, all-consuming anger. Just as another woman might be infatuated with love, so this girl is infatuated with loathing for the man who bought her. What draws her to me, partly, is the sweet possibility of revenge.

[THIRTY-THREE]

"Sweet"—a nice clean soft coffee free of any harshness.

—L. K. SMITH, Coffee Tasting Terminology

THE DINNER IS A GREAT SUCCESS. AS WELL AS ARTHUR BREWER, Pinker has invited the older Lyle, now an honorary ally in the war against Howell's, and several other free-marketeers. Emily finds herself hoping that she will be placed near the MP. Sure enough, when they go in to eat she finds that she is sitting directly on his left, which both pleases and alarms her. She is not worried because of the responsibility of entertaining him—she has no doubts about her ability to converse intelligently on political matters—but because she knows her father would not have placed her here unless he thought it would suit both of them.

Sure enough, no sooner has the soup been cleared than Brewer turns his attention away from the woman on his other side to talk to her.

"So," he says with a smile, "what did you think of Lyle's attempt to break the sugar monopoly?"

"It was very dramatic," she said. "But tell me—as a Liberal—is there not an inherent contradiction within Free Trade?"

He raises his eyebrows. "In what way?"

"If the price of, say, sugar is being kept artificially high, does that not allow men such as Sir Henry Tate to look after his workers better?"

"It does," he agrees, "although it does not oblige him to."

"Whereas if the market has its way, the workers will always be paid the bare minimum."

"Indeed."

"So Free Trade might actually work against the individual liberty of the worker," she suggests, "by denying him the opportunities which his freedom should bestow. He will not be free of disease, or free of poverty, or free of moral degradation. Nor will he have any opportunity or incentive to rise above his current station."

He looks at her, delighted. "Miss Pinker—Emily—you have summed up in one eloquent nutshell the debate which is currently preoccupying our party."

"Really?" She is absurdly pleased by his compliment.

"Gladstone, of course, thought that if you simply left everything alone—*laissez faire*—it would all work out for the best. But we are starting to discover the drawbacks of that approach. Did you know that half the men who were called up for service against the Boers had to be sent back to the factories? They were simply unfit to fight. What some of us are talking about now is something called constructive liberalism, or positive liberty—government safeguarding the freedoms and well-being of the individual."

"Meaning what, in practical terms?"

"Nothing less than a complete change in the role of the state. We would take on, in fact, many of the responsibilities of enlightened employers. For example, why shouldn't all workers be entitled to some form of medical care? To sick pay? To a pension, even?"

It is all she can do not to gasp. "And this will be your policy?"

"It will."

"How will it be paid for?"

"Well, not by import duties on coffee or tea, obviously—we are committed to reducing those. We are discussing a sort of national insurance scheme, into which every worker would pay according to his or her ability." He smiles. "I should stress that there is a long way to go. Even within the party, Gladstone has left a long shadow. And"—he glances down the table—"some of those whose support we need to enlist are not yet convinced."

"How can I help?"

"Are you serious?"

"I have never been more serious about anything in my life." It is exactly what she has always believed in: some middle way between the paternalism of enlightened Tories and the ferocity of the free market. But radical . . . exciting . . . not some dreary compromise but a completely new way forward. It is enough to make her pulse race.

"Would you be prepared, even, to do constituency work?" he says doubtfully. "In my own ward, Ealing, we are in sore need—"

"Yes! Please! Anything!"

"What's that?" Pinker calls genially from the head of the table. "Brewer, what are you scheming with my daughter?"

Arthur keeps his eyes fixed on her as he answers. "Miss Pinker is volunteering, Samuel. I had no idea she was so interested in politics. Of course, I would ask your permission first. . . ."

Pinker smiles indulgently. "What Emily does in her spare time is up to her. If my daughter can be useful to you, Arthur, by all means rope her in."

[THIRTY-FOUR]

"Rich"—indicates the gases and vapours are present in a highly pronounced intensity.

—LINGLE, The Coffee Cupper's Handbook

NEXT AFTERNOON, AS WE TRY TO DOZE, THERE IS A TERRIBLE commotion. I wake up, groggily, to the sound of gunfire. One of the Bedouin is being held down by three others. He is pleading, the words pouring from his mouth in an unending stream. He is made to stand up, pushed to the ground again, kicked savagely, babbling protests all the while. It seems he was caught making off with some of Bey's trade goods.

An impromptu court is convened—a circle of squatting Bedouin, a chair for Bey in the center, chairs to one side for Hector and me. Sensing that something unpleasant is about to happen, I try to decline mine, but the Bedouin are unhappy.

"You must watch, Robert," Bey says, his voice flat. "As far as they are concerned, they have done us a great favor by bringing him to justice."

Reluctantly, I sit. The man is brought into the circle and forced to his knees in front of Bey. There is a brief exchange: a few sentences, no more. A sword is produced. It is offered to the merchant.

Two Bedouin lift the accused man to his feet. He is stretched out, a man grasping each arm. His stream of protestations rises to a shriek. Bey walks toward him. The blade swings. One of the men holding the prisoner falls back; a moment later, the prisoner falls the other way.

The man who was holding the prisoner's left hand is still holding it. The prisoner, meanwhile, is staring in shock at a gushing stump. The blood heaves out in ghastly, pumping gouts.

Casually, without hurry, one of the camel drivers fastens a tourniquet around the bloody wrist and helps the prisoner away. The severed hand is tossed to the ground in front of Bey, who ignores it. Dropping the sword, he strides out of the circle. The Bedouin, who have so far maintained a watchful silence, turn to each other and chatter politely, for all the world as if they are spectators at a private *soirée.*

I SEE BEY later by the luggage, looking somber. I do not mean to disturb him but he walks over.

"I suppose you think that sort of thing bad form," he says curtly.

"I make no judgment."

"If I had not carried out that sentence—which is the sentence according to their law—they would have killed him. But they would also have looked on me—on you, on all of us *ferengi*—as weak, impotent men. And out here, that could be dangerous."

"I understand."

"Do you?" He scans my face as if he seeks there some other reaction, different from my words. Whatever he sees there seems to satisfy him, because he grunts and says, "If people drinking their coffee in London only knew what it *really* cost, eh, Robert?"

NOW WE ARE climbing into the mountains. Castles, quite ruined, perch on inaccessible rocks, their battlements patrolled by eagles and kites. We see cattle, small and lean, their heads topped with tall horns in the shape of lyres. Even the villages have changed. Instead of the humped tents of the nomads, there are settlements of wood and straw, the people round-faced, flat-nosed, like Aborigines. It is a strange mixture of the medieval and the prehistoric: if a crusading knight on his charger were to turn the next corner I would scarcely be surprised.

WE MAKE CAMP by a highland lake filled with pelicans and buy fish from a villager. The dazzling, glittering scales are like something beaten out of metal. Fires are lit: the fish are speared on twigs and roasted. The Bedouin murmur to each other as they eat, then one by one they go to sleep.

The ground is hard and the night cold. I get up and move closer to the fire.

A sudden flare illuminates a face opposite me. She is staring into the embers. Bright, fierce eyes reflect the flames, as does the polished skin. Beneath the headcloth, a face of elfin beauty. Any girl in London would kill for those cheekbones.

"I can think about nothing but you," I whisper.

For a moment I think she can't have understood. Then she says sharply in her lilting accent, "Don't say that. It's what *he* says."

"Perhaps it's true."

She makes a scornful noise. "Did he tell you how he got me?"

"Yes."

"He likes that story. I don't suppose it occurred to him I would rather have been bought by the other man."

"Would you?"

She shrugs. "Before the sale we had to go and collect our things. I knew where there was a glass tile with a crack in it. I worked at it until the broken glass came away in my hand. Then I wrapped it in my clothes. When my new owner—whoever he was—tried to take what he had paid for, I planned to use it to cut first his throat, and then my own."

Her eyes turn back to the dying flames. "Night after night I waited to die. But Bey did not come. That could only mean he was going to sell me. But he did not do that either. I was puzzled . . . and then I began to see. He wanted to own me, but he also wanted to preserve me, like a precious object which he alone may take out of its box, to gloat over and then put back."

She turns to look at me, raising her chin. In the half-light I can see her teeth, very white, behind her open lips.

I lean toward her. A moment's hesitation, and then my mouth touches hers. She takes my head in her hands, says breathlessly, "They can buy me and sell me. But my heart is my own."

We kiss again, more deeply. She looks around, at the sleeping shapes. "We must be careful," she warns. "People have died for less." She takes our blankets and pulls them over our heads, covering us.

There, in the darkness—in the cave of the blankets, like a child's game—there is the smell of her breath: myrrh, cinnamon, violets, musk . . . and the taste of her skin, her tongue, the sweet warmth of a kiss, the sounds she makes, her gasps.

And the words she whispers, as she nuzzles my lips: *"I have been waiting all my life for you."*

[THIRTY-FIVE]

"Leather"—this is the powerful, animal smell of well-tanned hides.

—LENOIR, Le Nez du Café

SO NOW EMILY ADDS LIBERAL POLITICAL WORK TO HER OTHER interests. Three afternoons a week she takes the train from Waterloo to Ealing to help in Arthur's constituency office. Amongst the volunteers are several other suffragists. It is interesting work—more than interesting: it is thrilling; this sense of comradeship and endeavor, all these different people with their differing backgrounds and motivations joining forces in the service of an ideal.

For all ideals are linked. That is what Emily sees now—that the world is divided into those who want to exploit it for their own ends and those who want to change it for the benefit of all. If you are on the side of change, you make common cause with other idealists. Whether your particular interest is suffrage, prison reform, the Poor Law, or pensions, you are all on the same side, working together for power.

And Arthur—he is the leader of their little group, but he wears his leadership lightly, always remembering to thank the volunteers for their efforts on his behalf. Sometimes he takes small groups of helpers to tea at the House of Commons: when he invites Emily to join one of these groups, she is all the more pleased because she knows he is not singling her out for attention. He shows her up to the Ladies' Gallery, from where women are allowed to watch the House at work, hidden from view behind a kind of iron grille. The debate is about the war—the Liberals are pressing the government to guarantee the jobs of those who have been sent abroad to fight. Emily is amazed by the boisterous atmosphere: the House reminds her of nothing so much as the sugar pit at the Exchange. But the aggression, the fighting, is even more ritualistic here. She sees men howling insults at each other yet, five minutes later, casually throwing their arms across each other's shoulders as they leave the chamber.

Arthur asks a question. He makes himself heard with dogged courtesy, and seems to win a small point of order. He sits down to a grave chorus of "Hear hear"; afterwards, when she meets him in the lobby, he is flushed with triumph. "Did you see how I harried the Admiralty?" he cries. "They will not be happy about that." She congratulates him. A group of half a dozen men hurry past. One of them pauses. "Good work, Brewer," he says jovially, punching him on the arm.

"Thank you, sir," Arthur says proudly. The man's eyes—his charming, twinkling eyes—turn to Emily.

"And who is this?" he says.

"Miss Emily Pinker, Sir Henry Campbell-Bannerman. A great reformer," he adds for her benefit.

"And what do you think of our Parliament, Miss Pinker?"

"It is wonderful," she answers truthfully. "There seem to be so many people here who are trying to get things done—to move forward."

"Indeed, although there are almost as many trying to do exactly the reverse," Sir Henry says, shaking his head comically. The other men around them laugh easily. For a moment she is suffused with the warm glow of inclusion in this clever, energetic, able comradeship.

"Miss Pinker has a special interest in female suffrage," Brewer says.

"Ah! And as you may have noticed," Sir Henry says, indicating the young men around him, "all of us here at present are male. We call it the mother of parliaments, but exclude those who might be mothers from its chambers. Perhaps, Miss Pinker, we will see a day when you not only have the Vote, but might even be voted for."

"Do you really think so?"

He smiles, as if to ask how she can doubt it. Then with a nod he has gone, already deep in conversation with an aide. The retinue follows in his wake. She can feel the force of his optimism still lighting her up like a flame.

After Arthur has said goodbye to her, escorting her to the Underground station at Westminster Bridge to catch a train back to Limehouse, she feels quite bereft, as if she is being banished from the Garden of Eden by a stern but kindly angel.

[THIRTY-SIX]

ANOTHER DAY'S TRAVEL. BUT THE LANDSCAPE AROUND US HAS changed. Now the hillsides are terraced for agriculture. From the high passes, looking down, it is as if someone has run a giant comb over the earth.

Sometimes I glimpse a stand or two of a bush with dark, waxy leaves. Hector nudges me and grunts with satisfaction. "See that? Coffee."

Intrigued, I ride my mount alongside one of these bushes to examine it more closely. The whole plant is dotted with tiny white blossoms, the petals sweet-smelling and fragrant when I crush them between my fingers; they are dense, almost like cactus, plump with perfumed sap. The smell is of coffee, but there is also a faint aroma of honeysuckle and jasmine that rises above even the reek of my sweat-dirtied travel clothes.

Underneath each branch hang pendulous yellow cherries, fat and full of pulp. I pull one off and bite it experimentally. But the flesh is bitter, astringent as the inside of a lemon.

The scent, I discover, is strongest in the evening. As night falls, tendrils of that distinctive coffee-bush aroma hang in the darkness, brushing my palate. I break them as I pass, spider's webs of scent that float, gossamer-like, drifting slowly from place to place on the still air.

AT EACH HALT Fikre makes us coffee, fragrant and strong. When she wipes the cloth over my face I feel the subtle pressure of her fingers. She strokes me smoothly, slowly, lavishing precious moments on my lips, my eyelids, the side of my nose. I can hardly breathe. These caresses feel as if they last forever, but I suppose they can actually last no longer than she spends doing the same to Hector or Bey.

Before she leaves me, there is always a coffee bean, pushed into my hand. Or, if she cannot manage that, somewhere else—my collar, between the buttons of my shirt. I find them later as I ride: small, light touches somewhere on my body, making their presence known, like the piece of grit at the heart of a pearl. And sometimes there is a glance, a brilliant smile for my benefit alone, quickly averted; a flash of white teeth and white eyes in the depths of her headscarf.

THE DAYS are hot, stifling, windless. My eyelids droop as if under the effect of some drug. The rhythm of the camels enters my head, becomes a slow, incessant rhythm of sex.

Obscene lascivious reveries dance around my dazed head like gnats. I could shoo them away but I know that they will return within moments.

ANOTHER STOP. Only once do I manage to talk to Fikre. As we are unloading the animals, we find ourselves hidden from the others by the camels.

"In Harar there is a warehouse Bey is trying to sublet," she says urgently. "It used to belong to a French coffee merchant. Say that you will take it."

"Very well."

The camels wheel about, and before anyone can see us she is gone.

I AM TOWARD the back of the column, so I do not see at first why the caravan has halted. I join the others, who have drawn up on a ridge.

Below us, nestled in the bowl of a fertile alpine plain, is an immense lake. Beyond the lake is a town. Even at this distance we can see the walls and fortifications that surround it; the long, ragged flags fluttering from its rooftops; the brown clay houses and the white onion-shaped minarets—and the scavenging birds who wheel over it endlessly, like flies circling a rotten fruit.

"Harar," Bey says unnecessarily. "We have arrived."

[THIRTY-SEVEN]

"Clove"—this delicious complex smell is reminiscent of cloves, sweet-william, the medicine cabinet, vanilla and smoked products. It is prized and appreciated for its delicate, spicy complexity that gives depth to coffee.

—LENOIR, Le Nez du Café

YOU SMELL IT AS SOON AS YOU ENTER THE WOODEN GATE: THE pungent, earthy smell of roasting beans, wafting from a dozen windows. Coffee sellers wander the streets, silver flagons under their arms. In the bazaar, stalls are piled high with jute sacks, their contents spilling from them like polished beads. This is a city of coffee.

Ibrahim takes me round the French merchant's storehouse, a fine double-story building overlooking the market. It is empty, apart from a few personal effects belonging to its former occupant. There is a ledger written in French, some letters, a tin chest containing some books, a camp-bed. The whole place gives the impression of having been abandoned in a hurry. According to Bey, it was an unfortunate case. The merchant arrived in Africa as a young man, eager to make his fortune in the coffee business, but got mixed up in some dubious schemes. Eventually he lost the use of a leg. He went back to Marseille, but his sister later wrote to say he had died. Bey is only too pleased when I say I will take on the lease.

Meanwhile, Hector engages a headman, Jimo, with experience of coffee farming. My companion refuses to stay in Harar a moment longer than is absolutely necessary.

"We'll leave tomorrow. As soon as we've bought our seed crop."

"A few days won't make any difference, surely."

"That's where you're wrong. You're a farmer now, Robert; you have to start working to the seasons. The rains—"

"Oh, the rains. I keep forgetting the rains."

He mutters an expletive under his breath as he turns away.

IN THE MARKET I find not only coffee but saffron, indigo, civet musk and ivory, along with a dozen fruits I have never seen before. I also find Fikre, buying food.

She is wearing a dark red robe, the top looped over her hair. She turns her head, and my pulse quickens at the sight of that perfect profile.

"You must not be seen with me," she murmurs, picking up a mango and pressing it with her slim, dark fingers, as if its ripeness is all she is interested in.

"I've taken the French merchant's house," I mutter. "Can you meet me there?"

She is giving the seller some coins. "I'll try to come at dusk."

Then she is gone—a dark red robe slipping into the shadows.

AT DUSK I am waiting.

I wander round. There are dozens of small wasps' nests in the corners of the rooms, and a parrot is nesting under one of the ceilings, the floor below spattered with its guano. I pass the time by poking among the French merchant's papers.

> Item: 1 bundle of colored wools. The blue merino is good stuff, as is the red flannel, and at the price I am offering it you have nothing to fear, except for worms if it is kept too long, but at present it is in good condition. . . .

A sound. I look up. She is there, hurrying toward me, her feet bare on the wooden floor. Her eyes, under the red hood, are bright. She stops. For a moment we stare at each other—if we are to step back from the brink, it must be now. Then I open my arms, and with a gasp she runs to me. Her skin tastes of coffee: she has been working amongst Bey's sacks all day, and her lips and neck still carry the smoky, toasted flavor of roasting beans. And something more, a *mélange* of spices, scents: cardamom, rosewater, myrrh.

Eventually she pulls away. "I didn't realize it would be like this," she whispers, placing a hand on my cheek.

"Like what?"

"That I would want you so much. Like hunger."

I feel her fingers slipping under my shirt, cool on my bare skin, as we kiss again.

"I can't stay," she says. "I only have a few minutes, but I had to see you."

She is squirming against me. I push back against her, on fire. "We have to wait," she says, almost to herself.

"Wait for what?" I gasp.

Every sentence takes an age, the words slipped in between kisses. "For him to go away. Back to the coast with his coffee."

"Then what?"

"Don't you see? I'm going to give myself to you. It's the only way."

HER EXPRESSION is triumphant. She has it all worked out. She is going to sleep with me—to shatter her precious virginity. Bey's investment will have been wiped out as surely as if he had taken his wealth and scattered it in the desert. This will be her grand revenge on the man who bought her.

"When he finds out, he'll be furious."

"Yes," she says. "He will kill me. But he's killing me anyway, keeping me like this. And if we can have one night . . ." She looks into my eyes. "It will be worth it. At least I will die knowing what love is."

I am sick with apprehension and lust. "There must be another way. Less dangerous—"

She shakes her head. "Don't worry, he will never know it was you. Even if they torture me before I die."

"You don't have to die," I say urgently. "Listen to me, Fikre. No one has to die."

"It doesn't matter," she whispers. "A night of love, and then death. It's enough."

"No. Fikre, I promise I will think of something—"

"Kiss me," she says. I do. "I am ready for what he will do to me. We have to wait until he goes away. Just until then."

With a groan I release her. She steps away from me, hesitates, looks back at me one last time. Then all that is left of her is that scent—coffee and rosewater and spice.

[THIRTY-EIGHT]

Yamara
August

My dear Hunt,

We have now left the last vestiges of civilization behind and are trekking deep into the forest in search of the land we are to farm. It is like traveling into the Stone Age—there are no buildings, except thatch huts; no tracks, except those made by animals, and so dense is the canopy overhead that we can no more see the sunlight than can earthworms in a flowerbed. Occasionally we come across clearings containing enormous wooden phalluses the height of a man, painted with gaudy designs. We assume they are some kind of ju-ju *or fetish.*

We encounter curious natives—each valley seems to play host to a different tribe. The bucks sport ivory bangles and copper earrings, and the girls dye their hair scarlet or daub their faces with whitewash. Everyone—men, women and children—smokes huge stogies made from rolled-up tobacco leaves, and no one does much in the way of work. Yesterday I traded a fishhook for a necklace of lion's teeth. The lion was a meat-eater, to judge from the smell, and not one in possession of a toothbrush. But I fancy it will cause quite a sensation when I am next in the Café Royal.

Something else has happened to me—something so strange that I hesitate to write it down, in case you think me perfectly mad. But I need to confide in someone, and it certainly can't be Hector. Here goes, my friend: I seem to have fallen in love. Yes: unlikely as it sounds, here in the middle of the wilderness I have begun a grand passion. The object of my affection is a girl called Fikre—an African—I know, even more unlikely; and a servant as well, of a sort. But she is highly educated and has had the most extraordinary life. It is, as you may have guessed, a rather delicate situation—the lady in question is already attached to someone else, someone for whom she has no affection whatsoever. Whatever happens, I can't see how I could ever marry her, and it would be awkward to break off my engagement to Emily while I am the manager of her father's plantation, so it is ticklish on every score. All I know is that I never felt like this about anyone before—and I think she feels the same way about me. I am riding along in a sort of delicious reverie, thinking about our last encounter with a dazed smile on my face. Hector has accused me of chewing khat, *which is the local narcotic! But far from being stupefied, I feel more alive than I have for months.*

I have no idea when I shall be able to post this: perhaps I will be able to give it to someone to take to the coast. Sometimes, looking down through gaps in the forest at the endless valleys filled with green, I have the sense of stepping across a threshold, as if I am about to push through a great hedge and vanish utterly from view.

Yours,

Robert

PART III
The Law of the Jungle

New districts have been opened up, supplying fresh fields for enterprise and capital, and changing by their prosperity the face of regions which, though once clothed in dense jungle, and now patched with the luxuriant green gardens characteristic of the industry, and dotted with the white bungalows of European superintendents. To gaze over the tract thus changing hands—from Nature's to Men's—is an experience not easily forgotten; the fair and fruitful plantations already won from primeval barbarism lying along the hollows of, it may be, a wild upland valley, surrounded on every side by the swelling masses of forest only awaiting their turn to come under the woodman's axe.

—LESTER ARNOLD, Coffee: Its Cultivation and Profit, 1886.

Every now and then a man's mind is stretched by a new idea or sensation, and never shrinks back to its former dimensions.

—OLIVER WENDELL HOLMES,
The Autocrat of the Breakfast Table

[THIRTY-NINE]

"Coffee blossom"—this is the sweet perfume of the lovely white flowers of the coffee tree that used to be called Arabian jasmine in the seventeenth century because the two plants are so similar. The essential oil of Jasminium grandiflorum, *fruitier and more highly perfumed than that of Sambac jasmine, is what gives us this cheerful note in coffee.*

—LENOIR, Le Nez du Café

DAWN ROSE OVER THE JUNGLE, LIGHT AND SOUND SWEEPING through the canopy together, the first glimmers of day greeted as always by a cacophony of calls, screeches, roars and rattles that slowly subsided into the lethargic mutterings of morning. Up on the hill, the white men snored in their camp-beds. In the native village the women put wood on the communal fire, pounded coffee, and went to the ravine to shit before waking their husbands. The dawn was chilly: breakfast was taken squatting around the fire, wrapped in brightly colored blankets.

There was only one topic of conversation: the visitors. There had been white men before, passing through the valley with their long caravans of animals and provisions; but these were different: they had built a house. True, it was a very bad house, too close to the stream, so that it would be infested with ants when the rains came, and too close to the ravine, so that their animals would sooner or later end up breaking their legs; but a house nevertheless. What did they want? No one knew.

There was one amongst them who was particularly uneasy. Kiku, the medicine woman, sat on her own, deep in thought. It was true that the white men did not seem warlike, but her fear was that their arrival might herald something even more worrying than war. She did not know what this thing might be, or even where her foreboding came from, so perhaps it came from the *ayyanaa,* the spirits of the forest, who sometimes told her things that could not otherwise be known. And so she sat apart, trying to listen to the forest, as another person might tune out the voices around them in order to listen to whispers from another room.

She realized now what the forest was afraid of: change. This surprised her, because although it was in the nature of men to fear change, change did not affect the forest. Like water, it could be stirred up: like water, it could be moved around, but like water it would always return, eventually, to its own level, and all the things that a man had done to it in his lifetime would, sooner or later, be erased.

"I tell you what it is," a young man called Bayanna said. "They have come to kill the leopard."

There was a general nodding. Of course—the leopard. For some months now there had been sightings of a leopard in the valley, causing those with young children great anxiety. If the white men had come to hunt it, everyone would benefit—well, perhaps not the leopard, but everyone else: the white man who killed it would be able to make a tunic of the leopard's skin, while the villagers would be safer. The only person in their own village who had ever killed a leopard was Tahomen, their headman, and that was twenty years ago, when he was a young man. Although he still wore the animal's skin on occasion, it had been eaten over the years by grubs and other insects, and these days it was looking somewhat the worse for wear.

Because they wanted the leopard to be the reason the white men had come, there was general hope it was. Hope quickly turned to agreement, and agreement to certainty, so that soon everything was settled except who would show the strangers where the best places to hunt for a leopard were.

The forest told Kiku that the white men were not interested in leopards, but it did not tell her what they were interested in. Perhaps she had not heard the forest correctly, or perhaps the forest did not know; perhaps the white men's forest was so far away that understanding was taking time to travel, as a gust of wind took time to pass from one side of the valley to another. So for the time being she kept her own counsel.

JUST THEN they heard the sound of crashing and clanking, followed by an irregular thumping on the path as two people wearing boots, and a third who was not wearing boots but who was equally unused to walking through the forest, approached the village. The villagers were astonished, and in some cases alarmed. Some of the women seized their children and hurried into their huts for safety; others took their children and hurried outside, the better to see what was going on. The crashing had by now been augmented by the sound of voices, booming and guttural, speaking words the villagers could not understand.

"It be here somewhere, sah," one voice was saying.

"I expect they'll have fled intae the trees, in any case," another said confidently. "Your native mind, Wallis, does not function like your working man's back home. It has been proven that their blood is considerably thinner, and their methods consequently more lethargic. Och, what's that in there?"

"It looks to me as if we have found their habitation, Hector."

The villagers watched, nonplussed, as three men strode into the clearing. Two were immensely tall, white-skinned, with outlandish clothes: one of these was rendered even more alarming by his bushy red beard, while the other was wearing a suit of green alpaca wool and a white pith helmet. The third man, a dark-skinned Adari, wore a robe of patterned cloth and was carrying a long stick, and he looked about him with a haughty demeanor.

"Berrah well," he said, gazing contemptuously at the villagers. "Who be headman this savage place?"

"Just a minute, Jimo," the red-haired man said. He strode forward. "Nae listen, all of ye," he boomed. "We have come here," he pointed at the ground, "to grow coffee." He pointed at the coffee which one of the surprised villagers was drinking from a wooden cup. "If you work for us, and work hard, you will be well paid."

There was a short silence. Bayanna said, "I think he wants coffee before he goes to shoot the leopard." The villagers nodded, relieved. Of course! Bayanna said helpfully to the visitors, "I will lead you to the beast." Aware that they did not understand what he was saying, he pointed to Tahomen's leopard tunic and mimed throwing a spear. "Dish-dash?" he said hopefully.

"Dish-dash, is it?" Hector chuckled. "Excellent—I thought we would be able to strike a deal with these fellows. Tell them: tomorrow we chop forest." He began miming the actions of a man chopping a tree, or possibly beating a mortally wounded leopard to death with a club.

Another young man was by now disputing Bayanna's right to lead the white men to the leopard. "Me! Me! I take you to the leopard!" he interrupted, jumping to his feet. He pointed at himself, then began enthusiastically miming the clubbing of leopards.

"Capital," the red-haired man boomed. "It appears we have our first woodsman. And you, sir? Yes? And you?"

Other young men were now pushing themselves forward, eager

to be among the sizeable group who would be handsomely rewarded simply for leading the white men to the leopard. "You see, Wallis?" the red-haired man said, turning to his companion. "Observe the action of a simple contract upon the savage mind! Observe the universal language of Commerce, breaking down the barriers between species in an instant! It's a braw sight, is it not?"

"Absolutely," the other white man said doubtfully. "Er—should we explain to them that we have bought this land? That we are now, so to speak, their landlords?"

"I doubt whether that'll be a concept their primitive minds can grasp." Hector pointed to the woods with both hands. "Forest—all of it—chop!" he shouted.

The hunting party understood that their advice was being sought on whether to seek the leopard in that direction, to the east. Many agreed, encouraging Hector with nods and smiles. Others, mindful that the leopard was actually to be found to the west, were of the opinion that it made more sense to go that way. After all, they suggested to the first group, the white man would hardly be happy if he was taken many miles on a fruitless journey.

Those of the eastern faction retorted that, on the contrary, it would be deeply impolite to tell the white man he was an ignorant idiot on their first meeting: the correct thing was to agree with him, even if he was plainly wrong. A vigorous debate ensued, during which the eastern party happened upon an unanswerable argument: if the white men were taken to the west, and actually found the leopard, they would soon be gone, whereas if they were taken to the east as they had requested, they would need to go on subsequent expeditions to the west, thus making further payments of *dish-dash* a much more likely prospect.

Jimo was moving among the young men, dispensing cards. Each card, he explained, was divided into thirty days. Each day the men chopped trees, they would have their card marked, and when they had accumulated a full month's worth of marks they would be paid. The young men of the hunting party understood him perfectly—these were the tickets that proved you had been chosen as a champion leopard tracker. Some of those who had been chosen broke into a dance, in which they leapt up and down energetically and mimed the leopard's death.

"Aha!" the red-haired man cried. "We have been here only a few moments, but see how we have galvanized them! We shall have this glen cleared in no time!"

"It does seem as if we might," the other man said.

Kiku was watching these preparations with an increasing sense of anxiety. It looked to her as if the white men were actually talking about chopping down trees, rather than killing leopards. It was not that which bothered her—the villagers chopped down trees themselves, if they needed green wood for building huts. No: what was bothering Kiku was the fact that when she looked at the two white men, she could see quite clearly that they were both, in their different ways, enchanted. And if she was not mistaken, at least one of the enchantments was a powerful charm of love.

THAT NIGHT the young men of the village held a dance, to bring good luck to the hunting of the leopard. The more noise they made, the more likely it was that the *ayyanaa* would hear them and bless their enterprise, so they deliberately made as much as possible, hollering and whooping, helped by plenty of fermented beer.

"Christ, what a din," Hector, half a mile away in his camp-bed, grumbled. "Don't they realize they'll be working tomorrow?"

"What do we do if they don't turn up?"

"They'll turn up. You saw how keen they were for *dish-dash*."

"Yes." In his own camp-bed, Robert was silent for a moment. "Odd, isn't it, that they've never tried to cultivate this coffee themselves?"

"Odd? Not really. Why should they? They've never had anyone like us to show them how."

"But nothing they do is remotely like farming, is it?" he persisted. "Or at least, not the sort of farming we do. They don't seem to have any desire to . . . tame the jungle. I'm just wondering why not. Whether perhaps they've tried it and found it hasn't worked. You know—almost as if they might know something we don't."

Hector snorted. "You're looking at it the wrong way round as usual, Wallis. It's us that knows something they dinnae." He reached out to the pressure-lamp, which burned dimly on the packing-case table between them. "Time to turn in."

The hiss of the lamp died; darkness filled the room. The drums and shouts from the native village seemed louder than ever.

"Good-night, Hector."

"Gu'night."

HE DREAMT of Fikre: of her slender black body crouching above him, her clear pale eyes holding his as nameless pleasures flowed back and forth between their loins. "Soon," she whispered in that lilting accent. "Very soon. When Bey leaves Harar." He half woke. In the darkness, an animal laughed at him. Down in the village, the endless throb of the drums was like a new heartbeat, echoing the pulse in his groin.

THE VILLAGERS were getting drunk, and their thoughts too were turning to sex. The young men enthusiastically danced the dance of leopard-killing, but really they were dancing to impress the young women, who in turn were dancing the great cheer that women made when the body of a leopard was brought back to the village, which was really a dance of encouragement to the men.

Kiku sat to one side, watching. Dancing was best left to the younger girls, in her opinion—once your breasts started to flap up and down rather than jiggle invitingly, leaping into the air was no longer quite so attractive. In any case, she already knew who would be leaving his spear outside her hut that night. Bayanna had made a great show earlier of bringing her food, reminding everyone who was watching that they were sleeping together. She did not mind, partly because he was an energetic lover, if a little pleased with himself, but also because she had her own reasons for sleeping with Bayanna.

At that point one of the reasons came over and sat down next to her.

"You do not dance," Tahomen said.

"I'm too old to dance," she answered casually. Which, from her tone, one might have thought a remark of no more consequence than Tahomen's. In fact, it was pushing the conversation neatly right to the nub of their disagreement.

Tahomen grunted. "Of course you're not. Who told you that? It's ridiculous."

You *told me that,* she wanted to say. *Not with words, but when you took Alaya as your second wife.* She looked across the fire to where the girl danced with the rest of the younger women. Curse her—her breasts were like little half-formed gourds, and when she jumped they scarcely moved.

"Alaya dances well," she said.

"Yes," Tahomen agreed gloomily. He too knew exactly what was behind his problem with Kiku. *Why are you being so unreasonable?* he wanted to say. *Of course I have taken another wife. How could I not? First, because I am the headman—whoever heard of a headman with only one wife? Second, because I have to have children, and you have not provided me with any.* But he did not say any of these things, because he knew that Kiku already knew them. Instead he said mildly, "Bayanna's spear has been spending a lot of time outside your hut."

Kiku scratched a zigzag in the dust. "It is a very busy spear."

"And he is a good spearman." Tahomen left the briefest of pauses. "He says."

Kiku did not want Tahomen to think that he could undo the hurt he had done her with a few clever jokes at her lover's expense, so she hid her smile by looking down at the pattern she was still scratching.

"And thus you have been too busy to come to my hut," Tahomen observed.

"As you have been too busy to come to mine."

"Even if I wanted to visit you, Bayanna's spear has been there."

"But you have not been to visit me, so it makes no difference."

"How do you know I have not?"

Because I was listening for you, she wanted to say. "Because you have been too busy with Alaya, of course."

" 'A new wife is like a coffee bush: both must be picked quickly,' " he quoted.

"Exactly." And then, because she could not help it, she quoted another proverb back at him. " 'A man has many wives, but a wife has many lovers.' "

He nodded. Like many of their proverbs, the one Kiku had just spoken expressed the importance above all of *saafu*—balance and reciprocity. "But you know, that proverb does start by saying 'a man has many wives.' "

Aware that she had just blundered into a trap, Kiku bridled. "Of course. No one is saying that you should not have wives. Have three. Have four! Have all the wives you like!"

Tahomen sighed. "Just because I have taken Alaya as my wife, it does not mean I think any the less of you. You are still the senior wife."

"What do you mean, 'still'? I was never the senior wife before. I was the *only* wife."

"I meant, you will always have respect."

Respect. *What good is respect,* Kiku thought, *when what you want is breasts, babies, and to be adored? What good is seniority, if it means you are too old to be loved?*

Tahomen sighed again. "Perhaps when Bayanna takes his spear somewhere else, then."

They sat in silence for a time. Tahomen said, "This leopard."

"Yes?"

"Do you really think the white men have come all the way here just to help us kill it?"

She shrugged noncommittally.

"It bothers me, too," he said. He spat into the fire. "In any case, I'm glad they don't want the leopard. I'm rather hoping to take care of that myself."

"You!"

"Yes. Why not?"

"People in your age-clan should leave the hunting to the younger men."

"You think I'm too old?" Tahomen said in mock astonishment. "Is that what people say, that I'm too old to kill another leopard?"

She sighed. Tahomen had a way of turning whatever you said back on yourself. *Look,* he was saying, *I'm getting older, too. Do you see me moping about it?* And—though she would never have voiced the thought out loud—in the unspoken row they were having with each other, she was forced to shout, *No! But it's different for you! You can just take another wife!*

On the outside, of course, she just grunted.

Tahomen spat expertly into the fire again. "There's more than one way to catch a leopard, in any case," he said thoughtfully.

"Yes. And in my experience, all of them end in the people trying them getting killed."

"Well, we shall see."

[FORTY]

WELL BEFORE DAYBREAK THE COOK, KUMA, WOKE THE TWO white men with strong black coffee. Outside, Jimo waited with a line of stupefied, hungover villagers. Many had daubed themselves with magical patterns for the occasion; some had even painted their faces to represent the whiskers and spots of the animal they were about to hunt. Some were carrying axes, some clubs, some spears.

"Like children," Hector said with a sigh. "Spears to chop trees! Imagine! Jimo, get some more axes out of the store."

When all the men were properly equipped, the chopping party filed into the jungle, Hector leading them uphill until he reached the highest point. He pointed at the trees. "Here! Cut these!"

The villagers looked bemused. "Bwana say chop trees!" Jimo shouted. "One time! One time!" *Now.*

The villagers looked at each other. If they stopped to cut these trees down, there would certainly be no hope of finding the leopard today.

"Come on, boy," Jimo said, roughly pushing one of the younger men toward a tree. Reluctantly, the man hoisted his axe and began to chop.

"Good! Next boy! Chop!" Jimo shouted, leading the next man to the adjacent tree. Soon he had a line of nonplussed villagers all hard at work chopping trees.

When the trees were almost chopped through, Hector had Jimo move the men on to the next row down. Again they chopped until the trunks were almost severed, and again they stopped before the trees actually fell. The villagers worked sullenly now—they had realized there was to be no leopard hunt after all, but there was still the promise of *dish-dash*. They grunted questions to each other as they chopped—what could all this wood be for? The strangers must be building a vast hut, or perhaps a series of huts. But why were they not finishing the trees off, and instead leaving them half severed like this? It must be the white man's way, but why?

They carried on like this until they moved forward another row. Now one of the trees in the way was a *quiltu,* a sycamore. Automatically the villagers parted, moving to left and right so that it would not be chopped.

"Over there!" Hector called. "They missed one."

Jimo took one of the men by the shoulder and led him back to the sycamore tree. "Chop!" he commanded.

The man looked first startled, then puzzled, then alarmed. The other villagers halted their own work to explain the problem to the visitors. This, they explained, was a tree sacred to women, from which the women's *siqquee* or ritual sticks were made.

"Make them stop jabbering," Hector said to Jimo, who drove the protesting villagers back to their own trees. "Robert! Time to show them that we don't ask them to do anything we're not prepared to do ourselves." He pointed to the base of the tree. "You take that side."

The villagers watched in appalled silence as the white men's axes spat wood. It was hard work, and both men were sweating profusely by the time the job was done—or rather, almost done: once again, a narrow cone was left at the heart of the tree.

It was early afternoon when Hector finally called a halt. By now some thirty or forty trees had been half chopped. They all trudged back up the hill, where Hector had the men finish off the very first tree they had worked on. With a great crash it fell—but its way was impeded by the tree below, which somehow bore its weight. That tree too was felled, and that too leaned against its neighbor on the downhill side. The combined weight of both trees was now being supported only by the forest canopy that stretched down the hill.

The third tree was a giant, tall and top-heavy. As it came crashing down, the trunk splintered: men leapt away as its vast bulk kicked into the air. Its branches slammed into the next tree down. With a sudden crack, that tree gave under its weight—and then the next did the same, and the next, the hillside turning into a great surging tidal wave of tumbling trunks and churning branches. The avalanche swept everything before it, even trees that had not been touched by the axes, toppling like dominoes all the way down the slope. It was as if some all-powerful giant had puffed his cheeks and flattened the jungle under his breath. The sound rippled like thunder away from the cutters, and then toward them again, back and forth, a roar that echoed from every side of the valley. Birds flung themselves upward: dust exploded through the falling branches: everything seemed to bounce and settle in slow motion.

"Now *tha',*" said Hector, gazing with satisfaction at the exposed hillside, "is the best damn sight in the whole damn world."

• • •

In the village Kiku heard the noise and froze. All around her there was screaming as women, suspecting an earthquake, ran to find their children. Kiku realized immediately that it was not an earthquake, but what it was she could not say. It was something completely outside her experience: the forest seemed to be collapsing in on itself, the way skin tore when you caught it on a rock. In the huge, raw gap, amongst the flotsam of broken trunks and upturned branches, she could see men, tiny at this distance, moving along to the next part of the hillside.

That night the villagers sat round the fire and discussed what had happened. It was plain to everyone what the white men were about now. There was to be no leopard hunting: it was the forest itself that the newcomers had come to slay. Yet what did it mean when a whole forest, which was composed of spirits as well as trees, was destroyed like this? When a person died their spirit climbed into a tree: when a tree was felled, its spirits joined the spirits of the other trees around it. What would happen now to all the hundreds, thousands of spirits the white men had set loose this afternoon? Nobody knew, because no one had been in a situation like this before.

Some of the older men believed that the young men should withdraw their labor. For the younger men, though, the damage to the forest was not so important as the fact that the white men were promising to reward them for their help. These young men could sense that everything was about to change, and saw that it might be to their advantage. Instead of being at the mercy of the jungle, as in the past, now the villagers would be able to control it, just like the white men. Some of the younger men, in particular, had found the method by which the white men had cleared the hillside both brilliant and thrilling. They relived over and over the sound of the breaking tree trunks—you had to have been there, they assured the other villagers: it was like the mightiest storm that any of them had ever heard, and all made by man! That they could work for people with such powers, and become rich at the same time, was an unimaginable piece of good fortune.

[FORTY-ONE]

"I AM SEEING SOME PEOPLE TODAY," PINKER SAYS DIFFIDENTLY. "I wonder if you would care to join me."

Emily looks up. "Oh? What people, Father?"

"They work for an American concern—that of Mr. J. Walter Thompson." Pinker grimaces. "Quite why Americans have to put both dates and initials in the wrong order I shall never know. Anyway, they are the people who have been advising Arbuckle's on their advertising. Now they have an office over here. They have written to me to say they have some new ideas on how to sell to the female market. I thought perhaps you would be better placed than I to judge whether they are right."

"I would be fascinated."

"Good." Pinker consults his watch. "They will be here at eleven o'clock."

RATHER to her disappointment, only one of the advertising men is an American. His name is Randolph Cairns, and he is almost exactly the opposite of what she had been expecting—instead of a personable, go-getting huckster, Mr. Cairns is quiet and polite and fussy, like a schoolteacher or an engineer.

"How are you marketing your brand at present, Mr. Pinker?" he inquires genially.

"With methods you yourselves, I believe, pioneered in America," Pinker answers promptly. "Every packet of Castle Coffee has a voucher on the wrapper, which can be redeemed for a ha'penny off the next purchase."

"That's all well and dandy, sir. But I think you misunderstood my question. I did not ask how you were selling your product—I asked how you were marketing your *brand*."

Her father looks confused.

"The product," Mr. Cairns explains, "is what you *sell*. The brand is what people *buy*."

Pinker nods, but Emily can tell he is still as baffled by this as she is.

"To put it another way"—Cairns fixes them both with a lofty stare—"your brand is the expectation people have of your goods. Indeed, I would go so far as to say that the actual product plays very little part in it." He sits back in his chair. "So. The question is, how do we create an expectation of superiority?"

He seems content to let the question hang in the air. Emily wonders if he is waiting for her or her father to come up with the answer.

"Sir?" It is one of Cairns's own retinue who leans forward—a young man who, Emily can now see, is both personable and eager.

Cairns nods. "Philips?"

"By psychology, sir?"

"Exactly." Cairns turns back to Pinker. "Psychology! The time will come, sir, when businessmen realize that customers are simply bundles of mental states, and that the mind is a mechanism which we can affect with the same exactitude with which we control a machine in a factory. We are scientists, Mr. Pinker—scientists of sales. We do not employ guesswork or hot air—we stick to what *works.*"

Emily can see that her father is mightily impressed. "And what does that mean—specifically—for Castle?" she interjects skeptically. "How would it change what we do?"

"No more coupons," Cairns says decisively. "We need to create a favorable impression—a mood. We are trying to woo the consumer, not to bribe her." He nods to Philips, who pulls some newspapers out of a case.

Cairns laces his fingers on the table. "First, you have to get yourselves out of the old-fangled notion that what you sell is coffee," he announces. "What you sell—what the housewife buys—is love."

"Love?" Pinker and his daughter look equally astonished.

"Love," Cairns says firmly. "To serve your husband a great cup of coffee—what better way is there, for a wife, of showing her love?"

Once more his question hangs in the air. But this time Philips does not bob up to answer: it is, Emily realizes, meant to be rhetorical.

"The smell of coffee is the smell of happiness," Cairns continues dreamily. "Why, when my wife makes me coffee, it is a pleasure for her, because she knows it gives me pleasure. And"—he holds up a finger—"she has the reassurance of knowing she cannot show her devotion any better way than to serve me Castle."

"How does she know it?" Emily asks. She cannot decide whether this extraordinary spiel is brilliant or nonsensical or some higgledy-piggledy mixture of the two.

"Because we will tell her, of course." Cairns turns to Philips, who opens the first newspaper with a flourish.

The page he is holding up has been pasted in: it is, she realizes, a mock-up of the advertisement they are proposing. A man sits in his shirt-sleeves drinking coffee. There is a wide grin on his face.

Behind him, holding a coffee-pot, is a smiling wife. Some trick of perspective makes it seem as if she only comes up to his midriff. The headline reads: *Every husband's right—every woman's duty.* In smaller type, at the base of the page, it says: *Don't disappoint him! Make the right choice—choose Castle!*

"It is . . . different, certainly," Pinker says. He looks helplessly at his daughter. "Emily? What do you say?"

"It seems somewhat negative."

Cairns nods gravely. "That is intentional. In sales the negative principle, it has been proven, is more powerful than the positive."

"Well, if it has been proven . . ." Pinker says, relieved.

Cairns gestures at Philips, who holds up a second advertisement. *"If you love him—show it. Choose Castle, and he'll know it!"* he reads aloud. *"A meal is always a feast with a lovely woman at the foot of the table, a pot of hot Castle Coffee in her hand."*

"Hmm," Pinker says. He looks baffled.

Philips holds up a third advertisement. A wife stands next to her husband, who is seated. From behind his cup of coffee, he beams at the reader. *"His pleasure—her satisfaction! Now he knows it's Castle, he's CERTAIN she gives him the best!"*

"But there is absolutely nothing here," Emily says despairingly, "about quality. About the raw ingredients—the proportion of mocca, whether we use Bourbon coffee or Typica—"

"The housewife does not care about that sort of thing," Cairns says dismissively. "She cares about pleasing her husband."

"Well, *I* care," Emily says. "I can only give you my opinion—"

"Exactly," Cairns says. "But we do not go by opinion, my dear—yours or mine. Opinion is subjective. We have tested these concepts—tested them with *real* women." Emily wonders for a moment if he means she does not fit into that category. "What we have in mind is nothing less than a coordinated military campaign. We identify our targets; we calculate how to make the maximum impact upon them, and then we devise our strategy." He taps the table. "This is the new, forward-thinking approach to advertising. These advertisements will *sell*."

WHEN THEY have gone Pinker says, "I sense you are not sure."

"On the contrary, Father, my mind is quite made up. There is something deeply unpleasant about appealing so directly to a woman's insecurities."

"Now, Emily." He looks at her fondly. "Could your reaction be connected at all to your political beliefs?"

"Of course not!"

"I have never criticized your involvement in female suffrage. But you must agree that it makes you less . . ." He hesitates. "Less able, shall we say, to see the position of the ordinary woman."

"Father—what nonsense!"

"As Mr. Cairns said, these concepts of theirs have been tested—we know they will work. And if we do not take this new, psychological approach, I am worried Howell's might. And then we will be left behind." He nods. "We must steal a march on Howell somehow, Emily, and this may be the way to do it. I am going to tell Mr. Cairns to go ahead."

[FORTY-TWO]

WITHOUT THE PROTECTION OF THE BIG TREES THE DELICATE shoots and creepers of the forest floor, dotted with orchids and butterflies, quickly shriveled in the sun. The fallen wood was ready for burning almost immediately. As soon as the wind was coming from the right direction, Hector organized the men to light a series of fires along the northern edge of the valley.

If the felling had been spectacular, the burning was even more so. The flames ran back and forth across the cleared land, filling it with a new growth that reached almost as high as the original canopy: a blazing, crackling forest of fire that sprouted, died and propagated itself over and over again during the course of a week. Sometimes the fires slowed to feast on one particular fallen tree; sometimes they carpeted a clearing with a low, flickering sward. At other times the flames were almost invisible in the brilliant sunshine as if the air itself were liquefying in the intense heat.

The natives were no strangers to fire, of course, but on this scale it seemed to fill them with a kind of superstitious terror, and they carried out our instructions with increasing reluctance. Hector swore he had never known workers so undisciplined; the result, he assumed, of our being pioneers. Whatever I thought of him personally, I could not be anything other than glad he was there. I would have been completely incapable of overcoming the hundreds of daily obstacles that faced us without him.

After the burning the blasted hillsides resembled nothing so much as a smoking moonscape filled with gray snow. Here and there the remains of charred trunks poked out of the gray, while a couple of giant trees which had somehow survived both the felling and the conflagration intact stood alone in the vast expanse, their lower branches shriveled like lace.

"Best fertilizer in the world," Hector said, reaching down into a knee-deep drift of ash and rubbing some in his hands. I did the same: it was powdery, unimaginably soft, still warm days after the burning. As it dissolved to dust between my palms it released a waft of ashy, sooty aroma. "Coffee exhausts even the best ground, Robert: you're fortunate to have plenty of land here. Come on, let's go home."

"HOME" WAS Wallis Castle, a colonial estate which came with the right of shooting through the parishes of Abyssinia and Sudan, comprised of an entrance hall, dining room, drawing room, library, breakfast room, countless bedrooms and their dressing rooms, with the unusual feature of their combination in one circular space about fourteen feet in diameter. In other words, Hector and I were now living like two tinkers in a squalid native hut of mud and grass thatch. The thatch rustled all night long, and occasionally small poisonous wriggling things dropped out of it to visit us (in that respect it was not so very different from my staircase at Oxford). The floor was earth, although we had put down two zebra skins, bartered from the natives, to carpet it. Jimo was rather surprised that we were not going to share this accommodation with a goat—apparently, a good supply of goat's piss on the floor kept down the jiggas, whatever they might have been—but we decided that, on balance, we would stick to rugs and slippers.

Our chief enemy was boredom. Darkness came early in the tropics, and although we had kerosene lamps we had only enough fuel to use them for an hour or so each night. Hector surprised me by asking me to read aloud from my small library: tentatively I opened *The Importance of Being Earnest,* and he chuckled at the opening lines:

ALGERNON. Did you hear what I was playing, Lane?
LANE. I didn't think it polite to listen, sir.
ALGERNON. I'm sorry for that, for your sake. I don't play accurately—any one can play accurately—but I play with wonderful expression. As far as the piano is concerned, sentiment is my forte. I keep science for Life.
LANE. Yes, sir.
ALGERNON. And, speaking of the science of Life, have you got the cucumber sandwiches cut for Lady Bracknell?

So I carried on, and eventually he took the book from me and gave a rather fine falsetto Gwendolen—"Pray don't talk to me about the weather, Mr. Worthing. Whenever people talk to me about the weather, I always feel quite certain that they mean something else. And that makes me so nervous." Heaven knows what Jimo and Kuma must have made of it, let alone the other natives; the strange Scottish falsetto emerging from our hut, the nocturnal gales of laughter, and the rapturous applause with which Hector greeted my Lady Bracknell. He even started to address me as Ernest when we were out and about on the farm.

But it was all unreal—a kind of dream, a hallucination. I participated in the daily routines of the plantation, but my real life was lived after the hurricane lamp had been turned off for the night and Hector's snores liberated me from his world of pegs, plantings and labor. Then, as darkness blew into the hut, filling it with the contrapuntal music of the jungle at night—so much noisier than the jungle by day—Fikre stepped toward my bed on silent feet, whispering, "Soon," and "Now"; straddling my body with her knees, so that if I just reached up I could shape her hips, her waist, her hanging breasts, between my hands. . . .

Sometimes I summoned other women I had known—even Emily. But her face always wore a slightly fastidious expression, as if lending her body to these fantasies was a distasteful duty that was keeping her from more important matters back in England. She was—quite literally—a distant memory now, less real to me than the whores whose bodies I had once been intimate with.

It was like the Ingersoll watch Pinker had given me before I left London, and which I had tried to keep to European time. Once it wound down in Zeilah, there was no easy way to reset it. It seemed easier to adapt to the local hours, and ultimately to abandon the use of a watch altogether—for watches are like the Guide: only of use if the person you are talking to has the same equipment as you. That is how it was with Emily. I did not suddenly fall out of love with her, but the part of my heart which should have kept ticking away with the thought of her ran down, and somehow never got restarted.

ONLY ONCE did I recall her in a different way. The villagers had quickly realized that if they suffered any minor medical mishaps in our employment, such as a finger gashed with an axe or a foot pierced by a chopped branch, we would dress and bandage the wounds more effectively than their own healer woman could. Diachylon, in particular, originally just one more baffling component of our medicine chest, turned out to be a marvelous invention; a mixture of linen and antiseptic ointments which hardened over a wound and kept it free from both physical damage and infection.

One day a native woman brought us her sick child. The infant was horribly lethargic, and although it was running a high fever its pulse was deathly slow. Even on the black skin one could see the yellow tinge of jaundice.

"This is no business of ours," Hector said abruptly. "The woman doesn't even work for us."

"Pinker would want us to do what we can."

"Pinker would want us to conserve the medicines for our own employees. And to make sure that the child is baptized, so that at least its soul is saved."

I thought: *but Pinker's daughter would disagree.* I dug out our Galton, and deduced the baby was suffering from yellow fever. According to Galton about half of infant cases resulted in death, but I gave the child some laudanum anyway. It slept more easily after that, but the next day it began to bleed from the nose and eyes, and I knew that it was hopeless.

I DROPPED various hints to Hector that I would need to go into Harar soon, all of which he ignored. Then, one night, soon after we had turned in, we heard a commotion outside. Jimo came running into the hut, gabbling breathlessly.

"Massa come one time, one time. *Marrano* eat coffee babies."

We grabbed our rifles and headed outside. There was a little moon, and we could see shapes crashing around in the nursery beds. As we got closer we made out a whole herd of warthogs, grunting ecstatically as they grubbed through our precious seedlings.

We chased them off and set Jimo to stand guard. In the morning we could see that they had wrecked the crop. It was a disaster, one Hector blamed on himself.

"I should have made fences. It never occurred to me that scavengers could do so much damage." He sighed. "It looks as if ye'll get your trip to Harar after all, Ernest. This will all need to be replaced."

"What a pity," I said, although inwardly I was exultant. "I'll go tomorrow."

TOMORROW. Tomorrow and tomorrow and tomorrow . . . That night I barely slept, my brain feverish with erotic imaginings.

As I left the camp next day, Hector had the workers burning again. Long after I had left our valley I could still tell where in that endless, rolling expanse of hills it lay by the smokestack that towered over it, its huge black branches spreading across the sky like some giant new species of tree.

[FORTY-THREE]

"Honey"—this note is redolent of flower-scented honeys. It also brings to mind beeswax, gingerbread, nougat and certain types of tobacco. Phenyl ethylic aldehyde, isolated in coffee, evokes this scent very well.

—LENOIR, Le Nez du Café

ONCE IN HARAR, I ALERTED FIKRE TO MY PRESENCE BY SENDing her a note, claiming to need her help with some translation. A servant brought her reply—something equally innocuous and guarded. There was no reference to Bey: that meant he was away. The gods were smiling on us.

I waited. And waited. The anticipation was unbearable—my very senses seemed tuned more tautly, as orchestra players before a concert retune their instruments to a higher pitch. I passed the time improvising a bed from sacks of coffee, spread with silk shawls. It was surprisingly comfortable, the beans shifting under my weight to make a soft, yielding hollow.

And then—so lightly I barely caught the sound—the door downstairs opened. I heard footsteps hurrying on the stairs.

Her beauty, each time I saw her, was still a shock: the dark, angular face, the light, piercing eyes, the slender body wrapped in a saffron-yellow robe.

NOW THAT we were finally together, it was as if neither of us wanted to begin. She made me coffee—the delicate, fragrant coffee of the countryside—as she had done in the desert, watching me solemnly as I drank the first cup. I remembered what Bey had told me about the coffee ceremony, that first time in his tent: that it is also a ceremony of love.

With a sudden rush then, desire overwhelmed me. I unwound the robe from her body with an impatient tug, until she was standing before me naked—or almost naked: she was wearing a thin chain belt on her slender black hips. It was hung with piastres, the golden discs swinging and glittering against her skin as she moved toward me.

I, who had made love to many women—some compliant, some desultory, some resentful, some furtive, but all of them, in their different ways, eager for it to be over—had never known anything like this: what it was to love someone whose passion was as great as my own, who gasped and quivered and trembled with pleasure at my every touch. She smelled of coffee: there was the taste of it in every kiss, the perfume of the roasting ovens in her hair. . . . Her hands were coffee; her lips were coffee; it was there in the taste of her skin and the glistening clear liquid in the corner of her eyes. And—yes—between the dark thighs, where the skin opened like a series of petals to reveal the honeysuckle-scented pinkness within, I found a single, tiny bean, a hard nub of coffee-flavored flesh. I slipped it into my mouth and gently chewed on it; as if by magic, even when I had eaten my fill, there it was again.

I was determined not to cause her any pain—to go slowly. It was Fikre herself who finally became impatient. Twisting on top, she eased herself onto me until she met a slight resistance; then, leaning forward so that she could look directly into my eyes, pressed herself down. She winced once as something gave, and then I was fully possessed of her. A smear of purple cobwebbed our bellies, briefly, soon rubbed away by the circular movements of her hips.

Her eyes blazed with triumph and fury. "Whatever happens," she whispered, "now I have won."

And then—something I had never seen before, although I had read of it—as we fucked she was gripped by a series of shuddering spasms, deep within herself, almost painful in their intensity, the effects of which passed through her body and even made themselves visible on her skin, the way an explosion underwater will briefly churn the surface. After each of these spasms her body went limp, and she covered my face with kisses, murmuring with delight, until suddenly her back would arch again, straining and gasping as the pleasure took her again. I felt muscles inside her squeezing me as each spasm took hold. I realized then that all the whores who had ever moaned and panted in my arms had been doing so in feeble imitation of this. Perhaps not one of them had ever felt the real thing, nor had I ever stopped to wonder what they might be getting out of it besides money.

LATER THERE WAS more coffee, and more love, and then she lay in my arms and we talked. We did not speak immediately of Bey, or anything serious: that was the world outside, the world we had renounced. Instead she told me about the French merchant who had lived in the house before me.

"It was a very sad story. In his youth he had been very beautiful—and a prodigy: he wrote poems that were lauded by all the great men of letters. One of them, another poet, took him to be his pupil. But he also demanded that the youth become his lover.

Eventually the boy shot him with a gun. Yet in a strange way, being that man's catamite had also been the source of his talent. Afterwards he never wrote another word: he came here to the end of the world instead, and lived his life as if he were already dead."

"Who told you that?"

"Ibrahim. Why?"

"It's a good story. But if there really had been a French boy genius like that, I would have heard of him."

"You think Bey made it up?"

"I think Bey exaggerates."

She smiled.

"What?"

"He will have no need to exaggerate when he hears about this."

"But he must never hear," I said. Now that the madness of our coupling was over, it was hard to keep the fear in check. What we had just done was so much more than a crime. I had taken another man's woman, violated his property and ruined his investment, all in a few minutes. I had no idea what kind of legal system there was in Harar, but I suspected that my status as a British subject would offer scant protection. Already a laughingstock for the way he had handled Fikre, Bey would know that the only way to regain any sort of credibility would be to exact a revenge of such voluptuous cruelty that even his enemies would be impressed.

"What is it?" Fikre lifted herself up so she could look into my eyes.

"Nothing."

"You were wondering what he will do," she guessed.

"How did you know?"

She placed her hand on my cock. "Like a snail you drew in your horn."

"Ah."

I was struck by the fact that what we had done could not be

undone. It was no use saying "We must never see each other again," or "we must stop this before it is too late." It already was too late. We had done the single, terrible thing which would condemn us both. But even that was a kind of freedom: there was no point in turning back.

With the third cup of coffee she brought a sprig of *tena adam*. We made love slowly, almost reflectively, all urgency gone. I remembered something else Bey had said about the coffee ceremony—that the third cup was the blessing, the one that sealed the transformation of the spirit. But in truth that had happened to me long before.

AFTERWARDS we slept, and woke together, and lay in an unspoken union of smiles and silence. "We will think of something," she said, breaking into my thoughts. She stroked my stomach with the backs of her fingers, lightly. "When I first saw you—it is true, my only thought was that it would be a wonderful revenge on Ibrahim. I wanted to die anyway, and I wanted to cause him as much embarrassment as possible. But now . . ." One finger circled my navel gently, as one might rub the rim of a glass. "Now I do not want this to end."

"Nor do I. But it's hard to see how."

"Perhaps I can seduce him. Then he will believe he deflowered me."

"You'd do that?"

"Of course. If it meant I could be with you sometimes."

I thought about Bey heaving his fat body on top of her, his wet mouth on hers, slobbering, where so recently mine had been. "He would know you weren't a virgin."

"There are ways of pretending—little bags of sheep's blood that burst when you do it. It would not fool a doctor, but it might fool a man in lust—such a man believes what he wants to believe."

"Too risky. Besides, imagine if it didn't work—if he refused you. He'd know for certain something was up."

"What, then?"

"I don't know. I'll think of something." It was like a refrain—one or the other of us was always saying it: *I'll think of something.* The words reassured, like a mother's soothing comforts. *Don't worry. Go back to sleep. It'll be all right.* It would not be all right—we were doomed—but the words worked their magic all the same.

"I must go." She sat up and reached for her robe.

"Not yet."

"I have to. The servants will be suspicious. I tried to make sure no one followed me but even that is not certain."

"Don't go." I reached for her breast.

"There's no time." But she shivered with pleasure and lay back anyway. "Be quick," she breathed, bringing up her knees to open her thighs.

She lay underneath me, supine, holding my face between her hands, one palm on each cheek; her eyes fixed intently on mine. This time there were no spasms inside her, but as my pace quickened she drew her legs even higher, the pink soles of her feet almost by my ears, and whispered *yes, yes, yes* until I had spent: then she kissed me, got up, cleaned herself unselfconsciously with the water I had brought to make coffee, and was gone.

FEW PEOPLE realize how salty coffee is. In its fresh state, the salt is hidden: it acts as a buttress for the other flavors, and is responsible for a fleeting bitter aftertaste that is one of the drink's pleasures. But if you leave a pot for a hour or two, so that some of the liquid evaporates, you will find the saltiness intensifies to such an extent that the coffee is almost undrinkable. That is why the coffee ceremony is only three cups long: the third cup is the last that can be extracted before the coffee becomes as briny as tears.

But there is a fourth cup that can be taken, a cup that is not named: the cup that is drunk, however bitter, by the lover, lying alone in his bed, as he pictures his loved one slipping through the dark streets in a saffron-yellow robe, back to the house of the man who owns her.

[FORTY-FOUR]

"Wild"—a gamey flavour often found in Ethiopian coffees.

—SMITH, Coffee Tasting Terminology

WEEKS PASSED. LIKE A HIBERNATING ANIMAL I MADE DO with my store of recollections, recalling the smooth, cool, spicy sleekness of Fikre's skin, the taste of her nipples . . .

"I must say," Hector observed one morning as we walked between the work gangs, "you're taking this remarkably well, Robert. I confess I thought you'd be pining for your auld Regent Street haunts by now."

"Regent Street? It's a funny thing, but I don't miss Regent Street in the slightest. In fact, it seems to me that my old life in England was remarkably dull, compared with here."

"Is that so?" Hector seemed quite taken aback. "We'll make an adventurer of you yet."

"Speaking of which, though," I said casually, "I'll need to go into Harar again soon."

He frowned. "Again?"

"I do understand that it'll be much more difficult to leave the farm after you've shipped out. But that's all the more reason to do as much trading as I can before you go, wouldn't you say?"

Reluctantly he said, "I suppose so."

"Good. That's settled, then. I'll go on Sunday."

We had reached the brow of the hill: below us, the gangs were working on digging the planting pits, one every six feet, along the lines of white tape we had marked out. Hector gazed down at them. "Look at those lines, Robert. When all's said and done, Civilization is just straight lines and bonnie white paint."

A SOUND was coming toward us through the jungle—the low, desultory chanting of men who sing not to give voice but to keep a marching rhythm. Everyone stopped work, Hector and I included, and gazed expectantly at the dripping trees.

"No stop!" Jimo shouted. He had acquired a switch these days, a long whippy branch which he swished through the air to give emphasis to his shouts. "No stop!" The villagers reluctantly turned back to their work.

Through the trees two long lines of men were coming toward us. No, not just men—women too, laden down with cooking pans, bags of maize, even small children tied in papooses around their backs. They were blacks, but quite unlike the blacks of our village. These were short and swarthy, with wavy hair and heavy eyebrows.

"The coolies," Hector said with satisfaction. "I wondered when they'd get here."

The front man of each column gave a command. The newcomers stopped, swinging their packs to the ground and crouching down beside them.

"Where have they come from?" I asked, puzzled.

"Ceylon. They're Indians—Tamils. Fantastic workers. Not like these Africans."

"But how have they got here?"

"We ordered them, of course." Hector seemed impatient with my questions as he strode up the slope toward the men's leader. He was standing waiting for us, his head lowered respectfully.

"You had them shipped over?"

"I had them recruited. They pay their own passage." Hector extended his hand to the head Tamil, who placed in it a sheaf of grubby papers.

"I'm surprised they can afford it."

"They can't." Hector sighed, as if having to explain to a simpleton. "There is no work for them now in Ceylon. So they have signed on with a gang-master to be shipped here. The cost of their sea-passage will be deducted from their earnings. We buy their contracts from the gang-master, so that his expenses have been covered, and the Tamils will get work and food, and everyone will be happy."

"I see," I said, although in truth I still could not understand how the mechanism of economics had somehow magicked these people so many thousands of miles from their homes.

THE TAMILS were a surly lot. Their habitual expression was a heavy scowl, quite unlike our local villagers, who were always laughing. But I could not deny that they were remarkable workers. Within days they had erected three large huts—one for the men to sleep in, another for the women, and one where, Hector explained, the coffee beans would be sorted. When they dug planting pits they managed three hundred yards for every sixty covered by the locals.

"It is because they are indentured," Hector said. "They work hard because they owe money."

• • •

A FEW DAYS later he assembled the African villagers in our camp. Going to the crate which held our farm tools, he took out a couple of European-made axes.

"These are good axes—very expensive," Hector said, showing them. "They cost hundreds of rupees. None of you could afford one."

Jimo translated this: there was a general nodding.

"But for our workers, it will be different. If you agree to work until our coffee harvest comes, we will give each of you an axe of your own. Or for women, a hoe."

Jimo translated again. This time there was a puzzled silence.

"You do not have to give us any money now," Hector explained. "You will pay us back one rupee a week, from your wages."

Jimo translated. Now there was a hubbub of noise. Those who had grasped the concept were explaining it to their slower neighbors. Others had leapt up to examine the axe, running their hands over the smooth, lathe-turned shaft, touching the mirror-like surface of the head, the greased cutting edge, murmuring with amazement.

"There is more," Hector shouted over the noise. "See! Over here!" He went to the crate containing our trade goods. "Fishhooks! Mirrors! They are all available on credit to those who sign up!" He held up a glass necklace and shook it. "See?" It was plucked from his hand by a wondering villager.

He turned to me with an expression of satisfaction. "They'll all agree. How can they not? It's the best offer they've ever had."

"But once they've paid off their debt, mightn't they decide to go and farm their own land with these tools?"

"Yes, in theory. I think you'll find only a very few manage to do that." He rubbed his hands together with satisfaction. "The beauty of it is, we'd have had to get more tools anyway. This way everybody wins."

IN THE VILLAGE that night there was plenty to talk about. Kiku, a veteran of these debates, knew the best policy was not to put her own view forward too soon, but to consider what the other women said before using her seniority to bring them to a collective agreement. However, it was difficult in this case, because for the first time since she could remember, no one else seemed to share her point of view.

"What is going to happen to the forest, once we all have these axes?" she asked plaintively. "What will happen to the trees?"

"But there are many trees, and so few of us. It seems only right that we should be able to chop them down. Then we will have made more *saafu,* not less, because the numbers will be more evenly balanced," someone said. To Kiku's annoyance it was Alaya, Tahomen's new wife, who had spoken, and to her even greater annoyance the others seemed to be impressed by Alaya's logic.

"Saying that we shouldn't use axes to chop trees—isn't that like saying that we shouldn't use pots to carry water?" someone else added. "We have enough work to do already without making life more difficult."

"And I for one don't mind hoeing," Alaya added, "if the hoe is a good one, although of course I will probably stop when I am with child."

The other women nodded. When Alaya was carrying Tahomen's baby, it stood to reason that she would not work. But they admired the fact that she was prepared to work hard until then. Not all headmen's wives were so industrious.

Kiku could almost hear these thoughts going through their heads, and when the women looked at her, waiting for her response, it was as if she could see the question forming in their eyes,

And Kiku? She does not bear Tahomen's child, but neither does she want to do his hoeing! That is the real reason she does not want us to have hoes and axes—she might have to do some hard work herself, for once in her life!

"This hoe of yours," Kiku said.

"Yes?" Alaya beamed.

"How will you pay for it when you are with child?"

Alaya frowned as she thought about this. The question had clearly not occurred to her. Then her brow unfurrowed. "If Tahomen has an axe," she announced, "he can pay for my hoe, and his axe, by chopping trees."

There was a collective sigh as the women drew in their breath. The headman himself, chop trees? As if he were no better than any other man? But then—and once again Kiku could almost hear the thought as it took shape in their minds—why should it not be so? Why should the headman be exempt from physical labor? Let him work alongside his barren wife!

It was the realization that she had been out-maneuvered by Alaya that made Kiku say baldly, "Well, I don't agree."

"But you don't have to agree, do you?" Alaya said. "Let those who want axes, and are prepared to work for them, have them. The same with hoes. We can all choose for ourselves whether this is something we want to do."

There was another shocked silence. The idea that this decision might be a matter for each individual, rather than the tribe, was also completely novel. Kiku could see the women looking at each other, trying it for size—and then nodding. Alaya was right, they were thinking; why should we be bound by what others want to do? Let those with strong, young husbands who are prepared to work hard do so, and earn their axes! Some would prosper—not all, obviously, not the very old or the very young or the infirm, but they were not the ones who had to do hard physical labor without the benefit of axes in the first place.

In that moment, Kiku knew it was all over. You could not stop these changes, any more than you could stop water when it wanted to flow downhill. But she was uneasy: she did not know what was coming, or where it would all end.

The next day they all signed up for the new contracts, even Tahomen. But as she looked at the necklaces which now adorned each woman's neck, Kiku could not help thinking that they looked more like the chains worn by slaves than anything the villagers had ever fashioned from the forest.

[FORTY-FIVE]

RATHER TO EMILY'S IRRITATION, MR. CAIRNS'S CONDESCENDING advertisements have been a great success. Whether it is their message, or simply that Pinker's has drawn attention to itself by running such an ambitious campaign, she is not certain, but Castle Coffee is now the best-selling packed coffee in the grocers' stores. As there is currently a massive expansion in that sector, with people like Thomas Lipton and John James Sainsbury opening vast new emporia as aggressively as Pinker's is expanding its coffee business, the new way of marketing suits all parties. Sainsbury can place an order for Castle knowing he will get exactly the same product in every one of his shops, while Pinker knows the massive demand his advertising is creating can be satisfied through sufficient outlets. Lipton in particular has become almost a business partner; when he suggests a version of Castle which is pre-ground, to go along with his own innovation of tea packaged in small porous bags, Pinker readily agrees.

"But pre-ground coffee will not last as long, or taste so good, as beans freshly prepared," Emily points out.

"Perhaps there is a small difference—but not every woman has leisure to grind coffee these days. So many women have jobs, Emily. You would not want women to be penalized for working, would you?"

Of course she would not, and so she drops her objections—not that he would take much notice of her opinion anyway, she suspects. Her father has a whole army of advisers now, secretaries and factotums and a new breed of assistant called *executives.* The language of business is changing along with the business itself. She has noticed that he sometimes refers to the warehouses as *depots,* and to Castle as *the product.* From the ledgers, she can tell that they are buying no more fine coffee than before; the expansion is being fueled by ever-increasing quantities of the cheaper stuff, leavened with a sprinkling of good arabica. True, the product is cheaper, too—just enough to undercut Howell's—but most of the money they save on raw materials is going to fund their advertisements. Expansion, not profit, has become the objective.

One day her father takes her into the street to show her a remarkable sight. Parked at the curbside are three petroleum vans painted in the Castle livery, black and gold, their engines filling the street with turpeny fumes. Each bears the same picture of a castle that dominates Pinker's packs, above which are the words *Castle Coffee—choice of the discerning wife.*

"It was Cairns's idea. As the vans drive round London making deliveries, people will see them and think of ordering Castle."

"I suppose we should be grateful he did not put something about Love," she mutters.

THE ONLY PART of their empire which does not thrive, in fact, are the Temperance Taverns. Sometimes Emily accompanies her father on visits to these establishments, trying to puzzle out the problem.

"It cannot be the concept," Pinker says, looking around at one almost deserted coffee-house. "Look at Lyons—they sell their tea through grocers, just as we do, and yet their cafés seem always to be full."

"Perhaps it is the location. Lyons tea shops are on busy streets, so that women can stop off for a few minutes during shopping trips. Whereas our taverns are in residential areas."

"That is because they were converted from public houses." Her father sighs. "I think I may have misjudged the public this time, Emily. And if they cannot make money we will have to close them down."

"But I thought the taverns were the reason—the reason for everything? Or is Temperance no longer your aim?"

"Temperance is the objective, of course. But perhaps the means will be different—perhaps it will be packet coffee that will change the working man's habits."

"While there are still public houses, and alcohol, there will still be drunks," she reminds him.

He shrugs. "Perhaps, but a business that does not make money cannot be the instrument of change. We will do nothing yet. Perhaps the market may turn."

[FORTY-SIX]

I LAY IN FIKRE'S ARMS, SATED. SHE HAD PERFUMED HER SKIN with myrrh smoke before she came to meet me, standing naked over a brazier as the Bedouin women did, and now the fragrance mingled with the liquors of our lovemaking, the smell of sackcloth and the aroma of coffee beans from our impromptu bed.

I laughed suddenly, thinking of the Guide: so many categories, yet ultimately one simply went on instinct: *yes, I want this, now; this is good.*

"What are you thinking about?" she asked, stirring in my arms.

"A very stupid experiment I carried out before I came here." I explained about the Guide, and Pinker, and the boxes of samples—

"But I want to see them!" She had jumped up—her energy was never stilled for long: minutes after lovemaking she would always want more: more sex, more talk, more passion, more planning. "Are they here?"

"Yes, somewhere."

I located the case with the scents and brought it to her.

"Which is your favorite?"

"This one, perhaps." I opened the phial marked "apple." For a moment I thought it must have evaporated—there was almost nothing there: then I caught a faint whiff of something bland and uninteresting, as insipid as milk. "But it seems rather horrible now." I held it out to her.

She sniffed it and shrugged. "It's so faint."

"You have changed the way I smell things."

"Africa has done that."

"You and Africa."

I went back to the bed and she came back to me. "I found one of his poems," she said.

"Whose?"

"The Frenchman's, the one who used to live here. Do you want to hear it?"

"If I must."

She sat cross-legged on the coffee sacks, naked and unselfconscious, and began to read aloud. "Enough," I said after a few moments. "Fikre, stop. It's just—sound without meaning."

"It's as if he's drunk with words," she insisted. "Can't you hear it?" She jumped up and walked around the room, beating the rhythm with her free hand as she declaimed,

" 'Est-ce en ces nuits sans fond que tu dors et t'exiles,

Million d'oiseaux d'or, ô future Vigueur . . .' "

I could not help smiling—her energy was like that of a child, and on her lips the French phrases, however nonsensical, were deliciously erotic. "Come back to bed."

" 'Mais, vrai, j'ai rop pleuré! Les Aubes sont navrantes . . .' "

"I want to fuck again."

"Well, I don't. I want to shout this poetry!"

I grabbed her ankles and tipped her up onto the bed. She fought me, scratching and fighting and laughing and trying to roar her poem as I took her. Even when I was inside her that strange, almost demonic energy was not dissipated—she twisted herself so that she was on top of me, and even when I had spent she did not stop, but rode my softening manhood and spat at me,

" '*Ô que ma quille éclate! Ô que j'aille à la mer!*' "—digging her nails fiercely into my stomach.

It was doggerel, of course it was—but there was something in its cadence, in the simple savage drumbeat of its rhythm, that throbbed and echoed in my blood.

I thought: *I am not a plantation manager. I am not a coffee merchant. I am certainly not a husband.*

When all this is over, I promised myself, I will write again—I will rediscover that savage, exultant succubus who used to live inside me and write verse.

"I'VE HAD an idea," Fikre's voice said.

"Hmm?" I was drifting off to sleep.

Something hard and light and dry dribbled between my teeth. I spluttered and opened my eyes. She was pouring coffee beans into my mouth from her hand. She grinned and ate the rest herself, chewing them straight from her palm with quick, fierce movements of her teeth, like a cat crunching bones.

"You eat unground beans?" I said.

She nodded. "They're good."

Experimentally, I tried some. She was right—they were good: the pure taste of coffee, undiluted.

"And besides, you needed to wake up." She paused. "My idea. I have decided we must kill Ibrahim. It's the only way."

"How would we do a thing like that?"

"You must hire a gang of *bashibazuks*—the mercenaries. They will kill him and then you and I can be together."

"Unfortunately, you're mortgaged. He told me so in the desert.

Even if he died, the moneylenders would take you to cover the debt."

Her eyes flashed. "How I hate him." She threw herself back onto the bed. "When this is over, we must find a way to make sure the world stops being like this."

I grunted. "That's the least of our worries."

She reached out to stroke my face. "Now that I have you—now I've got *this*—I want to live. To be with you."

"I'll think of something," I promised.

That comforting lie again.

[FORTY-SEVEN]

"Caustic"—caused by bitter replacing sweet in the basic taste modulation.

—LINGLE, The Coffee Cupper's Handbook

IN THE QUIET OF THE NIGHT THERE WAS A SCREAM.

Kiku knew immediately that this was not the scream of someone who has stepped on a snake or hit their hand with a maize pestle. This was not even the scream of someone in pain. This was the scream of someone who is trying—desperately, inarticulately—to tell others that something is terribly wrong.

She rushed out of her hut. Alaya was stumbling down the path from the white man's camp, one hand folded across her chest, the other clutched to her mouth as if she were trying not to choke.

Together Kiku and a few other women who had heard the noise helped her inside one of the huts, and little by little the story spilled out. A man had approached her, but she had not been interested in him—or at least, only enough to agree to go to his hut.

He had said he had a gift for her, and sure enough he had given her a necklace. But she had not wanted to give him what he wanted in return, so he had hit her—had knocked her to the ground—then taken what he wanted by force.

"What man was this?" Kiku asked. "Who did this thing to you?"

"Vanyata Ananthan," Alaya whispered.

It was the Tamils' foreman. This made the situation even more complicated. The workers feared the foremen far more than they feared Massa Crannach or Massa Wallis. It was the foremen who could assign you to an easy job such as hoeing or a hard job such as moving a fallen tree; the foremen who would flick you surreptitiously across the legs with a stick if they thought you were not working hard enough; the foremen who would dock your wages if you did not do as they wanted.

Kiku knew that if the villagers did not act together now, their lives would become impossible. She went into her hut and found her *siqquee* stick.

Every woman had a *siqquee:* you were given it by your mother when you stopped being a girl. It was made of sycamore, the women's tree—as was every other woman's stick. It was a symbol that you were all connected. When Kiku delivered a baby or boiled herbs to treat a fever, she tapped her stick on the forehead of her patient to show that she was using not only her own knowledge, but also the power of the *siqquee,* through which flowed all the power of the women who had come before her. Just to hold it gave you strength—not a man's strength, which could lift up rocks or wrestle, but a woman's strength, the strength to endure. With this gift of strength, though, came a responsibility. If a woman needed help in an emergency, all she had to do was to take her stick, step out of her hut, and call out the special words of the *siqquee* shout. It was a kind of alarm; each woman who heard it was bound to stop what she was doing and come to join the shout.

Kiku touched her stick to her forehead, gathering its strength. Then she went outside and shouted, *"Intala Aayyaa dhageettee?* Daughter of woman, do you hear?"

For a moment there was silence. Then, from one of the huts, came an answering call, *"Oduun na gahee!* I have heard!"

"I have heard!" another voice shouted.

From every direction women were coming at a run. All were calling that they had heard the *siqquee.* They gathered round Kiku and Alaya, facing outwards with their sticks raised, chanting the same question: *"Intala Aayyaa dhageettee? Intala Aayyaa dhageettee?"* until every woman in the village was there. The men gathered round them, shaking their heads.

Silence fell as they waited for Kiku to speak. She gathered her thoughts: it was important that the whole village understood exactly why this mattered.

"*Saafu* has been lost," she said. "First the forest was violated. You have heard some of the men round the fire saying that this is a good thing, that the white men can show us how to control the trees with their axes. But how will that restore *saafu*? *Saafu* means us and the forest living together, with neither having the upper hand."

Some of her audience were nodding, but outside her immediate circle of women, Kiku could tell the younger men were not convinced. "Now my sister Alaya has been attacked," she continued. "Today it was Alaya: tomorrow it will be the wives or daughters of any of you. And that is why you must say to the white man that we will not work for him anymore. Instead of teaching us his bad ways, he must let us teach him the way of *saafu*. Until then, the women are going to cross the water."

"Crossing the water"—that was ritual language. It meant that the women were going to withdraw from the life of the village. There would be no childcare, no cooking and no family life until peace and order were re-established.

Kiku led the women away, into the jungle. As they passed the men Tahomen stood up and said formally, "Without women the fire will go out. We men must do what we need to restore *saafu*."

I RETURNED from Harar to find the plantation in a state of uproar. It seemed the African workers had called some kind of strike. It did not affect the Tamils, so there was no real threat to the smooth running of the farm, but Hector was keen to restore order as quickly as possible.

"That man should not have done what he did, of course, but it's actually quite timely. We need to show these people that their obligation is what matters, not their own feelings."

A court was assembled. A shamefaced Tamil was brought before it, and with all the villagers watching he readily confessed what he had done. For this he was fined ten rupees.

"So," Hector said, looking round at the villagers, "this matter is settled. You can all get back to your work."

Even when this had been translated, the villagers did not move.

"What's the blether now, Jimo?" Hector demanded.

After some conferring, Jimo reported that the villagers wanted the fine to be paid to them, rather than to the court.

"Absolutely not," Hector said, shaking his head. "That is not how justice works."

"And they want the man sent away, sah," Jimo said softly.

"What? Out of the question. He has paid his fine. Don't they understand that this is an end to it?"

It seemed they did not understand. Even when Hector angrily dismissed the court, the villagers refused to return to work.

"Find me the lassie," Hector said impatiently. Eventually Alaya was brought before him and ordered to shake the Tamil's hand, to show there were no hard feelings. The girl stood there, eyes lowered, refusing to do any such thing, and although the man took her limp hand and shook it, the watching villagers looked, if anything, more mutinous than before.

"This has gone far enough." Hector got to his feet and strode angrily into the circle of villagers. He raised his voice. "Justice has been done. If you do not work, you will be in breach of your contracts." He took a hoe and thrust it into the girl's hand. "Here, take it." She took it without looking at it. "Now go. Back to work."

No one moved.

"Jimo—beat her," Hector snapped.

"Sah?"

"Twelve lashes with the whip. Then choose one of the men and give him the same."

Jimo motioned to two of the Tamils, who came and held Alaya while he struck her across the shoulders and back. She wailed but made no attempt to move. When she was released she sank to her knees. The Tamils pulled a man from the watchers, dragging him into the circle by his wrists, as if persuading a reluctant dancer to join in with the festivities. He too was given a dozen strokes with the whip. Then another villager was seized—

"Hector," I said, repulsed. "For God's sake, man. You can't beat them all."

"Of course I can." He turned to me. "Robert, this is your plantation. If you can't maintain discipline, you might as well go home. How will you keep order after I'm away, if you won't show them who's in charge?"

Jimo, sensing our disagreement, looked from one to the other of us, waiting for orders.

"Well, Robert? What's it to be? Will you thrash them? Or d'you have a better notion?" Hector demanded.

I hesitated. Emily, I knew, would have said that she did have a better idea—would have thrown herself between the beater and his victim if necessary. But what did I know of plantation work?

Hector clearly thought any scruples I might have were just lily-livered squeamishness. And the truth was that I was relying on him to show me how it was done.

"Very well," I said heavily. "If you have to beat the wretched brutes, then beat them."

"Carry on, Jimo."

Jimo raised his stick and brought it down on the man's back, whipping him without expression until the allotted number of blows had been given. When he went to the next man the villager raised his hands in a gesture of submission and muttered something.

"He says he will work, sah," the overseer reported.

There was an audible gasp from the watchers—a strange sound, more of horror than anger, I thought.

"Good." Hector turned to the villagers. "Who's next? You—will you work? You? And you? Excellent."

There was no more resistance. It was as if the villagers were shocked to discover that their feeble insurrection would not stand up to Hector's determined assault on it. I felt almost sorry for them.

In two weeks, I thought, *I will be back in Harar.* It was all I could think about. *Fikre.*

AFTER THE BREAKING of the strike, Hector instituted some changes. The villagers' round huts were taken down, and the flat area on which they had previously stood was cleared for use as a drying floor. The villagers were installed in long wooden buildings like the Tamils', the men in one hut and the women in another; so that, as Hector said, there were no Africans and Indians anymore, only plantation workers.

A few days afterwards I found a little shape made of grass on the floor of our hut. It reminded me of the corn dolls that field workers used to weave at harvest time when I was a child. But this figure had one of Hector's shoelaces woven through it. Pushed right through the middle of the body was a tiny piece of wood, like the broken sliver of a whip.

[FORTY-EIGHT]

As soon as I could I returned to Harar. But when Fikre came to the merchant's house her face was clouded with fear.

"Bey is here," she said as soon as she had slipped through the door.

"Can you stay?"

"No. It is too dangerous. But I had to see you. He means to sell me."

"What?"

"He lost money on his last shipment. Now he cannot afford to pay for the coffee he has bought. He has been thinking about it as he crossed the desert, he said—thinking and crying. He was weeping when he told me; he said he loved me, that he cannot bear to sell me, but he says he has no choice."

"What did you say?"

"I said I do not care who owns me." She spoke scornfully. "A slave is a slave."

"I'm not sure it's wise to anger him just now, Fikre."

"He wants to pretend he is not a bad man. Why should I give him that satisfaction?"

"But this means you'll be sent away—"

She laughed hollowly. "No, it doesn't."

"It must."

"Listen, Robert," she said, as if explaining to a child. "Before I am sold, I will be examined by a midwife. Any buyer will insist on that. So I will be discovered. And then they will certainly kill me, unless I can do it myself first."

"You're not to kill yourself."

"It will be better than the alternative. At least I will be free to choose the moment of my death. Now I must go. Will you kiss me?"

"You're not to die," I said, pulling away and holding her. "No one is going to die. I promise I'll think of something."

[FORTY-NINE]

"Muddy"—a dull indistinct and thickish flavour. Can be due to the grounds being agitated.

LINGLE, The Coffee Cupper's Handbook

❧

HECTOR STEPS SILENTLY THROUGH THE JUNGLE, HIS RIFLE raised. In front of him Bayanna raises his hand. Both men freeze.

"There, sah," Bayanna breathes.

Hector peers into the trees. The stripes of brilliant sunshine and deep shadow are very like a leopard's coat—so like it, in fact, that it is impossible to say for certain whether there is anything there. He thinks he sees a flicker of movement, but it might be no more than a leaf twisting in the wind.

"This way, sah," Bayanna whispers, moving forward on silent feet.

Hector has not yet told Wallis that, when the other man goes off on his jaunts to Harar, he is hunting a leopard. For one thing, he can imagine Wallis's sneering comments if he fails. No: the proper way, the manly way, is to shoot the thing first, then leave the animal's skin on the floor of their hut to await Wallis's return, its magnificent head and snarling jaws all the comment that is needed. "Oh, aye," he'll say casually. "Thought I might as well have a little sport while I'm here."

Behind them a twig snaps. Kuma the cook pads to Hector's side. He is carrying the second gun and a box of bullets.

"I don't think it dere, sah," he says, peering ahead of them.

"Quiet, Kuma."

"Yes, sah. Sorry, sah."

If only it were not so dark, here under the canopy. The three men advance a little further. There is a small stream, and then a cluster of rocks. It is, Hector thinks, just the sort of place which, if he were a leopard, he would choose to—

There is a sound like a huge chain rattling. A shape hurls at them, curving through the air, claws slashing. Hector brings the gun to his shoulder and fires in one smooth, practiced movement. The leopard falls to the forest floor, writhing. Hector watches: it is a magnificent beast, and the fewer bullets he uses, the less damage will be suffered by the pelt.

Finally the animal stiffens and is still.

"By God," Hector says, approaching it warily. "The brute's enormous." He feels a surge of excitement. The beast is dead, and he has killed it. Wallis can sneer all he likes—this victory, and the spoils, are his alone. He might even—

There is a screech, another roar, and something else flies through the air. The second leopard is smaller, but it is also fiercer. Although Hector reaches back for his second gun, Kuma has recoiled involuntarily, and Hector's hand finds only air before the creature is on him. The powerful jaws lock into his neck, tugging. He hears someone yell. Bayanna hits it with his stick, and then Kuma too is pounding it with the base of the rifle. As the animal opens its jaws to snarl, Hector struggles free. The leopard snaps at his face twice more, and Hector's vision seems to shrink into a tiny dot.

ON MY RETURN I found him in our hut, still in his bush clothes, the camp-bed stained with his blood. While Kuma unwound the bandages I opened up our medicine chest.

"Here, sah," Kuma said softly. I turned. One side of Hector's face looked as if it had been sliced open with a filleting knife. His left cheek was laid quite bare, so that I could see his teeth through the wound: the other side bore three deep gouges from the animal's claws, from the bloody ear all the way down his neck. It was quite dreadful, and probably hopeless.

As I was looking at the damage Hector opened his eyes. One of them was filled with blood.

"Oh, Robber'. It's ye."

"I'm here, Hector. I'm going to patch you up and fetch a doctor."

He chuckled—or rather, tried to: a thin wheeze was all that escaped his lips. "Wha' doctor, man? Nearest doctor's in Aden."

"I'll think of something."

"Aye." He closed his eyes. "Dinnae let them eat me."

"What?"

"After I'm dead. Ye promise, now? Make sure I'm . . . properly buried."

"Talk of burial is somewhat premature, since you're not going to die."

He tried to smile. "Aren't I?"

"No."

"You're a foolish pup, Wallish."

"Hector, I find it quite extraordinary that even on your—" I almost said "deathbed," but caught myself in time, "sickbed, you are insulting me. Surely you know it's bad form to anger your surgeon."

"Surgeon, is it?"

"It looks," I said, "as if surgery might be required. And in the absence of a Harley Street physician, the resident locum is one Dr. R. Wallis."

A faint sigh escaped his lips.

"I'll patch you up as best I can," I added. "And then we'll get you to Harar. There's bound to be someone there who can help." I turned to Jimo, and said more confidently than I felt, "I'll need some boiled water, Jimo, and the waxed thread and needles."

I got four spoonfuls of the Chlorodyne down his throat and got to work. It quickly became apparent that even that potent mixture of laudanum, tincture of cannabis, chloroform and alcohol was incapable of entirely dulling the sensations of my needlework, and I had to get Jimo and Kuma to hold him down, one on the shoulders and one on the legs. The screaming made it hard to concentrate, and the job was not one I would want to boast about. When I was finished his face resembled a badly darned pair of trousers, with a ragged corkscrew of waxed thread holding his cheek together, but at least it was done.

I am not ashamed to say that afterwards I took a long draught of Chlorodyne myself. I fell immediately into a multicolored sleep, in which I dreamt that I was back in Limehouse, analyzing coffee with Emily, Ada and the Frog. In my dream Emily turned to Ada and said, "What is the next liquid we must cup?" to which her sister replied, "Oh, blood, I think": I was then served three tiny porcelain dishes of dark red liquid, which I cupped daintily with a spoon. No sooner had I pronounced on the flavors it contained—meat broth, copper, vegetation—than Emily turned to me and said, in a voice that was Ibrahim Bey's, "Now I know you will never betray me."

• • •

THAT EVENING Hector seemed a little better, and managed to swallow some stew which Kuma spooned between his lips, but by next morning he was running a fever. I gave him the Dover's Sudorific, and some Warburg drops, but he was soon streaming with perspiration, his face swelled so much he was almost unrecognizable.

"Kuma," I said, "fetch the medicine woman. Perhaps she can help. And start the boys making a stretcher."

The medicine woman brought herbs and barks with which she prepared a poultice. Having applied it to Hector's wounds, she proceeded to chant over him in a high voice, accompanied by ritual flicks and movements of the hands. Again, for a while this seemed to be efficacious: toward evening Hector regained consciousness. But he could open only one eye now: the other was too swollen in its socket.

"Robber'?"

"I'm here."

"Plant the seeds."

"What are you talking about, Hector?"

"The new coffee berries—ye got them in Harar?"

"Yes, I have them. But don't exert yourself—"

"Keep the seedlings shaded with banana leaves. And keep them weeded. Don't use the Red Gang for weeding, they're idle bastards."

"Very well, Hector."

"Ye've made a good start here. It'll be . . . it'll be civilized one day, if ye only keep going. That's the important thing—civilization. Not us. We're dispensable."

There was a long silence, broken only by the medicine woman's murmurs and the painful seesawing of Hector's breath.

"Tell Emily I'm sorry."

"Emily?"

"Aye. Look after her, Wallis. She's a grand lassie."

"Of course," I said, mystified.

"Dinnae let them eat me."

"No one wants to eat you, Hector. With the possible exception of that damn leopard."

"After ay'm dead, I want ye to burn my body. Promise, now?"

"I keep telling you, Hector, it isn't going to happen." I got up and went to the door of the hut. "Kuma? Where the hell's that stretcher? We'll start for Harar as soon as Massa is well enough to travel."

I turned back to the bed. The medicine woman was bent over Hector's prostrate head, gesturing, as if she were miming pulling a rope out of his mouth, hand over hand. When she reached the end of her imaginary rope, she seemed to take something off and throw it up into the air.

Hector sighed. "Thank ye."

A kind of shudder passed through him—one could almost sense the struggle of the body to live, the terrible exertion of the life force that would cling on at any cost. Again the medicine woman mimed the pulling-out and throwing-off. This time Hector just nodded, faintly. Then, with a sudden violent groan, he was still.

MORE WOMEN came up from the village to prepare the body, while I had the men dig a grave. I waited outside the hut, occasionally taking deep draughts of the Chlorodyne.

The medicine woman came out with Hector's bloodstained clothing. I nodded toward the fire. "Burn it."

She hesitated, then took something from one of the pockets and handed it to me. It was a small sheaf of papers—letters, it looked like, tied up with a very old, faded ribbon.

"Thank you. They may be something that should be sent back

to his people." I pulled the ribbon and glanced at the topmost letter. For a moment, I thought I must be hallucinating again. The sender's address was one I recognized. It was Pinker's house.

My darling Hector . . .

I turned the letter over. It was signed *"Your loving Emily."*

I HESITATED—but not for long. Hector was dead, and Emily was thousands of miles away. In those circumstances, scruples hardly seemed to matter.

My darling Hector,

By the time you get this I suppose you will be in Ceylon! How exciting—I cannot tell you how jealous I am, & how much I wish I could be with you. Four years—it seems forever—but I know that you are going to be such a success, and your plantation will do so well, that my father will surely drop his objections before the end of your time there. And in the meantime will you write to me, and tell me everything that you see, so that I can experience it through your eyes, and drink in every moment along with you? How I long to be married properly, so that I can be out there by your side, and not have to live our life together through this medium of pen and paper! I have an Atlas, and every day I calculate how far your little boat must have traveled (just now as I write this you are off the coast of Zanzibar), and try to imagine what you must be seeing . . .

There was more—there was so much more, but none of it mattered: everything was there in the first few lines. *My father will surely drop his objections. . . .* Hector and Emily. Engaged. It seemed unthinkable, but the evidence was there in front of my eyes. Not only had she once loved Hector, but she had loved him physically, unreservedly, intensely. That was what came through in those love letters, above all—the passion with which she described their affair, the longing with which she looked forward to their union: how very different from the friendly but guarded tone of her letters to me.

There was no year on the letters, but it was possible to work it out. Hector had gone out to Ceylon when Emily was eighteen. Reading even further between the lines, there had been some sort of scandal. *I wanted to come to Southampton to see you off, but Father thinks the less we are seen together just now the better . . .*

I leafed through the letters until I found what I was looking for. There it was, about half a dozen letters in.

If we were impetuous it was only from a surfeit of affection: we are not the first, nor will we be the last, to have "jumped the gun" a little—or at least, it would have been a little, had my father not intervened and turned a few weeks into four long years. . . .

She had slept with him. Behind the euphemisms, the truth of what had happened was clear. Miss Emily Pinker, brought up in the Modern style—too modern, Pinker might have reflected; or perhaps he put it down to the lack of a mother's steadying influence—had thrown herself away on this dour, unprepossessing Scot.

Certain things made sense now: the time I had compared a particularly delicate coffee to a maiden's breath—no wonder Pinker had not drawn attention to it; no wonder her cheeks had been pink. And when he had realized what I wanted from her, he had said that they must avoid, not a scandal, but *another* scandal. I thought nothing of it at the time, but he must have been aware that her reputation might not survive another battering.

I plunged on through the letters. Gradually one became aware of a shading of tone—Emily, for her part, was not so gushing or so girlish; she seemed to be responding more frequently to comments or objections made in Hector's half of the correspondence. And then, finally, after more than a year, there it was:

I do not see how you could be said to be "releasing" me, since I am hardly bound to you by anything more than love—a love I had thought was mutual. I never saw you as being under any kind of obligation or contract, and hope you did not view me in that light either. But if the attractions of travel and adventure are really so much more delightful than family and domesticity, as you say, then of course we must not be married. I cannot in any case conceive of anything more repellent than being wedded to someone who did not wholeheartedly desire it—or me.

It was strange how everything suddenly swung round, like a compass when you take a new turning. I hadn't liked Hector, yet he had somehow become my friend. He had been my only companion—the only white man—within a hundred miles, yet it turned out I barely knew him. Emily I had understood even less; the irony was that I knew more about her now, when she was three thousand miles away, than I had done in London.

There was one more letter, not so faded.

Dear Hector,

I hardly know how to respond to your last letter. Of course I am delighted that you are considering settling down. I am flattered, too, that you still think of me after all this time. But I have to say that after so long apart I can hardly consider you as a potential husband. Indeed the manner of our separation, and the sentiments you expressed at the time, caused me no little anguish, and if I consequently tried to stop thinking of you with that affection which I had hitherto felt, it was because you yourself indicated that I should do so. However, I cannot stop you coming to England, and doubtless my father will want to invite you to our home, so let us try to remain friends, at least. . . .

That was dated 7th February. Eight weeks before she had started working with me on the Guide. So much hurt and misery, and I had been completely unaware of it.

THAT NIGHT, the drums started up in the village. When we came to bury Hector next morning, I discovered that the eyes and testicles had been taken from his corpse, gouged from the groin and face in great bloodless wounds. "It is for *ju-ju,*" Jimo said mournfully. "White man's body plenty big magic." He mimed someone eating. I stumbled outside and vomited, dry heaves that produced nothing but a terrible retching agony in my stomach. Sickened, I changed my mind about burial, and had them fill the pit with kindling. I watched Hector's flesh shrivel and burn like an overcooked spit-roast: the fat dripping into the flames made them splutter and turn green. It seemed to me that some of the natives watched with a faintly regretful expression, as if to say that it was all a terrible waste.

AFTER THAT I entered a numb daze of horror. As well as the Chlorodyne there were the other drugs, and the emergency whisky. I even tried Jimo's *khat.* It had a bitter, slightly astringent quality, not unlike chewing lime leaves. At first I thought it did nothing, but gradually I became aware of a faint tingling sensation, as if I had become too big for my body and were somehow seeping out of every pore, like a gas. I maintained this state of gaseous intoxication for about a week, chewing a little more every time the effects wore off, before eventually falling asleep and waking with a terrible headache.

And then I realized that, somewhere in that drugged ethereal haze, I had come to a decision.

Dear Emily,

I'm afraid I have some very tragic news. Poor Hector is dead. He was attacked by a leopard, and although I did what I could to save him the wounds became infected almost overnight.

He expressed a wish to be cremated, a wish I carried out immediately after his death. While sorting through his things I came across the enclosed letters from yourself. I have read them—probably I should not have done so, but there it is. Given what they reveal, you will not be surprised to learn that I do not intend to marry you after all. However, I should make clear that this was something I had begun to consider even before I read this correspondence. Briefly, I have fallen in love with someone else.

I wish you the best of happiness in your future life.

Yours—I was going to write "faithfully," but perhaps in the interests of precision I had better say "sincerely,"

Robert Wallis

So now I was free.

[FIFTY]

"Astringent"—a dry feeling in the mouth, undesirable in coffee.

—INTERNATIONAL COFFEE ORGANISATION,
The Sensory Evaluation of Coffee

"LET ME BE SURE I HAVE UNDERSTOOD THIS CORRECTLY." IBRAHIM Bey frowned. "You wish to buy Fikre from me?"

"I do."

"But why?"

"I am in love with her."

"One cannot love a slave, Robert. This I have learned through bitter experience."

"Nevertheless, I wish to buy her," I said stubbornly.

"Robert, Robert . . ." He clapped his hands. "Let us take coffee, and I will endeavor to explain to you why this is a foolish course of action."

We were in Bey's house, in a room filled with rugs and filigree lanterns. The reception rooms in these Harar houses were on the second floor, to catch the cool breezes that trickled down from the mountains toward the end of the afternoon. Ornate carved screens provided privacy from the street, although sometimes one could look down and catch the rolling eye of a camel, just a few feet below.

I said, "I am perfectly serious, Ibrahim. And I assure you I shall not change my mind. But of course I will take coffee, if you wish."

Mulu brought us tiny cups of thick, fragrant arabica. The honeysuckle fragrance reminded me of Fikre, of the sweet coffee taste of her body. I closed my eyes. *Soon you will be mine.*

"So," Bey said, putting down his cup. "Does this strange idea have anything to do with poor Hector's death?"

I shook my head.

"But were he alive, he would have forbidden it?"

"He was not my keeper."

"Your business is coffee, Robert. Not slavery."

"This is not a business matter, Ibrahim. I heard you were thinking of selling. I want to buy. That's all there is to it."

"It is true, unfortunately, that I am compelled to sell her. I wish it were not so. But you realize that for you to sell her on would be impossible? Whilst the Emperor tolerates the buying of slaves, no one but an Arab may sell them."

"It makes no difference—I do not intend to sell."

He gave me an anguished look. "Your future father-in-law would be furious if he knew about this conversation."

"Mr. Pinker," I said carefully, "will never find out."

"Robert, Robert . . . I think I told you I had to mortgage everything I owned to buy her. It was a moment of madness, one I deeply regret. If I could stop you from making the same mistake, I would." He paused. "And I think perhaps you do not appreciate just how costly a girl like that actually is."

"Name your price."

He said softly, "One thousand pounds."

I reeled. "I must admit, I had not realized it would be so much."

"I told you it was extortionate. I am certainly not trying to profit by the deal. My conscience—and our friendship—prevents me from doing that, at least. One thousand pounds is what I paid."

"She is worth less now, though."

He frowned. "How so?"

He does not suspect. Be calm. "Because she is older."

"True. What price do you think is fair?"

She is worth nothing, I wanted to shout. *She is no longer intact.* "Eight hundred. It is all I have."

"I bargained for her once, and I have regretted it ever since," he said heavily. "I will not bargain now. I accept your offer, Robert, although it will leave me considerably out of pocket. Will you want to have her examined?"

"Of course not. You are not the only man of honor here."

"Please, Robert. Don't do this. I can take her to Arabia and sell her there. Take a day or two to reconsider—"

"Will Austro-Hungarian dollars be acceptable?"

He nodded helplessly. "Indeed."

"I'll have the money brought round tomorrow."

"And I will instruct my lawyer to draw up the necessary papers." He shook his head. "I fear that when you come to your senses you will somehow blame me for this. And when that time comes, you will no longer be my friend."

I have been tupping her behind your back, you fat oaf. "I can assure you that I am going into this with my eyes wide open." I held out my hand.

Still he hesitated. "They say that when you have shaken an Englishman's hand, there can be no going back on the deal."

"That is correct."

He took my hand in both of his. "Then I will shake your hand, Robert. But I tell you frankly that it is with a heavy heart."

• • •

EIGHT HUNDRED POUNDS. It was, as Bey had said, extortionate. It meant using not just my advance from Pinker, but all the money for the expenses of the plantation, and what little I had made from my own trading.

It was the money that, had things turned out differently, would have enabled me to marry Emily Pinker.

But I would still have fifty or so left. It was not much, but the coffee seeds were planted and paid for, there was enough to pay the villagers, and my other needs were few. Once the crop was growing, I might be able to borrow against its eventual sale. We would be able to survive. Then, once we had some money coming in, we could leave—not for England, of course, but to some other part of Europe: Italy, perhaps, or the South of France. We would exist outside society: artists and rebels, free from the strictures of conventional morality.

THE CHEST of dollars was too heavy for one man, so I went into the market to find two soldiers to carry it. I took my pistol, in case of robbers, and together we threaded our way through the maze of brown streets.

Darkness rose up around us as if it were being poured into the city from some gigantic pot. But Bey's house, when we finally got there, was full of lights—tiny candles in filigree lanterns, flickering like stars.

The lawyer, a taciturn Adari, was waiting in the second-floor sitting room. He asked me some questions to make sure I understood what I was doing. I answered him patiently, all the while shooting glances at the door to see if Fikre was going to join us. But of course Bey did not want to risk a scene: as far as he knew, she was greeting this development with her customary fury.

The lawyer presented me with a document in Arabic. "This is her provenance—a bill of sale from the house which last sold her. Do you wish to show it to a lawyer of your own?"

"There is no need."

He shrugged. "And this is a document certifying that she was a virgin when she was sold." He placed another document in Arabic in front of me. "I understand you do not wish to have her examined?"

"There is no need," I repeated.

"Very well." He laid a third document on the table. "You will have to sign this, to say that you accept her as she is."

I signed. This time there was also a translation, in poor but tolerable English. *I, the undersigned, do hereby accept the slave known as Fikre, in recompense whereof . . .* I scanned it and signed that, too.

"And finally, the bill of sale." The lawyer looked at Bey. "Will you count the money?"

"Robert would not cheat me," Bey said firmly.

Again I signed my name, while Bey signed the receipt.

"She is yours," the lawyer said to me. I glanced at the door, but he was handing me a last piece of paper—a simple certificate, bearing a few lines of Arabic text. "This is to confirm it. If you ever set her free, you must tear this up."

"I understand."

Still she did not come.

The lawyer took a final cup of coffee. It was Bey's best, or so the merchant informed me. I could not taste a thing, only a longing for Fikre that saturated my senses and spread like honey through my veins.

Finally, the lawyer left us. "Robert," Bey said seriously, "you know that I believe you will regret this one day. When that day comes, I want you to remember that it was you who insisted I sell, and not the other way around."

"I understand."

At last Fikre came into the room, her face sullen. Mulu was behind her, carrying a coffee sack. "I have given her some clothes and so on," Bey explained. "As a slave she cannot own anything, but they go with her."

"Thank you." I took the sack. There were tears in Mulu's eyes, but he said nothing as he handed it to me.

I held out my hand to her. "Fikre—will you come with me?"

"Do I have a choice?" she said furiously.

"No."

WE MAINTAINED the pretense until we were around the first corner. Then I could stand it no longer. I pulled her into a doorway, kissing her, running my hands around her waist, reaching up for her head, pushing it against my lips, devouring her.

At last we pulled apart. "So now I am yours," she said, grinning.

"Exactly."

"And do you know what you are going to do with me?"

"Well," I said, "whatever it is, I think it's going to involve quite a lot of sex."

[FIFTY-ONE]

"Caramel"—tasters should be cautioned not to use this attribute to describe a burning note.

—INTERNATIONAL COFFEE ORGANISATION,
The Sensory Evaluation of Coffee

OF THE DAYS THAT FOLLOWED I FIND I CAN WRITE VERY LITtle. I can describe the elusive aroma of an Indian Malabar; I can find the words to distinguish between the coffee of Trinidad and that of Tanganyika; I can define the subtle variations between the different grades of Java. Yet of the dozens—scores—of fucks that Fikre and I enjoyed in that period following my purchase of her from Bey, the most ecstatic sex of my life, I can barely recall in any detail more than two or three, let alone find the words to describe them. And yet they were all different, as coffees are different—or even more so, for we worked our way through every possible permutation two bodies would allow.

What I can remember—but still, alas, cannot easily describe—is the sense of physical delight, the playful intoxication of a world reduced to just a room, two bodies and a bed, our lovemaking interrupted only by occasional forays to the market for food. Even those were remarkably infrequent: when we were hungry we simply chewed handfuls of beans from our makeshift mattress and, revived, fell back to pleasuring one another. Or sometimes we would go out to the market, thinking ourselves ravenous, and come back only with great armfuls of flowers, as if we could live on nothing more substantial than their heady fragrance, coffee, and each other's flesh.

The juncture of her legs was the altar at which I knelt, the cup at which I made my communion. I was Ali Baba, whispering *Open sesame* at the cave, my tongue uncurling like a caliph's slipper. I was a hummingbird, slipping my beak into the dew-filled calyx. And she, in turn, knelt before me, adoring me with her mouth, her eyes fixed on mine even as I pumped my seed over her lips, her cheeks, garlanding her perfect black shoulders with opalescent pearls of semen. They too tasted of coffee, she told me as she licked them from her fingers; flavored by the beans that were our addiction and our constant diet.

She was entirely without shame, and loving her, I became shameless, too. There was nothing she would not try, no point at which she would say "enough." If she was very sore, she would ask me to buy opium in the market: we smoked it the Arab way, in a bubbling *narghile.* Between *khat* and coffee and opium and sex, the days passed in a blur of sensations. "To burn always with this hard, gem-like flame, to maintain this ecstasy, is success in life," the aesthete Walter Pater had written. I knew the truth of it: I lived more intensely in that room than I had ever done before, or would do since.

Sometimes, when I was sleeping, I would half-wake to find her playing with my bollocks, rolling them around in her fingers, staring at them, quite fascinated. Around and around they went in her palm, prodded by her fingertips. . . . I asked her once what it was about them that so riveted her. She said, in a voice that sounded almost mesmerized, "Because these are the center of everything. Without these, there is nothing." I did not understand what she meant, nor did I try to—she had a tendency to mysticism at times. In any case, the prodding of her fingers had aroused me, and I was ready to slide inside her once more.

And then, at last, the banquet of our senses reached its final course. We were sated, and though we still fucked at the least opportunity, it was like having your wineglass refilled when it is still almost full; you do not need to drain each drop. Our minds began to turn at last to the future.

"WHAT DO YOU mean to do?"

"I'll have to go back to the plantation. The seedlings will need to be transplanted. It isn't fair to let Jimo deal with it on his own, and I've neglected the place."

"Shall I come with you?"

"I warn you, it's pretty rough. There are no feminine comforts."

"I can do without those."

"Then come."

"Robert . . . ?" she asked.

"Yes?"

"Do you have any plans for me?"

I gestured at the bed. "This is as far as my planning went."

"I meant my . . . status."

I laughed. "Do you want me to marry you? A white dress, church? All the ceremonies of the bourgeois?"

She shook her head. "I want to be free."

"We *are* free."

She looked at me intently. "Robert, what I have done with you—I do it because I love you, not because you have a piece of paper."

She was waiting, I knew, for me to say that I would tear the papers up. Why did I not? It would have proved my love. And yet something held me back. It was, after all, an irrevocable gesture. And deep down, I think I still needed to feel I had that authority over her—as if the love and the ownership were somehow linked.

I made a joke of it. "But I fully intend to sell you just as soon as I find someone better"—something like that, or possibly it was even more clumsy, I can't now recall. Whatever it was, I think I saw something harden for a moment behind her eyes. Then she nodded her head, meekly, and the subject was dropped.

SHE ONLY MENTIONED it one other time. We were in bed, our bodies pivoting together in the slow, easy dance of lovers who are not in a hurry. A butterfly beating its wings in the sun.

She whispered "Yes," and "Now," and then she suddenly took my head in her hands and said fiercely, "If you give me my freedom, I will give myself back to you. All of me. I will be utterly yours."

I groaned and said, "I love you."

Not quite the same thing, you see.

A COUPLE of days before we left for the plantation, we came back from the market to find Mulu sitting on our doorstep. Fikre embraced him so happily that it was several moments before he could hand me Bey's letter.

My dear Robert,

Mulu is pining without Fikre, and I have no work for him here, so I have taken the liberty of sending him to you. He needs no pay, only his food and lodging. You will find him a good servant so long as he is allowed to tend to Fikre's needs as well as yours. If you do not want him, send him back. If you keep him, there is no need to pay me for him—unlike Fikre, his value is very small, though I shall be sorry not to have him.

Your friend,

Ibrahim

There was no question of returning him—Fikre was overjoyed to see him, and he her. It was, I suppose, lonely for her sometimes, deprived of female company. But I was not used to having a eunuch around—it made me uncomfortable, if the truth be told, the way the two of them were together, almost like two girls, chattering away in a language I could not understand. Sometimes he would help her dress, or bathe, and that too seemed strange to me. Their intimacy was more like that of a lady and her maid than that between a man and a woman.

Once, getting up at night to piss, I found Mulu engaged on the same errand. He half-turned—I glimpsed the terrible scars of his mutilation, shining zigzags of tortured flesh, pink on the black skin. In all other respects he had the genitals of a child.

He gave a cry of embarrassment and turned away, hiding himself. I said nothing—what was there to say? It was horrible—ghastly—but there was nothing I could do.

[FIFTY-TWO]

"Acrid"—a burnt flavour, sharp, bitter, perhaps irritating.

—SIVETZ, Coffee Technology

THE POST FROM HARAR IS SLOW, AND IT IS SEVERAL WEEKS BEfore Robert's letter arrives, bearing the franks of many countries. It is the Frog who brings it, running from the hallway to deliver her prize, panting, into Emily's hands.

"Please may I read it?" she begs. "Please?"

"I haven't read it myself yet. Besides, Robert's letters to me are private."

"Please may I have the stamp and the envelope and please may you read me the bits that aren't private?" the Frog says hopefully. "Look—it's got something in it. Has he sent you a present?"

Emily does not answer. She has opened the letter, which is more of a package, containing as it does her old letters to Hector. For a moment she does not understand; then she goes white. She scans the note.

"What is it?" the Frog demands. "Is everything all right?"

"No, it isn't," Emily says. She gets to her feet. "I had better find Father. I have some very bad news about Hector. And Robert—Robert has . . ." Words fail her, and then the Frog is treated to the extraordinary sight of her oldest sister—her capable, efficient, all-powerful older sister—bursting into tears.

SOME TIME LATER, Pinker comes out of his study to find the Frog waiting.

"Philomena," he says, sitting down next to her, "I'm afraid your sister has had a shock."

"I know. Robert has jilted her."

"I—" He shoots her a look. "However did you know that?"

"I asked Ada why Emily was crying and she told me."

"I see. Well, you must be very especially nice to Emily now. For example, it would not be nice, perhaps, to use the word 'jilted.' They have simply decided that their future lies apart."

"But if he hasn't jilted her, why is she crying?"

"The other bad news is that Hector became very ill in the jungle. Sadly, he has passed away."

"Was he buried?"

"Yes, he was."

"He wasn't eaten by cannibals?"

"No. There was a short, dignified service, with a coffin, and a sermon, and all the natives saying prayers."

The Frog thinks about this. "He probably got to heaven quicker from Africa than he would have done from here. Because Africa is in the middle."

"Exactly." Pinker gets to his feet.

"Who will Emily marry now, if she won't marry Robert?"

"Well, in due course she will meet someone else she likes, and that is the person she will marry."

Something suddenly strikes the Frog—a thought so appalling

that it forces her pouchy, frog-like eyes open as wide as they will go. "Robert will go on writing to *me,* though, won't he?" she says anxiously.

"I doubt very much if he will," her father says, shaking his head.

Then, to his astonishment, he finds he has not one daughter in tears but two.

[FIFTY-THREE]

WE FOUND THE PLANTATION IN A BAD WAY. EVEN THOUGH it was mid-morning when we arrived, the workers were nowhere to be seen. The digging of planting pits, which had been proceeding at the rate of around fifty feet a day before I left, seemed to have slowed to less than a tenth of that, and although Hector and I had marked out with tapes the lines the gangs should follow, the new pits staggered randomly around the hillside as if dug by a giant mole. Without Hector's iron discipline, it seemed, the place was incapable of functioning. But the worst of it was in the nursery beds. The leaves of the new seedlings were discolored with a faint spotting of rust-colored circles, like the foxing you find on the pages of old books.

It was some kind of fungus. I could not understand it. Hector and I had carefully examined all the wild coffee bushes in the nearby forest, and none of them had showed any signs of ill health. I felt a sudden pang of regret—Hector would have known what to do. Instead, I turned to the pages of Lester Arnold, who advised washing the affected plants with a solution of soap and strong coffee.

When it became clear the coffee seedlings were going to die

anyway, we had to decide what to do next. There was money to buy another lot of seed crop, but only one: after that we would be unable to pay the workers.

I explained all this to Fikre one evening as we ate.

"You are worried," she said.

"Of course I'm worried. If the next lot die, there won't be any more—there's simply no more cash." I spoke more forcefully than I had meant to: the anxiety was a strain.

She was silent a moment. "Do you blame me?"

"Of course not."

"But if you hadn't bought me, there would be more money."

"There's no point in going down that road. What's done is done."

It was not the most tactful thing I could have said. "So you do regret it," she persisted.

"Fikre, can you stick to the point? I have to decide what to do."

For a moment her eyes flashed again. Then she seemed to check herself. "Have you thought of growing coffee as the natives do?"

"The natives *don't* grow coffee. They just pick the berries that grow wild in the forest."

"Quite. Perhaps you do not need all this." Her arm took in the cleared hillsides, the nursery, the rows of planting pits. "You could turn your diggers into foragers. They could bring you the wild coffee, and then you could pay them for it and take it to market at a profit."

"It's not how Lester Arnold says to do it."

"Lester Arnold isn't here."

"Maybe not, but his book is the only guide I've got. I can't disregard his proven commercial methods for—for coffee grown willy-nilly in the jungle." I sighed. "There is one other thing I could try. There's a white man, an ivory trader, down in Zeilah. His name's Hammond. He told me if I ever wanted help I should get in touch."

"But how can this trader help you?"

"The Emperor needs guns—everyone says so—he's buying every half-decent rifle that reaches Harar. White men—men like Hammond—can get them sent up from Aden. With the profit I'd make from that, I could set the farm straight."

"What will the Emperor do with these guns?"

"Hector thinks—thought—he wants to expand his territory into the Interior."

"To turn them on the natives, in other words."

"So long as it's only blacks he's butchering, it's no concern of ours."

She glanced at me. I had forgotten, for a moment, the color of her own skin. "You know what I mean," I said impatiently.

"It is a risky business."

"I'm not sure I have a choice. Anyway, I'm going to sleep on it."

"I see." She turned away. "Let me know what you decide."

"I certainly will. After all, it affects you too, darling."

Dear Hammond,

I am writing to ask a favor. You said you might be interested in doing a little trading with me. If that is still the case, can you get me as many of the latest Remingtons as an Englishman's credit will buy, and send them up to Harar? If anyone asks, say the boxes contain tools for the plantation. For reasons which I will not go into, I need an urgent source of funds, and there is a ready market for goods such as those at present.

I am enclosing twenty Austro-Hungarian dollars as a down payment.

Best,

Wallis

I sent the letter with an agent who passed on his way to the coast, although I knew it could take weeks or even months to get a reply.

Meanwhile, I was busy—too busy. It was as if the plantation was jinxed. The seedlings that were not diseased were attacked by black ants. A warthog got into the nursery beds and wreaked havoc. The workers became increasingly truculent. My feet became infested with jiggas, which had to be dug out with the point of a needle. The rust disease spread amongst the remaining plants, never quite wiping them out but preventing them from thriving. I replanted the diseased seedlings in more spacious beds, re-dug the nursery with fresh soil, and planted fresh seeds where the old ones had died. Some days I fell asleep without even taking my boots off, which at least prevented more jiggas from getting at them.

And yet, and yet . . . Every night, as evening fell—those ridiculously early equatorial nights, blackness falling like a blanket over the jungle—the kingfishers and parrots flashed to and fro in the dusk, colobus monkeys swung effortlessly through the trees overhead, and fireflies tumbled through the darkness like magic. Fikre and I ate together, the hissing lamp our only companion. It was hard not to feel a sense of satisfaction at those moments. Whatever I had thought I might end up doing when I was sent down from Oxford, never, in my wildest dreams, had I imagined anything like this.

[FIFTY-FOUR]

If the pain were a coffee, Emily sometimes thinks, she would be able to enumerate its myriad components. Heartbreak, of course, but heartbreak is only one element of what she is feeling now. There is humiliation—the knowledge that for the second time in her life, she has made a fool of herself. Her father and Ada love her too much to say "I told you so," but they did tell her, and she ignored them: now it turns out they were right about Robert all along. Failure—she feels stupid, useless, incompetent. How can she ever hope to change the world, when she can't even pick a husband? Anger—how dare he: betraying her like this with just a few casual lines, as if he were canceling a subscription to a newspaper? But the elegant, icy brevity of the note, she realizes, was part of the message. Loneliness—she misses him, she would give anything to have him back. She remembers afternoons cupping coffees here in her father's office, the descriptors bouncing back and forth between them like musical phrases, a duet, a private sensual language conveying so much more than the taste of coffee. . . . And then there is an emotion for which there is no word, or none that she can think of, the terrible wrenching amputation of a physical desire that will now never be expressed. She feels like some misshapen, stunted grotesque, an old-maid-in-waiting. . . . *Damn you, Robert Wallis,* she thinks as she collects suffrage petitions. *Damn you,* she thinks as she takes minutes for Arthur's constituency meetings. *Damn you,* she thinks, as she wakes in the night and remembers suddenly what has happened, why her eyes are sore and her nose inflamed, and waits for the tears to come yet again, as inevitable as a bout of fever.

[FIFTY-FIVE]

"Twisty"—a coffee with characteristics that are dubious as to its reliability.

—J. ARON & CO., Coffee Trading Handbook

❧

"I'LL HAVE TO GO TO HARAR," I TOLD FIKRE. "I NEED TO REPLACE those seeds."

"Of course. Do you want me to come with you?"

I hesitated. "Could you bear to stay here? The boys will work better if there's someone to keep an eye on them."

"Of course. There are a few other things you might get, for the house—I can give you a list."

"That would be grand." I looked at her. "You know I love you?"

"Yes, I know it. Come back soon."

• • •

My business in Harar was swiftly concluded, so I thought I would look in on Bey and see if he had heard from Hammond.

There was something different about his house. The filigree lamps that had hung from the balcony were gone: that was it. I knocked on the door. It was opened by a man I did not recognize.

"How can I help you?" he asked in French.

"I am looking for Ibrahim Bey."

He smiled mirthlessly. "As we all are. Bey is gone."

"Gone? Where to?"

The man shrugged. "To Arabia, perhaps. He left suddenly, to avoid his creditors."

It made no sense. "Are you sure?"

He laughed, grimly. "Certainly—I was one of them. I was lucky: I had this house as my security. The scoundrel had been planning this for some time—there was nothing left to sell."

A thought suddenly struck me—a thought so awful that I could not quite bring myself to think it through. "Do you by any chance read Arabic?"

He nodded. "Yes, a little."

"May I show you some documents?"

"If you wish."

I went back to the French merchant's house and found the papers I had signed when I bought Fikre. Retracing my steps through the streets, I knocked again on the ornate, carved door of the house where Bey had lived.

The man spread the papers by the window and looked through them. "This is a bill of sale," he told me.

Thank God—

"It is a receipt for ten crates of the finest pistachios in Cairo. And this one," he tapped another document, "is a loading bill for a consignment of coffee. And this," he held up the certificate of ownership, "is a letter. A note, rather. It seems to be addressed to you."

If you ever set her free, you must tear this up . . .

"Are you all right?" he inquired solicitously. "Perhaps you would like some coffee." He called some words in Adari, and a servant entered with a pot.

"No. Please—what does it say?"

"It says: 'My friend, do not judge us too harshly. It is surprisingly hard to make money in coffee anymore, and my debts have been mounting for years. When you are less angry, I hope you will recall that you paid only what you wanted to. As for the girl, forgive her. She is in love, and this was the only way.' "

I didn't understand. What did it mean? What way was the only way? For what was I having to forgive Fikre? How did he know that she was in love with me?

Unless . . .

Something else flitted into my brain, a series of separate memories that suddenly joined together and made a coherent pattern.

"It wouldn't fool a doctor, but it might fool a man in lust—such a man believes what he wants to believe."

I had to get back to the farm.

IT WAS IMPOSSIBLE to hurry that journey—the jungle clutched at you, it caught at your feet and tangled them with vines, it reached out to you with branches and leaves, placed its hand on your chest and said *wait;* it sapped your strength and exhausted your will.

Besides, I already knew what I would find.

Fikre gone. Mulu gone. A note, fluttering on the camp-bed.

Don't try to find us.

And then, in a slightly different hand, as if she had turned back at the final moment, unable to leave without this last, hasty explanation: *He is the only man I have ever really loved.*

I WILL NOT try to describe how I felt. Perhaps you can imagine it. Not just despair, but grief—a complete, crushing, suffocating horror, as if the whole world had collapsed around me. As if I had lost everything.

But then, you see, I had.

IN THE END, it is the stories we tell ourselves which are the dangerous ones, the ones that kill us or save us or leave us stranded in the middle of a jungle, three thousand miles from home.

They must have planned it long before they met me. Perhaps that was what they were doing while Hector and I were kicking our heels in Zeilah: going over the details, getting the nuances right, making the whole package—the lure—so perfect, so *delectable* that I couldn't help but swallow it.

Was the bait concocted specially for me? Certainly, the coming of an Englishman must have galvanized them. And such an Englishman: young, naive, impetuous, oblivious to everything except the sap roaring through his veins . . .

Tales told in the desert. Jeweled webs, spun to ensnare an unsuspecting fly. Perhaps some of them were even true. For example, I think Fikre probably had been brought up in a harem, as she described—how else could one explain her languages, her education? I suppose it was unlikely she had been a virgin when we met—she certainly knew how to give a good performance in bed. That would have been why she needed to seduce me, of course: so that I would waive my right to have her examined.

But one fact was indisputable: they all needed money. Bey to pay his debts, Fikre and Mulu to start a new life together. And I had money—a strongbox full of it. I had paid for sex before, that was obvious to them, but the sort of sums a man would pay for that were paltry compared with what they wanted.

They knew that the real prize was to get me to pay for love.

I COULD NOT know exactly how the story played out. But I could start to thread together possibilities, likelihoods; to construct different versions of events and test them against each other for authenticity, as a man might strike two coins against each other and listen for the ring that says, this one is counterfeit, this real. . . .

And so, painstakingly, I became a maker of tales myself.

IT STARTED in a harem, somewhere in the far reaches of the Ottoman Empire. A slave sale. A young merchant who should by rights not have been there, amongst all those wealthy courtiers. And a game of chess—a game the merchant lost to a slave girl, full of fury and resentment.

He must have seen then how clever she was, how agile her wits were even under pressure. And they would both have seen the rich young courtier who was to be her fate.

Whose idea was it? Fikre's, I imagine. After all, she had nothing to lose. Perhaps she muttered it even as she beat him.

If you help me, I will help you.

What do you want?

To be free.

How can I possibly help with that?

Buy me.

With what? He will easily outbid me.

However much it costs, I will make sure you profit on the deal.

She would have looked at him then—not pleading, but with

that level gaze I had come to know so well. But she still would not have known it was going to work, not until Bey came into the bidding at the last minute, waving his arms excitedly like a man possessed by a sudden infatuation.

And then the years of planning. Mulu, I imagine, joined them later, although it is possible he came from the same household, sold off as a job lot when the girls were disposed of.

Love without kisses is not love.
A spear without blood is not a spear. . . .

Mulu and Fikre. They loved each other completely—I could see that now. How could I have missed it? It was a kind of love between a man and a woman that I, in my ignorance, had not even conceived of. A love that was nothing to do with sex.

And yet, and yet . . . Suppose Bey had promised his slaves their freedom if they could get me to part with the money. That did not explain, surely, those weeks in which she and I fucked so incessantly, when she woke me from sleep with the touch of her hand, rolling my balls in her cupped fingers. . . . If it was Mulu she loved, why give herself to me so enthusiastically?

He is the only man I have ever really loved. . . .

But Mulu was not a man, was he? Not in one sense. So perhaps she had simply wanted to know what love was really like, no—what *sex* was really like, before committing herself to a lifetime without it. Perhaps she even hoped to make it work—the three of us, master, slave and servant—to give her body to one, and her heart to the other, all living together under one roof; until I, with my clumsiness, my refusal to listen to her, had made her realize that such an unconventional ménage was impossible.

Or perhaps—my thoughts raced ahead, found a further explanation, wanted to reject it but could not—perhaps it was not just sex she had wanted.

There was one other thing a eunuch could not provide.

I remembered her words as she gazed, fascinated, at my balls, cupped in her fingers. *Without these, there's nothing.*

That was why she had fucked me so insatiably.

She hoped for a child.

I HAD NEVER withdrawn from her. It was another way in which I had been blind to the future. Yet one only had to read Darwin to be reminded that all this—the lust which had propelled me blindly from one disaster to another—was ultimately just an expression of the same power which made the coffee bushes explode with blossoms.

What a fool I had been.

I had not just wandered into their trap; I had embraced it, tying its threads around myself with a shout of joy. Lust had blinded me, had shackled me; had led me, as if by a chain tied around my cock, down the road of skulls to Harar, and this.

God is not a watchmaker. God is a pimp.

[FIFTY-SIX]

"Soft"—characterised by an absence of any predominant taste sensation on any part of the tongue, except for a subtle dryness.

—LINGLE, The Coffee Cupper's Handbook

❧

ARTHUR BREWER COMES INTO HIS CONSTITUENCY OFFICE, A letter in his hand. "This one will have to be answered, I'm afraid. Some Poor Law Guardian who absolutely knows for a fact that anyone in his parish who doesn't work is a malingerer . . ." He stops. "Emily. Are you all right?"

"Hmmm?" She starts to turn toward him, then realizes he will see that her eyes are sore and red. "Yes, of course," she says, turning back to her typewriter.

"Perhaps you could dash something off—something placatory and utterly noncommittal." He places the letter on the table next to her. "Are you quite sure you're well?"

To his amazement she takes a great shuddering gasp. Her hand flies to her mouth, as if she has just hiccuped or made some other embarrassing *faux pas.* "I'm sorry. I shall be fine in just a—" But she cannot go on. Great gasping, racking sobs convulse her body.

"My dear," he says, appalled. Like a magician there is a handkerchief in his hand. She takes it—it is soft and thick and white, the linen perfumed with a warm, cinnamon-stick cologne. Trumper's, she thinks automatically—her father wears it, too. She buries her face in its vast, comforting folds. A hand touches her shoulder, then descends to the middle of her back, patting her gently while she weeps.

When she has recovered enough to speak he says gently, "What is it?"

She is torn between the urge to tell him everything and the need to conceal her stupidity, her over-trustfulness, her shameful, feminine gullibility. "Nothing. A disappointment, that's all."

"But you're upset. You must take the rest of the afternoon off." His face lifts. "I know—we'll go to a moving picture. Have you seen one yet?"

She shakes her head.

"You see! We are surely the last two people in London not to have been. I have been working you too hard."

She dries her eyes, manages a smile. "It is we who have been working *you* too hard."

"Well, whichever it is, the remedy is in our own hands." She tries to give back his handkerchief. "Keep it."

As he escorts her to the door, his arm still protectively around her shoulders, she realizes that she has forgotten how pleasant it feels, to be looked after like this.

[FIFTY-SEVEN]

"Harsh"—primary taste sensation related to the presence of bitter-tasting compounds.

—LINGLE, The Coffee Cupper's Handbook

❦

TAHOMEN CROUCHED IN THE TREES, QUITE STILL. THE MUD streaked on his chest and shoulders exactly echoed the pattern of the sunlight as it splashed through the canopy, making him almost invisible. His fingers were lightly curled around the haft of an axe. The metal head had been dulled with mud, lest sunlight catching on steel gave him away, and the haft had been cut down to half its length, so that now it was as good for throwing as it was for chopping wood.

He had been waiting like this for three hours, not far from where Massa Crannach had been attacked. It was possible the leopard had taken fright and already moved on, but he did not think so. Insects landed on his skin; the dried mud on his arms flaked and itched. A *gongololo,* a huge orange millipede, made its way along a twig, dropped onto his leg, then rolled onto the layers of fallen leaf that covered the forest floor, where it vanished.

Distracted momentarily, Tahomen looked up. Twenty feet away, a shadow in the trees flashed white and pink as a leopard yawned, showing its teeth.

Tahomen fought the urge to stiffen, although his fingers tightened on the axe. He could have sworn he made no sound, but even so the leopard's head swung up, its nostrils flaring.

It was too far to risk a throw. For long minutes they both waited.

In one lithe movement the leopard got to its feet, picking its way delicately over the twigs and saplings. Its coat glowed in the green gloom of the forest like the embers of a fire. Tahomen forced himself to be still. There was no more than ten feet between them now. Another few feet, and he would strike.

The leopard mewed quietly. From somewhere behind her, two cubs, each no bigger than a hare, ambled forward. When they reached their mother one immediately dived under her stomach and began to suckle; the other, braver, leapt for a passing blue butterfly, patting it with enormous paws.

So that was why the leopard had attacked Massa Crannach. Tahomen had suspected it all along, but now he was sure. She had been protecting her young, not avenging her mate.

The leopard had rolled onto her side now, batting away the greedy cub which wanted to suckle. That one turned to watch its sibling, copying its movements by jumping at the butterfly with an open mouth. It was a lucky snap: the cub could hardly have looked more surprised to find itself with a butterfly in its jaws. For a moment it had a bright blue tongue, then it opened its mouth and the butterfly fluttered drunkenly away.

Tahomen found himself thinking about Kiku, and their children who had died as babies. He wondered where in the forest their spirits had ended up.

The mother made another sound and the three leopards moved on through the forest. They passed within a few feet of Tahomen, the mother still too engrossed in her cubs to notice him.

If I am going to strike, he told himself, it must be now.

When they had gone, he stood up. He was stiff from having hidden for so long: it was another sign, he thought ruefully, that he was no longer as young as he had been. This had probably been his last chance to kill a leopard.

As he walked back toward the village he unlooped the leather necklace on which were strung Massa Crannach's testicles and eyes and tossed it into the forest. He had no need of their *ju-ju* now.

AS HE NEARED the village he heard a strange sound. It seemed to be coming from within a thicket of thorn trees. Carefully, Tahomen separated the branches with the haft of his axe and peered inside.

Massa Wallis was lying amongst the tangled thorns. His clothes were scratched and filthy, his hair matted with weeds, and he seemed to be weeping.

Tahomen hacked his way into the thicket and pulled Massa Wallis out. But it was clear there was something more deeply wrong than just having got stuck in a thorn tree. His eyes did not focus, and he was moaning and mumbling under his breath.

Tucking the axe in his belt, Tahomen got his arms around the white man and helped him toward the village.

[FIFTY-EIGHT]

"Delicate"—characterised by a fragile sweet-subtle sensation just past the tip of the tongue when the brew is first sipped.

—LINGLE, The Coffee Cupper's Handbook

ARTHUR MEETS SAMUEL PINKER AT HIS CLUB. THEY DISCUSS certain issues of interest to them both—the rise of Independent Labor: what will it mean for the two traditional parties? Then there is the war in South Africa, currently dominating the newspaper headlines: how will it affect the Empire?

Increasingly, Pinker is thinking about world issues. Lever Brothers, with their Sunlight soap, have shown that it is possible to market a product made in Britain abroad. Why, it is even being *made* abroad, with satellite factories in Canada and Brazil! Why should Castle not follow suit? After all, the Dutch and the French drink even more coffee than the British, and it so happens that in the Castle symbol Pinker's has an image which is universal. He has been studying the way Lever's has done it: opening a factory here, setting up a processing plant there, sharing the cost wherever possible but always maintaining control. It is the way forward, he is sure of it. Just as nations are currently stitching together complex alliances in foreign policy, so the companies behind those nations must come together in a similar way.

There is a difficulty, of course—a political difficulty. Some of the newspapers are saying that these business alliances are not good for the customer—that they are little better than cartels themselves. It is nonsense, of course: there is the world of difference between two companies agreeing not to compete too aggressively in certain areas, and something like the coffee syndicate, where a small number of grandees, governments and wealthy plantation owners have banded together to deny those same companies access to raw materials. He is confident that Free Trade will prevail, but the case needs to be put in the right way, and delivered to the right ears in government. . . . So he and Arthur Brewer have much to talk about.

Eventually they are done, and sit puffing at two cigars while they finish their drinks. But something, Pinker can tell, is still troubling the younger man.

"Mr. Pinker," Arthur begins.

"Samuel, please."

"Samuel . . . There is something I have been meaning to ask."

Pinker makes an encouraging gesture with his cigar.

"It's about Emily," Arthur says with a diffident smile.

Pinker's eyes narrow, although he says nothing.

"I have said nothing to her, of course, and would not do so without your permission. But I find that she and I have many interests in common, and she is such delightful company—a credit to the way you have brought her up, if I may say so."

Pinker raises his eyebrows.

"I was wondering if I might be permitted to get to know her a little better," Arthur explains.

"Permitted?" Pinker says, barking cigar smoke like some furious dragon. "Permitted? You want my permission to woo my daughter?"

Arthur, holding his nerve, nods. "That is correct."

Abruptly Pinker's face creases into a smile. "My dear fellow, I was hoping that you already were."

[FIFTY-NINE]

THE RAINS HAD COME AT LAST. A GREAT DELUGE OF GRAY WAter poured from the sky as if from a gigantic waterfall.

Meanwhile, the villagers discussed the question of what to do with Massa Wallis. The Tamils took little part in these discussions. Now that the farm had no effective master, and they had no certainty of being paid, they slipped off into the jungle in ones and twos, looking for other plantations to work on.

The water got into the farm buildings, so the villagers took them apart and used the wood to construct round huts with thatched roofs which they knew would be waterproof. The rain softened the ground, so they took up some of the diseased coffee seedlings and put down yams and maize. After all, there was plenty of coffee in the jungle already, and a man could not fill his belly with coffee.

It seemed, however, that one man was going to try. Massa Wallis stayed in Kiku's hut, existing only on coffee and *khat,* sleeping for a few hours at a time before waking again, sometimes sobbing and banging his head against the ground in his madness.

"The enchantment is wearing off slowly," Kiku said to the

others, "and there is little we can do to hurry it. So he might as well chew, if it helps the pain."

ONLY ONCE did Massa Wallis rouse himself from his torpor, and that was when a trader arrived at the farm, an agent for one of the new companies that were bringing goods in and out of the jungle. He was accompanied by two mules, each of which had strapped to its back a hefty wooden crate. The trader, a Somali, was dressed in the clothes of a white man, a thing the villagers had never seen before.

"I am delivering the goods that Mister Wallis has ordered," he informed an astonished Tahomen. "Where is he?"

Tahomen was further astonished to see Massa Wallis emerge from Kiku's hut, his eyes bright. "My guns!" he shouted. "The guns have arrived."

The crates were unloaded from the mules, and Jimo was set to work levering the crates open with the edge of an axe. There was a note, which Wallis opened and scanned.

Wallis,
I am sending twelve of the latest Remingtons, as requested. If you think you can sell more, send more money.
Yrs, Hammond

"Sell more?" Wallis muttered. "Of course I can sell more. Get that open, will you Jimo? At last—"

He stepped forward and pulled something heavy out of the crate. Quickly he unwrapped it from its oilcloth covering.

It was a device such as the villagers had never seen the like of—four rows of buttons set on levers, and then above those, a wide semicircle of teeth, which gave the machine the appearance of being topped by a grinning jawbone. For a moment Wallis seemed quite stunned. Then he put the machine down and started to laugh. For long minutes he continued to cackle, doubled up as if in pain, tears streaming from his eyes. The villagers smiled politely, unsure of the exact nature of the joke but ready to be amused.

"Hammond, you bloody fool," Wallis gasped. Looking at Tahomen, he spoke a series of words that were incomprehensible to the headman. "He's sent me a dozen bloody typewriters."

AFTER THE ARRIVAL of the crates, the white man retreated once more to Kiku's hut. It was as if he had been placed under a new spell of death: he simply turned his face to the wall.

"Will he die?" Tahomen asked his wife.

"Perhaps, if he wants to. It's not like having a curse put on you by a sorcerer—Massa Wallis has cursed himself. Only he can decide if he will let it be lifted."

Every morning she made him coffee, thick and dark, murmuring the old prayer as she ground it:

Coffee-pot give us peace
Coffee-pot let our children grow
Protect us from evil
Give us rain and grass.

But Massa Wallis left the coffee untouched, and only chewed more *khat*.

I WILL ASK the forest what to do, Kiku decided. She went into the jungle and sat very still, listening to the myriad whispers of the *ayyanaa*. Already the land that had been cleared for the coffee plants was thick with weeds: soon the trees would start to spread inward from the jungle, and eventually the great hole in the forest would close up again, as skin grows back to close a healing wound.

As so often, the forest did not give her any answers directly. Instead, it allowed her mind to settle, until the answer became obvious and she realized that it had been staring her in the face all along.

[SIXTY]

"Medicinal"—a secondary coffee taste sensation related to "harsh."

—LINGLE, The Coffee Cupper's Handbook

THEY CARRIED MASSA WALLIS INTO THE HUT THAT WAS RE-served for healing and laid him on the floor. The hut contained a firepit, but no smoke opening in the roof. In the firepit Kiku had heaped up a good mound of leaves and bark from the iboga bush. There was coffee, too, because coffee made the iboga more powerful, and a paste made from crushed iboga roots.

As the acrid iboga smoke filled the hut, Kiku cut away Massa Wallis's clothes and painted his body with the patterns of his age-clan. Then she took the bowl of paste and carefully smeared some on his lips and gums, before doing the same to herself.

"What are you doing?" he murmured.

"Where we are going, we will go together," she promised him in Galla. Then she sat down beside him to wait, her hand resting lightly on his wrist so that the *zar* spirits would not come and fly off with him without taking her as well.

• • •

TIME IN THE dream hut was rarely the same as time on the outside, but even so it seemed to Kiku to be an unusually long while before she felt the tapping of the spirits on the roof as they arrived. Massa Wallis stiffened, and lifted a few inches off the floor as the *zar* tried to hoist him on their shoulders, but Kiku held him firmly until they deigned to notice her.

"Who are you?" one of the spirits asked her threateningly.

"I am his guide, to see he is safe."

"Why? He does not belong to you."

"He is our visitor. I must look after him."

She could hear the *zar* conferring amongst themselves. "We are not your *zar,*" they said at last. "We have come a long way to take this man. This has nothing to do with you."

"You are not our *zar,* but this is our hut, and he is under the protection of our hospitality. He has been painted with our markings."

"We have far to travel, and you will not be able to turn back."

"Even so, I am ready to come with you," she answered.

THEY FLOATED UP, over the valley, and for the first time Kiku was able to look down and see the changes that the white men had made—not just the physical ones, like the clearing of the forest, but the complex webs of kinships and clan bonds that the iboga paste made visible, and which had been even more savagely decimated than the trees. Though the forest would heal itself, she did not know if the tribe's social structure had the same resilience.

On and on they flew, over Harar and over the desert, over the great sea and mountains locked in snow. They flew to a place that was strange even by the standards of iboga journeys, a place full of gray stone boxes and many straight lines, and she understood that this was the white man's village.

The *zar* tried to separate them, but with an effort of will Kiku held on to Massa Wallis, turning as they dropped down so that he was riding on her back, so she saw what happened next as if through his eyes.

A MIDDLE-AGED woman stands at a table. She is working her way through a great pile of leaflets, folding them and placing them in a neat stack. Just as it looks as if the stack must topple, another woman, rather younger, comes in and takes them, removing them to another table where they are matched with envelopes. It is clear they have been working this way for some time.

Both women have the multicolored outlines people acquire after you have taken iboga, but it is possible to tell that this younger one is well featured. From the way Massa Wallis catches his breath at the sight of her, Kiku realizes that this woman is important to him. So they move over to the second table, where they watch her putting leaflets into envelopes.

The woman cannot see them, but her delicate nostrils flare and she turns in their direction, a puzzled expression on her face. For a moment she seems to sniff the air.

"Mary?" she calls.

The other woman looks up.

"Can you smell coffee?"

"No. Only printer's ink. And I have cut my fingers three times on these dratted leaflets. Shall we stop for some tea?"

"Yes, you must certainly stop," a man says, entering the room. "It will be our first piece of legislation—no one shall fold constituency leaflets for more than two hours without a tea-break."

"In that case we shall have to work on. Because we have only been doing this forty minutes," the younger woman says drily. But her face lights when she speaks to the newcomer.

"I'll put the kettle on," Mary says. As she passes the younger woman she murmurs, "I may be a while—that kettle is a slow one."

When she has gone there is a silence. Kiku might not understand the white people's words, but their silence is another matter altogether. In Galla there are many kinds of silence, from the awkward pause to the companionable hush, and she sees immediately that this particular silence is one of flirtatious anticipation.

"There is a meeting tonight," the man begins. "I am afraid I am expected to attend, but I was wondering—if you are not too tired—if you could bear to come with me, as my guest."

"What is the subject?"

"Home Rule." He spreads his arms. "We must find a way to get a bill through the Lords. As it stands, the landowners have made it clear they will block any attempt to settle the Irish question."

"I should like that very much, Arthur."

"Really? You would not be bored?"

"I should be fascinated," she assures him. "Will Sir Henry be there?"

"He is the main speaker."

"I will look forward to it, then. They say he is a wonderful orator, and in any case, it will be a pleasure to accompany you."

On Kiku's back, Massa Wallis gives out a terrible sob.

WALLIS WAS getting heavy now, and the outlines of the people in the room more colorful. It was time to leave. Kiku felt the *zar* placing strong hands under her arms, lifting her. But they had come too far and stayed too long: Wallis was so heavy, and Kiku so tired, that the *zar* could not raise them. For a moment it seemed they would not be able to leave. It happened in some cases, she knew: people fell into the iboga trance and for one reason or other never returned, condemning their spirits to wander the earth forever, invisible and homeless. With a great effort she launched herself into the air. She felt the *zar* tugging, and then they were airborne again, drifting over the seething termite nest that was the white man's village, slowly at first, and then with mounting speed over the sea.

BACK AT THE healing hut, Massa Wallis fell into a deep sleep. Kiku spoke the charms that thanked the *zar* for their help, wishing them a safe journey back to where they had come from. Then she took a sharpened porcupine quill and carefully dipped it, first into the iboga ash in the firepit, and then into the tribal markings on Massa Wallis's chest. The sharp tip pierced the skin: the gray ash, still slightly toxic, would make the skin raise and harden in the dotted pattern that described Robert Wallis's initiation into his age-clan.

WHILE WALLIS slept, Kiku went to seek out Tahomen. "I have had a thought," she said diffidently.

He knew her too well to believe that it was really only a thought. "Go on."

"I think Massa Wallis should have Alaya as his servant."

Tahomen tried to digest this. "Why Alaya?"

"Because she is the prettiest of the young women."

"You want her to share his bed?"

She shook her head. "I think he is too sick for that just now. But a pretty face will be good for him. And it will give her something to do."

Tahomen looked into the distance, still busy digesting. Even by Kiku's standards, this suggestion was a lot to get one's head round.

"If Alaya does become the white man's servant," he said, "she will not be there when I wish to go to her."

"Then it is lucky that you have another wife."

"So Bayanna's spear will no longer be outside your hut?"

"Bayanna's spear . . ." Kiku said thoughtfully, "does not always fly quite as straight, or as far, as he would like to think."

Tahomen cackled. "Are men so very simple," he asked, "that a pretty face alone can lift a curse?"

"Are you saying my suggestion is obvious?"

"Of course not," Tahomen said hastily. "Just simple. Which is a very different thing."

"Hmm," she said, mollified. "Well, yes, men are simple. But so are women, when it comes down to it."

"Why? What do women want?"

"They want . . ." She paused. "They want never to be asked what they want."

"Oh, spare me your riddles, old woman," he grumbled.

She pushed him, hard, on the shoulder. "Less of the old," she said. "I'm not so old, for example, that if you start coming to my hut again . . ."

"Yes?"

She shook her head. "Let's just say the forest has made me a promise."

"Oh," he said. She saw that he understood, and she saw, too, that he was not going to spoil everything by putting it into words, this hope she had. That was one of the things that made her love him, she realized: it was the fact that, generally, he knew what not to say.

[SIXTY-ONE]

It is a strange courtship, not least because much of it takes place in the run-up to a general election. There is all the intense activity of a political campaign: writing leaflets, printing leaflets, folding leaflets, going from door to door delivering leaflets; attending meetings, organizing debates, lobbying, touring the constituency. . . . It is thrilling, but they are rarely together for more than a few minutes at a time; he is the general, and she among the foot soldiers. Arthur demonstrates his affection by inquiring, tenderly, if she is not working too hard, by telling the other volunteers that he must insist she takes a short break, now, with him. Her frailty becomes a convenient myth between them: the unspoken reference is to her tears, that time in his office, and the gift of a handkerchief scented with Trumper's cologne. . . .

It becomes clear to the others that the two of them have an understanding. His chivalry, and his gallantry, have become focused on her. When, at a public meeting, he talks about the Vulnerable, his eyes seek out hers in the audience. When he speaks of the Role of Woman, it is one particular woman he favors with a smile. When he talks about the Liberals as the Party of the Family, he catches her eye and looks grave, so that she cannot help smiling, and has to stare at the floor for fear she make him grin, too.

She does not think about Robert Wallis. Or if she does—because however hard she tries, it is impossible, sometimes, to tell her mind what not to think about—it is only anger, of all those initial emotions, which she still feels. At these times she does not feel at all like the frail little woman Arthur believes her to be. At these times she still feels like finding that stupid, feckless, self-centered young man and giving him a bloody great thump on the nose.

THE ELECTION coincides with the return of thousands of soldiers from the war against the Boers in South Africa. The Conservative government organizes victory parade after victory parade. Sometimes it is hard to tell the election and the celebrations apart.

The Conservatives retain power by a comfortable margin. Afterwards, Pinker is enraged to discover that William Howell, of Howell's Coffee, has been knighted; ostensibly for his services to philanthropy, but actually—everyone knows—for his contribution to Conservative party funds.

Senior Liberals complain that support for issues like female suffrage is keeping them out of office. What is needed, they argue, are policies designed to appeal to *electors,* rather than to those who have, by definition, not got a single vote to cast in their support. Sick pay, pensions, unemployment benefit—these are the ways to appeal to the working man.

In London, the Suffrage Union redoubles its efforts to win influence. Emily works as hard for them as she ever did for Arthur's constituency. She looks frail now—she is terribly thin; but her eyes are bright, and in any case, the thinner and frailer she is, the more Arthur seems to dote on her.

• • •

FOR ARTHUR, the disappointment when his party lost the election has been tempered by the fact that, in his own constituency, his personal share of the vote has gone up. He is an important man now among the Liberals, a possible future minister.

It is time to settle his domestic affairs. Luckily, he has found the perfect minister's wife: hard-working, right-thinking and, thanks to her father's endeavors, wealthy. There is nothing more natural than to make a proposal of marriage.

It is a low-key proposal—deliberately so: they are neither of them enamored of histrionics. He takes her to the terrace of the House of Commons. It is evening; the endless to-ing and fro-ing of traffic along the waterway has quietened. Arthur speaks at some length, impressing upon her that this is not a step he takes lightly, that no one has a higher regard for the sanctity of love, expressed in its purest form as a lifelong union between two people, than he does.

"In conclusion," he says, "I should like your permission to speak to your father, and ask him for your hand."

"Oh, Arthur," she says. It is not entirely unexpected: he has made his regard for her clear over these last weeks. "The answer is yes—of course it is yes."

Of course it is yes. How can it not be? This is what she has always wanted. She is a Rational person: to walk away from this now, from everything she has ever envisaged for herself, would be a deeply irrational thing to do.

If, over the coming days and weeks, she has doubts—and she does have doubts—then those too are only natural. It is a big step, a change in both their lives. And if, when he speaks of marriage, it sometimes seems to her that he means by it something different, something more abstract and possibly rather nobler than she does, then that too is only to be expected. He is an idealist: it is one of the things she most admires in him.

It is not love which will sustain their marriage: rather, marriage will sustain their love—she fervently believes it. Nevertheless, she cannot help wondering what will happen if it is not so.

PINKER SEES that he has been wrong to rely on politicians. If something needs doing, it is Business that will do it. Sales of Castle are at an all-time high and his coffers are full. True, Howell has copied his strategy and launched his own packaged coffee now, under the name Howell's Planter's Premium, but Pinker is confidently one step ahead. He expands into other forms of packaging—half-pounds, quarter-pounds, even a new kind of container, the vacuum tin, that allows him to store ground coffee for weeks at a time. The copywriters at the London office of J. Walter Thompson call it the "everlasting coffee." They are busy turning out a dozen ads a week, all of them drumming home the message that Castle Coffee is a vital ingredient of a happy marriage. *("When you make him that special cup of Castle . . . you're making a home!")*

He spends long hours in his office, plotting and scheming and thinking.

[SIXTY-TWO]

On the whole, Kiku decided, things were working out. Alaya was pleased to be looking after someone as important and distinguished as Massa Wallis. Wallis, although he was still not speaking much, was eating again, and working every day in the forest, picking coffee. And Tahomen and she were spending several nights each week together, not always to make love—because, although she might still be young enough to have a child, she was certainly too old to be wearing herself out like that—but talking, and wondering aloud how things were going, and sharing the village gossip, and sleeping nestled into the familiar shapes of each other's bodies. And although it was too early to say whether she would be given another child, and certainly much too early to know if this one would stay with them or be called away, the whispers of the forest were reassuring.

But the question of Wallis was still not finally settled, and at last Kiku judged that the time had come. She waited until the council of the age-clans had gathered to discuss a number of village matters, and then she raised her *siqquee* stick to indicate that she had something to say.

"Sons of woman, daughters of woman," she began.

Tahomen nodded to her. "Speak, and we will listen."

"You will recall," she said, "that when the white men came, *saafu* was broken. The forest was unhappy; but the forest knew to wait. Now the fields they cleared are full of weeds and bushes, and the trees are growing back.

"But do not think that everything is going back to the way it was before. Already, stories reach us of other white farmers, coming to other valleys. Already traders are coming to this place, with their crates of goods to sell, looking for things to buy or exchange.

"The forest can grow back, but it cannot defend itself against the next white man who comes, wanting to tear it down and plant straight lines. We can tell the white man his plants will die, that warthogs will eat his seeds and the sun will shrivel his seedlings, but the white man will not listen to us, because that is his nature."

"What do you suggest?" somebody asked. "Or are you like the dog who barks when the hyena is gone?"

She shook her head. "I am like the spider who says: one cobweb is easily broken, but a thousand cobwebs may tie down a lion. What I suggest is this. We have been paid money by the white man, money for our work. Instead of using that money ourselves, we must give it back to him."

There was a long silence as the villagers pondered this odd proposal.

"Massa Wallis cannot stay here," she explained. "Until he goes, there will not be *saafu*. To get back to his own valley he needs money—a lot of money. If we give him back the money we have earned, he will have enough."

"But then we will have no money to buy clothes, or to buy food for our children. All the work we have done for the white man will have been wasted," a listener objected.

"Yes—but when he has gone, we will still be able to pick the wild coffee berries from the forest, and take them to Harar to be sold. They will be worth more than before, because the white men have shown us how to wash off the pulp and dry them in the sun. Then we will all share the money that we make. And, most importantly of all, no other white man will be able to come and say, 'I think I will have this land now.' That is not how it works: they would have to find Massa Wallis and buy the land back from him, and he will be a long way away."

"Surely the forest already belongs to us," someone objected.

"It should, but it does not. There is nothing we can do about that now. That is what I mean when I say that things have changed."

"And why should we help this man?" somebody else asked. "Why does he deserve our generosity?"

"We should help this man," Kiku said, "because he is a man, the son of a woman, just as we are the sons and daughters of women."

There was a long silence. Then Tahomen cleared his throat. "Thank you, Kiku," he said. "You have given us much to think about."

THEY TALKED for days. That was their way: what might look like aimless chatter was actually a slow process of reaching consensus, looking at an issue from many different points of view, testing each against the proverbs which constituted their received wisdom, until at last a collective agreement emerged. It was a very different decision-making process from the white man's. That assumed the most crucial thing in any situation was speed, not agreement, and therefore allowed orders to be imposed on the unwilling in the name of discipline. The villagers had no discipline, but they did have something far more powerful: the need for *saafu*.

[SIXTY-THREE]

"Caramel"—this wonderful smell evokes that of caramel, coffee, grilled pineapple and strawberries, which is not surprising as all four of these contain furaneol. This scent is a powerful flavour enhancer and an important part of the aroma of coffee.

—LENOIR, Le Nez du Café

❧

I AM SITTING IN MY HUT AS DUSK FALLS. IT IS THE BEST PART OF the day, the part when the pain of Fikre's absence is dulled by the prospect of the approaching night. Below me in the valley, clouds gather and bubble. Tropical birds dart suddenly amongst the tree canopy, flashes of brilliant color amongst the gloom. I am struck by how dandified they are: one, with a long orange streamer for a tail, bobs and weaves in and out of the creepers; another, iridescent in blue, hops impatiently from one leg to another; a third fluffs up his red throat feathers self-importantly as he twitters—for all the world like a trio of fops in a café.

Tahomen appears, walking slowly up the hill toward me. He is dressed in his chief's finery: my old alpaca jacket, worn over a piece of cloth wrapped at the loins. Behind him is Kiku. The medicine woman's hair has been colored with red dye, and at her throat is a necklace of ebony beads. Behind her is Alaya, and behind her, a long line of villagers. But there is none of their usual frivolity: this procession is conducted in an eerie, watchful silence.

Tahomen stops in front of me.

"Massa Wallis go home," he says. Solemnly, he places two coins, thalers, on the ground by my feet. Then he walks on a little way and squats down to watch.

Kiku says something in Galla. She too places a couple of coins at my feet.

Alaya smiles at me and gives me one thaler. The person behind her does the same, and the person after that . . . Those who have no money donate a mirror, or a glass necklace, or some other trinket given to them by Hector and me. One elderly gentleman fishes in his loincloth and produces a half-smoked cigar, which he adds to the pile. Those who have nothing else deposit a handful or two of coffee beans.

To an outsider, it might look as if they are giving me tribute: I am sitting there in my camp-chair like a king on my throne, and they are filing past me one by one, making their obeisance. But it is I who is humbled, who bows my head as each passes, my hands clasped together, tears flowing from my eyes, saying over and over, *Galatoomi. Galatoomi.*

Thank you.

NEXT DAY Jimo and Kuma and I load my few possessions onto a mule. I take only what I can sell in Harar; the rest I leave for the villagers. To this day, perhaps, somewhere in the high mountains of Africa there is a village which enjoys the use of a Gasogene Rechargeable Sodawater Maker, a wooden lavatory seat, a copy of the *Yellow Book* for April 1897, a cracked Wedgwood coffee cup, a dozen Remington typewriters, and various other appurtenances of civilization.

The very last thing I come across is a stout mahogany box containing a number of glass tubes of scent and a pamphlet headed *The Wallis-Pinker Method Concerning the Clarification and Classification of the Various Flavours of Coffee. With Notes, Cupping Charts and Illustrations, London, 1897.* It is too heavy to fit on the mule, and quite worthless, but I am pleased nevertheless to see that both the samples and the text have defied Hector's prediction, and survived intact the terrible heat of the tropics.

PART IV

Milk

[SIXTY-FOUR]

"Aftertaste"—the sensation of brewed coffee vapours, ranging from carbony to chocolaty to spicy to turpeny, released from the residue remaining in the mouth.

—LINGLE, The Coffee Cupper's Handbook

❧

"THEY SAY THE PRICE OF COFFEE WILL SOON BE DOUBLE WHAT it was last year." Arthur Brewer glanced from his paper to his wife. "In New York, apparently, investors who speculated on a fall are throwing themselves off skyscrapers rather than pay their debts."

"You make it sound as if suicide were an economy measure," Emily said tartly, pushing her eggs to the side of her plate and laying down her knife and fork. "Presumably the poor creatures thought they had no choice."

Arthur frowned. He had not really meant to initiate a conversation about the day's news, only to fill the silence over the breakfast table with an occasional observation. Mainly he did this to show that by reading the paper he was not actually neglecting his wife—in fact, now he came to think of it, it was almost as if he was reading it for both of them, filleting out the little titbits that were appropriate for her consumption. The glance of silent reproach she gave him every morning when he picked up *The Times* while they ate, a glance that was already habitual, was surely unjustified. And the way she coughed ostentatiously when he lit his pipe . . .

He turned back to the paper, looking for something with which to change the subject. "I see there is a move to have Oscar Wilde's remains transferred to the cemetery at Père Lachaise. They're even talking about raising some sort of memorial."

"That poor man. It's a disgrace that he was sent to prison in the first place. When his only crime—"

"My dear," Arthur said mildly, *"pas devant les domestiques."* He nodded to where the junior maid, Annie, was clearing the sideboard.

Emily seemed, he thought, to sigh a little, but she said nothing. He sipped his tea and turned the page.

The doorbell rang, and the maid went to answer it. Both of them, without appearing to, listened to see who it was.

"Dr. Mayhews is in the drawing room," Annie announced. Immediately Arthur was on his feet, dabbing at his lips with a napkin.

"I will go and explain matters to him first," he said. He did not add "man to man," but it was clear that was what he meant. "If you wait here, my dear, I will send Annie up when he is ready to see you."

EMILY WAITED. Occasionally the rumble of male voices penetrated from the drawing room next door, although they were too indistinct for her to catch the words. It hardly mattered, however. She knew what Arthur would be saying.

She poured herself some more coffee. The Wedgwood cups were a wedding present from her father. The coffee was not Pinker's, though. After Castle had started being so heavily advertised to the middle classes, it was no longer considered quite good enough for tables such as Arthur's. In fact the coffee he bought—or rather, that his housekeeper bought for him—was little better, a cheap Brazilian masquerading as a Java mix, but Emily was picking her battles one by one. The issue of the housekeeper's honesty was not one she was inclined to fight just yet.

"WE HAVE BEEN married for almost two years," Arthur explained. "And she is . . ." He stopped. "This is somewhat difficult for me."

Dr. Mayhews, a bony man in his early fifties, said, "You may be sure that you can tell me nothing I have not heard many times before."

"Yes, of course." Even so, Arthur hesitated again. "After our marriage, my wife seemed to undergo a change. On our honeymoon she was delightful, but since that time she has become increasingly . . . opinionated. Shrewish, one might almost say, if one were being judgmental. She becomes easily distressed. She kicks against the restrictions of married life—well, perhaps that's only natural; it's a big change from the freedom she enjoyed previously. Her father spoiled her, in my opinion. She has always been spirited—that I have no problem with. But this present mood of hers—she can be silent one hour, then so vociferous it is hard to get a word in edgeways. And this is not just women's chatter: she will converse on radical ideas, politics, with as much frantic passion as a *sans-culotte.* Sometimes she barely seems to make sense." He stopped, aware that he was perhaps mixing up a medical history with his own resentments. But Dr. Mayhews was nodding gravely.

"Is there conjugal incompatibility?" the doctor inquired delicately.

"Well, of course— Oh." Arthur realized what the other man was asking and blushed. "Not on the honeymoon. But afterwards."

"An excess of amativeness?"

"Sometimes, yes."

"And at those times, is she wanton?"

"Really, Doctor. This is my wife we are speaking about."

"Of course, but I must be fully aware of the facts."

Reluctantly, Arthur nodded. "Sometimes, yes. Shockingly so."

"And is she any easier after intercourse? In her mind, I mean?"

"Yes, generally, she is. Although that can also be when she is most difficult." He cleared his throat. "There is something else. When we married, my wife was not intact."

The doctor raised his eyebrows. "Are you quite certain?"

"Yes. It gave me quite a shock. I have been wondering if it could somehow have a bearing on her present condition. Whether she has been affected by some unsavory experience in her past."

"It is certainly possible. Does she suffer from nervous inefficiency or exhaustion?"

"I suppose she does, at times."

"Have you ever suspected hysteria?" the doctor asked quietly.

"She has never screamed blue murder, or fainted in company, or run down the street in her nightgown, if that is what you mean."

Mayhews shook his head. "The word 'hysteria' is a diagnosis, not a description of a kind of behavior. It applies to malaises emanating from the female parts—hence the term, from the Greek *hystaros,* or 'womb.' There are differing degrees of hysteria, just as there are degrees of severity in cases of influenza, or leprosy, or any other sickness."

"And you think hysteria may be the problem here?"

"From your description, I am almost sure of it. Does she over-indulge in coffee?"

Arthur stared at the doctor. "Yes, she does. Her father is a coffee merchant. She has always drunk copious amounts."

Mayhews shook his head again. "The female is very different from the male," he announced. "The reproductive force is so strong that it can irradiate every part of the frame. When it becomes disordered, as it may do all too easily—even from something as simple as an excess of coffee—it can carry its confusion into every department, even into the deepest recesses of the mind itself. Are you familiar with the works of Dr. Freud?"

"I have heard of him."

"He has proved that these complaints are generally hysteroneurasthenic in origin. Once the pelvis becomes congested . . . Have you noticed any unusual turgescence? Any abdominal humidity?"

Arthur nodded miserably. "I thought it was just—the way she is built. A sign of her passionate nature."

"Passion and hysteria are very close cousins," the doctor remarked darkly.

"Can it be cured?"

"Oh, yes. Or rather, it can be treated. And it may become less acute with time. Generally women are less prone to these problems once they have a child, the body having fulfilled its natural function."

"So what is to be done?"

"I will examine your wife, but I am quite clear in my mind that she will need to be referred to a specialist. Don't worry, Mr. Brewer. There are a number of excellent practitioners dealing with this sort of malady."

THREE DAYS later the motor car drove Emily to Harley Street for her appointment with the specialist. It was a prosperous area, the consulting rooms grander than the old doctors' warrens around Savile Row. A line of vehicles waited by the curb, and the street was thronged with people going in and out of the imposing doorways. Most, she noticed, were women.

"You may wait," she said to Billit, the chauffeur.

He nodded and flipped down the step so that she could alight onto the pavement. "Very good, ma'am."

Number 27 was the widest and grandest of the doorways. She entered and gave her name to a uniformed doorman. "Please, take a seat," he said, indicating a row of chairs. "Dr. Richards will be with you shortly."

She sat and waited, closing her eyes. God, she was tired. It was exhausting, this constant fighting with Arthur. Not that they were fighting exactly, that was not the right word. It was more that they were chafing, struggling against the harness each had slipped on with their wedding, as if the marriage were a coach and they were two horses, unaccustomed to the task, pulling in different directions. She had tried so hard, initially, to be the wife he wanted her to be. She was meant, she knew, to manage him by hints and suggestions, by showing him what made her happy rather than by nagging or needling. But the truth was that she liked a good argument, always had. Arguments between friends, it seemed to her, were simply the quickest way for two intelligent people to exchange strongly held opinions. But to Arthur, an argumentative wife was a blatant challenge to his authority. He—it transpired—desired silence, order, acquiescence; while she desired . . . She wasn't sure quite what she desired, exactly, but certainly not the suffocating boredom of the house in Eaton Square, its endless succession of high rooms filled with the beating of clocks, like so many mechanical hearts, and all the important issues of the world reduced to this: "the woman's sphere"; a few yards of domestic territory, and even that only held in fiefdom from her husband.

The problem had not been the marriage itself so much as the expectations that went along with it. It was one thing, apparently, for her to deliver leaflets and sample coffees when she was single; as an MP's wife her function, suddenly, was ceremonial. She was expected to be at Arthur's side for every social visit, every tea party, every debate—never to speak, but simply to applaud him indulgently, a visual embodiment of the Approval of Woman.

Yet, simultaneously, he had been betraying her. The word was a melodramatic one, but she could think of none better. The Liberals, for whom she and countless other suffragists had worked tirelessly over the years, had suddenly decided to drop female suffrage. Campbell-Bannerman himself—the jovial, kindly leader she had met in the House of Commons—had pronounced it a "distraction." And Arthur, to whom she was by this time engaged, had gone along obediently—no, enthusiastically—with his party's new line. "It is politics, my dear. And politics is simply a question of priorities. Would you really put votes for women ahead of pensions for miners?" It had been clear from his tone that he now considered the former a kind of indulgence. "Come," he had added, "we must not let this change anything between us. The bonds between a husband and a wife are, surely, strong enough to survive a political disagreement." He did not appreciate that her feelings for him and her political principles sprang from the same impulse. It had not been a matter of political strategy; it had been a question of trust.

Arthur was not a cruel man, but he was a conventional one, and if the conventions were cruel then the man would be as well, without ever quite realizing or intending it. Too late she saw that not all idealists are radicals. In the House, Arthur expressed his political personality through a fanatical devotion to that institution's myriad regulations and points of order; at home, he expressed it with disapproval and sniping . . . and now this ridiculous business with Dr. Mayhews.

Strangely, though, being told she was ill had brought out a tenderness in Arthur that had previously been absent. He had known what role to slip into at last: the protective husband. Perhaps he felt a little guilty, too, now that he was able to categorize her behavior as a malady rather than a character defect. So he had started bringing her cups of tea, ordered a series of special restorative dishes from the cook, and inquired solicitously after her health at every opportunity. It was driving her mad. And if she professed the slightest opinion on any subject, his face adopted an anxious expression as he reminded her that Dr. Mayhews had left instructions that passion was, for the time being, best avoided.

Passion! It was lack of passion that was the problem, not a surfeit of it—God knew she had tried to show him that. After so long bound by the different but equally restrictive codes that curtailed the behavior of an unmarried woman, she had actually been looking forward during their engagement to what she thought of as the greater freedom of the marriage bed. From the men who had adored her thus far, she had come to expect a certain amount of adoration as her right. But the reality had been shatteringly different. After the initial awkwardness—inevitable, she suspected, for two intelligent people of their time and place—she had just begun to hit what she thought of as her stride when the honeymoon came to an end, and with it, any apparent inclination Arthur had to continue its pleasures. Relations took place, but they were perfunctory. Any signs of pleasure on her part seemed almost to put him off: once or twice her enthusiasm had alarmed him so much he had actually brought proceedings to a halt. Evidently his taste for orderliness in domestic affairs extended to the bedroom as well. And so she had resigned herself to remaining unfulfilled in that respect. It was not so great a hardship—it was, after all, the condition in which she had lived most of her adult life—but it was a disappointment.

Of course, she knew perfectly well no visit to a doctor's was going to change anything, but to have refused to go, in the face of Dr. Mayhews's diagnosis, would have put her in the wrong. Mayhews might even have had her carted off to an asylum—it had been known to happen. So here she was.

"Would you tell my driver to bring the car to the door? There are so many, I am not sure which is mine."

She looked up. The woman speaking to the doorman was someone she knew—Georgina Dorson, the wife of one of Arthur's friends. "Hullo, Georgina," Emily called.

The other woman turned. "Oh—Emily. I didn't see you there. So you are on Dr. Richards's list, too? He's a wonder, isn't he?"

"I wouldn't know. This is my first consultation."

"Ah," Mrs. Dorson said dreamily. "It is a most exhilarating cure. I feel quite a different person after he has treated me. More alive."

"I'm glad to hear it." She did not actually seem terribly alive, Emily thought. The other woman continued to regard her with a strange, beatific smile, as if she had been doped. Emily made a mental note not to take any drugs Dr. Richards might prescribe.

"Anyway, there is our car. And my driver. Goodness, I shall probably sleep all the way home. I am quite exhausted. But he is a wonder, my dear. A wonder. Whatever did we do before doctors like him?" Georgina put out a hand to steady herself as she went down the steps.

"Mrs. Brewer?"

Emily turned. The speaker was a good-looking young man in a smart suit of modern cut, his hair neatly brushed and his smile broad. A silver watch chain hung like a second, bigger smile across the flat front of his waistcoat. She would have taken him for a prosperous young banker, or possibly the assistant to a Minister of State, something of that sort, rather than a doctor. "I'm Dr. Richards," he said, shaking her gloved hand. "Will you follow me?"

He walked briskly toward the rear of the building. "In here," he said, pushing open a door.

The consulting room contained a desk, a screen and a couple of chairs. He indicated where she should sit, then took the chair next to hers.

"Now then," he said cheerfully, "what seems to be the trouble?"

"I think I am."

He raised his eyebrows. "Oh?"

She liked him, she realized—or rather, he was likeable, which was probably not quite the same thing. "I seem to be a disappointment to my husband."

Dr. Richards's smile broadened. "Well, I have read the letter of referral from Dr. Mayhews, in which he certainly suggests something of the kind." He nodded to some papers on the desk. "For the moment, though, I am more interested in whether your husband is a disappointment to *you*."

"What do you mean?" she said, wondering whether to admit the truth to this young man. It might still be some kind of trap; he would report to Dr. Mayhews, and Dr. Mayhews to Arthur. . . . "Arthur has my complete loyalty."

"Naturally. But perhaps you have need to be loyal?" he inquired, fixing her with his quick fair eyes. "Loyalty—that suggests a bond of duty, Mrs. Brewer, rather than of love."

"Love!" she said, still unsure how to respond.

"Perhaps love . . . has not turned out to be all that you hoped."

"Yes," she said. It was ridiculous, but the urge to confide in someone was so powerful, so compelling, she felt her pulse begin to thud. "Love has not been quite what I imagined."

He took a stethoscope from the desk and pulled his chair even closer, his knees almost between her own. "I will just listen to your heart rate," he said, placing the cup between her breasts. At his touch she felt the pounding in her chest increase.

"It is a little rapid," he said, unhooking it from his ears. "Do you sleep well?"

"Not always."

"You find yourself fretful?"

"Occasionally."

"And do you know what Dr. Mayhews believes to be the cause of this?"

"I believe he mentioned to my husband some kind of hysteria."

He raised his eyebrows. "I see by your expression you do not agree."

She hesitated. "May I speak in confidence?"

"Of course."

"I find it hard to believe that I am suffering from an illness when the circumstances which occasioned this difficulty are clear, namely my marriage to a man who turns out not to like me very much."

Dr. Richards nodded. "That is an understandable reaction."

"Thank you," she said, grateful to have found someone at last who did not actually consider her defective.

"However," Richards said briskly, "since we may not change the circumstances, it is the reaction we must try to alter. We are going to treat you, Mrs. Brewer, and I mean that in both senses of the word. What do you know of the undulatory theory of health?"

She shook her head. She felt, obscurely, that she had revealed too much, and now she was angry with herself.

"Science has discovered that all existence is based on oscillation." The doctor laced his fingers through each other and fixed her with his cheerful gaze. "In the cells which make up animal tissue, it is a small variation in oscillatory velocity which produces a viper or a vertebrate, a mountain lion or a milkmaid. All nature literally pulsates with the life-force! And for woman in particular, who is the source of life, the healthy specimen is she whose blood oscillates in unison with the natural laws of being. If we induce that harmony, you will instantly feel the benefits. Every nerve will be refreshed, every fiber will tingle with reawakened powers. Rich red blood will be sent coursing through your veins. You will be invigorated, vitalized and energized. Many of my patients leave these rooms with as much buoyancy of spirits as if they had been drinking champagne."

"Then why don't they?"

"Why don't they what?"

"Why don't they drink champagne? Surely it must be cheaper."

Richards frowned. "Mrs. Brewer, I do not think you appreciate what I am telling you. We are going to restore tone and vigor to the entire system. We will reawaken your feminine energy."

"And how—precisely—do you intend to do this?"

"Rhythmotherapy. Or, to be more precise, by the operation of the percussive principle upon the afflicted tissue. The sensation is a soothing one, I assure you, but it will quickly draw out the hysteria. Behind that screen you will find a gown; if you put it on, I will show you through to the treatment room."

SHE PUT ON the gown, a shift of thin cotton that tied down the front. In the next room was a table padded with leather on which a sheet had been spread. There was some kind of apparatus built into its base—she saw an electrical engine and several mysterious objects made of what appeared to be gutta-percha, connected to the motor by wires, like the ends of a skipping-rope. "Please," Richards said, pointing to the table.

He turned a switch, and as she climbed up onto the couch the engine began to thrum.

AFTERWARDS, when it was all over, she dressed with shaking fingers, and sat slumped in his chair while he performed some tests on her reflexes and pulse.

"Your heart rate is already improved," he observed.

"I am glad to hear it."

"And the pelvic congestion Dr. Mayhews writes of—can you feel that it has eased?"

"I certainly feel different," she said numbly.

He glanced at her with a smile. "Almost as if you had been drinking champagne?" He turned back to his desk and began to write up his notes. "Take a few minutes, Mrs. Brewer. Many of my patients experience a feeling of torpor after the treatment. It is perfectly normal—a sign that the hysteria has been vanquished, at least temporarily."

"Temporarily?"

"In most cases there is no cure for the hysterochlorotic disorders. It is necessary to return periodically to repeat the treatment."

"And how frequently would I need to do that?"

"Most of my patients find once a week is about right. I should mention that many supplement my own approach with treatments from my colleagues. In this building alone we have Dr. Farrar, who offers the ascending douche—directing a stream of pressurized water to the relevant area is a very reliable method. Then there is Dr. Hardy, who specializes in electrotherapeutics, whereby a mild faradic current is applied; Mr. Thorn, who is an expert in the administration of the Swedish Massage, and Dr. Clayton, who provides electric fustigation of the womb. We even have a proponent of the Viennese talking cure, Dr. Eisenbaum, whilst in the basement there is a fully functioning water spa equipped with various forms of hydraulics."

"I see. And how does one pay for all of this?"

"By account, of course. A bill will be sent to your husband every month."

"Is it expensive?"

He appeared surprised that she had asked. "These are costly premises, Mrs. Brewer. Then there is the equipment . . . So effective a treatment does not come cheap."

WHEN SHE HAD GONE he checked his watch. He still had a quarter of an hour before his next appointment.

Taking up his pen, he reread what he had already written, making a few corrections as he did so. He added:

> One observes almost immediately the penetrating effects of the oscillatory apparatus. After some minutes, the body begins to shake violently, signaling the onset of the hysterical paroxysm. There is a cry; her body curves into an arc and holds this position for several seconds. One then observes some slight movements of the pelvis. Shortly after, she raises herself, lies flat again, utters cries of pleasure, laughs, makes several lubricious movements and sinks down onto the right hip. Following this, she is transformed: the quick impatient nervousness displayed before treatment is replaced by pleasantness of disposition, the frown is chased away by a smile, the characteristic suppressed fury of the hysteric is supplanted by calmness and sweet reason. Truly the discovery of the statuminating principle is one that will come to transform psychiatric medicine in the coming century.

He frowned. Only the day before he had read a paper by a man called Maiser, who had proposed that these women could be treated at home, by their own husbands, and that "what we currently call treatment is no different from what any attentive spouse does for his wife." It was absurd, of course. Quite apart from anything else, hysterics made excellent patients: they neither recovered nor worsened, and in most cases returned for years of treatment. Picking up his pen again, he wrote:

> The mechanisation of the treatment is undoubtedly key to its success. However, the anatomical skill and manual expertise of the physician, born of long practice, are what produces results.

There was a knock at the door. He put down the pen: his next patient was here.

[SIXTY-FIVE]

Dr. Mayhews had been right; Arthur noticed a change in his wife immediately. After visiting the specialist she had slept for most of the afternoon, but the following morning she had been almost like a different woman. She seemed . . . He searched for the term. Calmer, that was it. There was a quietness about her that he had not seen since their engagement. And she no longer objected when he read the newspaper at breakfast. Only her lungs seemed unimproved—she still coughed when he lit his pipe after meals, but perhaps one couldn't have everything.

They were having breakfast together in a companionable silence later that week when he laughed out loud at something he read.

"This writer. Most amusing," he said. "Some of the things he saw in Africa . . ."

"Would you like to read me some of it?"

"Oh, well. Probably you have to know the context." He shook out the pages. "About the French, you know. At Teruda," his disembodied voice said.

"Really."

"Name of Wallis. Robert Wallis." He put the paper down to pick up his pipe. "Are you all right, my dear? You seem pale."

"I do feel a bit off color. And the room is quite stuffy."

He looked at his pipe. "Would you like me to wait a few minutes before I smoke?"

"Thank you."

"Or you could always go into the sitting room."

"Yes, dear," she said, getting to her feet. "Perhaps if I sit near a window I will feel better."

"Well, be careful not to catch a chill."

"If I do catch one, I shall be sure to release it again immediately."

He stared at her. "What?"

"I was joking, Arthur. I don't know why. I was thinking of something else at the time."

"Good heavens," he said, returning to his paper.

LATER, AT DINNER, there was another incident. He was explaining to their guest, a visitor from France, that the Liberals were the most reforming government that the country had ever seen—that they had transformed the lives of the working classes beyond recognition—

"If you are a man, that is," his wife interjected. "For the women, there is to be no change."

Their visitor smiled. Arthur shot his wife an anxious glance, fearing that she was about to mount her hobby-horse. "Remember your condition, my dear," he murmured as Annie helped their guest to some vegetables.

His wife looked at him; then, somewhat to his surprise, she nodded meekly and remained silent for the rest of the meal. It was extraordinary, Arthur thought, what a difference a medical diagnosis could make.

[SIXTY-SIX]

SHE HAD BEEN WONDERING IF THE EFFECTS OF DR. RICHARDS'S oscillator would be different on her second visit. Perhaps the force of her reaction was due to years of pelvic congestion, as he had called it, and there would be no shattering, overwhelming release of hysteria this time. In fact the reverse turned out to be true. It took only a few minutes before she felt the palpitations building up in waves, anticipating the uncontrollable, terrifying onset of the paroxysm.

Afterwards she once again sat in his chair, watching him write up his notes. She liked the way he wrote—quick and deft, the pen flicking upward in fast little gestures before looping down again as it formed letters and words. *Flick* . . . *flick* . . . There was something hypnotic about it.

"What do you find to write about me?"

He did not look up. "Some of it is technical."

She thought she saw a circumflex. "Is that French?"

He said reluctantly, "Some of it, yes. The pioneering work was done at the Salpêtrière Institute in Paris. The French medical terms are the accepted ones to use. And," he hesitated, "they ensure privacy."

"For the patient, you mean?" But he did not mean that, she saw immediately; he meant for him, for the notes, lest anyone find them and think that what he did was improper. She leaned forward. *Trop humide . . . La crise vénérienne . . .*

Seeing her looking, he shielded the page with his arm. "A doctor's notes are confidential."

"Even from the patient?"

He did not reply.

"I would have thought," she said carefully, "that what we do here—the nature of the treatment—makes such niceties redundant."

He put down his pen and gazed at her. His eyes—gray-blue, untroubled, rather beautiful—regarded her thoughtfully. "On the contrary, Mrs. Brewer. It makes niceties all the more necessary."

"Do you have many patients?"

"Above fifty."

"Fifty! So many!"

"The mechanization of the apparatus makes it possible."

"But it must also make it harder for you."

He frowned. "In what way?"

"You must like some of your patients more than others."

"What difference would that make?"

She was fishing for compliments now, she realized, but somehow she could not stop. "It must be easier with those you find congenial. Or those who are pretty. Whom you find pretty, I mean."

The frown deepened. "Why would that have anything to do with it?"

Desperately she said, "Are you married, Dr. Richards?"

"Really, Mrs. Brewer. I must ask you to stop asking me these questions. If you wish to talk, you should make an appointment to see Dr. Eisenbaum for the Talking Cure."

"Of course," she said, recoiling. She felt a sudden, irrational urge to cry. *They were right after all,* she thought: *I am simply a hysterical, foolish woman.*

THE CAR WAS waiting outside, but she instructed Billit to drive home without her. "I shall walk to John Lewis," she told him. "I need to buy some handkerchiefs."

As she walked south down Harley Street she was struck by the number of women coming in and out of the buildings. How many of them were there for the same reason she was? It seemed inconceivable that they were all being taken into these grand, high-ceilinged rooms and swept to hysterical paroxysms.

She walked on, crossing Cavendish Square, then turned toward Regent Street. This was the edge of respectable London: immediately to the east lay the slums of Fitzrovia, while to the south was Soho. Glancing down Mortimer Street, she saw a line of prostitutes leaning against the railings, unmistakable in their grubby, old-fashioned dresses, their faces made up like music hall caricatures. There was a time when she would have crossed to talk to them, fearless in her enthusiasm for saving them, but she was no longer quite so fixed in her certainties.

She did not go into John Lewis: it had been the walk she had wanted, the chance to burn off some of the heaviness she had felt after Dr. Richards's treatment. And, if she was honest with herself, some of her embarrassment, too, the shaming realization that he had no more feeling for her than if he had been operating on a bunion or a broken bone. How easy it was to confuse attention with affection! It was the same with Arthur. These men did not dislike women, exactly, but they had a sort of template in their heads of what a woman should be. For them, any deviation from the norm required intervention, as if one were a clock that must be set back to the correct time.

As if to mock her, she passed directly underneath a giant billboard advertising Castle Coffee. A bride and groom, still in their wedding clothes, were toasting each other with cups of Castle. The headline read *I VOW . . . to give him Castle. What every husband wants!*

If only, she thought, marriage were so simple.

A noise on the other side of the road caught her attention. A small group of women had gathered on the pavement. One of them held a placard: *DEEDS NOT WORDS!* It was so exactly what she was thinking herself that for a moment it felt as if someone had written it just for her. Two of the others were unfurling a banner on which was written in black paint *Votes for Women*. The group raised a ragged cheer, causing a few passersby to stop and stare. Rather than be seen gawking, Emily turned to watch their reflection discreetly in a shop window.

"Are you shopping here, sister?" The words came from a woman standing beside her.

"I am not, no. I am walking home."

"Then you will not mind if I do this. Please, step back." The woman raised her hand and made a stabbing motion at the window. Emily jumped, but then she saw that the woman was only scrawling the downstroke of a huge V with a lipstick concealed in her hand. In a few moments the same slogan that was on the placard had been written in three-foot-high oxblood letters across the front of the window.

Up and down the street came shouts and cries of outrage as other windows simultaneously suffered the same fate. There was the crash of breaking glass. A policeman's whistle sounded. Nearby, someone yelled. " 'er—down there!" A man was pointing in their direction. "That's one of 'em!" The woman suddenly looked panicked.

"Quick, take my arm," Emily said. She took a step forward and hooked the woman's arm in hers. Then she swung her round to face the street. "Look down there, as if you can see something, too," she urged her companion. "But whatever you do, don't move." Sure enough, a group of four men rushed past them, going in the direction in which the two women were looking, their feet pounding on the pavement. She felt the other woman's body tense, then relax.

Emily said, "I think they've gone."

"Thank you." The woman's eyes were shining with triumph. "We have struck a blow for freedom."

"But what have shop windows to do with votes?"

"We have had enough of talk. We have a new group: we are going to make a nuisance of ourselves. Unless we do that, we will never get anywhere."

"But if you are a nuisance, you may annoy the men so much they never give us anything."

"Give?" They were walking down toward Piccadilly now, the woman striding along confidently as if she knew where she was going. Somehow, though, neither of them had relinquished the arm by which they were joined. "You make equality sound like a treat—like a bunch of roses or a new hat. It is not. It is our right, and the longer we go on asking for it politely, the more we give men the false impression that they can choose to deny it to us. Do you have money?"

"I'm married."

"But you had money of your own, before? Then you pay taxes. There isn't a politician alive who believes in taxation without representation—until it comes to women. Why should they be allowed to take our money off us, when we can't tell them how to spend it?"

"Believe me," Emily said, "I am strongly in favor of votes for women. I have been an active member of the Union for years. I'm just not sure about being a nuisance."

"Then come to a meeting and let us persuade you. Tonight, if possible."

Emily hesitated. The other woman said impatiently, "Here, I'll write down the address." She scribbled something on a card and handed it to her. "We will awaken the feminine force!"

They were almost exactly the same words that Dr. Richards had used. And then something else struck her. This woman seemed more energized by her act of vandalism than she, Emily, had felt after Dr. Richards's treatment.

She felt a sudden surge of excitement. "Very well," she said impulsively. "I'll come."

[SIXTY-SEVEN]

"Fiery"—a bitter charcoal taste generally due to over-roasting.

—SMITH, Coffee Tasting Terminology

IT TOOK ME TWO YEARS TO GET BACK. PERHAPS FORTUITOUSLY, my attempt to travel up through the Sudan coincided with a small military standoff between Britain and France, subsequently known as the Teruda Incident. I discovered I had some ability as a foreign correspondent, and starvation was averted, for the time being at least. From Egypt, I wandered up to Italy. I spent the summer on the shores of Lake Como; the same period during which I finished, and destroyed, a novel about a man who falls in love with a slave. It was a dreadful book, but writing it was the next part of putting all that behind me, and once the flames had eaten into the very last page of the manuscript, I knew, finally, that I was free of her.

For I discovered something important, during that long return. I had loved Fikre, perhaps not as she deserved to be loved, but with an absolute physical passion, and even something a bit more besides. Despite what had happened, I found that I hoped she was finally happy. That may not seem like much of a discovery, compared to the naming of Lake Victoria or pinpointing the source of the Nile. But for me it was new territory, to be marked in full on the hitherto blank atlas of the heart.

IN THE TIME I had been away, London had reinvented itself yet again. Oscar Wilde, John Ruskin and Queen Victoria had all died within a few months of one another, just as the century ended; all those redoubtable Victorian queens escorting one another to the grave. Now, instead of Pater and Tennyson, people spoke of J. M. Barrie and H. G. Wells. The streets were full of what Pinker had called autokinetics, but which were now known as motor cars. The electrophone had become the telephone, and one could use it to speak to anywhere in the country, even to America. And the mood—that indefinable perfume of a city—had changed, too. London was well lit, well run and well regulated. The bohemians, the decadents, the dandies—all were gone, chased from the half-shadows by the electric streetlights, and in their place the respectable middle classes had taken over.

I had intended to avoid Covent Garden. But old habits die hard, and I had some business in Fleet Street which took me in that direction—a few small articles on my travels I had managed to place. I left the offices of the *Daily Telegraph* with a check for twelve pounds in my pocket. Almost unconsciously, my feet led me to Wellington Street. Much had changed here too—there were shops and restaurants where once there had only been houses of pleasure. Number 18, however, was still as it had always been. Even the furnishings in the second-floor waiting room seemed the same, and if the Madam did not recognize me, so much the better—I was not certain I recognized her either.

I chose a girl and took her upstairs. She too was new, but she was practiced enough at her profession to see that I did not want to be disturbed with chatter, and after exclaiming at the strange tattoos on my chest she let me get on with it. But something was wrong. At first I thought I was simply out of practice. Then I realized what it was: it felt strange, somehow, to engage in the sexual act without trying to give pleasure. I tried to remember how I used to do it, years previously. Or had I simply taken for granted that all those groans and moans meant I was doing it properly?

I reached around and stroked various parts of her: she gasped obligingly, but she was play-acting. I tried rubbing and stroking harder, and it seemed to me that she sighed.

I stopped. "Will you do something for me?"

"Of course, sir. Anything. Though you may have to pay a little more—"

"This isn't a . . . service. Or at any rate, not one you normally provide. I want you to show me how to give you pleasure."

She sat up, smiling, and ran her hands up and down my arms, and rubbed her soft breasts against my chest. "You give me pleasure with your big hard cock, sir," she breathed. "When you give it to me hard and strong."

"I wish that were true. But if I touch you—here—gently, and move my fingers so—is that nice?"

"Ohhh! It's exquisite, sir. Don't stop! Don't stop!"

Now it was my turn to sigh. "No. Tell me truthfully."

She looked confused. I thought: *The poor girl doesn't know the rules of this game. She's trying to work out what to say.*

At last she said tentatively, "Everything you do to me is nice."

"Do you have a boy friend? A fancy man? What does he do for you?"

She shrugged.

"Lie down," I said. "I'm going to touch you, and when it gets better, tell me."

Still confused, she lay down on her back and submitted to my fingers. "But sir," she said after a while, "why do you want to do this?"

"I want to know how to please a woman."

There was a pause. Then she said in a voice that was very different, "Do you really want to know?"

"Of course. I wouldn't ask otherwise."

"Then give me another pound and I'll tell you."

"Very well." I fetched her the money.

She put it somewhere safe. As she climbed back on the bed she said, "You've just done it."

"What? Ah." I smiled. "The money."

"That's it, mister. Now I'm pleased as punch."

"I meant in bed."

She shrugged. "Same difference."

I persisted: "But suppose I wanted to make you feel . . . what your customers feel. How would I do that?"

"Doesn't work like that, though, does it? I'd be out of a job else. If women needed what men need, there wouldn't be places like this."

"You know—you're right," I said, struck by the profound truth of what she had said.

"Well, I'm only stating the bleeding obvious. D'you want me to frig you off?" She gestured at my cock. "You've paid for it."

I would like to say that this scene ended with me nobly refusing to have her do any such thing, and that the conversation we had just had was more precious to me than a frig. But it would not be true.

SOMETHING ELSE: as I was leaving she said, "You know, I liked talking to you. You can come back, if you want."

"And give you more money?"

She laughed. "That too."

I liked her. I never saw her again, but I liked her. For a few minutes on a sunny afternoon we had talked honestly, and got on, before conducting our business and going our separate ways. Perhaps, I thought, it is as much as one can ask of a civilized life.

MY ARTICLES appeared, and for a few weeks I knew what it was to be fêted. There were invitations to private houses—*soirées* at which I was expected to thrill the company with tales of bloodthirsty savages and the exotic otherness of Africa, all neatly wrapped up with the convenient platitude that Trade would one day turn the place into another Europe. I disappointed. In my articles I had been forced to water down my opinions or face having my pieces rejected, but in the drawing rooms of Mayfair and Westminster I was less circumspect. I pointed out that the only bloodthirsty savages I had met were wearing white skins and the khaki uniforms of the French and British armies; that what we now called Trade was simply a continuation of slavery by more devious means; that the natives I had lived among were as sophisticated in their way as any society I had come across in Europe. People listened to me politely, and then said things like, "But in that case, Mr. Wallis, what is to be Done with Africa?"

And I answered, "Why, nothing. We should clear out—admit we don't own any part of it, and just go. If we want African coffee, we should pay Africans to grow it. Pay a bit more, if necessary, so that they have a chance to get themselves started. It'll be to our benefit in the long run."

It was not the answer they wanted to hear. London just then was in the grip of a strange coffee mania. The Brazilian government was now part of the growers' cartel, and was supporting the world price with huge loans taken out on the London Stock Exchange: these were generally over-subscribed within hours of being issued, and as the price climbed ever higher, people were scrabbling to invest in whatever way they could. Nobody wanted to be told that this economic miracle was founded on despair and misery. Those who had started the evening hanging on my every word had let go their grasp long before the end. That suited me: I was not there to make myself popular.

But I was also aware, sometimes, of sidelong glances, even before I had had my say: older women who hurried away their unmarried daughters, husbands who steered their wives to the other side of the room. I was disapproved of, it seemed, and not only for my opinions on Africa.

At one of these occasions I met George Hunt again. My old friend had grown fat and affable: he had his own magazine now, a literary journal called something like *The Modern View.* After I had driven away my listeners with my own modern views, we walked together to his club, and ensconced ourselves in a fine drawing room on the second floor, where he ordered brandies and cigars.

We chatted of this and that for a while, and then he said suddenly, "Did you know Rimbaud?"

"Who?"

"Arthur Rimbaud, the French poet. Don't tell me you've not heard of him?" I shrugged. "But that's extraordinary. He was based in Harar, like yourself—a coffee merchant, too, though he would have been working for a French concern. His verses are quite remarkable—though I gather he had stopped writing by then: he wrote most of them while he was still a youth, the catamite of that old toad Verlaine, here in London. . . ." He stopped. "You really knew nothing about this?"

"Someone told me about him," I said tersely. "I'm sorry to say I didn't believe a word of it. And no, we didn't overlap—Rimbaud left Harar just before I arrived. In fact, I took on the lease of his house."

"Incredible." Hunt signaled to a club servant for two more

brandies. "Of course, his time out there was somewhat scandalous. There was a rumor about a native concubine—some slave girl he bought off an Arab trader, and then abandoned when he went back to France. But he was a broken man by then, they say."

I nodded slowly. There was a small click in my mind, and suddenly my story rewrote itself yet again. *She speaks English like a Frenchman. . . .* What else might such a man have taught her? The knowledge that some people will tell themselves any lie for love? But these were things to be mulled over another time, in private.

Hunt was taking a pull on his cigar. "But I imagine out there that sort of thing isn't altogether unexpected. Doubtless you had some adventures in that line yourself." He regarded me with greedy eyes.

"Are his poems any good?" I asked, ignoring his question.

He shrugged. "They're revolutionary, and these days that's what matters. *Vers libre*—that's what they're all writing now. The Irish poets are quite interesting at the moment, then of course there are the Americans—everyone wants to be Whitman—English poetry's shot to hell." He tapped ash into a saucer. "But you were going to tell me about your escapades."

"Was I?" I said shortly.

"You wrote to me at the time, as I recall . . . Something about falling in love with a native?" he prompted, undeterred. He glanced around. "Come on, man. No one can hear us. And of course I shan't repeat any . . . interesting confidences."

I suddenly understood why I had been the object of those disapproving glances. "So there's been gossip?"

He smirked, then hastily backtracked as he remembered that if there had been, it could only have originated from him. "Speculation, Robert, speculation. There *was* a native girl, though, wasn't there? A Hottentot Venus?"

"There was a girl," I said. "And I did fancy myself in love with her, for a while."

"I see." He puffed at his cigar again, and watched me through a skein of gray smoke, thick and soft as wool. "Perhaps it's a tale you would prefer to set down on paper. I need authors, you know."

"My poetry days are over."

"I wasn't necessarily referring to verse." He picked up his brandy and addressed its amber depths. "I don't only publish the *View.* There are books for discerning gentlemen readers as well. I get those printed in Paris."

"Pornography, you mean?"

"If you like. I thought perhaps—now that you're a writer, and presumably one in need of an income . . . And the African slant could be terrific. I hear those women, with their hotter blood, are quite something. What about a Negro *Fanny Hill,* or a *My Secret Life* amongst the natives? I know it would sell."

"I'm sure it would," I said, setting down my glass. "But I am not the man to write it." Suddenly I felt quite nauseous. The smoke from his cigar caught in my throat, sour and bilious. I got to my feet. "Good-night, George. Find some other mug to provide your titillation."

"Wait," he said quickly. "Don't be too hasty, Robert. You must know you can't live off Teruda forever. My writers—I look after them. An article here, a poem placed there . . . You're just the sort of man who could benefit from being read in our pages. We've published Ford Madox Ford, you know."

"Go screw yourself, George."

He smirked wearily. "Don't be so bloody conventional."

As I walked out he called after me, "I see Pinker's daughter Emily sometimes."

I stopped in the doorway.

"She made a rather good marriage. To a complete crashing bore. You're well out of it there."

I did not turn round. I continued on my way.

[SIXTY-EIGHT]

EMILY WAS A CHAPTER IN MY LIFE THAT I KNEW WAS CLOSED, but her father was another matter. Finally, I could put it off no longer. I went down to Limehouse and sent my card in to his office.

He made me wait—of course. As I sat in one of the anterooms I watched an endless procession of porters and storemen filing past me with jute sacks on their shoulders—not filing, in fact, so much as *marching,* each man moving at a smart pace out to where a line of lorries waited in the street. I wondered why they did not store them in the warehouse, but perhaps that had been put to other uses now.

Then I saw a face I recognized—Jenks, the secretary, although he was clearly rather more than a secretary now: he had two assistants running after him as he hurried back and forth directing the loading. "Jenks," I called out.

"Oh, hullo, Wallis. We heard you were back. And you've cut your hair." It was a strange comment: I had had many dozens of haircuts since I saw him last. "We wondered when we would see you." He continued moving as he spoke, so that like his assistants I was obliged to get to my feet and follow him. "There," he said to one of them. "Up there, on the third floor. Do you see? Space for at least another five hundred."

I stopped, silenced by what I saw in front of me.

The warehouse was not just full: it was crammed. On every side walls of coffee sacks reached up toward the roof. There were no windows—just a couple of arrow slits in the endless heights, where sacks had been piled up against the real windows, and a sliver or two of light sneaked past. Squeezed in between the great stacks were tiny pathways and winding corridors, staircases made of sacks, wormholes . . . there must have been over fifty thousand bags in that warehouse alone.

There was an open sack near where we stood. I reached down and pulled out a few beans, sniffing them. "Indian typica, if I'm not mistaken."

Jenks nodded. "Your palate was always accurate."

I looked up to where the towers of sacks vanished into the gloom. "Is it all the same? What's it for?"

"You had better come upstairs," Jenks said.

PINKER WAS SITTING at his desk. The tickertape machine was chattering quietly to itself; he was holding the paper tape in his cupped hands, reading the symbols and then dropping it, picking it up again almost immediately to read the symbols that had replaced them, like someone drinking from a fast-flowing river.

"Oh, there you are, Wallis. Back at last," he said, as if I had just been down to the West End for lunch. "How was Africa?"

"Africa was not a success."

"So I surmised." He had still barely looked at me, continually running his thumbs over the strange rubric emitted by the machine.

"The warehouse is very full," I commented when he said nothing further.

"That?" He sounded surprised. "That is nothing. You should see the bonded stores. I have four now; all larger than this, all filled to capacity. I am having to rent extra space until it is over."

"Until what is over?"

He looked at me then, and I was struck by how much like Emily he was, physically. But in his eyes there was a strange light, a kind of nervous excitement.

"My army is almost ready, Wallis," he said. "We are nearly at strength."

HE HAD HAD a revelation, Pinker explained. He had grasped, finally, that the coffee market was cyclical. If the price went up, plantation owners planted more, but since those seedlings took four years to produce a crop, the effects on the market were not felt until then. Four years after a price rise, therefore, a glut occurred, the coffee that had been planted in the years of shortage coming onto the market in ever-increasing quantities, until over-supply caused the price just as inevitably to fall, and plantation owners either went out of business or switched to other crops. Four years later, this then caused another shortage; prices rose, and the planters expanded all over again.

"An eight-year cycle, Wallis. As immutable, as inexorable, as the waxing and waning of the moon. The cartel can mask it, but they cannot eradicate it. And once I realized that, I knew I had him."

"Had who?"

"Why, Howell, of course." Pinker smiled tightly. "He will be howling soon enough." He stopped, and looked almost surprised. "You have made me witty, Robert."

He had been waiting years, he said, for the cycle to come around to the point at which the price would be under pressure from the natural rhythms of the market.

"And that moment is now? I thought the consensus in London is that the price will go higher?"

He shrugged. "The Brazilian government claims it will. They have this new scheme—valorization, they call it. They are taking out vast loans to buy up their farmers' coffee, and so smooth its passage on to the market. But it cannot last. The market is like a river: you can only dam it for so long. When the dam bursts, it will take everything with it."

He crossed to a map of the world which dominated one wall. "I have been making my preparations, Robert. You have seen some of them downstairs—but those are just the visible ones. It is the invisible ones that will make the difference. Networks—alliances—treaties. Arbuckle on the West Coast. Egbert's in Holland. Lavazza in Milan. When we act, we act together."

"You have formed your own cartel?"

"No!" He spun round. "We have formed the opposite of a cartel—an association of companies who believe in freedom, the free movement of capital. You rejoin us at an auspicious moment."

"Ah—I have not come to ask for my job back. Just to apologize."

"Apologize?"

"For letting you down."

He frowned. "But all's well. Emily is satisfactorily married. Hector's death, of course, was a tragedy—but it was an accident of his own making: these things happen. And in the meantime, Robert, I am in need of someone with your expert knowledge of coffee."

"What you have in your warehouse now is scarcely coffee."

"Yes. And do you know something? Thanks to our advertising, the customer believes it tastes better than the finest arabica. If you put a cup of Castle and a cup of Harar mocca side by side, it is the Castle they would prefer. A housewife's nose, it seems, is even more easily led than what is in your trousers."

"You despise your customers," I said, surprised.

He shook his head. "I do not despise them. I have no feelings for them whatsoever. In a successful business there is no room for sentiment."

"Be that as it may, I have no place here. I intend to make my living by my pen from now on."

"Ah, yes—I read those articles of yours. They were amusingly written, if a little misguided. But Robert, there is no reason at all why you should not continue to write for the newspapers as well as work for me. In fact, it might be useful. I could suggest some avenues for you to explore, set you right about certain matters—"

"That isn't quite how it works."

"Then you will want to settle up." His voice had barely changed, but there was a dangerous glint in his eye that had not been there previously. "Three hundred a year, wasn't it? And you managed—what? Six months? Let us say you owe a thousand, and not bother with the small change." He held out his hand. "A check will do."

"I cannot pay you," I said quietly.

He smiled thinly. "Then you had better stay with us until you can."

ON MY WAY out I encountered Jenks again. I had the feeling he had been waiting for me.

"Well?" he said.

"He seems to want me on the staff again."

"I'm glad to hear that, Wallis."

"Are you?"

"Yes." He sighed. "The old man—I sometimes think he has gone a little odd, you know. Perhaps together we might be able to . . . well, to calm him."

[SIXTY-NINE]

THE CURIOUS THING WAS THAT PINKER ACTUALLY SEEMED TO have no real use for me. Occasionally he would seek me out and deliver a lecture about the evils of price-fixing or the iniquities of the Exchange. Sometimes he would have Jenks bring me cuttings extolling the success of the Brazilian scheme—a "model for a prosperous future; one that will surely be followed closely by those endeavoring to bring stability to sugar, rubber, palm oil, and every other world market," as one writer put it: in the margin Pinker had scrawled a single word—FOOLS.

Once, when he had delivered himself of a particularly biting critique of his opponents, he glanced at me and said, "Make a note of it, Robert. You will never remember it precisely unless you do."

"But I am unlikely to have any need to remember it."

"Write it all down," he insisted. "That way, when you come to tell the story, you will not have to guess—you will have the proof."

"The story?" I said, my mind still on which pocket I had left my pen in. Then I realized what he meant, and why he wanted me around.

• • •

"HE MEANS me to be his biographer," I said to Jenks when we were alone.

He nodded. "He thinks he is making history. He always has. Emily used to record his utterances. Since she married he has had no one else to do it."

"Speaking of Emily, do you ever hear from her?" I asked, casually.

He stared at me, and some of the old antagonism returned to his voice. "Why would I?" he said coldly. "She is married now, she has her own concerns. She does not need to mix with the likes of you and me."

AFTER THAT I did what was required of me, and kept a record of my employer's observations in my notebook—the same notebook in which I had once recorded my own poetic jottings.

I did pick up some snippets of Pinker family news. Ada had stayed in Oxford and married a don; Philomena had "come out," as the phrase had it, going to society parties and mixing with a crowd of artistic types in Bloomsbury. There was no longer any reason for them to come to their father's offices. As for Emily, since her marriage she was effectively barred from taking part in the business.

"Her job now is to be a wife, and a politician's wife at that," Pinker said testily, the only time I mentioned it. "Doubtless she will soon have her own family to concern herself with. And in the meantime, we have a business to run."

He ran that business in ways that were increasingly unconventional. For example, quite without warning a dock strike crippled movements of coffee in and out of the Port of London. This was not in itself unusual—there were often strikes in those days—but what was curious was that there were strikes at exactly the same time in Antwerp and New York.

The price of coffee to the ordinary shopkeeper rose accordingly. But on the Exchange it was a different story. Coffee was being kept in ships that were waiting to unload: the Thames, the Hudson and the Scheldt backed up like faulty conveyor belts. Nobody could buy any more until the dispute was resolved, and the price dipped sharply—until the Brazilian government stepped in and supported it.

For those who had stored coffee outside the Port of London, of course, there was no difficulty: they could sell at a handsome profit. I remembered that endless line of porters marching out of Pinker's warehouse, and marveled at the extent of his planning.

HE MADE a fortune that week—but it gave him no satisfaction. Victory, not money, was what he craved.

"That was a skirmish, Robert. We have probed their strength. The real battle is to come."

He began to instruct Jenks and myself in the workings of the Exchange. If Emily had taught me to cup, and Hector to farm, then it was Samuel Pinker who taught me about the mysterious alchemy by which wealth is created in the City.

"We sold half a million sacks of coffee this month, and made a profit of two shillings on every one. Now then. What if we'd had ten million bags under contract?"

"There is not so much coffee in the supply chain," Jenks said, baffled.

"Yes. But suppose our bags are hypothetical. What then?"

"Then we would have made twenty times the profit," I said.

"Exactly." Pinker nodded. "And all from adding a few zeros to our position. So. We want those ten million bags. Where shall we find them?"

Jenks threw up his hands. "It is a riddle—a nonsense. The coffee does not exist, and nothing we can say will make it otherwise."

"But it will exist in the future," Pinker insisted. "What if we could bring it back here to the present, where it will be more use?"

Jenks made a noise that suggested he thought the conversation had become ridiculous.

I said slowly, "If someone had a contract to supply that coffee at a later date . . ."

"Yes?" Pinker said eagerly. "Go on, Robert."

"And if you could buy that contract—well, its value would go up or down depending on whether the current price meant it was likely to represent a profit or a dud."

"Exactly," Pinker said with satisfaction.

"But how does that help anyone?" Jenks demanded.

"It would mean, for example, that a grower could take out insurance against a future fall in prices," I said. "He could buy a contract which assumed they would fall, and make a small profit to offset the greater loss from his crops."

"Yes," Pinker said. "But there is more to it than that, Robert—much more. Think of it as a time-bargain—a contract in four dimensions. A man might create such a contract who had never grown a bag of coffee in his life—he could always buy the goods in to fulfill the contract if need be, but there would never be any need: he could simply replace one contract with another when the time came. He would be growing . . ." He paused, searching for the word.

"He would be growing capital rather than coffee," I said.

"But what does this have to do with us?" Jenks said plaintively. "We have a coffee—Castle Coffee. People drink it. People choose it over our competitors' product. We have a duty to ensure that it continues to be there, on the shelves, and not merely in some hypothetical sense."

"Yes," Pinker said, with a sigh. "We have a coffee. And you are right, Simon—we must not be unduly distracted by the time-bargain. No matter how fascinating its possibilities."

JENKS BELIEVED our employer had gone a little mad. Certainly, Pinker had some strange notions. On one occasion he bounded into the office Jenks and I now shared and announced that we were to look into controlling the weather.

"I beg your pardon?" Jenks said, nonplussed.

"Specifically, frosts. Frosts in Brazil kill millions of coffee plants, but they are apparently unpredictable. What if there is a pattern? A cycle, even? What if—oh, a dry summer in Australia, say, or a typhoon in Jamaica—what if that could make a frost more likely in the highlands of Brazil?"

"I have never heard of such a thing."

"Look into it, though, will you? I have a sense about these things."

And so we contacted various meteorological societies, and a succession of strange men with even stranger devices traipsed through Narrow Street. One man brought along a contraption in which a dozen live leeches were attached to tiny bells by wires: when the atmospheric conditions were inauspicious—a circumstance to which leeches, he assured us, were particularly sensitive—the leeches would contract, thus tugging their bell-ropes. Another claimed that weather was determined by the conjunction of the planets, like a horoscope; another, that summer rainfall over the Pacific was a certain predictor of winter frosts in Brazil. Pinker listened to all of them with the same rapt attention. But then—

"Proof! I want proof!" he would mutter and, restlessly, search for the next charlatan to come and gull us.

SOMETIMES he referred to stocks and shares, and other more esoteric forms of contract, as *financial instruments.* It was an apt description: he was like nothing so much as a musician, or a conductor, beckoning great symphonies of cash flow into existence with a perfectly timed wave of his hand.

Jenks could not hear these invisible melodies. I think he saw himself as the practical one, the diligent servant who ensured that his eccentric master always had a clean shirt to wear and socks on his feet. It was Jenks who dealt with the advertising agency now, Jenks who negotiated terms with Sainsbury and Lipton. In that commonsense world—a world in which women bought coffee because you told them it would make them better wives, and store owners bought coffee because you offered them a better profit—he was completely at home. It was the more philosophical, notional world of the Exchange which flummoxed him.

Pinker said to me one day, "You have a feel for finance, Robert."

"That seems unlikely, given that I have never managed to stay out of debt for more than a day or two in my life."

"I'm not talking about money. I'm talking about finance—a completely different matter. And I suspect it is precisely your attitude to debt which is the reason. Simon cannot shake off the idea that borrowing is a bad thing—that money owed must be earned, and creditors paid off. But in this new world of hypothetical coffee and time-bargains, one can buy and sell debts and contracts just as profitably as one can sell beans." He stared at me, drumming his fingers on the table, and once again I was struck by the nervous energy which animated him these days. "You see it, Robert, don't you? We are no longer just traders in sacks and beans. We are traders in *obligations.* And just as an emperor might call on ancient loyalties to raise an army, so we too can make these obligations work for us—to shape the market. Imagine it, Robert! Imagine what we might do with such a force at our command!"

[SEVENTY]

The same coffee, served at the same time, will exhibit slightly different aromatic characteristics to different people. Similarly, the same coffees will show slightly different characteristics when served to the same person at different times.

—LINGLE, The Coffee Cupper's Handbook

BY NOW BOTH THE ARTICLES AND THE INVITATIONS HAD ALMOST dried up, just as Hunt had predicted. But there was an At Home in Pimlico which I went to, more to fill myself up with canapés and wine than because I wanted to tell yet again the story of Teruda.

And there she was.

She had her back to me, but I knew her instantly. When she turned away from the person she was talking to, and I saw her in profile, I saw that she had changed. She looked a little more careworn, and her hair was not so bright. Styles had changed while I was away: it was the women now, not the men, who were the peacocks. But the expensive lace blouse she wore looked as if it should belong to someone else.

She was not one of the group who hung on my words, but her husband was, and he called her over—like a fool. "May I introduce my wife?" he said. "Emily has a particular interest in Africa, Mr. Wallis."

Her handshake was brief, her expression impassive.

"Indeed," I said, "Miss Pinker and I are old acquaintances. We both worked for her father."

At that the man flushed. "She is not Miss Pinker now."

"Of course. My apologies, Mrs.—?"

"Brewer," she said. "Mrs. Arthur Brewer."

"And she was never actually employed by her father, I should make that plain," Brewer said nervously, looking around to see who might be listening. "Before her marriage she used to lend a hand with his papers and so on, but these days being my wife gives her plenty to do."

"Indeed," I said, "there is nothing wrong with employment."

She raised her eyebrows at that, just a little. "Do you have employment, Mr. Wallis?"

"Not as much as I should have."

"You are once again a *boulevardier*?" she said, with a hint of her old asperity.

"I meant, not enough to fill my time. Your father keeps me on his staff, but I have little to do there."

"Oh, but you are a writer," Brewer said. "I read several of your pieces on Africa—they were most evocative; one could almost smell the dust—" And he was off, chattering away, while my eyes remained locked on his wife.

Yes, she had changed. There was less bloom on her cheeks now and more sharpness to her face. Her eyes had a slightly bruised quality, as if she were not getting enough sleep. But there was also a belligerence in her gaze that had not been there before.

Brewer was still rattling on. Clearly he had no idea that she and I had once been engaged. I wondered at that. Why had she not told him? But perhaps, I thought, any woman would want to keep the way I had behaved to her a secret.

It was hopeless. I could not speak with her there, and besides, people were starting to stare—her husband might not have known of our previous connection, but there were some in that room who did, and out of the corner of my eye I saw one or two women already whispering behind their hands. I said to Brewer, "Sir, I agree with everything you have said so far, and since that leads me to believe that I must certainly agree with everything else you have to say, there seems little point in prolonging our conversation." I nodded at his wife. "Mrs. Brewer. It was good to see you again."

I moved to the other side of the room. Behind me I heard Brewer say "Well!" in a hurt tone. I did not care that I had offended him: I cared only whether his wife would come after me.

She did not, directly—could not, with so many eyes on us. I was prepared for that. I circumnavigated the room, talking briefly to this person, then that . . . allowing myself to be swept, as if by accident, into quiet corners, discreet nooks.

Still she did not come. Until, finally, just as the room was beginning to thin, I turned and found her behind me, replacing an empty glass on a tray.

"Tell me one thing," I said quietly. "Are you happily married?"

She stiffened. "You're very direct."

"There's no time for diplomacy. Are you happy with that man?"

She glanced over at where Arthur was holding forth. "Is happiness the purpose of a marriage?"

"I'll take that as a no. May I see you?"

She was silent for a moment. "Where?"

"You tell me."

"Come to Castle Street tomorrow at four." She put the glass down. "You know, Robert, you've become really quite fierce," she murmured as she moved away.

• • •

FIERCE: that was one word for it. What I had felt, when I looked across that room and saw her profile—even before I met the look of tired accusation in her eyes—was a fierce emotion, certainly. But it was rather more than that.

I have experienced, in my life, desire for many women; tenderness for a few; affection and admiration for even fewer. There were some who were a challenge; some who were a diversion; others for whom my lust itself was a kind of sweet ecstatic torment.

But there was only one woman for whom I ever felt that awful ache, that gulping, yearning emptiness and despair. And what made it even worse was the knowledge that it might so easily not have been this way—that I had once had fulfillment almost within my grasp, then simply threw it away: had smashed it as surely and savagely as a child smashes a nut to pieces with a stone.

Love without kisses is not love, the Galla warriors sang. What is it, then? What is this thing that remains after mere desire has departed? What is the name for this thing without kisses, that burns more fiercely than a kiss—this thing more terrible than love?

Without her I am hollow, a vessel waiting to be filled.

Without her I am nothing, a book without words.

THE NEXT DAY I was there at four, and she was not. The café was closed up, its windows shuttered, and from the air of decay it had clearly been that way for some time. I noted that, although Pinker had changed the sign that originally said Pinker's Temperance Tavern, he had been unable to resist leaving some indication of his philanthropic purpose. Underneath the windows an inscription painted on the black wood still read: *For he shall be great in the sight of the Lord and shall drink neither wine nor strong drink.* No wonder the place hadn't prospered.

I paced up and down, waiting. It was after five when she finally appeared, walking purposefully down the street toward me.

"In here," she said, producing a key.

I followed her inside. Dust sheets covered the marble tables, but the coffee-maker behind the bar looked clean. Emily went to a cupboard and pulled out a jar of beans. "These are fresh."

"How can you be sure?"

"I brought them here myself, last week."

I did not understand. "Why?"

"I come here sometimes on my own to drink good coffee. What we have at home is awful. And occasionally I need a quiet place to meet . . . certain people. Somewhere my husband is not aware of."

"I see."

She glanced at me sharply. "Do you?"

"I'm not going to judge you for taking lovers, Emily. God knows I've had my share of those."

She ground the coffee, and the aroma filled the room.

"Is there anyone at the moment?" I asked.

She smiled. "A lover?"

"What's funny?"

"It's just that you're very blunt these days. No, I don't have a lover at the moment. I find myself rather too busy for that."

I watched her for a while. "What kind of coffee is that?"

"I thought you might know without me telling you."

I went over to her and smelled the beans she was grinding. The scent was fragrant, but not as floral as the coffees I had come to know in Africa: there was a brightness, too, a lemony sharpness . . . "Jamaican," I said.

"Actually, it's Kenyan—the large berry. It's only recently started to come onto the market. I get it from a specialist importer in Spitalfields."

"Yet another thing I have got wrong, it seems."

When the coffee was done she carried it to one of the tables. I picked up my cup: as well as the lemon and fragrant notes, there was a rich black-currant depth. "It has been a long time," I said at last, "since I had a cup as good as this. I'm surprised you still own these cafés, actually."

"We don't. They lost money and had to be sold. But when I found out that the new owners intended to turn them back into public houses, I insisted on keeping just this one. I don't think Arthur has even realized it exists—he is only interested in the stocks and shares, the ones that make money." She sighed. "It's the law of the jungle, isn't it—survival of the strongest, and the rest be damned."

"Having spent some time in a jungle," I said, "I can tell you that its laws are considerably more complex than one imagines."

She put down her cup. "Robert?"

"Yes?"

"Will you tell me how Hector died?"

So I told her the whole thing, leaving out nothing except the detail about the eyeballs and the testicles. As I spoke, the tears poured silently down her cheeks. She made no move to brush them away, and although I longed to kiss them off her pale skin I did not move toward her.

"Thank you," she said softly when I had finished. "Thank you for telling me, and for what you did, as well. I know you weren't fond of Hector, but I'm glad you were there at the end. That must have been a comfort to him."

"You loved him."

"I was very young."

"But you loved him . . ." Now it was my turn to hesitate. "You loved him fully. Not as you loved me."

She turned her head away. "What do you mean?"

"As you told your father that morning in his office, you and I were friends. We were never lovers."

Somewhere outside, there was a sudden rattle as a noisy knot of children ran down the street, running their sticks along the railings. There was a shout, an excited cry, and then they were gone again.

"What I told my father," she said, "was that I wanted to marry you. That should have been enough, surely."

"But you were in love with Hector."

"That was already long over. As you are presumably aware, since you read my letters. He preferred his bachelor freedom. And you—" she turned to me at last, and her eyes were accusing, "you fell in love with someone else soon enough."

"Yes."

"Who was she?"

"Her name was Fikre."

"And did you . . ." She made an ironic gesture. " 'Love her fully'?"

"I did."

"I see."

"Emily . . . I have done a lot of thinking, these past few years. I asked you to meet me today because I wanted to apologize."

"To apologize!"

"Yes. My letter. I was—discourteous."

"Discourteous!"

"It would mean a great deal to me if you were able to forgive me."

"Let me get this straight, Robert," she said, setting her cup down rather firmly in its saucer. "You are asking my forgiveness for the manner in which you broke off our engagement, and for nothing else?"

"I am aware that there are probably other things—"

"Well, let us just think what those other things might be. You asked my father for my hand in marriage, without ever happening to mention to me that you were thinking of doing so. You spent every evening after we had been together in the fleshpots of Covent Garden—did you think I didn't know? Jenks saw you there on more than one occasion, and he was only too happy to pass on that information, believe me. You went off to Africa in the most fearful sulk, and you wrote me those horrid letters in which you made it quite clear that you felt trapped, even before you fell in love with someone else—"

I looked into my cup. "Believe me, I would do anything—anything—to make amends."

She made a scornful noise.

"Is it too late?" I asked.

"Too late for what?"

"To put all that behind us. To start again."

She said incredulously, "You mean, to be your . . . to be what that woman was to you?"

I glanced at her. Two spots of color burned in her cheeks. I said slowly, "I want to hold you, and to be inside you, and for us to make each other feel . . . well, I can't explain that part of it in words, but perhaps you already know. All I can tell you is that learning to feel pleasure—the pleasure of love—is like learning to taste—your palate changes, just as it does when you learn to cup coffee."

"And this is what you have learned on your travels, is it? How to insult women?" she said furiously.

"I had rather thought that the continuation of my feelings for you after so long was a compliment."

"Anyway, it's quite impossible."

"Because of Arthur?"

"Not in the way you imagine."

"Perhaps in time—"

"No. You don't understand. First, because I am not that sort of woman. Don't protest, Robert, there's nothing either of us can do about it. Second, because I can't afford a scandal."

"But what about the others? The men you meet here?"

"Those I meet with here are women."

"Oh . . ." I said, baffled. "But why?"

She looked me in the eye. "We need somewhere private to plan our criminal actions."

I still didn't understand.

"I am what's called a suffragette," she explained. "Although it is a name we dislike intensely. An attempt by the newspapers to make us sound like silly ineffectual females."

"Ah." I thought about it. "There's been a certain amount of criminal activity, hasn't there—slogans painted on walls, women trying to demonstrate in the House of Commons—"

"That was us. At least, some of it."

"But what will happen if you're caught?"

"We'll go to prison. And it isn't 'if.' It's 'when.' "

"You might be lucky."

She shook her head. "There'll come a time when the movement will need prisoners—martyrs, if you like. Imagine it, Robert: these 'silly girls,' these 'suffragettes,' actually prepared to be imprisoned for our cause. They won't be able to call us the feeble sex then."

"And your husband?"

"He doesn't know. He's bound to find out sooner or later. But I'm prepared for that."

"Perhaps he'll divorce you."

"Not him. It would look bad."

"And—why is it so important? I mean . . . the chance to elect an MP . . . to send some pompous oaf like Arthur to the House—is it really worth risking prison for?"

She looked at me with a gaze that contained only utter certainty. "It is the only way left. They promised it to us so many times, and every time they lied. Does one MP matter? Perhaps not. But to be denied it—to be denied the recognition that we are human beings with rights as great as any man's—that matters. When an army advances, Robert, it isn't they who choose the place of battle but those who want to oppose them. Voting—representation—is where those who oppose us have made their stand. The House of Commons is their citadel. And so we must storm it, or accept forever that we are not their equals."

"I see."

"Will you help us?"

"Me!" I said, astonished. "How?"

"This café—if our group is to grow we'll need places like this. Somewhere where messages can be left, and meetings held, and where people who are interested can come to find out more. I've been looking out for someone to manage it for me. Yesterday, when you said you were at a loose end, it struck me that you would do it very well. I could ask my father to release you, for the afternoons at least. I'm sure he would agree to that. And you could live above the shop—there are two floors upstairs, completely empty: it would save you paying rent."

"I'm flattered, Emily, but surely you can see it's impossible. I have had articles published, things are starting to happen for me. I can't give up my freedom still further."

"Oh yes. I see perfectly." Her voice trembled with anger. "When you said just now you would do anything to make amends, that was just another pose, I take it? When you asked me to sleep with you—that was just a pretty speech? You talk about the pleasures of sex readily enough—so long as it is pleasure without responsibility, just another one of your 'exquisite sensations.' Do you remember that phrase, Robert? It was how you described kissing me, once. It was a long time before I realized just how horrible that was—what it said about how you saw me." She glared at me. "You had better go."

There was a long silence. "Oh—very well," I said.

"What are you waiting for, then? Go." She turned away, preparing to ignore me.

"No—I mean 'very well, I will run your blasted café.' "

"Really?" She sounded surprised.

"I said so, didn't I? Don't ask me why. I seem to have a ridiculous inability to say no to anyone in your family."

"It would be a considerable undertaking," she warned. "Once it became known that this is where we gather . . . Put it this way, you'd best keep a pickaxe handle behind the bar."

"I'm sure we'll cope."

Her eyes narrowed. "You do realize I will never sleep with you?"

"Yes, Emily. I do understand that."

"And the salary will be quite small. You will not be able to afford your usual cohorts of whores and concubines. Why are you smiling?"

"I was just recalling a previous negotiation with a Pinker over the terms of my employment. I am sure that whatever I am paid will be sufficient for my modest needs."

" 'Modesty' is not a word I readily associate with you."

"Then perhaps I can surprise you. However, I do have some conditions."

"Such as?"

"I'd want to get rid of those ridiculous mottoes. It's going to be hard enough to get people to come here without them thinking I'm going to lecture them about the joys of temperance."

"All right. What else?"

"No blends. I'm damned if I'll take coffees from all over the world, only to mix them all up into one nameless sludge."

"And you really think you can make a profit that way?"

"I have no idea," I said. "But then, do you really care? I suppose I hope to avoid making a loss."

She put out her hand. "In that case, Robert, we have ourselves a deal."

[SEVENTY-ONE]

Experience is essential in developing a complete flavour language and comprehension of the tremendous number of flavour nuances that hide in the background of general smell and specific taste sensations we know as coffee. Gaining this type of experience takes time. There are no short cuts.

—LINGLE, The Coffee Cupper's Handbook

❧

EMILY HAD BEEN WRONG: PINKER'S REACTION TO OUR PROPOSAL was not, initially, favorable. It was, I assumed, the impropriety that bothered him—his married daughter employing someone who had once been close to her. I emphasized that my role would be limited to helping to set the place up, and eventually he relented.

"One thing, though, Robert. Remember this: we cannot turn back the clock. Our failures are best forgotten. It is our successes that we take with us into the future."

At the time I was not sure whether he meant my failure in

Africa or my failure to marry his daughter. That there was another possibility did not occur to me until many years later: that he might have been referring not to me but to himself, and his own relations with Emily.

FOR THE NEXT few weeks I was busy. There were builders to oversee, staff to hire, lawyers to wrangle with—there was a brief legal skirmish when it became apparent that we could no longer call it Castle Coffee: in the end we renamed it the Castle Street Coffee House, and everyone was satisfied. I met Frederick Furbank, the importer who supplied Emily with her Kenyan. To my surprise the fellow had heard of me; indeed, was positively proud to make my acquaintance. "Robert Wallis?" he cried, pumping my hand. "The same Wallis who created the Wallis-Pinker Guide? I have to tell you, sir, that a modified version of that system has now been adopted by all the smaller merchants. Wait until I tell the others that I am buying coffee for Wallis!" It was strange to think that I had created something that had a life of its own. But I felt no great pride of authorship: in truth the driving force had been Pinker, not me.

Furbank and I tasted some coffees together and made an initial selection. It was remarkable to see how quickly the Africans were taking over from the South Americans in terms of quality, and how the wet-process coffees were leaping ahead over the dry-process ones. . . . We talked coffee-trade jargon happily for several hours, and by the end of it I knew Emily had a supplier who would not cheat her.

Once the café opened I was busy in a different way: supervising the waiters, attending to the Toselli machine, even washing cups and dishes when the occasion required. And almost from the start, there was a steady stream of women who came there looking for information. You could always tell which those were—their expressions both determined and anxious as they slipped through the door, as if they had had to steel themselves for this irrevocable step.

THE MILITANT suffrage movement—the Cause—was growing quickly now, fueled by reports in the newspapers about what was happening in Manchester and Liverpool. Emily and her co-conspirators spent long hours in the back room, debating everything—their constitution, their ethics, what was legitimate action and what was not, how to make their case. For a movement whose avowed slogan was "Deeds not words," there certainly seemed to be an awful lot of the latter. They talked of rousing all London, but never seemed to have enough postage stamps.

There were times, in fact, when I thought it was all just an enthusiasm—a girlish adventure. But then, at the end of their interminable meetings, they would put on their hats, tie up their boots, and, instead of getting on the omnibus to go home, head off in ones and twos to daub slogans on government buildings with buckets of whitewash, or to flypost walls with their manifesto. Molly, Mary, Emily, Edwina, Geraldine and the rest, no longer "angels in the house" but angels of vengeance. These night-time escapades, I admit, filled me with misgivings. It had been indoctrinated in me from an early age that women were frail creatures, and I found the notion a hard one to shake off.

"You need not stand there glowering," Emily said one night, as she prepared to go and plaster bills on Chelsea Bridge. "If you're worried, come along."

"What makes you think I'm worried?"

"It is something to do with the way you've polished that cup so thoroughly you've almost punched a hole in it. Really, I shall be perfectly all right, but come if you want—it would be useful, actually, you could hold the bucket while I apply the paste."

"Very well. If you need me, I'll come."

"I didn't say I needed you, Robert, I said you would be useful."

"Is there a difference?"

"As my father would say, a distinction."

We hailed cabs in the street—five ladies with rolls of proclamations under their arms, each carrying a small bucket of wallpaper paste and a brush, and myself. If the government ever decides to smash this sedition, I found myself thinking, they will not find it so very difficult.

Emily and I alighted on the Embankment. She began to unroll the posters—but despite the mist there was a brisk wind and it was no easy matter to get them covered with paste.

"You would never have managed this alone," I said as a bill rolled across the bridge for the fourth time. I sprang to retrieve it.

"Yes, well, you have the satisfaction of knowing that you were needed after all," she said crossly, clutching at her hat.

"You're annoyed!"

"Of course I'm annoyed. I can't get the dratted things to stay on the brickwork." She pushed a sheaf of bills at me. "If you're so useful, get them up yourself."

"Gladly."

I stuck them up while she kept a lookout. "K.V.," she said suddenly.

"What?"

"K.V. That's what one says when a policeman appears, is it not?"

"Oh—you mean *cave.* From the Latin—" I glanced across the bridge. Two policemen were even at that moment strolling across from the Lambeth side toward us. "Actually, one says 'Run!' "

There was the sound of a whistle, and then thudding feet echoed across the bridge. "Faster!" I urged, taking her by the elbow.

WE WORKED our way toward Parliament Square, flyposting any public buildings we passed on the way. Then, by Westminster

Bridge, we saw a motor car. It had been parked by the side of the road, the chauffeur evidently having gone off for a bite to eat. On the bonnet was a government flag.

"That's the Home Secretary's car," Emily said.

"Are you sure?"

"Certain. Arthur knows him. Come on, let's flypost it."

"What!"

"It's a wonderful opportunity," she said impatiently. "He's much more likely to read a bill posted on his own motor car than on a bridge. And just to make sure, we'll flypost the inside as well."

"But Emily—you can't."

"Why ever not?" She was already unrolling some bills.

"Because it's . . . well, it's a car. It's a lovely machine. A thing of beauty."

"Oh, in that case," she said sarcastically, "let's wander round until we find something ugly and flypost that instead, shall we? Robert, I can't help the fact that the Home Secretary has chosen a particularly nice machine to be driven around in. The message is what counts."

"But think of the poor chauffeur—the trouble he'll get into."

"It's unfortunate, but there you are," she said, sloshing paste onto the backs of four or five bills. "Keep a lookout, will you?"

"This isn't fair play," I protested, even as I did as she asked.

"The thing about women, Robert," she said as she applied the greasy back of the first bill to the car's pristine metalwork, "is that we are not gentlemen. And we are not playing the game, we are fighting the fight."

"Oi!" There was a shout. I turned. Our friends the policemen had spotted us again.

We pelted down numerous side streets, until at last I drew her into a quiet, darkened doorway, the porch of some grand house. We waited, listening. The streets were silent.

"I think we've lost them," I said. "We should give it five minutes, to be sure."

"Isn't this wonderful?" she said. Her eyes were shining.

"Wonderful?" I said doubtfully.

"You always wanted to be a rebel. And now you are."

"And you are my helpmeet."

"Other way round, surely. You're *my* helpmeet. And very good you are, too."

I could not help it—those flashing eyes; the panting lips; the rise and fall of her chest as she caught her breath . . . it was all so like a situation in which someone wants to be kissed that I kissed her.

She kissed me back—I was sure of it: deeply, lingering, with a sigh of pleasure. But when I went to kiss her a second time she stopped me with a hand on my chest.

"We must find you a wife, Robert," she said quietly.

"What do you mean?"

"You and I—we are friends now, aren't we? We have thrown over the trivialities of romance for the deeper bonds of comradeship."

"Don't mock me, Emily."

"I'm sorry. I was just trying to—make light of it, I suppose. But I meant what I said, before. You and I are pals. If you want any more you must find someone else."

"I don't want anyone else," I said. But I let go of her shoulders.

[SEVENTY-TWO]

GRADUALLY I MADE SOME FURTHER CHANGES TO THE CAFÉ; increasing the number of tables, bringing in colorful advertising posters such as those I had seen in the coffee bars of Italy and France, and creating a long shelf behind the counter for bottles of absinthe and other aperitifs. Emily bore all this without comment, but when I spent a week's income on a vast display of peacock feathers she stopped me.

"What on earth is this, Robert?"

"There used to be something similar in the Café Royal. It gives the place atmosphere, don't you think?"

"Atmosphere," Emily said decisively, "is exactly what we do *not* want."

"Oh?"

"Atmosphere—by which you actually mean, I think, the decadent ambience of a Parisian brothel—no, let me finish—suggests something superficial. It is conversation and the exchange of ideas we need here, not feathers and fripperies. I have something more like a Methodist meeting hall in mind—plain and earnest and functional."

"Why on earth would anyone want to come to such a place?"

"Robert, it appears to have escaped your notice that we are planning a mass insurrection. They will come for the politics, not the peacocks. As for your absinthe—has anyone actually ordered one?"

"Not as yet," I admitted. "You suffragettes are an abstemious lot."

"Thank goodness. Let us serve coffee, and be done with it."

I did as I was asked, but I could not help thinking that the suffragettes would have been just as happy drinking tea, or water for that matter. Such little expertise as I possessed was wasted in that place.

THE GOVERNMENT had learned from the suffragettes' successes in Manchester. In London they had decided on a different policy, that of belittling them. The impression they gave was that the militants were over-excitable females with nothing better to do, rather than the threat to natural order they had been portrayed as in the North.

CABINET PUDDING

Take a fresh young suffragette, add a large slice of her own importance, and as much sauce as you like; allow to stand on a Cabinet Minister's doorstep until at a white heat; mix freely with one or two policemen, well roll in the mud, and while hot run into a Police Court; allow to simmer; garnish with a sauce of martyrdom. Cost—a little self-respect.

"IT IS SO VEXING," Emily said, throwing the *Daily Mail* to the table. "We are like gnats attacking a rhinoceros."

"Even gnats are a nuisance in a cloud," Geraldine Manners said. "We must hold a march."

Edwina Cole sighed. "Doubtless the *Daily Mail* will inform its readers that it is not ladylike to march."

"Then we shall not call it a march. We will call it a procession—they can hardly object to ladies doing that."

THE PROCESSION was planned for Easter Monday. The newspapers called it the "Ride of the Valkyries" and "the charge of the petticoat soldiers," but all that was water off a duck's back to Emily by this time.

"Would you like me to come with you?" I asked.

"Why not?"

"Shall I bring my pickaxe handle?"

"Oh, I doubt you will have any need of that. We are only organizing a procession—the pitched battle can wait until another occasion."

THEY WERE to march—or rather, to process—from Trafalgar Square to Westminster. There the women would present their petition to the House of Commons. Emily had no idea how many people would turn up. Two hundred, said the *Daily Mail*. Where they got that figure, I had no idea: I suppose they were striking a balance between a number large enough to justify to their readers that it was in the newspapers at all, and one so small that the marchers could not actually be said to represent a significant part of the population.

We got to the start well before the advertised time. My first thought was that Emily had done well—the place was already crowded. But then with a sinking feeling I saw how many of those milling about were men. Looking vulnerable in the patch of green in the middle of the square, fifty or so women and a few male supporters stood waiting, nervously.

As we started across the square a policeman stopped us. "If you stay here hi will arrest you for causing han obstruction to the pavement," he said to Emily. Some of the men watching us applauded enthusiastically.

"I am not on the pavement," Emily replied calmly.

"Ho yes you are," the policeman retorted, bodily picking her up and placing her on the pavement. Emily gasped. Then I heard a shout from the men at the back: "Jostle her!" The mass of male bodies surged forward, bumping her slender figure into the road.

I turned to the policeman, appalled. "Are you going to allow them to do that to this lady?"

He stared at me without expression. "Wot lady would that be?"

WE CANNOT have been above sixty when we finally set off, and on either side was a mob of about two hundred. Some shook their fists, some howled abuse, but most just eyed the women with an interest that was openly sexual. Occasionally hostility sparked to violence. Two women were carrying between them a banner, beautifully embroidered with the words *Cheshire Women's Textile Workers Representation Committee.* I saw three men run toward them. Tearing the banner from the women's arms, they stamped and pulled at it until all that was left were broken sticks and rags trodden into a puddle. More policemen were standing not twenty feet away, watching.

Few of us in the procession were men, but we were a particular target. To begin with I did not understand why I kept hearing a peculiar clucking sound, until I also heard the shouts of "Henpecked! Henpecked!" and "Wash the dishes!"

I felt Emily push her arm through mine as we walked. "Just ignore it."

"On the contrary," I said, "I was thinking what a pleasure it is to be mistaken for your husband."

As we reached Westminster the crowd began spitting. Great glistening webs of phlegm flew through the air around us. One landed on Emily's jacket, where it hung on her lapel like a slimy, opalescent brooch.

"They will have to do better than that," she said grimly, pulling out a handkerchief.

As we entered Westminster Square the crowd pushed in behind us. In front of us, blocking the way to the House, was a line of mounted policemen. It seemed that we were not to be allowed to present our petition after all, but we could not go back, either.

All around us the chanting intensified as the bystanders took advantage of our immobility to taunt us further. And then, quite without warning, there was a commotion on our right. A group of men rushed into the marchers, grabbing the women and wrestling them to the ground.

"Why don't the police do something?"

"They are moving at last. Look."

It was true—the police had drawn their truncheons. But with a sickening sensation I saw that they were not pulling the attackers off: it was the suffragettes who were their targets. Female screams filled the air. We could not escape—the press of the panicking crowd all around us was too thick, and although we were pushed and pulled this way and that like seaweed on a rock, we always got swept back to the same place. The blue uniforms and their truncheons were twenty feet away—ten—within touching distance. I could see the sweat on the red face of the policeman nearest to me as he knocked a woman to the ground. She kicked out at him, and he clubbed her across the shins.

"Get behind me," I told Emily.

"It will make no difference."

"Do it anyway."

I turned and clasped her to me, turning my back on that blue wave as it prepared to break over us.

• • •

I WAITED in a cell for hours, bloodied, bruised, and thoughtful.

Allegiance is a strange thing. It can be intellectual—but it can also be visceral, a decision forced on you by events. I had no reason to care about the women's cause. But I had stood alongside them as they were attacked, and I saw now, quite suddenly, the natural justice of what they were trying to do. If their demands were really as trivial as the newspapers claimed, why go to such lengths to deny them? If females were really such gentle, precious creatures, to be ushered through doors and protected from traffic on pavements, why club them to the ground at the first signs of dissent? Were they really the meeker sex—or was it simply a fiction men had created, so that we could keep them that way?

As I pondered these unanswerable questions the door opened. A policeman looked in and said, "Come with me."

Still handcuffed, I was led down the corridor into a gloomy room lined with white tiles, like a bathroom. Emily's husband was sitting at a steel table. Next to him sat a dour-looking fellow in a black suit.

"Wallis," Brewer said, looking me contemptuously up and down. "I suppose I should have known."

"Known what?"

He leaned back, hooking his thumb into the watch pocket of his waistcoat. "When they told me that my wife and I had both been arrested, I was naturally concerned. To be in two places at once is difficult enough, but to have been making a civil disturbance outside the House while simultaneously denouncing it inside is surely quite remarkable."

"That particular mistake was not of my making, I assure you."

"No. It was mine. I should have realized that someone—or something—had infected my wife with this filth."

The idea was so ridiculous that I laughed out loud. He eyed me sourly. "What's so funny?"

"Where is she?"

"She is to be released on medical grounds."

"Why? Is she hurt?"

"None of your damn business," growled the man in the black suit.

Brewer said calmly, "She suffers from hysteria. Were you aware of that, before you dragged her into a riot?"

"Hysteria? Says who?"

"I do," the man in black said.

"Dr. Mayhews is her principal physician. It turns out that she has not been attending her appointments with the specialist for some time." Brewer eyed me with distaste. "In any case, she will now get the treatment she requires."

"If you have harmed her—"

"I am sending her to a private sanatorium in the country," he interrupted. "The fresh air and calm will do her good. And *you* will never make contact with her again. Do I make myself clear?"

"I intend to write a full account of today's procession—including the illegal activities of the police—and submit it to a newspaper."

"Please do so. You will find that no editor in this country will publish it. Take him back to his cell," he told the policeman.

With deliberate insolence I said, "I doubt very much that you will want my association with your wife to become common knowledge, Brewer." I gave the word *association* a particular intonation. I knew what he would take it to mean.

His face froze.

"If you have her locked up, I will publicize our relationship in every club and coffee shop in London."

He recovered himself. "The suffragists cannot afford that kind of scandal."

"Perhaps. But I am not the suffragists. And I will stop at nothing—nothing—to have Emily released."

"And if I do release her?" he said slowly. "What do I get then?"

"My discretion."

He snorted disbelievingly.

I shrugged. "It is the only guarantee you will get."

There was a long silence. "Throw this man out," he said at last. "Doctor, we will make alternative arrangements for my wife's treatment in London."

[SEVENTY-THREE]

"YOU DID WHAT?" SHE CRIED.

"I told him that I would keep quiet about the affair we are having if he let you go."

"I saw him just now," she said, appalled, "and he never so much as mentioned it."

"Perhaps he was too embarrassed."

"No," she said. "We underestimate men like Arthur. How good they are at keeping their true feelings hidden. It is why they will never give us power unless they are forced to." She looked at me. "So you struck a deal over me."

"It wasn't like that."

"You had no right to do it. Even if it had been true, you would have had no right."

"I'm sorry. I could think of no other way."

"And now I will have to face Arthur every day, and he will never say anything, but he will think he knows . . ." She sighed. "Well, I have lost the moral high ground, but it is my own fault. Perhaps it will do me good to be a little humbled."

"Of course," I said, "there is one possible compensation . . ."

"Oh? What's that?"

"If your husband thinks we are sleeping together, then we might as well be guilty as charged."

" 'Might as well'? What a romantic you are, Robert. I have never been propositioned so charmingly."

"But you see my point? What is there to stop us?"

"Apart from the little matter of you having given your word, and me having to face Arthur every morning over the breakfast table. Oh, and your slight propensity to go and fall in love with other women. I'm sorry, Robert. Even put so irresistibly, I find I am able to refuse that offer."

[SEVENTY-FOUR]

"Rio flavour"—a heavy and harsh taste characteristic of coffees grown in the Rio district of Brazil, and sometimes present even in fancy mild coffees.

—Uker's Coffee Buyers' Guide

As the price climbed ever higher, so the quantities of coffee pouring out of Brazil and the other South American countries turned from a deluge to a flood. Now there was a new shadow on the horizon—over-production. Who would drink all this coffee? True, the standardization of packaging had kept the price of the finished article in grocery stores down; but there was, surely, a limit to how much demand could be expanded. The price wobbled briefly—and still the supply rose, fueled by planting decisions made four or five years earlier. Pinker watched the markets like a hawk, waiting to pounce.

The Brazilian government announced that it would deal with any over-supply by destroying the surplus itself, before it reached the market. The stock markets approved. The inexorable rise of coffee, and the various South American bonds and currencies associated with it, continued unabated.

"I NEED YOU to go to Brazil for me, Robert," Pinker said.

I looked at him somewhat doubtfully. He laughed. "Don't worry. I am not expecting you to run a plantation this time. There are some matters I must investigate, and it has to be someone I can trust—someone who can see beyond the end of his nose."

He wanted me to scrutinize the destruction of the coffee, he explained, and make sure that it was really all it seemed.

"Oh, the theory is sound enough. Reduce the supply, and you control the demand. But it is quite one thing for a government to issue such a decree. Those who are required to carry it out will always have a conflict of interest. For any farmer, burning his coffee would be like burning money. And my experience of farmers, Robert, is that they are rarely more altruistic than they need to be."

I could hardly refuse to go—I was his employee, after all. There was a boat from Liverpool that would reach São Paulo in sixteen days, so I booked my passage.

It was a very different experience from my journey to Africa. For one thing there were no missionaries on board, no sermons about the need to keep up appearances or lighten the darkness. My fellow passengers had only one reason for their journey: coffee. In one way or another all of us were connected to the trade; the only trade, it seemed, that South America knew.

I did not tell them that I had another, secondary reason for my journey. Before I left London, Pinker had entrusted me with a message, to be delivered personally.

"Not to a secretary, not to a foreman, not even to a member of his family. Give it to him directly, and if possible stay with him as he reads it. I want you to tell me how he reacts."

He placed a letter in my hand. The envelope was sealed: it was the name on it which made me start.

Sir William Howell.

"To no one else, Robert," he said, watching me. "Place it in Sir William's hand, and tell no one else of its existence."

SÃO PAULO was like nowhere else I had ever been—a city of furious energy, new buildings rising on every side, palaces of stone and marble being built by barefoot men with rags for clothes and sticks for scaffolding. I thought: *This is what Africa might someday become,* but I could not quite believe it; I could not imagine those fierce African skies tolerating such ambition, such relentless, passionate activity.

Pinker had given me letters of introduction to the Secretary for Agriculture, who was only too happy to arrange for me to see the destruction of the coffee at first hand. I was taken to the docks at Santos, where a fleet of barges was being laden with sacks.

"These will all be dumped at sea," my guide said, with a wave of his hand. "And the same amount next week, and the same the week after that. As you can see, there are armed guards, to ensure no one helps themselves."

"May I inspect the sacks?" I asked.

"If you wish."

I walked past the guards to the stack of sacks and untied one. I sniffed it. The beans were unroasted and unmilled, but there could be no doubt: this was rough Brazilian arabica, the same coffee that was exported by the ton to San Francisco and Amsterdam. I took a handful and rubbed it in my fingers to be certain, then went to another bag to check that the contents were the same.

"Well? Are you satisfied?" the guide asked, a peeved edge to his voice.

"I am."

"Good. Then you can tell your employer that when the Brazilian government says it will do a thing, it does it."

PINKER HAD LEFT it to me how best to approach Sir William. In the end I decided that I would simply write to him, telling him that I had something for him. I gave my hotel address, but made it clear that by the time the letter reached him I would already be on my way.

There was a railway all the way from the coast into the hills—the same railway that brought the coffee down for export. The locomotive was an American one of the latest design, with a pointed cow-catcher on its front. For three days we chugged across endless valleys and up innumerable hillsides. But what was extraordinary was that in all that time the view out of my carriage window never changed. Every hill in that country—every valley, every vista—was the same. Stretching into the distance as far as the eye could see, like the grooves in a gramophone record, one saw nothing but shiny, dark-green lines of coffee. The bushes had been pruned so that they stood no higher than a man could pick, and one occasionally glimpsed peons tending to the plants, but for the most part the huge fields were as eerily empty as a desert—a desert of coffee. The original lush jungle had been pushed back into a few ravines and other inhospitable corners not worth cultivating, while the soil, as we gradually went higher, turned a deep brick-red, so dry and fine that in the least puff of wind it lifted, and seemed to drift over the fields like colored smoke. The lines of coffee were so straight, and stretched so far into the distance, that passing by them in the train caused one to experience strange optical illusions: sometimes they seemed almost to flicker and jump, as if the bushes themselves were in motion, striding with military precision into the interior.

When we stopped to take on coal and water, I chatted with the engine driver.

"This is nothing." He gestured at the combed, regimented landscape, one eye closed against the cigarette in his mouth. "Where you're going—up to Dupont—now that's a *fazenda.* Five million trees. Imagine! Me, I have twenty trees, and I consider myself a wealthy man. Imagine to have five million!"

"How does a train driver come to grow coffee?" I asked, astonished.

He laughed. "In Brazil, everyone grows coffee. I rent a little land with my wages, so I took up the maize and planted a few beans. With half the money I make, I buy maize; with the rest, I'll buy more land and plant more trees. It's the only way to make money."

"Aren't you worried about the government destroying crops?"

"They pay compensation, don't they? Well then, it's all the same to me."

AT LAST we reached the stop that marked the edge of Howell's plantations. There was a small platform, and on the other side of it another, smaller train was waiting.

"Howell's," my driver said. "He must have sent it down for you."

I stepped into a luxurious Pullman carriage, its glass windows engraved as finely as those of any West End hotel. Porters hoisted my bags into the luggage van, a whistle blew, and the train glided up into the hills.

The view was still of endless straight lines. But along with the coffee, one glimpsed other signs of human activity. There were roads cut through these fields: tractors and carts trundled along them, generating clouds of that colored dust. Men marched along in groups—work gangs, presumably, but unlike the lone peons I had glimpsed occasionally in the lower hills, these were wearing smocks, each group of one color, while the foremen had white bandanas tied around their heads. Water glistened in irrigation channels, while from time to time we passed huge terraces for drying the washed beans. I found myself wondering how simple farms, or even what Hector and I had tried to set up in Africa, could ever compete with an operation as vast as this.

The train drew into another station. Warehouses and some offices clustered around a central piazza. The porters were already unloading my luggage, so I followed it, and them, toward a long, low mansion which overlooked the estate.

"Mr. Wallis?"

The speaker was a small, swarthy man. Despite the heat he was wearing the full dress of an English bank official—starched collar, dark suit, spectacles, pince-nez.

"Yes?" I said.

"Sir William says you are to state your business to me."

"I'm afraid my message is for Sir William only."

"Sir William is not here."

"Then I will have to wait."

The man frowned. "That may not be permitted."

"Well, you can hardly ask him whether he permits it unless he is here, can you?" I said loftily. "You had better find somewhere to put me up until he arrives."

"I'll see to this, Novelli," a curt voice interjected.

I turned. A young man was walking toward us. He was rather less formally dressed than the man he had spoken to, but Novelli nodded obediently and withdrew.

"Jock Howell," the young man said. "And you must be Wallis. Do you mind telling me what the devil you want?"

"I have a message for your father."

"I'll give it to him."

I shook my head. "You can tell him that it's from Samuel Pinker. But I can deliver it only to him in person."

The young man scowled and stalked away. For an hour I remained where I was, until he returned.

"Follow me."

I followed him into the mansion. In the hall—lined with cool marble, the windows shuttered against the humidity outside—he knocked on a door.

"Come in," a voice answered.

I recognized Sir William Howell from the portrait on every pack of Howell's Planter's Premium. In the flesh he was smaller than I had imagined; leaner, more intimidating.

"Mr. Wallis," he said. "Shut the door, please."

I turned to do as he asked and found my way blocked by the son, who looked uncertain which side of the closed door he should be on.

"I'll call you if I want you," the old man told him brusquely.

When we were alone Sir William looked me up and down. "I hope you haven't come all this way just to see what a proper plantation looks like. I fear for you it is rather too late for that."

He clearly knew all about my own abortive attempts to grow coffee. "I have a letter for you."

"From Mr. Pinker of Narrow Street?" He sounded amused.

"Yes."

He held out his hand and I placed the letter in it. Picking up a letter knife from the desk, he slit the envelope open and pulled out its contents—two pages covered in Pinker's tidy writing.

Howell read it through once, and grunted—I thought, with surprise. Then he glanced at me and read it again. This time he seemed to weigh it more carefully.

Putting the letter down, he looked out of the window. I followed his gaze. The view was of a great expanse of plantation—twenty or thirty miles of it. "And you really know nothing of the contents of this letter?" Pinker must have said so in the text, since I had not.

"Nothing whatsoever," I agreed.

He said abruptly, "What sort of man is he? Pinker, I mean?"

"He's clever," I said. "But it's a particular kind of cleverness. He likes to dream—to imagine possibilities that no one else has seen. And then, more often than not, he's right."

Howell nodded slowly. "Stay here for a few days. Jock will show you around. My reply to your employer will require some thought."

THEY WERE as good as their word. For three days I was allowed to witness every facet of their operation, from the giant nursery beds which alone occupied more than a hundred acres, to the vast sheds in which the beans were pulped and processed. Even the terraces on which the beans were spread to dry in the sun were made of concrete, so that the red dust did not taint the finished product. The men who walked amongst them turning the beans with huge rakes went barefoot, their bodies lacquered with sweat.

There were two sorts of workers, Negroes and Italians. The Negroes were former slaves, Jock told me, but since abolition the company had recruited only Italian immigrants. The Italians worked harder, he said; partly because they had to pay off the heavy costs of their transportation, and partly because they were from better racial stock—by which he meant, I took it, that they were closer in color to himself.

"What happened to the Negroes they replaced?" I asked.

Jock shrugged. I understood him perfectly: once they were no longer slaves, they were no longer his concern.

The workers were housed in villages called *colonos,* each of which contained a bakehouse and a store where they could spend their wages. There was even a schoolroom, where the children were taught to count—counting, Jock Howell assured me, being one of the most useful skills a peon could acquire. All children, of whatever age, were excused school if their parents were on picking duty, the lowest berries on the bushes—those in reach of their little hands—being routinely left for them. Picking went on late into the night. More than once I myself saw families tramping wearily back to their villages in the dark, their heads bearing great baskets of picked beans, while a small child slumbered on the woman's hip.

"There are a great many children here," I commented.

"Of course. My father has always encouraged families."

"He likes children?"

Jock shot me a sideways look. "In a manner of speaking. These children will be our future laborers. And for the workers, there is no greater spur to industry than having hungry mouths to feed."

"What happens if they get into difficulties?"

"We never let anyone starve. A peon can always take a cash advance against his family's future earnings."

I remembered Pinker, and his time-bargains. "And how are the debts repaid?"

"By the children themselves, if necessary, from their wages."

"So these children inherit their parents' debts? And start their working lives in debt themselves?"

He shrugged. "It is better than slavery. And the workers seem happy. Judge for yourself."

It was true that the workers did seem contented with their lot, although I noticed that wherever Jock and I went we were accompanied by *capangas,* guards armed with rifles and machetes.

IN THE MANSION there were several white women who acted as maids and servants. I expressed my surprise that the estate had been able to recruit them, so far from the city.

Jock frowned. "Those women aren't white, Robert. They're black."

"I distinctly saw a white face in the kitchen as we passed this morning—"

"That was Hettie. And she certainly isn't white. She's a mustifino."

I wasn't familiar with the term, so he explained for my benefit. A mixed-race child was called a mulatto; the offspring of a white person and a mulatto was a quadroon; the child of a white person and a quadroon was a mustee, and so on, through octaroons, quintroons and mustifinoes.

"But where," I began, and then stopped. There was only one English family in Dupont. The question I had been going to ask was superfluous.

"HERE, THIS may interest you," Jock said, leading me toward one of the vast processing sheds. "It's where the coffee is sorted."

Inside, a long table snaked continuously around the room. At the back of the table was an open box like a trough. Sitting at the table were over a hundred Italian girls, from about ten to twenty years old. Each girl reached into the box, pulling out a handful of green beans which she spread in front of her. Then she examined them, picked out any bad ones and tossed them into another box behind her, at the same time sweeping the good beans through a hole in the table into a sack below. A high proportion of the girls were quite pretty, with the lustrous black eyes and dark skin of Italian peasants. As Jock and I entered the shed they looked up at us. They dug their bare pink toes into the sacks, and it seemed to me that they remained very conscious of our gaze as they continued in their work.

"Any of them would be glad to catch your eye," Jock murmured in my ear. "Should you find yourself at a loose end during your stay . . ."

I FOUND MYSELF at a loose end quite soon, as it happened. But try as I might to enjoy my pretty dark-skinned companion, I could never quite shake off the memory of Fikre, writhing on top of me in false ecstasy. And I could not shake off the disturbing sense that, whatever I did, Emily was watching it all, too—cool and sardonic: *So this is what you do with your whores and concubines.*

IN THE EVENINGS Sir William and his wife joined us for dinner. They kept a lavish table, with uniformed servants waiting on us hand and foot, refilling crystal goblets engraved with Howell's monogram, an elegant *H* motif, while Sir William spoke about the problems facing his country.

"You see this food, Wallis?" he said, indicating the spread in front of us. "Barely a mouthful has been grown in Brazil. As far as our peons are concerned, food is something that arrives on ships."

"They are quite right, of course," his son pointed out. "The coffee boats might as well bring grain on their inward voyage as travel empty."

"And so this country becomes ever more reliant on coffee," his father said. "Every peasant grows a few bushes. If we have overproduction it is not because of efficient estates like ours: it is because of all these little, low-grade producers, who are protected from competition by the valorization program." He stared into his wine. "Perhaps he is right, after all. Perhaps we must destroy what is weak, before we can build what is strong."

I did not need to ask who Sir William meant by "he."

ON ANOTHER OCCASION he said, "You know, Wallis, I was one of those who supported the abolition of slavery here."

I had not known that, and said so.

"Slavery is ultimately an inefficient way to run a plantation—it is like trying to work with donkeys rather than mules. The present system is far cheaper."

"How can it be?" I asked, puzzled.

"If you own a slave, you have capital tied up in him. Then you must feed him when he is sick, and pay someone to beat him when he is lazy, and feed his children even before they are old enough to be useful. . . . Abolition was a great change, and many opposed it for that reason, but it has turned out to be the best thing Brazil ever did." He drummed his fingers on the tablecloth. "Your employer, I think, is someone who understands about change."

"Indeed," I said, "it is his great preoccupation."

"I will write my answer to him tomorrow. You will be able to leave by mid-day—I will have Novelli order the train."

THE FOLLOWING MORNING he handed me an envelope addressed to Samuel Pinker. "You will know what to do with this."

"Indeed," I said, taking it.

"There is something else . . . You were shown, I believe, some coffee you were told was being dumped at sea?" I nodded. "You should know that our government is far too corrupt, and too greedy, to destroy anything that has a monetary value. Take a closer look, Mr. Wallis, and pass on what you learn to Mr. Pinker."

BACK IN SÃO PAULO I went down to the docks, without a government guide this time, and made some inquiries. There was a convoy of barges scheduled to dump sacks out at sea that evening. I found a fisherman with a small skiff, and paid him handsomely to take me out behind them.

Sure enough, about two miles out the barges pulled up alongside a freighter and began unloading their cargo onto the larger vessel. When they were done, the freighter steamed off toward the south while the barges returned to shore. I had managed to get close enough to see the freighter's name—the SS *Nastor*—and back on dry land I set about discovering what I could about her.

She was registered to a shipping syndicate; a syndicate, my researches soon told me, which included the son of the Secretary for Agriculture. What was more fascinating still was that she was bound for Great Britain by way of Arabia.

I could not conceive of any reason why a coffee ship should sail from one coffee-producing country to another—except for one.

I TELEGRAPHED Jenks, who tracked down a consignment of coffee from one of the *Nastor*'s previous trips. It was as we suspected; the sacks might be labeled mocca, but their contents were Brazilian. The SS *Nastor* had been shipping beans to Arabia. There, after a brief interval, they were reloaded and sent on to Britain, to be sold at what was a low price for mocca but a rather good price for Brazilian.

Back in England, Pinker was exultant—once again his instincts had been proved correct. "You must tell the world, Robert. Your Fleet Street contacts—have lunch with a few of them, and let them know how the Brazilian government betrays its commitments. But do it subtly—it should not look as if it comes from us: people will say we have an interest, and we must not let their cynicism get in the way of the truth." I did as he asked, and when articles appeared criticizing the valorization program, he professed himself well pleased. The market wobbled—and we milked the fluctuation for all it was worth.

But what had really delighted Pinker, I could tell, was the letter from Howell. I did not know what it contained, but the news was evidently good. "You have achieved exactly what I hoped, Robert," was how he put it to me. "Howell would have been suspicious had I sent some smooth-tongued ambassador. You told the truth, and that is what mattered."

[SEVENTY-FIVE]

If the coffee has picked up a taint or fault, the off-flavour begins to become detectable in the aroma of the freshly brewed coffee.

—LINGLE, The Coffee Cupper's Handbook

❧

WHILE I HAD BEEN AWAY THE SUFFRAGETTES HAD CHANGED their tactics, and were now heckling politicians at public meetings.

They would conceal a banner under their coats—they soon learned to have two or three of these, as the banners themselves were usually the first casualties—and sit in different places around the hall, never together. One woman would get to her feet and shout a question, unfolding her banner as she did so; while the stewards were ejecting her, the next would stand in a different part of the hall and repeat it.

I accompanied Emily on one of these outings, on a mission to interrupt a speech by a senior government minister. Perhaps he had got wind that something might occur. Anyway, after we had been waiting for half an hour a spokesman announced that the

Great Man had been delayed on parliamentary business, but that his place would be taken by the MP, Mr. Arthur Brewer.

I glanced across at Emily. She had gone quite pale.

"You need not do anything," I told her. "There are enough others to make a show."

She shook her head. "A principle is hardly a principle if it is dropped at the first sign of adversity. The others will be looking to me to do my part."

THE DEBATE began. Arthur spoke well—the writer in me noted and approved the clever phrases, the way he posed questions and then immediately answered them himself, the way he built up a rhythm of emphasis, one-two-three; all the tricks of the trade. His theme was Liberty and Security, and the balance that must be kept between the two; how the hard-won freedoms of Great Britain must not be thrown away, and how the first duty of the libertarian is actually thus defense—

To my right, a small figure in a smart green dress rose from her seat. Molly Allen, fearless as ever. "If you think so much of Liberty," she said in a high, loud voice, "don't keep it just for the men." She took out her banner and shook it. "Votes for Women!"

Uproar. Instantly three stewards were pushing toward her, but she had quite deliberately seated herself in the middle of a row. A furious clergyman sitting behind her tore the banner from her hand. "You may pass that one around," she said, unrolling another. "I have more, if anyone would like one." Then the stewards reached her—one on either side, and there was a tug-of-war as to which would manage to yank her to him.

On the platform, Arthur was watching all this with an expression of amused tolerance. "I see we have been graced by the presence of the ladies," he said with a smile. "But as I was saying—"

Geraldine Manners got to her feet. Geraldine was frail, passionate and nearly fifty years old; it was she who recruited Emily to the militants, after the episode in Regent Street. "Answer the question!" she shouted. "Will a Liberal Government give Votes to Women?"

Stewards charged toward that inoffensive little lady as furiously as if she were running at them with a rugby ball. She barely had time to unfold her first banner before she was dragged backwards from the hall by a steward.

Up on the platform, Arthur's composure did not waver—I had to admire the man: he seemed inoffensive enough, but he was doggedly, determinedly inoffensive. As soon as he could make himself heard over the hubbub, he raised his hand and said, "The lady herself has had to rush off"—laughter—"but I will address her question in her absence. The answer is: no." Thunderous applause. "Now to return to the real issue of the day, and one which will be close to the hearts of many in this room: Employment—"

From the back of the hall I heard Edwina Cole's voice. "Why do you take taxes from women when you won't let them vote?" She waited until they were all looking before she got to her feet, her banner in her hand. "Votes for Women!"

In their haste to reach her the stewards were climbing over the chairs. "Show some respect for your Member of Parliament," a man's voice cried angrily.

"He is not my Member of Parliament," she retorted. "I am a woman, I have no member." One or two people laughed at that, though others winced at the coarseness of the joke. Then she was pulled down. There was a shriek; it sounded as if someone had punched her.

Emily was still deathly pale. "There is no need," I said quietly.

She neither looked at me nor answered. She got to her feet—she was shaking, shaking like a leaf. She pulled out a banner. For a long agonized moment I thought she was going to lose her nerve.

"What about the women?" she called. "Why no votes for us?"

Brewer looked at her—and his smile froze. More stewards—those who had been unsuccessful in the race to get to Edwina Cole—thundered toward us.

"Very well," Arthur said slowly. "I am for Free Speech: I will answer this question." There was a ripple of applause, mingled with one or two boos. The stewards continued pushing through the crowd.

Arthur hooked his thumb in his waistcoat. "Madam, your friends have done us a great service today," he said with icy contempt. "They have illustrated far better than I could how dangerous it would be to give the vote to people like you—people who would abuse the democratic process without a second thought." Applause and cheers from the audience. "They remind us that women who can resort to this sort of behavior in seeking the vote would, if they were successful, resort to the same methods to obtain any other political objective. Those who will not behave as citizens cannot expect the rights of citizens."

More applause, over which Emily could just be heard, shouting, "Other methods have failed! It is precisely because—"

But Brewer was in full flow now, and the crowd had ears only for him. "Not only do they seek to achieve their ends by hysterical methods—they would incorporate that hysteria permanently in the political life of the nation. They seek votes for women—yet they are prepared to betray womanhood and all the gentle virtues of their sex to get it. What does that say about them? What kind of example do they set their children? What kind of message do they send to our enemies abroad?"

And thus he was back, neatly, where he wanted to be—and with the meeting giving him a standing ovation, too, just as the stewards were laying violent hands on his wife. "Get off me," she cried, flailing at the men as they pushed and pulled her along the aisle, but there was no question of them letting her go now.

She had dropped a banner behind her on the seat. I did not stop to think. I got to my feet. No one looked at me to begin with—we were all on our feet, clapping the glorious protector of our liberties, and a man amongst all those men was hardly noticeable. I shouted, "Votes for Women!" to get their attention, and, as soon as there was a lull in the noise, called out, "What does it say about your marriage, Brewer, that your own wife is a militant?"

There was a pause. People looked from one to the other of us. Just for a moment he seemed uncertain how to answer. Then he said languidly, "I have already given this subject far more time than it deserves. Do we want to talk about women—or work?"

The cry came back "Work," but by then I too was already being manhandled out of the hall by the stewards, with a few beefy kicks into my kidneys while they were about it.

THAT EVENING, of course, she had to confront him—what in those days we used to call a *mauvais quart d'heure.* He had arranged himself in their sitting-room, with his papers around him, waiting for her when she returned—the master in his domain.

She busied herself picking up her letters from the stand. He seemed quite composed, but she knew with Arthur that was no indication of his real mood.

At last he said, "I was surprised to see you at that meeting, this afternoon."

She took a deep breath. So they were going to talk about it. And she was going to tell him why she had done what she did—why she would not stop. This was hard—harder even than the meeting. It was one thing to stand and shout a slogan into a crowd; for a woman to stand up to her husband in his own home was unthinkable.

"You were already aware, I think, of my political views." She matched the even modulation of his voice.

"I was aware that you supported extremism. I had not known

that you were now actively engaged in attacking the democratic process."

"It is not a democratic process. Democracy requires the enfranchisement of the whole population, not just the male half—"

"Please," he interrupted acidly. "We have both had enough speeches for one day." She bit her lip.

He said, "What you forget is that when you behave like this it is my name you are trampling in the dirt."

"I hardly think—"

"First, because it is my name that you now carry—as a Brewer, the reputation of the family is in your hands. Secondly, because as my wife your actions reflect on me. If you attack me in public, people will think I behave badly to you in private."

"That is ridiculous."

"Oh? You were not there, I think, when your friend Wallis made that very point to several hundred of the electorate."

"Robert had no right to do that," she muttered. "I did not ask him to."

"Perhaps you have less control over him than you think. People like that will use your movement for their own ends. Just as he will use you for his own purposes."

"Arthur, you misunderstand. There is nothing between Robert and me."

"Well, it hardly matters now. Emily, I have made some decisions on this matter. I have decided that you must give up Wallis completely. And you must give up Votes for Women."

"What do you mean—give up?"

"Just that. You must no longer be involved. Not in any form."

"Arthur—I cannot agree to that."

"I am no longer seeking your agreement. I am overruling you. This is my decision. And as your husband I expect you to abide by it."

"And if I do not?"

"You are my wife—"

"But you are not treating me like your wife. You are treating me as something lower than a servant—"

"I would remind you of your marriage vows—"

"Is that what this is about? As if I have broken a contract of sale, and you would be recompensed?"

"For my part," he said quietly, "I meant every word of those vows. I made them before God, and I will honor them until my dying day."

He was so obviously sincere that for a moment she was caught off guard. "It did not feel that way when you spoke to me in that horrid fashion in front of all those people."

"The time and place was not of my choosing. Besides, I was trying to protect you."

"Protect me!"

"If I had not addressed you when I did, the stewards would have treated you far more roughly. As it was, they were forced to wait until I had finished. It calmed them down."

She was not sure whether to believe him, or if this was just a politician's way of retelling events to his own advantage.

"In any case," he added, "there is something else I wish to say."

"What is that, Arthur?"

"What Wallis shouted out . . . He asked what it said about my marriage, that my wife was a militant. It was offensive and personal—typical of the man. But I concede he may have a point. Our relations . . . Perhaps I have not been as attentive to domestic matters as I ought."

She saw, suddenly, where this might be leading.

"Dr. Mayhews is of the opinion that your hysteria will be eased when you are fulfilling the purpose for which nature intended you. Certainly I have noticed that few of these militants seem to be young mothers."

"That is because young mothers cannot leave their children—"

"Be that as it may." He paused. "I have decided it is high time we started a family."

"What!"

"Mayhews is in full agreement. Although you are somewhat delicate, he observes that it is frequently nature's way to strengthen the female frame during pregnancy, with corresponding benefits for mental robustness."

"Is this to do with politics?" She was aghast. "Has someone decided that your party is for the family?"

"All parties are for the family. Families promote stability—as you will doubtless discover, when you have one of your own."

"Arthur, I am too busy to have children just now."

"But you are not going to be busy, because you are going to give all that other business up," he said reasonably. "We will start immediately."

"What? Here? Now?" she said despairingly.

"There is no need to be vulgar." He stopped. "You would not refuse me this?"

"Of course not," she said dully. "If you will excuse me, I will go and ask Annie to draw me a bath."

"And I shall be up presently." He gestured at the papers. "I have some work to finish, but I will not be long."

Of the details of what followed, I cannot bring myself even to think. Emily would not, in any case, have spoken to me of such things. What little she did tell me she let slip only because I was cross-questioning her about Arthur's reaction to their encounter.

Finally she said—with a little gasp that was attempting to be a laugh—"We are trying for a child."

"Are you serious?"

"Arthur is—very serious. You cannot imagine how seriously—well, never mind." She sighed. "I am not certain whether he means to punish me with pregnancy, or whether he genuinely believes it will cure me of the Cause."

"But you will let him?"

"I have no choice. As he reminded me, I made certain vows."

"It was when you made them that you had no choice. After all, one cannot call in one's lawyer to rewrite the wedding vows clause by clause."

"No. Perhaps it would be better if one could, though I suspect we would still get into just as many muddles. In any case, it is not quite as simple as you put it."

"Why not?" I said, and then saw what she was getting at. "You *want* a child?"

"A family. Yes. Why do you look surprised? It is what most women want. And Arthur, as my husband, is the only person who can furnish me with that. For this, at least, I need his cooperation."

"But you cannot be a mother and a militant."

Two red spots had appeared on her cheeks. I should have recognized the signs; I knew her so well.

"Why not, exactly?" she demanded.

"Well—take yesterday. When those stewards manhandled you. Imagine if you had been pregnant."

"Perhaps if I were pregnant they would have seen the brutishness of their actions."

"But what if they had not?"

Her eyes flashed. "If men cannot be trusted, they have no right to be throwing us out of meetings in the first place."

"In principle you are quite right, Emily—but what use will your principles be when you are lying in a hospital?"

"Are you saying that my duty to my children is more important than my beliefs?"

"Well—yes. I suppose I am."

"When did my husband walk into the room?" she cried. "And when will you get into your thick selfish skull, Robert, that principles are not something to be put on and taken off again like—like one of your stupid jackets."

"Actually," I said, "I possess very few jackets these days, a consequence of the low wages for which I labor. My employer is—"

"In any case, it is all your fault," she snapped.

"Mine?" I said, astonished.

"It was the insult you hurled at Arthur which prompted all this in the first place."

"Ah."

"Ah indeed. Though a slightly more abject *Ah* would be appreciated, given the price I am having to pay for it."

"Emily, I'm so sorry."

"Sorry! What use is being sorry?"

She could be maddening when she was cross. "I should not have said what I did. I wanted to rile him—it was seeing you being roughly treated, I suppose, and by him of all people."

She sighed. In a different tone, she said, "And I have to give you up. You and the Cause. He insists on it."

"I see. Well, this *is* serious—even more serious, I should say." I spoke lightly, but my heart lurched. "What are you going to do?"

"I cannot give up the Cause," she said briskly, not meeting my eye. "I could give you up, I suppose, but since you and the Cause are now a job lot, and since I have already decided to defy him over the political side, I suppose you are here to stay."

"Does that mean—"

"No, Robert. It does not."

"How do you know what I was going to ask?"

"Because it is what you always ask. And the answer is always no."

THERE WAS ANOTHER consequence of that moment in the hall. I was working in the café one morning when a rather scruffy individual appeared carrying a notebook.

"Robert Wallis?" he inquired.

"Yes?"

"Henry Harris, *Daily Telegraph.* Can you spare five minutes?"

We talked about the Cause, and as usual he was curious about how a man had got involved. Then he said, "I gather you were mixed up in the Wigmore Hall disturbance."

"I was there, yes."

He glanced at his notebook. "Is it true that you asked Arthur Brewer about his marriage?"

"Yes."

"And was it really his own wife who had just been thrown out?"

"It was indeed," I said. He wrote it down in his notebook. "Will you print that?"

"Probably not," he admitted. "Him being an MP. But I've got friends on other papers where they take a less respectful line. These things have a way of getting around."

[SEVENTY-SIX]

THE NEWSPAPER MAN WAS RIGHT. NOT IN THE NEWS PAGES, BUT in the social diaries, the parliamentary sketches, the cartoons, there gradually appeared a nameless figure of fun: the MP who opposed suffrage but whose wife was a militant. *Punch,* previously so quick to mock the suffragettes, was equally happy to tease the establishment. There was one amusing cartoon of a couple at breakfast:

HON. MEMBER: Will you pass the salt, my dear?
HON. MEMBER'S WIFE: Will you pass a Suffrage Bill?

Well, I suppose it seemed amusing at the time.

For Emily, of course, it was no laughing matter. I remembered what she had said to me, years before, about marriage being a kind of legalized rape. The best that can be said of what she now endured is that I cannot believe Arthur enjoyed it any more than she did. I am sure he thought he was doing his duty, not humiliating her for his own pleasure.

She would not talk to me about it. Once or twice I tried to ask, tactfully, if there were any signs of pregnancy—but to do so was to risk having one's head bitten off. "You are like some horrible old peasant woman, always on about the bed linen," was one of the more printable replies.

[SEVENTY-SEVEN]

PINKER MADE MORE MONEY OUT OF THE MOVEMENTS IN THE coffee price after the revelations about the *Nastor* than Castle had generated in six months. The mood in Narrow Street was one of quiet triumph—but also shock: I think we had surprised ourselves by how effortless this new way of generating a fortune was. It required no warehouses, no machinery, no porters or menials to grade and husk and roast, just a few signatures on some time-contracts. It was profit without expense; profit that almost seemed to transform itself from a thought in Pinker's head to actual cash in the bank without the intermediary of any agency except his will.

He was generous toward his staff: they were all given bonuses according to their length of service. Those like Jenks who had worked for him for many years were now wealthy men.

To me, too, he was far kinder than he needed to be. Called into his office, I found him sitting in front of some ledgers.

"Ah, Robert. I am just going through the books, clearing up some anomalies." He smiled. "What a pleasure that is, to be able to cancel one's old mistakes with a stroke of a pen."

I nodded, though I was not entirely sure what he meant.

"I am going to write off the Ethiopian enterprise," he explained. "It is time to put all that behind us—to look to the future again. A clean balance sheet—a blank slate, waiting to be filled with new endeavors." He pushed the ledgers to one side. "You owe me nothing, Robert. Your debts are all annulled."

"Thank you," I said. "But—"

"From now on, you will be paid the same salary as Jenks or any of my other senior men. And like them, you will be given a bonus every year dependent on how well we fare."

"That is very generous. But—"

He held up his hand. "You are about to say, but you are an artist. I know. And that, Robert, is precisely why I value you so much, and why I wish to persuade you to stay. Some of the others . . ." He pursed his lips. "Some of them do not see the big picture. Or rather, they see it, but they fail to appreciate its beauty. Jenks, Latham, Barlow . . . I sometimes wonder if they really have the imagination to take a company like this forward. You and I, Robert—we understand that it is not enough to have a product. One must have a *vision*."

"You are referring to your political ambitions? Temperance, social reform and so on?"

He made an impatient gesture, as if brushing away flies. "In part. But those are small fry, Robert—too small. Art is neither moral nor immoral: it exists for its own sake. That is what you believe, is it not? Well, then—so too in commerce. Business for business's sake! Why not? Why should an enterprise not simply *exist*, with no other purpose than to be remarkable; to stand for ever, to be admired, and thus to change the way men think, or work, or live. . . . You will see it, Robert, in time. You will see how great this company of ours can be."

He seemed to be waiting for me to say something. "Indeed," I said politely.

"Let me be clear, Robert. I am offering you a position as one of my right-hand men. It is customary to say either yes or no."

I hesitated—but really there was no decision to be made. I still needed a job, and no one else was going to offer me one. I had no illusions about Pinker's splendid visions: I had no illusions about anything very much. The man was a Napoleon, but he was a damned capable one, and he paid handsomely.

"I accept with pleasure," I said.

"Good. Then that is settled. And Robert—you will be able to move out of Castle Street soon, hmm? You can afford better accommodation on the salary I am paying you. And my daughter, I hear, will soon have other things on her mind besides coffee."

IF PINKER THOUGHT he was forcing me to choose between him and his daughter, he was mistaken. Although I had no intention of moving out of Castle Street until I had to, I barely saw Emily now. All her energies were directed toward her political work.

As the suffragettes' struggle became more intense, so their organization became more autocratic. Previously there had been a constitution and elected officers, with decisions taken after a show of hands. Now the constitution was torn up. "The leaders must lead: the rank and file must carry out their orders," wrote Mrs. Pankhurst, their chairman—or, as she now styled herself, "Commander-in-Chief of the Suffragette Army." "There is no compulsion to come into our ranks, but those who come must come as soldiers, ready to march in battle array."

"But isn't this the exact opposite of what you believe in?" I said to Emily on one of the rare occasions when we managed to have a cup of coffee together. "How can you have an organization fighting for democracy which bans democracy from its own workings?"

"It is the result that counts, not the methods. And as she says, I joined of my own free will."

It seemed to me that the movement's objectives were becoming more important than its principles, but what did I know? Never having had much in the way of either, I was hardly in a position to pass judgment.

Emily was ordered to shout slogans at a certain minister; she did so. She was ordered to deliver handbills in a certain district; she did so. She was ordered to speak outside a factory in the East End; she did so, even though she was pelted with rotten eggs for her trouble.

One tactic of those who opposed them was to release mice or rats onto the stage when a suffragette was speaking, in the hope of provoking a girlish scream and thus rousing the audience to laughter. I was present at the Exeter Hall when they tried that with Emily. Without breaking her stride she reached down and picked up the mouse that was running round: holding it up so that the audience could see, she said, "I was a mouse, too, once. Now it is Asquith who is the mouse. And look!" She pointed to a large gray rat that was scurrying across the stage. "There is Mr. Churchill!" It got her a cheer.

But then, a few minutes later, I saw her stagger. At first I put it down to the heat—we were packed in tight; all meetings were packed in those heady times. Turning to the organizer, she said, "May I have a glass of water?" She had gone very pale. Water was fetched, but as she took the glass she staggered again, spilling some over her dress. I could hear the organizer saying to her in a concerned voice, "Are you all right? You look done in," and her answer, "I am a little faint." No sooner had she said it than she collapsed.

She was helped off the stage. I hurried round to the side door, and found her sitting on a chair, being fanned. "It's just the heat," she said, shooting me a warning glance. "It is very stuffy in there."

I did not dispute it, but we both knew that she was pregnant.

• • •

"Will you stop?"

She shook her head. "I cannot."

"If you go on like this you will damage yourself."

"What nonsense, Robert. Women have been giving birth for millions of years, and they have had to do much more arduous things during their pregnancies than making a few speeches. It is just the first phase, that is all—they say the sickness usually passes in a few weeks."

"Have you told Arthur?"

"Not yet. He and Dr. Mayhews will almost certainly try to hospitalize me. So for the moment I intend to keep mum, as it were."

"I am not at all happy about this."

"I cannot stop now, Robert. We are at a critical stage—one more push and I do believe the government will crumble."

Personally, I thought the opposite—one more push and the suffrage movement would burn itself out. But I did not say so.

My reticence was partly selfish: I knew that when her pregnancy became public knowledge, she would be forced to withdraw from politics, despite her protests. And once that happened, everything else would change. Castle Street would close. Once she became a mother, she would inevitably have to become a wife as well—the wife her husband wanted her to be.

I took my newfound wealth down to Sotheby's, where I bought a number of fine drawings by a Renaissance master, including one of an Italian girl's head which reminded me of Fikre. I spread my rooms at Castle Street with Turkish rugs, crowned my table with exquisite silver candelabra, and frequented the more expensive departments of Liberty's once again. It seemed, finally, that my life had settled its course. I was a coffee merchant, a hired man, working for the greatest concern in London. Art and pleasure were to be my consolations.

I NOTICED, though, that there was a darker tone to the Castle advertisements these days. As well as the smiling, pliable women of the early posters, a new type of wife was increasingly being featured—the rebellious female who got her just desserts. Women who had failed to give their husbands Castle were shown being scolded, spanked, or in one case having the offending liquid poured over her head, by husbands who demanded complete obedience in coffee as in everything else. A new slogan—*A Man's Home Is His Castle!*—accompanied texts such as *You have a right to good coffee: your wife has a duty to serve it. Don't be the victim of womanly penny-pinching!* There was even one which showed a woman holding a placard—clearly a suffragette about to abandon her husband to go on a march—with the caption *Who's in charge? Men, assert yourselves! If she's not serving Castle Coffee, it certainly isn't you!*

There was no doubt that battle lines were being drawn.

[SEVENTY-EIGHT]

Bitterness—this taste is considered desirable up to a certain level.

—INTERNATIONAL COFFEE ORGANISATION,
The Sensory Evaluation of Coffee

THE BUILD-UP TO THE ANNUAL BRAZILIAN CROP REPORTS HAD begun. Wild rumors swept the Exchange—that the figures would be disastrous, that the figures would be astounding, that frost or disease or politics or war was going to affect the harvest. At one point there was a sudden panic that the President of Brazil had suffered a heart attack: the price rose two cents a bag, forcing the Brazilians to intervene, before the rumors were proved to be unfounded.

Pinker watched all this with amusement. "They are chafing, Robert. The traders know the situation is unfeasible; they are simply waiting to be told which way to run. It is all grist to the mill."

"Some of my journalist friends have been asking if the market will turn."

"Have they indeed?" Pinker considered. "Tell them . . . tell them you believe it will fall, but that you cannot reveal why just yet. And Robert . . . you might like to explain to them how to take a short position in the Exchange."

"But if I do that, aren't we encouraging them to invest for themselves? What happens if we are wrong?"

"We will not be wrong. And besides, it will do no harm for them to have some personal interest in this."

He spent increasing amounts of time closeted with his bankers, but now he was having meetings with a different type of person as well—young men with sharply cut check suits and loud, confident voices.

"Speculators," Jenks said with a sniff. "I recognized one of them—Turner, he is one of the coming men in the City, they say. I believe he trades in currencies."

"What does it mean?"

Jenks shrugged. "The old man will tell us when he wants to."

Pinker was also poring over weather reports and other arcana. One day I found a Moore's *Almanack* on his desk: the margins were full of strange scribblings and notations in what could have been algebra, but might just as easily have been astrological signs.

"THERE IS to be another march," Emily told me. "This one will be the biggest yet—all the suffrage societies are coming together to organize it. They are calling for a million people, to fill the streets all the way from Hyde Park to Westminster."

"And I suppose you intend to go, despite your condition."

"Of course."

"They will not notice if one person is not there."

"If everyone said that, we wouldn't have a Cause at all. Robert, there are women who will make incredible sacrifices to be at that march—servants who risk losing their jobs, wives who risk a beating. The least I can do is walk alongside them."

"Let me take your place."

"What!"

"I mean it. If you agree to stay safely at home, I will go instead. And if you insist on going, I will not. So the numbers will be exactly the same."

"Do you really not see," she said, "why it would not be the same thing at all?"

I shrugged. "Not really."

"We are not simply tokens, to be counted. We are voices—*people*—who must be heard." She stared at me helplessly. "Robert, we cannot go on like this."

"What do you mean?"

She said quietly, "Ever since you came back from Africa you have been different."

"I have grown up."

"Perhaps. But you have also grown cynical and bitter. What happened to the happy-go-lucky show-off my father met in the Café Royal?"

"He fell in love," I answered. "Twice. And both times he failed to see that he was making a bloody fool of himself."

She caught her breath. "Perhaps my husband is right. Perhaps you and I should stop seeing so much of each other. It can't be easy for you."

"I can't give you up," I said brusquely. "I'm free of the other one but I can't be free of you. I hate it but I can't stop it."

"If I really make you so unhappy, then you should go." Something about her voice had thickened. I looked at her: the corner of her eye was glistening. "It must be the baby," she gulped. "It is making me tearful."

Seeing her crying, I could not quarrel with her. But neither could I go on as we were. She was right: the situation was becoming impossible.

• • •

AT NARROW STREET I found the porters unloading sacks from the warehouse. "What's going on?" I asked Jenks.

"It seems we are selling our stocks," he said drily.

"What—all of them? Why?"

"I have not been privileged to be given that information. Perhaps he'll tell you more."

"Ah, Robert!" Pinker called, spotting me. "Come along, we are off to Plymouth. Just you and I—the train leaves in an hour."

"Very well. But why Plymouth?"

"We are meeting a friend. Don't worry, all will become clear in due course."

WE SAT IN first class and watched the countryside go by. Pinker was strangely quiet; there were fewer impromptu lectures these days, but I had noticed, too, that he was more relaxed when he was in motion, as if the furious headlong impetus of the train somehow soothed his own restless need for activity.

It was remarkable, I reflected, how little his appearance had changed. He must have been almost sixty by now, but I never heard him talk of retirement. If anything, he simply seemed to feel a greater sense of urgency.

I pulled out a book.

"What are you reading?" he asked.

"Freud. Interesting enough, although it is almost impossible to tell what he is driving at sometimes."

"What is his subject?"

"Dreams, mostly." And then something made me add maliciously, "Although in this chapter, fathers and daughters."

He smiled slightly. "I am surprised he can cover it all in a chapter."

• • •

"I AM WATCHING the sheep, Robert," he said a little later, looking out of the window. "It is a curious thing: when the train passes them they panic, but they always run in the same direction, the direction the train is headed, even though it would be more logical to run the opposite way. They are running from where the train *was,* you see, not where it is going; they cannot take its motion into account."

"Well, they are only sheep," I said, not sure what his point was.

"We are all sheep—except those who decide not to be," I thought I heard him mutter to the glass.

I MUST HAVE dozed off. When I opened my eyes I found that he was looking at me.

"Each time we buy and sell on the Exchange, we make a profit," he said softly, as if he were merely continuing some conversation I had missed the beginning of. "But there is more to it than that. Each time the Brazilians are forced to intervene and buy up more coffee, they have to put more into storage, which costs them money. And so every profit we make puts more pressure on them. The last thing they want now is a good harvest—they cannot afford to store the surplus from the years they already have. A frost might have saved them, but there have been no frosts." He shook his head. "I cannot believe it is an accident. I really cannot. But what does one call it? What is the word?"

I nodded, but he said no more, and I soon went back to sleep.

AT BUCKLEY, a small country station near Plymouth, a car was waiting. The doors bore a small monogram, a heraldic *H.* I tried to recall where I had seen it before. Then it came to me—it was the same device I had seen on the *fazenda* in Brazil. "That's Howell's monogram," I said, surprised.

Pinker nodded. "We are going to his English home. We both felt it would be more discreet than meeting in London."

HOWELL'S ENGLISH HOME was an Elizabethan manor house. Sheep grazed on either side of the long drive; through gaps in the parkland one got glimpses of the distant sea. Gardeners were busy clipping hedges, and a gamekeeper with a terrier in his coat pocket and a gun under his arm touched his cap as we swept past.

"A fine estate," Pinker commented. "Sir William has done well for himself."

"Have you ever thought of getting somewhere like this?" I did not need to ask if he could afford it now.

"It is not to my taste. Ah! There is our host, come out to greet us."

THEY CLOSETED themselves together in a drawing room for half an hour before I was called in. The space between them was strewn with papers; legal documents, they looked like.

"Come in, Robert, come and join us. Sir William has brought us a gift." Pinker held out a large envelope. "Take a look."

I slid out the pages and scanned them. It made no sense to me at first—a list of foreign names with figures next to them, and a series of subtotals at the bottom.

"Those are this year's crop figures from the fifty largest estates in Brazil," Sir William said.

"How on earth did you get them?"

He smiled. "That is a question best not asked. And certainly best not answered."

I looked at the figures again. "But this comes to more than Brazil's entire annual output."

"Fifty million bags," Pinker agreed. "Whereas the Brazilian government declares only thirty million."

"What happened to the rest? Has it been destroyed?"

Sir William shook his head. "It is an accounting trick; or rather, a series of tricks. They have built in false figures for wastage, downgraded certain estates, created losses that do not exist—anything, in short, to make it look as if they produce less coffee than they actually do."

I did not have to ask why they should want to do that. "If the Exchange knew about this . . ."

"Exactly," Pinker said. "Robert, I think you should have a lunch or two with your journalist friends. It must be carefully timed—we need the news to start coming out next week. Not all at once, mind. We want to start a panic, and investors always panic more when they know they are ignorant of the real facts."

"Are these figures accurate?"

Howell shrugged. "Enough for our purposes—they will bear reasonable scrutiny."

"You must say only, Robert, that there is to be a great scandal," Pinker continued. "Then, when a statement is made in the House of Commons next Wednesday—"

"How do you know a statement will be made then?"

"Because I know who will be making it, and why. But that is only the start of it. There will be a Trade and Industry investigation announced, and the monopolies committee will call for sanctions against Brazil—"

My mind was racing. "Trade and Industry—that's Arthur Brewer's ministry, isn't it? And he is the chairman of that committee."

Pinker's eyes twinkled. "What is the use of having a son-in-law in the government if one cannot provide him with information on matters of national interest? But even then we will not release the figures—not all of them: you must feed different parts of the document to different newspapers, so that no one quite has the whole picture. They will all be guessing, speculating, and the speculation will feed on itself—"

"The markets will stampede."

"The markets will realize the truth: that they have been too trusting. The Brazilians release their own figures on Thursday. And those figures, we may depend on it, will be another fiction—a gross underestimate. The difference is, this time people will be able to see it." He crossed his legs and leaned back in his seat. "This is the moment, Robert," he said softly. "I have waited seven years for this."

He was perfectly calm; they both were. I knew then that everything he had done—the speculating, the mastering of the new financial instruments, the approach to Howell, even the seeding of my contacts in the newspapers—all had been carefully directed to this end. What I, and the markets, had taken for changes of direction had in fact been only the most terrible, implacable patience.

I turned to Sir William. "If the market crashes, it will ruin you."

"I used to think so," he said quietly. "Like every other damn fool producer in the world, I used to think we needed to support the price of coffee. But it is not so. It is the others—the less efficient producers—who will go to the wall first. When it is all over, and the price settles, my plantations will still make a profit—a small amount per acre, perhaps, but healthy when taken across the operation as a whole." He nodded at Pinker. "It was your employer who did the sums."

"That was what he sent you," I said. "That was what was in the letter. Sums."

"Why should Sir William's efforts support farmers less successful than himself?" Pinker demanded.

Howell nodded. "Life will be much easier when only the big

fazendas are left. We can do business with each other: the leeches who sit in São Paulo and suck our blood can fend for themselves for a change."

"The future is a smaller number of bigger companies," Pinker added. "I am certain of it."

I said brusquely, "But what about those smaller producers? What about the smallest ones of all? For twenty years they have been encouraged to plant coffee—to root up crops they can eat, and live off, in favor of a crop they can only sell. There must be millions of them, all across the world. What will happen to them?"

Both men looked at me blankly.

"They will starve," I said. "Some of them will die."

"Robert," Pinker said easily, "this is . . . This is a great undertaking we are embarked on. Just as, a generation ago, British men of vision and industry freed slaves from the yoke of tyranny, so we today have an opportunity to free the markets from the grip of foreign control. Those people you speak of—they will find better crops, more efficient ways to make a living. They will prosper and thrive. Liberated from the impossible constraints of an artificial market, they will turn to new enterprises and endeavors—some of which may fail, but some of which will transform and enrich their countries as coffee never could. Remember your Darwin: improvement is inevitable. And we—we three, in this room now!—are privileged to be its instruments."

"There was a time when I might have swallowed that nonsense," I said. "Not anymore."

Pinker sighed.

"You could make a fortune when this market correction happens," Sir William said sharply. *Correction*—how neatly the word implied the inevitable rightness of what they were about. "Only a handful of people in the world know what you know now. If you were to take a short position on coffee tomorrow . . ."

Pinker shot him a warning glance. "It is not just the money.

Robert, think what this opportunity could mean for you. Imagine the respect in which you will be held in the City! Sir William and I—we are old men; our time will soon be over, and then a new generation will come to the fore. Why not you amongst them, Robert? You have the aptitude—I know you do. You are like the two of us: you understand the need for bold gestures, big decisions. Oh, you are young, and sometimes misguided, but we would be there to steer you; you would profit from our hands on your shoulders, but you will make your own decisions, find your own adventures—"

"And then there are the investors," I said. "All those who have put their savings into coffee bonds. They will lose everything, too."

"Speculation involves risk. They have profited handsomely from our labors in the past." Pinker shrugged. "It is not them I am thinking of. It is you."

They looked at me, waiting. For a moment I thought they resembled nothing so much as two old dogs, their fangs bared, waiting for me to roll over and show them my neck.

I thought of Emily, prepared to defy her own husband to do what she thought was right. I thought of Fikre, bought and sold like a sack of beans, simply because of where and what she had been born. And I thought of my villagers—my age-clan—picking coffee berries, handful by careful handful, in the cloud forests of the Abyssinian highlands; coffee that would soon be almost worthless.

"I cannot help you," I said.

"You cannot stop us," Sir William said.

"Perhaps not. But I will not be part of this." I got to my feet and left the room.

[SEVENTY-NINE]

I WALKED BACK TO THE STATION, DOWN THAT LONG, ELEGANT drive; past the grazing sheep, the gardeners and the gamekeepers—that idyllic English scene, paid for by the sweat of a hundred thousand peons. Pinker had my return ticket: I traveled back to London third class, amongst men who smoked cheap cigarettes, on seats that stained my fine suit with coal dust.

THE PLAN Pinker was executing was remarkably simple. In the parlance of the Exchange, he was taking a short position. He would sell not only the coffee he had, but coffee he did not have—making contracts to supply it in the future, in the expectation that by then the price would have fallen and he would be able to buy it at a lower price than he had committed to sell for.

But short selling is not simply a bet on which way the market will go. In large enough volumes, short selling itself creates an over-supply, which in turn puts more pressure on the price. The over-supply is not real, of course—rather, it is the *expectation* of over-supply: there is no more coffee in the world, but suddenly there are more sellers than buyers for it; and traders, who after all owe money themselves, will take whatever they can get to close their positions—that is, to balance their books.

If that pressure combined with others—such as a market panic, when ordinary investors rush to sell—not even a government could buy enough to maintain the price. Pinker's plan would bankrupt the Brazilian economy, along with any other country foolish enough to stand alongside them. And the world price—the price coffee sold for, from Australia to Amsterdam—would tumble.

I had no doubt there was even more to it than that. Those currency speculators, and the other City men, would all be in on it, too: doubtless there were derivatives and swaps, loans and leverages, all the armory of modern financial tools trundling toward this little battlefield—but in essence it was as beautifully straightforward as a game of poker. Pinker and his allies would sell coffee they did not own: the Brazilian government would buy coffee they did not want. The winner would be the one who held his nerve the longest.

BACK AT Castle Street I found Emily preparing a banner. "Your father is going to crash the market," I said bluntly. "He is in league with Sir William Howell. Your husband, too. They are conspiring to cause a panic on the Exchange."

"Why would they do that?" she said calmly, continuing to tie up her banner.

"They will all make fortunes. But to be honest, I think that's only part of the reason. Your father is obsessed with making his mark on history: he doesn't care what happens if he can only do that. It is like an addiction for him. Whether he destroys or creates, does good or evil, makes money or loses it—I don't believe anything really matters to him except that it is Pinker who is behind it."

She rounded on me. "That is wholly unfair."

"Is it? When I first met you it was Temperance he claimed to champion—how will crashing the price help that? And then he used to talk of Africa, and how coffee would turn the savages to God—when did you last hear him speak that way? They were just ideas, to be plucked from the air and squeezed dry of whatever energy they might have. He never really believed in anything except himself."

"Do not tar him with your own brush, Robert," she said furiously.

I sighed. "Emily, I know that I have not been much use to the world—but neither have I done it much harm. What they are doing now—it is a terrible thing, it will cause untold misery."

"The markets must be free," she said doggedly. "If it is not him, it will be someone else."

"Is destroying people's lives freedom—or the abuse of it?"

"How dare you, Robert! Just because you have achieved nothing, you try to belittle him. I know what you are trying to do—why you are undermining him to me."

"What on earth do you mean?"

"You have always been jealous of my admiration for him—"

We quarreled then—not argued, but quarreled: both of us saying things that were designed to wound. I think I told her that she was only able to carry on with her campaigning because of money made out of other people's suffering; she told me that I was not worthy to clean her father's shoes; I think I might even have hurled some insults out of Freud. But what hurt her the most, I think, was the accusation that her father was acting without any moral thought or scruple.

"I will not stand for it, do you hear? He is a great man, a brilliant man—"

"I am not denying his brilliance—"

"He cares. I know he cares. Because if he did not—" And then she was gone, the door slamming on its hinges as she went.

• • •

I THOUGHT: *She will come back soon enough.*

I had not reckoned with her stubbornness.

PINKER, SO Jenks told me later, went back to Narrow Street after my departure as if nothing had happened. He gave Howell's figures to Jenks and instructed him to call the newspapers in my stead. The journalists were only too happy to help spread the rumors that would destroy the market; in many cases they had taken short positions themselves, on my own advice. Were Howell's figures true? The more I thought about it, the more I doubted it—but as he had said, they would bear what cursory scrutiny they needed to.

Jenks told me that when Pinker had taken care of that, he went into his warehouse. It was empty by then—every sack, every bean he owned had already been committed to the battle. He walked into that vast echoing space and called, "Jenks?"

"Here, sir."

"Sell them, will you? Sell them all."

"Sell what, sir?"

"All this, man." Pinker raised his hands, and his spinning gesture took in every last empty corner of the store.

"There is nothing here, sir."

"Can't you see them? My invisibles! My hypotheticals! Every alliance and future, every cent we can borrow, every contract we are good for. Sell them all."

ON THE DAY of the march, it rained—not a light spring shower, but a downpour such as you rarely get in England, rain so heavy that it was as if the gods were hurling great armfuls of marbles down at London's streets. Westminster was a quagmire of stinking mud. The endless ranks of bedraggled women set off anyway, but everyone had their heads bent against the slashing rain. In those conditions friends were soon separated, unable even to call to each other over the noise of the deluge, every marcher blind to everything but the churning, clinging mud around her own feet. . . .

At two-thirty, in the House of Commons, Arthur Brewer rose to ask a question. In his hand were Sir William's crop figures. Apparently, even in the House the rain made it almost impossible to be heard without shouting. When the lobby journalists realized what he was saying, that the rumors were confirmed, they rushed to the telephones, and then they rushed outside. . . . The honorable members, too, those with investments in coffee, were frantic trying to reach their brokers; when they could not, they joined the desperate exodus as well. Pinker had wanted a panic, but even he could not have predicted how swiftly it would grow.

She should not have been there. That much was obvious to everyone, in hindsight. When she collapsed in the mud no one noticed at first: they were all falling over, slithering and slipping in their boots and petticoats, and the streets were coming to a standstill in the confusion.

Perhaps if she had been more careful she would not have lost the baby. But we can never know.

AT CASTLE STREET, I watched the weather turn from sunny to stormy—black clouds, the color of a dark roast, gathering over the City. It may seem fanciful, but when the deluge started it seemed to me as if it was not rain but coffee beans that poured down on us from the heavens, drowning us all.

• • •

I HAD NO DESIRE to witness Pinker's victory in the Exchange, but the importer, Furbank, went. He told me later that when it was over—when the Brazilian government finally admitted defeat, and the numbers went into freefall—he was watching Pinker's face. He had expected to see the merchant exultant. But there was nothing in Pinker's expression at all, Furbank said: only a mesmerized, polite interest as he watched the numbers plummet, as if he were in a kind of trance.

A sound rippled through the public gallery. Those who had made fortunes rather than lost them—those who had seen which way it would go—were clapping; standing and applauding Pinker's astounding coup. But even then he seemed not to hear. There was only that intense, flickering focus on the blackboards below.

[EIGHTY]

"Tarry"—a taste fault giving the coffee an unpleasant burnt character.

—LINGLE, The Coffee Cupper's Handbook

THE RAIN HAD STOPPED AT LAST. AS FURBANK AND I CROSSED the river by Tower Bridge, the ships at Hay's Wharf were unloading their cargoes. But instead of taking the sacks of coffee into the warehouse, the porters were making a vast pile in the open area in front of the buildings.

"What are they doing?" Furbank asked, puzzled.

"I am not certain." As we watched, we saw a twist of smoke coming from the far side of the pile.

"They have set fire to it. Look!" The stack must have been doused in petrol: within moments, the flames were encircling it like a giant Christmas pudding. "But why are they burning it?"

With a sickening sensation I realized what had happened. "The new price—it is not worth the cost of storing it now. It is cheaper to burn it, and free up the ships for other goods." I looked down the river. From other quays along the bank—Butler's Wharf, St. Katharine's Dock, Bramah's, even Canary Wharf—came similar plumes of smoke. I smelled coffee on the wind: that bitter, beguiling perfume I always used to associate with the roasting ovens in Pinker's warehouse, spreading now like a thin, fragrant miasma over London.

I said, wonderingly, "They will burn it all."

IT WAS NOT just in London. Fires were being set across Europe—and South America, too, as governments bowed to the inevitable and instigated mass burnings of plantations that no longer stood any chance of being profitable. The peons stood by and watched, helplessly.

In Brazil, a journalist smelled the aroma of roasting beans from the inside of an airplane, nearly half a mile up. The smoke from the fires formed great clouds trapped by the mountains, and when the rains finally came, what fell from the sky still tasted of coffee.

I WILL NEVER forget that smell, or those days.

I walked the streets of East London hour after hour, unable to tear myself away. It was like something out of a nightmare. Gorgeous aromas of fruit and citrus, of woodsmoke and leather, filled the air. My lungs were so crammed with it that after a while I could not even smell it anymore—and then the wind would tease you, a new gust whipping it away, clearing your palate, flooding your senses again with the fragrance of roasting coffee.

And behind the fragrance, something darker and more bitter, as the beans went from roast to charred, and charred to burnt—crackling, melting, fusing together like hot lumps of coal.

I smelled Brazilian, Venezuelan, Kenyan, Jamaican, even mocca, all going up in those fires. A million cups of coffee, a burnt sacrifice to some terrible new god.

WHEN I WAS in Ethiopia, and began to learn a little Galla, the children of the village taught me some of their nursery stories. There was one about the origins of coffee—not that convenient Arab myth about the goatherd who noticed his goats being lively, but something much older.

Many centuries ago there was a great sorcerer, who was able to communicate with the *zar,* the spirits who rule—or rather, misrule—our world. When this sorcerer died the sky-god was sad, because now there would be no one powerful enough to keep the spirits in check. God's bitter tears fell on the sorcerer's grave; and where they fell, the first coffee bush sprang up.

Sometimes, when the villagers served each other coffee, they would say it to each other, as a kind of toast.

Here, the water is almost boiling. Let us drink God's bitter tears.

[EIGHTY-ONE]

I DID NOT GO BACK TO PINKER'S. A FORTNIGHT AFTERWARDS, AS I was locking up the café, I heard a knocking on the door. I went and shouted through it, "We're closed."

"It's me," a tired voice said.

I let her in. She had a coat on, and on the pavement was a valise.

"I came by cab," she said, "and now I have sent it away. May I come in?"

"Of course." I looked at the bag. "Where are you going?"

"Here," she said. "If you'll have me, that is."

I MADE COFFEE while she told me what had happened.

"Arthur and I had a row. Both of us said such things—well, you know how angry I can get. I told him he was nothing more than my father's creature, and for once he lost his self-control."

"He hit you?"

She nodded. "It was not even particularly hard—but I cannot stay with him now."

I thought: how strange, after everything that had happened—

the police beatings, the contemptuous speeches, the manhandling by stewards, the marital rapes—that it was this, a simple angry slap, which had finally tipped the balance.

As if reading my thoughts she said, "He has broken his own code, you see. Or I have broken it for him."

"What will you do?"

"I'll stay here—if you really don't mind."

"Mind? Of course not. I should welcome it."

"You do understand though, don't you, Robert—there must be no impropriety. People can say what they like, but we must know we have nothing to reproach ourselves for."

"Very well."

"Oh, don't look like that. In any case, I suspect between Arthur and the baby and Dr. Mayhews, I have been rather ruined for all that."

"You'll recover. And when you do . . ."

"No, Robert. I do not want to give you false hope. If you find it difficult simply to be my friend, then you must say so and I will stay somewhere else."

"WHAT DID YOU mean," I asked her later, "about Mayhews?"

"Hmmm?"

"You said that between Arthur and the baby and Dr. Mayhews you had been put off sexual relations. I understand the first two. I was only wondering about the third."

"Oh." She could not look at me, but her voice was firm enough. "Did they not tell you that I have been diagnosed with hysteria?"

"Yes. It's nonsense, of course. I have never met anyone less hysterical in my life."

"No, Robert. As it happens, they were right. I even received treatment from a specialist."

"What sort of treatment?"

She would not answer at first. Eventually she said, "They have an electrical machine . . . a kind of oscillating device. It draws out the hysteria. One has a sort of . . . convulsion. A paroxysm, they call it. It is quite shattering, actually. And that is how they know—know you are really hysterical. The paroxysm is the proof."

I cross-questioned her further, and little by little I began to understand what they had done to her. "But Emily," I said when she had finished, "this wasn't hysteria. This is simply what women are meant to feel—with their lovers."

"I cannot believe that."

"Oh, Emily. Listen—"

"No, Robert, I really do not want to talk about this."

Despite her injunctions, and my anger at what her doctors had done to her, it gave me a curious kind of hope—a hope that when she had put all that behind her, she might one day start to think about her experiences—about me—in a different light.

SOMETIME THAT NIGHT, very late, I woke up and heard the sound of weeping.

I went downstairs. Emily was sitting on the stairs that led to the café. She was in her nightdress, a crumpled ball of white, crying.

Her hair was loose. It occurred to me that I had never seen her hair unpinned before. I sat beside her and put an arm around her shoulder. She was so slight, there was almost nothing of her.

"I have failed," she sobbed. "I have failed at everything. I am no good as a wife, no good as a mother, no good as a suffragist."

"Shh," I said, "it will be all right," and I held her, very still and quiet, while she sobbed her poor heart out until morning.

[EIGHTY-TWO]

"Hard"—with particular reference to Brazils.

—J. ARON & CO., Coffee Trading Handbook

FOUR WEEKS LATER PINKER HOLDS AN EXTRAORDINARY GENeral Meeting of his board. Since the board consists of himself, Emily, Ada and Philomena, the meeting takes the form of a lunch—a lunch of celebration, the daughters assume, to toast their father's remarkable successes in the Exchange.

The sisters have not seen one another recently, and there is much family news to catch up on. Only Emily is a little quiet; but the others, tactfully, do not draw attention to this.

It is only over coffee—not Castle, as it happens, but a fine Kenyan longberry, served in Pinker's favorite Wedgwood china—that he finally brings up the business of the day, tapping the cup in front of him with a tiny silver spoon for silence. "My dears," he says, looking around the table. "This is a family occasion, but it is also a board meeting, and there are one or two matters we are obliged to discuss. I have asked Simon to take the necessary minutes—it is a formality, but one we have to observe." Jenks comes in and sits to one side, greeting the sisters with a smile. He balances a folder on his knee and takes out a pen.

"We are a family business," Pinker begins. "That is why we are able to have these meetings in this way. It is now seen as a rather old-fashioned way of doing things, I'm afraid. Public companies, listed on the Exchange, who open up their stock to the powers and opportunities of the market—these are the companies which, in the future, will have the resources and the flexibility to expand across the world."

"Are you saying you want Pinker's to float on the Exchange, Father?" Ada asks. She is a confident young woman now: marriage to a man she adores has softened her sharp edges and put a twinkle in her eye.

"Bear with me, Ada," Pinker says indulgently. "These companies, you may have observed, can also buy and sell each other. Already, in America, we are seeing the emergence of what they call conglomerates—companies which own more than one subsidiary. Here, too, old enemies are having to forge new alliances. Lyle and Tate, for example—two long-time rivals who are now forming a single entity."

He pauses to set the silver spoon down. "I have been having discussions with one of our competitors," he says. "A wealthy plantation owner. A combination of our interests would suit both parties: in Castle we have the stronger brand, and the better market share, while he has an expertise in the production of the raw material which, since poor Hector's death, we have been lacking. He is rich in assets; we are rich in cash. Together, I believe, we will create a company capable of taking on the world."

"Who is this person, Father?" Ada asks.

"It is Howell," Pinker says. "Sir William Howell."

There is a short, stunned silence. Philomena leans forward. "But could you work with him? Surely you hate each other?"

Pinker is very calm; indeed, he smiles at his daughters. "Somewhat to our surprise, we find that on the most important matters we have much in common. I doubt we will ever be friends, but we can certainly do business."

"He will double-cross you," Emily says.

Her father shakes his head. "He needs us even more than we need him. And don't forget, this company will be listed on the Exchange. There will be shareholders who hold the balance of power."

This time the silence goes on for some time.

"The announcement will be made tomorrow morning, when the Exchange opens. You should be aware that this will mean the end of Pinker's as a family firm. The new company will be run in a different way—it will have to be, the Exchange demands it. All the shareholders, for example, will be eligible to attend the General Meetings." He looks round the room. "I doubt if they will all fit into our little dining room."

Nobody smiles.

"Will we be shareholders?" Ada wants to know.

"You will have some shares, yes. But they will not be voting ones."

"So—effectively—we are being asked to sell?" That is Philomena's voice.

"Yes. You will all receive money—a great deal of money—from the sale of your shares to the new company."

"I don't know . . ." Emily says.

"I have thought about this long and hard," Pinker interrupts firmly. "If we are not to be swallowed up by one of the big American firms, we must become a big firm ourselves. And there is something else which has influenced my decision. Sir William has a son."

They stare at him.

"Jock Howell has been educated in all aspects of his father's business. After we have formed the company, he will need to come and run this side of things for a while, under my auspices of course, to complete his understanding. Then, in the fullness of time, when Sir William and I retire, he will be well positioned to take over the running of the entire, combined operation."

"You would give away your business—to Howell's son?" Emily is aghast.

"What choice do I have?" Pinker says quietly. "He has a son. I do not."

While the implications of this sink in, Pinker raises his cup. "I for one should like some more of that coffee now. Is there a refill?"

"So if one of us had been a boy—" Emily says with sudden fury.

"No, no, no," Pinker soothes. "It is not like that at all. But you are married, and to an MP—Ada and Richard have Oxford—Phil is more than occupied with parties and dances. Of course it cannot be any of you."

"I would have taken it over, if you had only asked me," Emily says. "I would have avoided marriage altogether, if that had been the alternative—"

"That's enough," her father says sharply. "I do not want to hear any criticism of your husband. There has been quite enough scandal as it is."

"Then there is a lot you do not want to hear, apparently," she says bitterly.

"Emily—I will not be spoken to like that."

She bites her lip. Mutiny and obedience battle it out on her face.

"I will have that coffee now," he says, gesturing down the table. "Jenks, thank you, you may go." Jenks closes his file and gets to his feet.

"Wait," Emily says.

"Emily, what are you saying? Of course he can go."

"We should have a vote," she says. She looks around the table, at her sisters. "If we all have shares, we should vote on this."

"Don't be ridiculous," her father says.

"That is the proper way of doing things, though, isn't it?" She appeals to Jenks. "Isn't it?"

Reluctantly he nods. "I believe it is even required, technically."

"And if we vote against it," she says, speaking to her sisters, "it cannot happen. We are the majority here."

"What in the name of heaven has got into you?" her father thunders. "Dear God, woman, this is not some suffragette meeting. This is my company—"

"*Our* company—"

"*My* company," he insists.

"You will not be able to argue with your shareholders like this, when you are listed," she points out, cruelly. "They may not even approve of your Jock Howell. Or perhaps he will have *you* voted off—have you thought of that?"

He stares at her, furious.

"All those against the proposal," she says, raising her hand.

"Enough," her father snaps. "Jenks, you may go. Record that the proposal was carried with no opposition."

"Yes sir," Jenks says. He leaves the room. There is a long, weighted silence, and then with a sudden cry Emily does the same.

[EIGHTY-THREE]

SHE KEPT A ROOM AT CASTLE STREET, AND AS THE TEMPO OF the unrest accelerated she spent more and more time there. In all that time I never heard her speak of her husband or her father disrespectfully; in fact, she rarely spoke of them at all. She and I were almost a household, albeit of an unconventional kind.

"ROBERT?"

I looked up. On the counter was a mahogany box. Emily opened it. Inside were rows of glass phials, and a number of cups and spoons for cupping.

The Guide.

She placed four small packets of coffee on the table and began to unwrap them.

"What are you doing?"

"The only thing we can do," she said. "These are Furbank's best new coffees—two from Guatemala and two from Kenya." She poured water carefully over the first set of grinds and looked at me. "Well?"

I sighed. "There is no point."

"On the contrary, Robert—there is every point. These are good, distinctive coffees—Furbank says so. The people who produced them should not go under just because they are forced to sell them at the same price as Howell's industrial product. There are still enough people in the world who care about coffee. They simply need a way to distinguish the good from the poor—and the Guide cannot do that unless you keep it up to date." She pushed one of the cups toward me.

I groaned. "What do you want me to do?"

"Taste them, of course. Aspirate, aerate, and ultimately expectorate. Ready?"

Together we pushed down the grounds and slurped a little of the coffee into our mouths.

"Interesting," she said thoughtfully.

I nodded. "An aroma of bananas."

"And on the tongue, a little natural roughness . . ."

"Even a touch of Muscat grapes."

The same tastes in both our mouths, on both our tongues, our lips: the sensations passing back and forth between us, like kisses.

"BLACKBERRY, or peach?"

"Plums, I rather think. Or possibly damsons."

"And something warming—roast meat, or maybe pipe tobacco."

"Roast meat? It shouldn't be—that would make it savory. Taste it again."

"I would say rather, the crust of a freshly baked loaf."

"Very well—I'll make a note. Will you change the cups?"

I SAID, "You know, we could start asking Furbank to source the coffees we sell here from African farms, instead of big plantations.

If enough people did it, it might give a few small farmers an alternative to working for the white man."

"I think it's an excellent idea."

"Of course, it will mean the coffee is more expensive."

"Will we make a loss?"

"I haven't the foggiest."

"Dear Robert; you really have no idea at all how to run a business, do you?"

"On the contrary—it's businessmen who have no idea how to do that, in my experience."

"Very well . . . What is that African proverb you are so fond of quoting?"

" 'A spider's web is easily broken, but a thousand spiders can tie up a lion.' "

"Exactly. Let us be spiders, and start weaving."

"NOW THIS ONE," I said, "reminds me of Africa. Blueberries, clay, and that spicy brown earth the beans were dried on."

"Well, I have not been there, so I can't say. But I can taste the spices—bay, perhaps, and turmeric. And there's something else—something faint . . ."

"Yes? What is it?"

"I'm not sure. But it is something sweet."

OUT OF THE ASHES of those fires, a tiny wisp of something worth preserving—not hope, exactly, but something fragile, delicate, ethereal as smoke: something that she and I shared in that room, and which was then shared with others—with Furbank, and other importers; with a few passionate customers, and then a few more; growing little by little, like a series of tiny messages that flickered around the world.

[EIGHTY-FOUR]

AND THEN, JUST AS EMILY HAD PREDICTED, THERE CAME A time when her movement needed martyrs.

THE SUFFRAGETTES' decision to start hunger-striking changed the mood of their rebellion. It raised the awful prospect of casualties: the government killing those whom it claimed to regard as the weaker sex.

The first hunger-strikers were quietly released from prison on medical grounds, but with the newspapers on the case it was impossible to do anything quietly anymore. So the government—some said at the instigation of the King himself—decided to subject those who would not eat to "hospital treatment": in plain English, forcible feeding.

There was a wave of revulsion. Women who had not previously supported the militants were both impressed by the hunger-strikers' heroism and horrified by the lengths to which men would go to keep power for themselves; while for the suffragettes, the violence being done to them warranted ever greater violence in return.

The government knew that to back down now would be taken as weakness. They also knew it would mean handing a million new votes to the other parties on a plate. This was a contest they could not afford to lose.

This was how the situation stood in September, when Emily was sent out to throw a stone through the window of the House of Commons.

"YOU NEED not go."

"Of course I need not. But I want to."

"There must be others—"

"And how would I feel then, if someone else took my place?" She shook her head. "You don't understand, Robert. If it is my fate to be imprisoned, it will not be a sacrifice. It will be . . ." She searched for the word. "It will be a privilege—the fulfillment of everything I have worked for."

I said miserably, "You grow more like your father every day, did you know that? Once you are committed to something there is no shaking you."

For a moment her eyes flashed angrily. Then she said calmly, "Yes, Robert. Of course I know I am just like him. And that is why it must be me, and not someone else."

SHE WAS ARRESTED on her first attempt. I wondered, afterwards, if she had even made sure she would be—if she had waited until she was certain the policeman was watching.

Her trial was remarkably quick. Since she was not denying the charge, there were no speeches for the defense. The arresting officer read his notes; the prosecutor said a few words; the stipendiary magistrate declared the sentence ten shillings or three weeks in jail.

Emily said calmly, "I will go to jail."

There was loud applause from the gallery, which was filled with suffragettes. The magistrate banged his hammer for silence.

"Do you refuse to pay your fine?"

"I refuse to recognize the authority of this court, which is paid for out of my taxes without my consent."

"Very well. Take her away."

I TRIED TO see her in the cells, but they would not let me. So I hung around outside with the rest of the crowd, hoping to get a glimpse of her as they moved her to Holloway. I spotted Brewer, dressed as if for a funeral. Pushing his way through the throng, he bellowed, "Happy now, Wallis? Or is there any further degradation you would wish upon my wife?"

"I have no more desire to see her in prison than you do," I answered miserably.

Just then the Black Maria left the court. It had to move slowly through the crush, its bell ringing to clear a way. There was nothing to be seen of Emily, in the back, but we set up a great cheering and clapping to try to encourage her. I could not help putting myself in her shoes, and imagining how she must have been feeling.

THEN I SAW another face I recognized. I hurried forward to catch her up. "Ada?" I called. "Ada Pinker?"

She turned. "Why, it's Robert." She stopped, and so did the woman she was with. "I didn't know you'd be here."

"Nor I you. Have you come down from Oxford? Emily told me you had married a don."

"Yes—the movement is very robust there; we haven't had the violence they've had here in London. Oh, Robert—I have a terrible feeling about this."

"As do I. Emily is so determined. I suspect she may be fixed on hunger-striking."

"We hope to be able to visit her." Ada indicated her companion. "We're family, after all."

I turned to the other woman. "I don't believe I've had the pleasure."

"Oh, you have, Mr. Wallis," she said in a voice that was just a little familiar. "Though I doubt it was a pleasure. I suspect your recollections of me will not be favorable ones."

My bafflement must have shown on my face, because Ada said, "Philomena is rather grown up since you saw her last."

"Good Lord—the Frog?"

The young woman nodded. "Though not many people call me that these days."

Now I looked at her more carefully I could just see an echo of the childish features I remembered. But the pouched, frog-like eyes had changed; or rather, her face had changed around them. Now they gave her an unusual appearance, like someone who has just woken up.

"I kept all your letters," she added. "I drove my sisters mad, demanding to know when the next one was going to come. I used to learn them by heart."

"I doubt very much they were worthy of repeated reading," I said. We were walking down the hill now, away from the court, along with the rest of the crowd.

" 'You can tell Ada that she is not doing at all the right thing pinning her hair back, if she wants to make herself marriageable,' " Philomena quoted. " 'Here the accepted way to do it is to knock a couple of your front teeth out, smear your scalp with ochre paint, and carve a pattern of zigzags into your forehead with a hot knife. Then you're considered quite a beauty, and asked out to all the dances.' You cannot have forgotten writing those words, surely?"

"Good Lord," I said again. I glanced at Ada. "Was I really so flippant? I do apologize."

"It's quite all right," she said drily. "My husband is an ethnologist, so I have become quite used to being compared disparagingly to those with ochre paint on their heads." We reached the tube station, and she stopped. "We are going west. Shall I let you know if we hear anything from Emily?"

"Please." I handed them my card. "And it was a pleasure to see you both again, despite the circumstances."

"You too," Ada said earnestly, and we all shook hands. As I took Philomena's gloved hand in mine she said, "I have always wanted to know, Mr. Wallis—did you write any more of your nonsense poems?"

I shook my head. "I am rather hoping to have left nonsense behind. Although these days there seems to be plenty being spouted by the government."

"Yes," Ada said, looking anxious. "They are very determined not to give in. I do hope Emily will be all right."

HER CELL was twelve feet by eight, the walls painted gray like the inside of a ship. There was a gas lamp, a small window too high to see out of, a plank bed and a chair. On the bare wood were two folded sheets and a pillowcase. Two buckets with tin lids stood under a corner shelf. The shelf held a prayer book, a card of rules, a piece of slate and a chalk. In the door was a small hatch. There was nothing else.

She spread the sheets on the bed and examined the buckets. One contained water, the other had clearly been used as a commode. The pillowcase was filled with straw; sharp golden shards pricked between the weave.

Every sound seemed to boom and echo and bounce cavernously back and forth down the endless corridors. She heard a distant rolling thunder of noise that gradually came closer: doors and shouts and footsteps. The hatch opened. A disembodied voice said, "Dinner's here."

"I am not eating," Emily said.

A tin bowl of soup appeared at the hatch. She didn't move. After a moment the bowl disappeared, leaving a faint greasy smell of warm root vegetables. The thunder rolled away. Eventually the gaslight dimmed—there must be a control outside, she realized, so that the wardress could turn it down: even that small freedom was denied her.

The next morning she lay on her bed, in defiance of the printed rules. The hatch opened. "Aren't you up yet?" a voice said in surprise. "Your breakfast's here."

"I'm on hunger strike."

The hatch closed again.

Then the stream of visitors began. The chaplain, the matron, the work supervisor—they all came to offer platitudes. "It is to be hoped," the chaplain explained, "that you can use this time for reflection, Mrs. Brewer—to improve yourself."

"But I do not want to improve myself. It is the Prime Minister I am hoping to improve." The chaplain seemed quite taken aback, and cautioned her against showing disrespect.

She was taken for a bath: the cubicle had a two-foot door across it, and the wardress came and looked at her every minute. There was a lavatory, but the door was again half-sized, and the chain was on the outside so that the wardress and not the prisoner flushed it.

When she was back in her cell the Warden visited, a tall, harried man who looked as if he should have been working in a bank. "Don't think you can make trouble in here," he warned her. "We've dealt with murderesses and violent thieves. We know what we're about, but if you don't give us any difficulty, you shall soon have your freedom again."

She replied, "You can release me from this place, but you

cannot give me my freedom. Only when women have the Vote will I have that."

He sighed. "You will address me as sir, while you are in my charge." He eyed her. "Your husband is a Member of Parliament, isn't he?"

She nodded.

"If there are any small comforts you require, let me know. Soap for example, or a better pillow . . ."

"I insist on being treated the same as any other prisoner."

"Very well." He turned to go, but seemed unable to. "The thing I don't understand, Mrs. Brewer, is this," he said, coming back abruptly into her cell. "If you are successful—if women get the vote—it will destroy all chivalry between the sexes, have you thought of that? Why should men treat women as any different from themselves?"

"Was it chivalry that prompted you to offer me soap?" she said quietly. "Or my husband's position?"

Lunch was brought—more soup, although the trusty who brought it called it stew. She refused it. A doctor came and asked her when she last ate. She told him.

"You must eat your dinner tonight," he said.

She shook her head. "I will not."

"The alternative is to be forcibly fed."

"I will not cooperate."

"Well, we will see. In my experience a lot of these people who talk about hunger strikes and so on only last a couple of days. After that their bodies tell them not to be so stupid."

He too left her. She waited a long time. There was an hour of exercise, walking round an outdoor yard in single file and in silence.

At dinner time—which was actually mid-afternoon—the wardress asked her if she would eat. Emily said she would not.

At dusk the lights were turned off. She lay on her bed, by now quite dizzy with hunger.

Through the echoing rumble of the prison, she caught the sound of singing. It was "John Brown's Body." The words were different, but she knew them: it was one of the suffragette anthems. With a rush of happiness she hurried to the serving hatch. Kneeling down beside it, she angled her head to the corridor outside and added her voice to the others.

"Rise up women, for the fight is hard and long,
Rise up in thousands, singing loud in battle song.
Right is might, and in its strength we shall be strong,
And the cause goes marching on."

The other suffragettes seemed very distant, her own voice loud and echoing in the little cell. Eventually a nearer voice shouted, "Shut up, will yer?" and she stopped.

SHE TRIED to sleep, but hunger pangs made it impossible to rest for more than a few minutes at a time. The next day she refused breakfast. The pain seemed to be getting less now, not more. Sometimes she felt despair, sometimes, without warning, great waves of exhilaration washed over her. *I can do this,* she told herself. *I can starve myself. They can control everything else, but my body is my own.*

Later that morning someone slipped a tray into her cell. On it was a freshly baked cake. It was not prison food: it must have been brought in specially. She folded her hands over her stomach to ease the pains and ignored it.

By the evening she was almost delirious with hunger. *I am lighter than air,* she decided, and the phrase seemed to reverberate round and round inside her empty frame. *I am lighter than air . . . I am lighter than air . . .*

Sometimes she thought she could smell coffee, wafting through the vent in the ceiling, but when she tried to identify the type, the fragrance shifted and changed like a will-o'-the-wisp.

The doctor came. "Will you eat?" he said brusquely.

"I will not."

"You are starting to stink, did you know that? It is the smell of ketosis—the body feeding off itself. If you go on with this, you will do irreparable damage to your system, starting with your reproductive organs. You may never be able to have a child."

"I know what the reproductive organs do, Doctor."

"You will ruin your hair, your appearance, your skin—all the things that make you so attractive."

"If that is a compliment, it is a very roundabout one."

"Then you may damage your digestive system, your lungs . . ."

"I am not going to change my mind."

He nodded. "Very well. Then we must save you from yourself."

HER SENSES, now, were extraordinarily clear—almost supernaturally so. She could distinguish between distant smells; could even will them into being. She caught a twisting, elusive whiff of fresh Kenyan—it had the aroma of black currant bushes; then, a moment later, the lovely smell of barley stalks, left standing after a harvest. A fruity note—that was apricots, the intense fragrance of an apricot preserve. . . . She closed her eyes and inhaled deeply, and it seemed to her the pain lessened.

EVENTUALLY four wardresses came into her cell. They had chosen the biggest women for this task: it was going to be impossible to resist.

"Will you come to the doctor?"

"No."

"Very well. Pick her up." Two came behind her and took her

by the arms. As they lifted her, another seized her feet. She struggled, but it made no difference. She was carried bodily to the corridor.

"Perhaps she'll walk now," one of the wardresses said.

There was a sharp pain under her arm. One of the women who had hold of her was pinching the soft flesh. Emily screamed.

"Come along, dear," the woman said.

She was half pushed, half dragged along the wing. She caught sight of faces peering through the food hatches. After her little group had passed, the prisoners banged on the doors and shouted. She could not make out the words: the echo swallowed everything. At last they reached the infirmary. The doctor she had met earlier was there, along with another, younger man, both wearing rubber aprons over their suits. On the desk was a length of tube, a funnel, and a jug of what looked like sloppy porridge. There was also a glass of milk. It was so incongruous that she almost laughed out loud, despite her terror.

"Will you drink your milk?" the doctor said.

"I will not."

"Put her in the chair."

The women maneuvered her by degrees into a large wooden chair. She had one on each arm now, pushing her down, and one on each knee. The younger doctor went behind her to hold her head back, while the other picked up the length of tubing. Dipping his fingers into a pot of glycerine, he worked them over the end of the tube. "Hold her steady now," he said.

She gritted her teeth, clenching them shut with all her strength. But it was not her mouth he went for. Instead, he pushed the tube into her right nostril. The sensation was so repulsive that she opened her mouth to scream, but she found she could barely make any sound, only an inarticulate gasp.

Another inch, and then another. She could feel the tube in the back of her throat now, making her gag. She tried to shake her head from side to side but the younger doctor had her too firmly in his grasp. There were tears on her cheeks; she felt a sharp pain in her windpipe, and then with a final sickening slither the thing was fully inside her.

"That should do it," said the older man, standing back. He was breathing heavily.

He fitted a funnel to the end of the tube. Taking the jug of porridge, he began to pour it into the funnel, raising the whole assembly into the air as he did so. Warm, choking liquid filled her windpipe. She coughed and retched, but the hot, thick liquid would not budge. She felt as if her head would burst—there was a pressure behind her eyes, a drumming in her ears, and a sensation as if she were drowning.

"That's a square meal's worth," the doctor said.

The tube was pulled from her nostril—a long, agonizing withdrawal. As it left her she vomited.

"We shall have to replace that," the doctor said. "Hold her still."

So the whole ghastly process was repeated. This time they waited a few minutes before taking out the tube. The doctor carried it over to a sink while Emily coughed and retched and spat.

"Take her back to her cell."

She said, "I'll walk back. And you're a despicable cat's-paw, to treat a woman this way."

"Oh, so a woman should be treated differently, now, should she?"

"If you were a proper man you wouldn't go along with this."

"Wouldn't save your life, you mean?" He waved for the wardresses to take her away.

THAT NIGHT she set fire to her cell, pulling apart her pillow and pushing handfuls of straw onto the gas burner. Then she barricaded herself in, wedging the plank bed under the door handle to stop them opening it. They had to chisel the hinges off to get to her. After that she was stripped and moved to a cell that had an iron bed, screwed to the floor.

That night, and all the next day, someone came and looked at her every ten minutes. At first she thought they were simply coming to gawp, and shouted at them.

"You are being close-watched," a voice answered coldly. "We are charged with making sure you cannot do yourself harm."

At lunchtime the matron came with a glass of milk, which she refused. "Try to eat a little," the woman coaxed. Emily shook her head.

Now that she knew what it was like, she was dreading the feeding. By the time they came to take her to the doctor again she was almost sick with fright. But there was nothing she could do: they knew what they were about now, and the tube was pushed in quickly. She cried as they did it, tears and vomit and the sour smell of the porridge all mixed up together. Then she fainted.

When she came round the doctor was looking at her anxiously.

"You had better stop this," he said. "You are a delicate woman, you are not fit for this sort of thing."

"Is anybody?"

"You are not used to rough treatment. It may damage you."

"You are a doctor. You should refuse to do it."

"Nobody cares," he said suddenly. "That's what I don't understand. You are sitting in here doing this to yourself and nobody on the outside gives a damn. What's the point of it?"

"To show that you can only govern with the consent of the governed—"

"Spare me your slogans." He waved at the wardresses. "Take her away."

As they escorted her to her cell one of the women said quietly, "They take taxes on my pay, so I don't see what right they have to say I can't vote." She glanced at Emily sideways. "And you were brave in there."

"Thank you," she managed to say.

"It's not true what he told you, anyway. You're in all the papers. Not the details, but people know what's going on."

That night she could not breathe properly—there was something in her windpipe, like a bit of food that would not budge. Then she was sick again, and there were streaks of blood in her vomit.

She could not face the tube the next day. She accepted a glass of milk from the matron, and then a little soup. But after that she went back on hunger strike.

[EIGHTY-FIVE]

I WAS IN THE CAFÉ, CLEANING THE COFFEE-MAKER, WHEN HER husband came. It was mid-morning—a quiet time. I suppose he had chosen it for that reason.

"So this is where you disseminate your poison, Wallis," a voice said.

I looked up. "If you are referring to my coffee, it is the finest there is."

"I was not referring to your coffee." He placed his hat on the counter. "I have come to talk to you about my wife."

I did not stop what I was doing. "Oh?"

"The doctors tell me that if she keeps this up, it will kill her."

"Would these be the same doctors who once pronounced her hysterical?"

"This is different." Something about his tone made me look at him. "She has been hurt. An attempt at forcible feeding that went wrong. It appears to have damaged her lungs."

I stared at him, appalled.

"We need to get her out of prison," he said. "Or at the very least, out of danger."

I found my voice. "Then prevail upon your government to give women the vote."

"You know that's not going to happen." He ran his gloved hand over his hair. Suddenly I saw how tired he looked. "This government will never give in. Quite apart from anything else, it would send the wrong message to our enemies. The Empire may look impregnable, but there are those in Europe who would take advantage of any domestic crisis. . . . What Emily is doing is dangerous for all of us."

"And why are you telling me this?"

"Because she might listen to you, even if she will not to me."

I thought, *It must have taken some courage, or at least an iron nerve, to come here like this.*

"I doubt that," I said, shaking my head.

"But you must try."

"As I understand it, it is not her wish to have anyone dissuade her."

"Do you love her?"

It was strange to be discussing such a thing, and with him of all people. But they were strange times. I nodded. "Yes."

"Then help me save her. Write to her," he urged. "Tell her she has done enough, that others can take up the fight now. Tell her you don't want her to throw away her life like this."

I said, "If I do write, and it weakens her resolve, she may never forgive me."

"But it must still be done. For her sake, if not for ours." He picked up his hat. "There's something else you should know. The government is talking about enacting a new piece of legislation. It will allow them to release hunger-strikers on probation."

"Why would they do that?" I said, puzzled.

"To avoid them dying in prison, of course."

"But if they release them, they will go out and create more unrest."

"Only if they are well enough. And if they are well enough, they will be re-arrested and returned to prison. That way, if they die, they will not do so in prison, as martyrs, but in hospital, as invalids. So you see, her protest will not make any difference in the end, not even to her own cause. You must write that letter. Will you do it?"

"I make no promises. I will think about it tonight—"

"One final thing," he interrupted. "If you can get her to stop all this, I will give her a divorce."

I said slowly, "I don't believe she wants a divorce."

"No, she doesn't. But it's not her I'm talking to. It's you." His eyes met mine levelly. "If you can persuade her to stay alive, Wallis, she's yours. I'm washing my hands of her."

WHEN HE HAD GONE I thought about what he had said. I was under no illusions about his motives—whilst I had no doubt that he did care for Emily in his own way, he was a type of man for whom love was indistinguishable from his own interests. If what he had told me was true, and Emily died, it would reflect badly on him. They would say what I had said—that he had let his own government kill his wife, while he stood by and did nothing. Better from his point of view to divorce her.

Brewer was a politician: he had known the best way to make his appeal to me. But it did not alter the fact that he was right. A letter from me saying she had done enough, couched in the right way, might change Emily's mind. She could be willful and stubborn, but I knew her well enough to know how to be persuasive.

I could not contemplate a world without her in it. I loved her, and I wanted her to live. As to whether she would ever marry me . . . I knew her too well to take that for granted, but I could hope.

Finally, after so long, we had a chance at happiness.

I stayed up late, drinking cup after cup of coffee. At last I took a piece of paper and a pen, and by the time dawn came I had written my letter.

[EIGHTY-SIX]

EMILY DIED IN PADDINGTON HOSPITAL, FOUR WEEKS LATER. Just as Brewer had predicted, the government released her on medical grounds rather than allow her to die in prison. There had been some hope that with proper medical care she might improve. But it was too late.

By the time of her death the suffrage movement had, despite all the government's efforts, achieved the unthinkable—a conciliation bill supported by the majority of MPs. The militants declared a truce. But even as it seemed that victory was finally within their grasp, Emily was fading.

I managed to see her a couple of times in the hospital, but she was very weak by then. She never regained the weight she lost in prison: her beautiful face, which had once seemed so fresh and full of passion, was reduced to angles, like something that had been hacked about with a knife. Her hair had lost its brightness, and her skin was very dark—when you looked closely it was lined with fine textures, like a piece of old muslin. Even her eyes were dimmed, and her voice, which was little more than a whisper, caught on her words as if she were stumbling over something in her throat.

Her mind, though, was as sharp as ever. I had brought flowers. "Thank you," she said hoarsely as I held them up for her to smell. "They're lovely, Robert, but next time you must promise to bring me something else. Cut flowers die so quickly: they make me think of death."

"What shall I bring you?"

"Bring me some coffee beans, and a grinder to grind them."

"Will the doctors allow it?"

"Not to drink. But I can smell the aroma of the grounds, and perhaps you could drink a cup for me."

I laughed. "That's the strangest order I've ever taken."

"I always associate you with the smell of coffee. It was so wrong, somehow, when you met me that time in Castle Street after you had been away, and you did not smell of it. But you smell of it again now, so that is all right."

"Do I?" The smell was so ubiquitous in Castle Street that I was no longer aware of it.

"How is the café?" she asked.

"It does well. The new Kenyan is very good, just as you predicted."

She closed her eyes. Then she said, in a voice that was slightly stronger, "I got your letter. Thank you."

"Did it make a difference?"

She nodded.

"Then I am glad."

Her hand reached for mine. "It must have been hard to write."

"It was the easiest thing in the world."

"Liar." She sighed. "I have written a letter to you, in return. You will get it when I die."

"There's no question—"

"Please, Robert. Don't insult me by pretending. The doctors

have been quite honest. My lungs have almost gone. They give me laudanum to dull the pain, but it dulls my mind as well. So when I have visitors I don't take it. Then I have pain, and when I am in pain I am in no fit state to see anyone."

"You're in pain now?"

"A little. They'll give me my drops when you've gone."

"Then I will go soon."

"Perhaps you had better. I am a little tired."

"But I'll come back. And next time I'll bring that coffee."

She died that night, in her sleep.

[EIGHTY-SEVEN]

IT ARRIVED A FEW WEEKS AFTER THE FUNERAL, IN A SMALL PACKing crate. Inside were some legal papers relating to the shop. A solicitor's letter, explaining that in full and final discharge of the estate of Mrs. Emily Brewer, deceased, he was obliged to inform me . . . et cetera. And then a letter in her own hand, the writing small and purposeful, as if she were conserving every ounce of effort.

My dear Robert,

I wanted you to know that I am leaving the café to my sisters. It is not much of a bequest, given how little profit it makes, but I was never able to be as unsentimental about business as my father, and I have been happy there. I hope you will decide to stay on, at least for the time being. The Cause needs Castle Street, and Castle Street needs you.

Robert, I believe that men and women will only be able to communicate properly when they are equal. That has got nothing to do with votes, you may say, but equal rights are a necessary first step along the way to what really matters.

That is why there is something I must tell you, however difficult it is for me to set it down in black and white . . . You recall that morning when I told my father that I wanted to marry you, and why? I think you have always assumed that the reasons I gave him then were my real ones. They were not. I told him only what I thought would persuade him most readily. There had already been one potential scandal with Hector . . . How could I stand there and tell him what I really felt, how much I desired you? But it is true. I have pictured it so many times—I have covered every inch of you with my kisses, have imagined what it must be like to be in bed with you. There—I have said it. I have always wanted more than anything to share that experience with you, and then to wake up in the morning and feel your warm skin against my back, and your breath on my neck, and to know that if I just reach around, you will be there. . . .

I was ashamed of it. We women are not meant to feel such passions, are we? After Hector, I swore to my father I had changed, that I was in control of my emotions, but the truth is I was not. And so I left too much unsaid. Then, later, with Arthur, when I might have said something . . . well, you know some of the reason I did not, but perhaps, too, by then I had become too much a prisoner to my principles.

You will fall in love again—of course you will, that is what happens. When you do, there is one thing that you must promise me. Tell her everything—about me, and about you, and what happened in Africa. Tell her your true feelings, and perhaps one day in return she will be able to talk to you about her desires.

There is something else I want you to do for me: I want you to write it all down. To tell our story. I know you can do it better than anyone. I am sure everyone feels their life has been lived at a great turning point—perhaps that is one of the remarkable things about life, that it is actually an endless succession of great turning points—but I feel that this story, this moment, above all must not be forgotten.

Tell the truth, Robert, and tell it kindly. In the end, that is all any of us can do.

Sometimes, when the longing for you was almost too much to bear, I reminded myself that men and women have been sleeping together for thousands of years; that millions of them do it up and down this country every day. But a friendship between a man and a woman is still a rare and precious thing. Robert, I love you—but most of all I am glad to have been your friend.

Your loving,
Emily

The only other things in the crate were another letter and a small mahogany box. I recognized the box at once: it was probably the last surviving example of the original Wallis-Pinker Guide.

The letter was the last one I had written to her, with a note from the solicitor: *Mr. Brewer has asked that this be returned to you.*

[EIGHTY-EIGHT]

Castle Street
April 28th

My dear Emily,

Your husband has been to see me. He is worried about your health—we all are. That will not surprise you: what may come as a surprise is that he made me an offer concerning your welfare.

He said that if you will give up your hunger strike, he will give you up—will stand aside so that you can divorce him. He does this, of course, in the mistaken belief that you and I are lovers, and that we will marry if you are free. He wants me to persuade you to follow this course of action.

My darling Emily, when I think of what joy it would be to be married to you, you must know that I cannot conceive of anything more wonderful. And yet I am not going to try to persuade you one way or the other. I do not tell you to give it up, or to continue with the strike. All I will say is that it is a great thing you have done, and that whatever you decide to do now, I will be proud of you. And I will never stop loving you.

The decision is yours.

With all my love,

Robert

{EIGHTY-NINE}

The flavour compounds found in the aftertaste may have a sweet characteristic reminiscent of chocolate; they may resemble campfire or pipe tobacco smoke; they may be similar to a pungent spice, such as clove; they may seem resinous, reminiscent of pine sap; or they may exhibit any combination of these characteristics.

—LINGLE, The Coffee Cupper's Handbook

❧

BREWER HAD BEEN RIGHT: EMILY'S SACRIFICE MADE LITTLE DIFference in the long run. At the last minute the government dropped its support for the conciliation bill. The militants, outraged, responded by calling for England to be made ungovernable.

What followed was chaos. Burning linen was pushed into letterboxes, government buildings and shops had their windows smashed, cricket pavilions and even churches were set on fire. Years later, the suffragettes liked to claim that theirs had been a peaceful insurrection, but that was not how it looked at the time. Prime Minister Asquith was a particular target. They tried to tear his clothes off while he was playing golf, and were prevented only by his daughter Violet, who beat them off with her bare fists. When his car slowed to avoid a woman lying in the road, a group appeared from nowhere and began striking him with dog whips, his head protected only by his top hat. A man mistaken for him was whipped at Euston Station; the Ireland Secretary had his kneecap damaged protecting him in Whitehall; an Irish MP sitting next to him in a carriage was wounded in the ear by a hatchet. Meanwhile, almost two hundred women were on hunger strike.

To begin with, like many others, I thought the government deserved whatever they got. We male supporters had been organized into a separate body by now. I broke a few windows and burned a few empty buildings myself, and each time I thought with a burst of satisfaction that I was doing it for Emily. But—again like many others—I eventually found that I did not have the same appetite for conflict that the movement's leaders had.

FOR ME, that realization came on the day we were to attack the National Gallery. The plan was for two of us to go in as if we were just looking at the pictures, then simultaneously produce butchers' cleavers with which to slash the paintings. The particular object of our attack was to be the Rokeby Venus, a famous nude only recently acquired by the Gallery. By this time all public buildings were being guarded by the police: for that reason, it was thought essential to send along a man and a woman together, as we would attract less notice.

I had not seen the Venus before. The canvas had pride of place in the rear gallery, underneath a skylight. The woman was lying on a couch, looking into a mirror. Her skin seemed to glow with life, and the dip of her back was so realistic in every detail that it was as if she was there, in the room with us.

I thought: That woman is dead now—has been dead for

centuries—but the sensual power of her gaze—the way Velázquez responded to it, as a man and as a painter—these will last forever.

I remembered a line from Emily's last letter—the letter that was, even then, folded inside my jacket. *To wake up in the morning and feel your warm skin against my back, and your breath on my neck, and to know that if I just reach around, you will be there . . .*

I stood in front of that painting, and when the clock of St. Martin-in-the-Fields struck four—the signal to strike—I found I could not move. It was the woman beside me who raised her cleaver: the woman who with a desperate cry slashed the long white back from shoulder to waist, so that the canvas hung limply in shreds, and one could see, suddenly, what had not been apparent before—that the Venus was only a painting, an illusion, utterly fragile.

The suffragette was immediately seized by the guards. I stood for a few moments in front of the ruined masterpiece, tears burning my eyes, then I turned and walked away. I dropped my cleaver into the fountain in Trafalgar Square and kept on going. It was the last time I was involved with the Cause.

Part V

Sugar

[NINETY]

"New crop"—a fresh light coffee flavor and aroma which enhances the natural characteristics of a coffee blend, particularly in flavour and acidity.

—SIVETZ, Coffee Technology

A YEAR PASSED. I VISITED EMILY'S GRAVE; I RAN THE CAFÉ AND maintained the Guide; I paid no attention to politics and still less to the arts. In truth, I paid little attention to the café either. There were hardly any customers now—the militants no longer needed a place to meet, and because I preferred to be left alone, I made no particular effort about those few who still came.

And then one day Ada and Philomena paid me a visit. I came in late, and found them looking around the place with a faintly perplexed air. Ada was running her gloved hand over the counters, inspecting the result with a fastidious expression on her face.

"Can I help you?" I said sourly.

"Oh, Robert, there you are," Ada said. "Perhaps you had better make us some coffee."

I sighed. "I'll get some Java. The mocca is too stale."

They exchanged glances, but said nothing while I prepared the coffee.

I had not seen them since the funeral. Then, of course, they had been in black. Now, as they took off their long, waisted coats, I saw they were wearing dresses of pleated, stencilled silk, with high, floppy collars and wide silk belts. Ada's was quite restrained, but Philomena had coupled a flowing dress of abstract pattern with a green cloche hat, from which a pheasant's feather stuck straight upright like a squaw's head-dress. For a moment I found myself reflecting that it was extraordinary what some people would wear. Then I caught myself. It was simply the new fashion—the ragtime style, it was called, after the musical craze from America. Dances like the Turkey Trot required loose-fitting clothes like these, although of course the split legs were good for shocking the older generation too. And although these new looks were a long way from Victorian corsets, one could still discern the influence of the Liberty Style of my own misspent youth.

I brought the coffee over, and we sat around one of the marble tables.

"You're aware we own this café now?" Ada asked.

I nodded.

"From what few accounts have been kept, it seems to be losing money."

"The location is wrong," I said brusquely. "This is a residential area. Nobody needs a place like this on their doorstep."

Again the two women exchanged glances.

"The thing is," Philomena said, "it seems such a shame to close it."

I said nothing. I thought so, too, but neither could I see any reason for keeping it open.

"Phil has some ideas," Ada said. "Would you like to hear them?"

I said with a shrug, "I suppose I had better."

I pulled a chair up. Philomena said, "You are quite right, I think, that this is not the best place for a café. But people do not only drink coffee in cafés. There is also the home to consider."

I snorted. "No one drinks coffee at home either now, as far as I can see. It's all packaged rubbish. Like Castle. Cheap beans, pre-roasted and pre-ground, then stored in paper packets on the shelves of Messrs. Lipton and Sainsbury until what little flavor it possesses finally evaporates."

"Well, quite," Philomena said. She regarded me with those sleepy, just-woken-up eyes. There seemed to be a submerged trace of amusement in them.

"We were wondering," Ada said, "why we can't sell people a quality coffee."

I looked at them, puzzled.

"You see, we grew up with coffee—fine coffee," she explained. "The sort of coffee that is now almost impossible to get hold of. It seems to us that, if we are finding it hard to get, then there must be others in a similar predicament. Not, perhaps, a vast number, but"—she allowed her eyes to travel around the empty and, I had to admit, somewhat run-down café—"perhaps enough to support a business."

"So what you are suggesting—"

"Is a small operation, not unlike Pinker's used to be," Philomena finished for her. "Essentially, it would be a shop with a couple of roasting ovens, the roasters not hidden away but proudly on display for all to see." Almost unconsciously she pointed with a delicate finger to the end wall, where, I could now see, there was just room for two small roasters side by side. "It will be the drama of the roasting which makes the difference—"

"And the smell—" Ada said.

"And the smell." Philomena inhaled deeply. "The smell of freshly roasted mocca! Imagine!"

"I *am* familiar," I said drily, "with what roasting coffee smells like."

"And the chimney—" Ada said, ignoring me. She pointed to a currently chimneyless corner.

Philomena nodded. "Wafting said aroma down the street . . ."

". . . so that even if you don't want a pound of Bogota to take home . . ."

". . . you might decide to call in and buy a cup instead . . ."

". . . or a jug . . ."

"A jug?" I said, puzzled.

Philomena turned her eyes on me. The sleepiness, I now saw, was an illusion. Her eyes were sharp and shrewd and quick. "Like buying a jug of beer for your supper. Why not a jug of coffee for your breakfast?"

"They do something similar in Africa," I admitted. "There the coffee sellers wander the streets of Harar at dawn, and everyone comes to their door to buy from them."

Philomena clapped her hand on top of Ada's. "You see? Robert is already seeing how it could work." She grinned at me.

"So we would roast and sell fresh beans," I said. "But wouldn't that mean we were competing directly with—well, with pre-packaged coffee? Such as Castle?"

Ada nodded. "But since Castle is no longer owned by us, that is hardly a problem. And let's face it, if we can't produce a better coffee than that, there's something very wrong."

"And *we* won't be spending money on advertising," Philomena added. "Just on good beans—African beans, if you wish it." She opened her bag and took out some sketches and photographs. "We will make it look nice, though." She placed them in front of me. "These are some tea rooms I visited recently in Glasgow. The style is *art nouveau*—extremely so. I thought perhaps something similar here." She waved her gloved hand at the space around her. "With your palate, and our investment, there is no reason why this place should not be a success."

"We would need to close," I said, studying the sketches. "This refit will take months."

"Three weeks," Philomena corrected me. "We start the day after tomorrow."

"Good Lord. Er—'we'?"

Philomena put the sketches away. "We are going to be quite hands-on employers. I hope that will not cause you any problems—working for a woman, I mean."

"But—this is hardly fitting work for Samuel Pinker's daughters, surely? You must be very wealthy women now."

"Really, Robert, have my sisters taught you nothing? We will decide for ourselves what is fitting."

"Your father won't be happy about it."

"On the contrary. You underestimate Father, Robert. He likes nothing better than to see his daughters succeed." She paused. "He sent his regards, by the way."

I grunted.

"There is not a bean of coffee in Narrow Street these days," Ada said. "The warehouse is a great big office now, with desks instead of sacks. But I think Father rather misses the old days. You should talk to him sometime."

"You really think he'll help you?"

The two sisters looked at each other. "Why would we want his help?" Philomena asked. "This is *business.*"

AT THE DOOR, just as they were leaving, Philomena turned. "Are you writing something about Emily?"

"What makes you think so?"

"Because she asked you to. I know—she told me."

I shrugged. "It's not quite as easy as that."

"But you are trying?" she persisted.

"I suppose I am. Why?"

"Because I should very much like to read it, Robert," she said simply. "So get on with it, will you?"

I WENT TO the window to watch them as they walked away. Philomena evidently already had some further ideas; she was pointing to the street corner, and then back to the café, talking animatedly to her sister as she turned. I caught her face in profile, the edge of that sleepy smile—

And I suddenly felt something stir in me, something I had not expected to feel.

Oh no, I thought. *Please no. Not that. Not again.*

[NINETY-ONE]

We opened the shop; we fell in love. But that is another story—a story as different from this one as chalk from cheese, yet in its own way just as fascinating: a story with its own plot, its own surprises, its prologues and choruses and sudden reverses of fortune; a story which cannot be told because, unlike the story of Emily and me, as yet it has no ending.

"To demand moral purpose from the artist is to make him ruin his work," said Goethe. Once, I would have defended that statement as if it were an article of religion. Now, having reached the end of my own brief memoir, I find the Victorian in me will not be satisfied without a moral—or perhaps, it is fairer to say, a conclusion. And since I am writing this to please no one but myself, a conclusion is what I will damn well write.

What have I learned?

I have learned what every man must learn, and no man can be taught—that despite what poets may tell you, there are different kinds of love.

I do not only mean that every love affair is different from every other love affair. I mean that love itself consists not of one emotion, but many. Just as a good coffee might smell of—perhaps—leather and tobacco and honeysuckle, all at once, so love is a mixture of any number of feelings: infatuation, idealism, tenderness, lust, the urge to protect or be protected, the desire to ravish, comradeship, friendship, aesthetic appreciation and a thousand more besides.

There is no chart or code which can guide you through these mysteries. Some must be sought at the end of the world, and some in a stranger's glance. Some can be found in the bedroom, and some in a crowded street. Some will burn you like a moth in their flames, and some will warm you with a gentle glow. Some will bring you pleasure, some will bring you happiness, and some—if you are lucky—will even bring you both.

The laugh of a woman, the scent of a child, the making of a coffee—these are the various flavors of love.

[NINETY-TWO]

I WAS GOING TO LEAVE IT THERE, BUT PHIL, HAVING READ OVER these pages, has some comments. That is the problem with having your wife double up as your employer: you are under her thumb twice over, and I know there will be no rest until I agree.

So, for the record, it is apparently not true that I was once promised "a very advantageous proposition—three aways for two poems." She also claims that the poem I then composed for her was far shorter than the one I actually give here, and not as good: it did not even rhyme properly, apparently.

She also says that Hector was a far more sympathetic character than I have made him out to be—"a rather dashing, romantic type, a sort of restless adventurer-hero, incredibly well read, fluent in several languages, an anthropologist before the term was invented." So perhaps I have done him a disservice—but if, as Oscar Wilde has written, every portrait is an accurate depiction, not of its subject, but of its creator, I feel justified in allowing my original, biased sketch to stand.

She feels, too, that my portrayal of Emily may be a little slanted, but for opposite reasons: love may have blinded me to her faults.

My sister was admirable in many ways, Phil has scribbled in a margin, *but she could also be inflexible and strict. She would certainly never have farted in front of me, for fear of encouraging me in what she called my heathenism, although Ada does remember some sort of competition they had in that regard in their teens. However, I think the more important point is that Emily was attracted to the militants partly because she admired their absolute autocracy—the way those suffragettes referred to Emmeline Pankhurst as "The Leader" always made me feel slightly nauseous. You don't mention anywhere that it was the moderates, not the militants, who eventually won us the Vote, and that not for years after the events you describe.*

As for the section on Fikre, Phil—who was, of course, not even there—has littered the margins with a series of exclamation marks—*!,* and *!!,* and even *!!!!* She reserves the full armory of her punctuation, however, for the scene in which Fikre and I first slept together at the French merchant's house, when Fikre served me coffee in the ceremony of love. Toward the end of that passage a note in the margin says, *What?!!! By my count this makes four (!) times—is this a different Robert Wallis we are talking about???* Well, she can choose to disbelieve me if she likes—but in answer to her question: yes, it is a different Robert Wallis; I was a young man then, and you cannot have the advantages of maturity without some of the drawbacks, too.

Tell them about ARTHUR, she has written under the last page. Actually, I was intending to do so, but somehow it didn't fit anywhere. After Emily's death, Arthur Brewer, MP, had a rather extraordinary change of heart. He began making speeches in support of suffrage. It would be easy to be cynical, and say that he had finally seen which way the wind was blowing; it would also be easy to take a more forgiving view, and say that her death, and the circumstances of it, made him realize that he had done his wife a great wrong. His own public comments on the matter could support either interpretation. Interviewed by the *Daily Telegraph,* he would say only, "My job is to represent my constituents' views in Parliament. It has become clear to me that a majority of them now want female suffrage, even if they deplore the methods which have done so much to discredit the women's cause."

Castle Coffee was for a time the most successful packaged brand in the country. But when Jock Howell took over he made some bad decisions; in particular, he failed to anticipate the way that instant coffee would transform the market after the war. The Castle name was eventually sold to another concern, who embarked on an aggressive price battle with a competitor which ultimately destroyed them both.

Meanwhile, several small importers were developing their own versions of the cupping guide, refining and improving on the work that Emily and I began. The Wallis Pinker Guide is no longer unique, nor even amongst the most comprehensive of those systems. But I like to think that, had it never existed, those later versions would never have become quite what they are today.

The coffee shop, needless to say, has prospered. The Pinker sisters were not being entirely honest when they visited me that day: I would refer you to a small but significant slip Phil made, when she asked me if I would find it difficult working for *a woman*—note the use of the singular. It quickly became clear that the plans, and the impetus to implement them, were all Phil's: she had asked Ada to come along with her that morning for support, and because—she admits it now—she already suspected that her relationship with me was going to be charged with feelings that were more than just professional.

After two years we opened a second branch, and then another, and another—and then we realized that, unless we were careful, we would have just the sort of business we both abhorred, in which you start to rely on numbers to tell you what is going on, rather than on the aroma of a roasting Java, or the mouthfeel of a Kenyan, or the taste of a freshly brewed Guatemala, bright and lively in the cup . . . So we stopped, and there are currently no plans to open any more.

I confess that I still retain a certain snobbery about blends. It seems to me that something should taste of what it is, rather than what you want it to be: the faults of a coffee are as much a part of its character as its virtues, and I for one would not wish to mask them. But Phil insisted, and I have mellowed enough to stock a few: they are amongst our most popular lines.

And then, five years after the events I have written about here, Phil and I produced a blend of our own. It smelled intensely of vanilla and meringues, burnt cream and crusty bread, and that faint, far-off whiff of sex that perfumes all newborn skin when it first emerges from the womb. She is absolutely perfect, and she rejoices in the name of Geraldine Emily Wallis.

For a reading group guide, an interview with Anthony Capella and a readers' message board, visit www.anthonycapella.com.

Acknowledgments

The Wallis-Pinker Guide owes a great deal to several cupping manuals both old and new, and in particular to *The Coffee Cupper's Handbook* by Ted R. Lingle, published by the Specialty Coffee Association of America. It also owes a debt to *Le Nez du Café,* a set of bottled aromas created by Jean Lenoir, and the accompanying booklet of sensory definitions co-authored by Jean Lenoir and David Guermonprez, translated from the French by Sharon Sutcliffe.

I have drawn on many books about coffee, including *Uncommon Grounds* by Mark Pendergrast, *Black Gold* by Antony Wild, *The Devil's Cup* by Stewart Lee Allen and *Coffee: The Epic of a Commodity* by Heinrich Jacob. What little I know about Victorian coffee farming I learned from *Coffee: Its Cultivation and Profit* by Edwin Lester Arnold, published in 1886.

I have moved around one or two dates in the history of the suffragette movement to suit my story, but the events themselves happened much as I describe. For primary sources I am particularly indebted to *Votes for Women: The Virago Book of Suffragettes,* edited by Joyce Marlow, and *Literature of the Women's Suffrage Campaign in England,* edited by Carolyn Christensen Nelson.

My descriptions of turn-of-the-century treatments for hysteria are based on *The Technology of Orgasm: "Hysteria," The Vibrator, and Women's Sexual Satisfaction* by Rachel P. Maines. What she relates sounds so strange to modern ears that I have taken the liberty of putting directly into the mouths of my fictional doctors some of the contemporary sources quoted by her.

Some of my descriptions of *fin-de-siècle* London, as well as various menus, meals and observations, are also taken from contemporary accounts, including *Scenes of London Life* by Henry Mayhew and John Binney, and *Dinners and Diners* by Lt. Col. Newnham-Davis, both archived on the excellent www.victorianlondon.org.

Robert Wallis's letters as he travels to Africa are based on several late-Victorian travelers' journals, such as those by Gustave Flaubert and Mary Kingsley—both far more enthusiastic explorers of that continent than Robert. I owe a special debt to Charles Nicholl's *Somebody Else: Arthur Rimbaud in Africa 1880–91,* and in particular to the section in which he re-creates Rimbaud's journey from Aden to Harar from the notes of Alfred Bardey, coffee merchant and adventurer.

For a description of a Victorian-era slave sale, I drew on *To the Heart of the Nile* by Pat Shipman. This is the biography of Lady Florence Baker, who was spotted at one such sale by the explorer Samuel Baker and who subsequently became his wife.

My heartfelt thanks go to those who read early drafts. In particular to Tim Riley, Judith Evans and Elinor Cooper: passionate advocates, indefatigable rereaders and tough critics; to Peter Souter for his early enthusiasm; and to my agents Caradoc King and Linda Shaughnessy for their help and commitment throughout. And of course Jo Dickinson and Kate Miciak, my editors at Little, Brown and Random House respectively, without whom *The Various Flavors of Coffee* would have been a very different brew.

The Various Flavors of Coffee is dedicated to my sisters:
Clare, Carolyn and Jane.

About the Author

Anthony Capella is a lover of all things culinary who lives in Oxfordshire, England. His previous novels, *The Wedding Officer* and *The Food of Love,* have been translated into twenty-two languages. He is at work on his next novel.